MAQ

THE SECRET WAR OF JOSEPH QUANTOCK

BING TAYLOR

This book is dedicated to the brave men and women of the SOE and the French Resistance, particularly Krystyna Skarbek (Christine Granville) and Paul Héraud, but above all to the late Francis and Nan Cammaerts, friends and mentors for most of my life.

Copyright © 2014 Bing Taylor

First published in the UK in 2014
by Middle Farm Press

British Library Cataloguing-in-Publication Data
A catalogue record for this book is available from the British Library
ISBN 978-0-9928896-1-6

Front cover: The Cross of Lorraine, symbol of the Free French in WWII

Editor: Kate Taylor
Designer: Kath Grimshaw
Cover Design: Lewis Heriz
Cartographer: Stefan Chabluk

Printed in Italy by L.E.G.O. S.p.A.
Published by Middle Farm Press
www.middlefarmpress.com

A list of characters can be found at the back of the book

MAQUIS

THE SECRET WAR OF JOSEPH QUANTOCK

BING TAYLOR

MIDDLE
FARM
PRESS

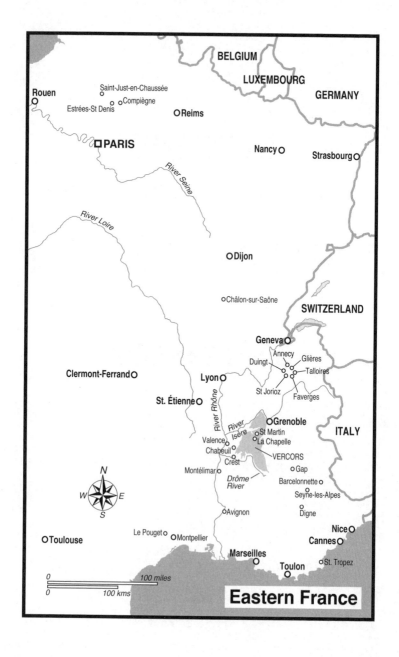

Eastern France

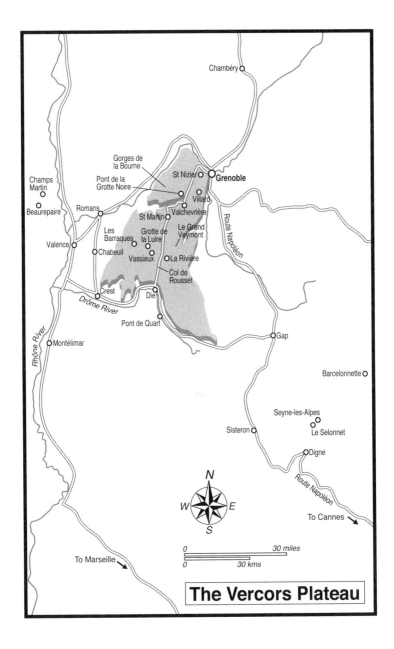

The Vercors Plateau

PROLOGUE

Had I not known differently, I would have guessed that he had sat in that wingback armchair all his life. Even when his body wasn't in it his spectral presence was there; the indentations from his back, the shine on the arms, the burns where his pipe had missed the ashtray and the hollows on the seat cushion.

Until a few months ago his upright figure could be seen every morning, at 7:00 precisely, leaving the house at 30, rue des Caves and wending its way slowly and with the help of a solid birch stick down Le Pouget's main street to collect his copy of The Guardian, specially ordered, at the tabac. On his return journey he would call in at the bar to take a small cognac with local men before they went off to work. They always treated him with great respect, partly due to his great height, partly to his great age but mainly due to the discreet red rosette of a Chevalier of the Legion d'Honneur in his buttonhole.

He would sit at the same table in the small bar where the owner would bring him his morning tipple. Before long, five or six farm workers would gather round him. Some sat, others stood as they thought up an excuse to question him – about life, about people, about politics but never about the war. It was what everyone really wanted to hear about but it was something no one ever felt they could ask him. He would answer each question in a slow, reasoned, school masterly sort of way, never repeating himself, never using an unnecessary word or an inappropriate one, and never an emotional one. He would stay fifteen minutes, no more, no less, before making his way back home where his daughter would have prepared breakfast.

The farmers would return to their positions at the bar. With varying degrees of unwarranted confidence they would exchange stories about the presumed wartime exploits of the man they called 'Le Grand Diable Americain'.

I first met Joseph Quantock, 'Le Grand Diable', soon after World War II had ended. I was a little boy at my father's side. He and Mr Quantock were great friends. Through the years I got to know him better. My family had returned to the States and I spent summer months staying with him at the school outside Montpelier where he was headmaster. He would take me camping with a group of other boys identified as troublemakers. We would learn how to sail, cook, tie knots, forage for food, build fires, make rudimentary shelters and cooperate with each other, rather than fight with each other. The aim was to turn our attention away from making trouble towards something constructive. By and large it worked.

Many years later, when I was a teacher in Africa and Mr Quantock was Professor of Education in a neighboring country, we spent a summer together driving around several East African countries where he had a job inspecting schools. It was then, huddled together in a government inspector's jeep, that he told me his story. He knew I was a writer and he warned me that I was not to write about it until after his death. And if I were to do so, I should write it as a work of fiction. I agreed.

Each day, driving hundreds of miles to the next school, he would give me a new installment. It was the story of his war, in his own words. A story he had never told before.

This is his story.

Bing Taylor, New York City, March, 2014

1

Somewhere over France, March 1943

Guided by the March moon, a lone Lysander makes its way across the English Channel and heads for the gap in flak defences near Quend-Plage. Once through the gap the pilot turns the aircraft swiftly to avoid attracting the attention of the fighter base at Abbeville. The night skies are unusually busy with Nazi Junkers flying between Paris and points east. The Luftwaffe pilots don't seem to notice the distinctive carrot shape of the unlit Lysander a thousand feet below.

On board the tiny plane are two secret agents on their way to be dropped inside Occupied France.

The older man is Charles Decosse, head of the Lyon circuit of the French Resistance.

The younger man is Joseph Quantock, a 26-year-old American. This is his first mission as an agent of the Special Operations Executive (SOE), the ungentlemanly warfare department set up in great secrecy by Winston Churchill in July 1940.

Its mission is sabotage and subversion behind enemy lines.

Within three days Decosse will be dead and Quantock will be a hunted man.

Groombridge, Kent. Nine months earlier

I stretch, throw back the sheet, jump out of bed and open the shutters. Looking forward to this moment each day, I light a post-coital cigarette and take a satisfying drag. On a distant hill farm buildings gather colour in the early-morning sun. The wheat in my neighbour's field waves contentedly in the breeze. No sound but birdsong. No sense of impending doom.

As so often these days, all that is lovely in the Kentish landscape fills me with foreboding. Like watching your innocent young sister frolicking in a field, knowing that before long she will be savagely raped.

For this is 1942. The world is at war and rumours of a German invasion are rife. For some reason, perhaps the sun on my face, I think again of Africa; dead bodies, panic, screams, poison. I feel like someone is standing on my chest. The blood flowing ever faster through my veins. Fuck Mussolini.

I stub out the cigarette, turn and catch sight of my naked body in the mirror. You wouldn't call me handsome. Attractive maybe. I've even been called sexy. I can't pretend it doesn't make me feel good. I'm fit, no sign of fat; three years of physical labour have seen to that. The scar that runs from my right hip and disappears into my pubic hair is not a botched appendectomy but the wound from a knife stab intended to emasculate me. I was working at a hospital in Marrakesh. Drug smugglers didn't take to me.

It's 7:00 a.m. The guys will be at the barn soon, waiting for their orders. I don't want to be late.

On my bed, half-covered by a sheet, Lucy Price, the red-haired upstairs maid at the big house, is silently watching me.

"Come back to bed Joey. I haven't finished with you yet."

She pulls down the sheet and S-shapes her body seductively to show the small of her back. She knows it drives me crazy. I walk over and gently spank her bottom.

"We've got to get to work Lucy Price. It's already late. Are you never satisfied?"

"Nope."

"Yeah, that's what I've heard…"

She hurls a pillow.

I lean down, pull back a wisp of hair that is sticking to her lips, and give her a kiss.

"We've got all summer, Lucy. Time isn't running out" I say, pulling on some clothes for the walk to the outdoor privy.

But Lucy thinks it is. She may be right. They tell me that when I first came to work on the estate eighteen months ago she bet the other girls that she'd be the first to get me into bed. She was. She says she likes me because I'm different: American, a French speaker, well-travelled. We have fun in bed and out, but she wants more. I'm not ready for more. Sometimes I doubt I ever will be. Everyone I've been close to has been taken from me, except François. But he lives in France. I hardly hear from him any more, thanks to the war.

The privy is dank and cold, but it wakes me up. I hurry back indoors to make the coffee. Lucy is already dressed and downstairs putting on her coat.

"Coffee Lucy?"

"Not this morning Joey. I'll get some at the big house."

A quick kiss, "See you later" and she leaves.

The coffee tastes bitter. It's strong and ersatz. I sit down at the kitchen table to lace up my boots for the walk across the fields.

The guys are waiting at the barn. I know by their expressions what to expect…

"Lucy's walkin' funny this morning Joey. Bit of a rough night was it…?"

"You look shagged out Joey, our girls too much for you? Better find youself some tame Yankee girl instead…"

I can't suppress a smile, "Alright, alright enough smart-alec remarks. We've got work to do."

No more comments. I allocate the jobs for the day.

Fifteen-year-old Tommy Knox and I walk down the front drive where we need to deal with a couple of chestnut trees that have blown down.

Too young to serve in the army, the guys who work on the farm are a good bunch. Despite what you might think we respect each other and make a good team. The people in the village are a different matter.

You know how people, especially village people, gossip. They say I'm on the run. There's a dark secret there. No doubt about it. An American working on an English farm? Not in the army? Got no family. Or so he says. He's up to no good. Mark my words. The Yanks have finally joined the war, haven't they? Why isn't he fighting?

You may believe it's cowardice or fear. You may be right. I've asked myself the same question, more than once. Deep down I know it's something else.

I began to question the rights and wrongs of war when I was teaching in Ethiopia. It was 1935 and Mussolini, wanting to expand his African "empire", took a liking to Ethiopia. One day his pilots strafed the marketplace in Makelle, where I lived, killing and maiming hundreds, mainly women and children who had walked many kilometres to sell their wares (spices, breads, empty bottles, tree roots) in the market. Two Italian bombers dropped what we later learned was mustard gas. I had nightmares for days afterwards just thinking about the Italian pilots laughing at their success all the way home to their girlfriends' arms and their mammas' pasta.

In civilian life they may have been decent people. As were their victims. War, like religion in my view, can turn otherwise decent people against one another. I want no part of it.

I think it goes back to my childhood. I read somewhere that children growing up in 'a loveless environment grow a shell around their hearts that can be hard to crack open later.' That's me, at the moment. My dad was an alcoholic sadist. He enjoyed beating me, his only son. As a result I was always pretty much a loner; still am. Frequently in trouble and in fights with other guys, I was often suspended from school and rebelled against the strictures imposed by any kind of authority.

I was ten when my parents were killed in a car crash. I was sent to France to live with my mother's brother, Uncle Sam, whom I'd never met. His name was never even mentioned in my house except when my dad lost his temper with me: "You go on like that young man you'll end up a fucking queer like your uncle."

In the event, my years in France were the happiest of my life… so far. Uncle Sam lived in a village, a hamlet really, near Paray-le-Monial in Burgundy. He was a small, bright-eyed, impish little man who always had a scarlet handkerchief tied around his neck, green corduroy trousers and red shoes. He looked like an elf. He was always kind to me and taught me more than I ever learned at school. His housekeeper, Mme. Joupin, had a son François who was my age, taught me French and became my best friend. François had a wooden leg but that didn't stop him. We even participated in the Ski Championships in Grenoble together.

After Uncle Sam died and left me the house and a bit of money I decided to travel. François looked after the house and rented out rooms. We agreed to share the profits. I ended up in Ethiopia where I got a job teaching at a secondary school in Makelle. It was the capital of Tigre, the Ethiopian province that borders on the Italian colony of Eritrea.

The summer after the massacre in the marketplace I left Makelle and bummed around Africa for a few years, ending up in Morocco where I worked in a hospital. I was transporting a truck full of drugs to a town outside Marrakesh when I was attacked by a gang of drug smugglers. I got away with cuts, two broken ribs and a stab wound to my groin. But I got away.

I made it to England, a country I had never visited, and got a job as a gardener in Suffolk. In late December 1940, shortly after Christmas, a guy telephoned to say that he had a letter addressed to me from François. We arranged to meet the following day at The French House Pub in London, a well-known haunt of the Free French and a rendezvous for anyone newly arrived from Nazi-occupied France.

I took the train down to London and found The French House Pub. I ordered a beer. The bartender and I had a friendly chat. Despite the number of people in the smoke-filled room, there was no one the bartender didn't know. Newcomers stuck out. He made it his business to find out who they were. When a new guy came in the bartender gave me the nod.

It was an uncouth little man with a puffy face and deeply stained brown teeth. He checked my identity, handed me the letter and made a quick exit. I bought another beer and sat down in a corner to read.

Maison de Tollecy
Prizy
Bourgogne

11 decembre, 1940

Joey, mon frère,

It is not easy for me to get letters to you these days. Even though Prizy is in the zone un-occupée (only by a kilometre or two) all our letters are read by the foul Pétainists and if people say things against the "beloved Maréchal" they are sent to Germany to work in the factories to make weapons to be used against their own people.

Already it is difficult to find food here. The butchers left town a long time ago. People fight like animals for a few litres of petrol. The peasants are barricading themselves against the refugees from the north who try to steal their food and are ready to kill for it.

Do you recall that bully Philippe Morseau? The one you knocked unconscious at school? Well now he has found his natural métier. He is Chief of Police in Paray. He and his friends are more German than the Germans. I am surprised he has not come for me yet!

A few of the lads and I are living in your house. We look after it as best we can. I am not charging them rent because they have no money and I knew you would not mind. It is for a good cause. We have formed a group, there are maybe twenty-five of us in all, from Prizy and the surrounding villages. We are training each other how to live rough and to use weapons and organize bits of sabotage to disrupt the Germans. Some people are thinking of starting a newspaper that tells us what is really happening in the war. Maybe I will write for it?

I wish you were here with us my brother. We would make a good team like we always did, did we not? Are you well? What is it like working on the farm? I know you will not be able to answer me but I like to ask the questions anyway.

I hope it will not be very long before we see each other again – in a Free France! I will look after the house for you. We repaired the broken window in the attic last week. We listen to La Beeb when we can.

Take care

Your brother,

François

I folded up the letter and put it in my jacket pocket. I had a moment of regret; that I couldn't be in France; that I couldn't be part of Francois' group. But it passed…

The following week I heard from an agency that there was a need for a forester in Kent. The job came with a house. I took the train down the next day.

That's how I've ended up here, two years later, stripped to the waist, chopping wood with Tommy Knox on Lord Horley's front drive as a large, black, chauffeur-driven military car glides by on its way to the big house.

2

Bosworth, the butler, escorts Colonel Buckmaster into the drawing room. "Good morning Lord Horley. All well I trust?"

"Fine Buck, thank you. Have a cup of coffee? I think it's still warm."

Horley walks over, closes and, somewhat to Buckmaster's surprise, locks the door.

The two men sit down. Both had attended Eton and Oxford. They've met before. The protocol comes naturally. They are immediately at ease with one another.

Buckmaster is tall with a military bearing, outsized ears, sharpened vowels, a bird-like nose and an overhanging lip.

Horley is short but every inch an aristocrat. He wears thick glasses and has a brain as sharp as his tongue when fully engaged.

Horley isn't even certain what Buckmaster does. All he knows is that he was one of the last people to be shipped out of Dunkirk and that he now works for some secret department in the Ministry of Economic Warfare that the PM and Hugh Dalton cooked up together; that it is entirely independent; responsible to no one but Winston Churchill personally; and that it eats up a lot of money which, in Horley's view, would be better off going to the official, and therefore accountable, armed forces instead.

He is about to find out more.

"Now Buck, since I am the minister responsible for funding your organization, among others, the PM has, at my request, agreed that you should explain to me exactly what it is you chaps are up to. All totally confidential of course."

Anticipating Buckmaster's reluctance to break his word of absolute secrecy, Horley shows him a letter from the PM to Sir Charles Hambro, deputy head of something calling itself the SOE, authorising Buckmaster to tell all.

Buckmaster shifts uncomfortably in his armchair. He has never uttered a word about his work before, not even to his wife. It seems there is no avoiding it now.

"Very well, Sir. A little bit of history first. As I understand it, the PM was frustrated by his predecessor's insistence on always playing by the Queensbury Rules which Churchill believed had resulted in ignominious acts of appeasement. He therefore ordered the creation of the SOE or Special Operations Executive. It was designed to be a clandestine department charged with the express objective of sabotaging the enemy's efforts in every way conceivable and aiding, arming and training Resistance movements in enemy-occupied territories."

Horley frowns. "What is Dalton's involvement?"

Buckmaster, aware of professional jealousies among ministers, treads cautiously.

"I believe, Sir, that Mr Dalton, as Minister of Economic Warfare, recommended to the PM that the organization should be set up entirely independent of the War Office machine. The PM was in agreement but the received wisdom is that he didn't want Dalton to be the man to run it."

"Very understandable" says Horley, pouring himself another cup of coffee.

Buckmaster continues "However Clement Atlee is a great Dalton supporter and as he was Leader of the Labour Party and a member of the coalition government, the PM was forced to listen to him. As a result on 16 July 1940 Hugh Dalton was charged by the PM to, in his words, 'Set Europe Ablaze'."

Horley looks despairingly at the ceiling.

"What's more, the PM decreed that the activities of the SOE must never be mentioned in parliament. Dalton was given absolute powers, subject only to the PM's approval."

"Dangerous stuff, Buck. It's got to be wound up as soon as the war is over. I'll see to that. Go on."

"Well, as you can imagine, Dalton had a real struggle to get support for his case. The military were viscerally opposed to the idea of a 'private army', particularly when they would have to compete with it for funding, as you would know better than anyone."

"Understandably, don't you think? Your people want to create social mayhem whilst MI6 want to operate without doing anything to alert the authorities."

Ignoring this remark Buckmaster continued, "The fall of France concentrated everyone's minds on matters at hand and diverted scrutiny from Dalton, thereby releasing him to set up the SOE relatively unencumbered. It is now the responsibility of Lord Selborne."

"What about those other shadowy Whitehall organizations? Don't the Foreign Office and the War Office have similar departments?"

"They did, Sir, yes but they have all been brought under the SOE umbrella."

"Well at least there's a saving there presumably? And where are they headquartered? In some secret bunker somewhere I suppose."

"No, Sir. In Baker Street. Number 64, formerly the Marks and Spencer headquarters. But it is expanding quite rapidly."

"Inevitably. It all sounds very fishy and open to misuse to me, Buck. Still I suppose it's all for a good cause. Thank you for illuminating me. I'd like to come and pay a visit one day."

"That would be a pleasure, Sir" said Buckmaster, determined that no such thing would happen. "I hope it helps to explain why we so desperately need funding."

"I'll do my best, Buck, but I can't promise anything. The armed forces will also fight tooth and nail for that money." He walks Buckmaster to the front door.

"Thank you, Sir. I know I can count on you," Buckmaster pauses, "By the way Sir, if you don't mind my asking, who is that young forester you've got working in the drive? Shouldn't he be serving his country? Looks pretty fit to me."

"Joseph? Well he's an American actually. Some sort of pacifist too. Surprising fellow. Speaks fluent French would you believe. Very popular here I'm told. Good worker."

Buckmaster gets into the passenger seat of his car and indicates to the driver that they should go. Before closing the door he says "Thank you Sir. Good luck with the PM."

Horley waves goodbye.

But Buckmaster's mind is already set on young Joseph, the forester. Bright, strong and speaks fluent French. Couldn't be better.

"Nutting, if those young chaps are still working on the trees in the drive I want you to let me out while I have a word. You can drive on and wait for me at the gate" he instructs the chauffeur.

Tommy and I are still at work when that same military vehicle draws up beside us and stops. I amble over, pulling on my shirt as I go.

"Need some help?"

A man in uniform gets out of the car. His car drives off.

"Are you Joseph?" inquires the uniform.

"Yup. How can I help?"

"I'd like a word if I may, in private?"

"And who are you, Sir?"

"My name is Buckmaster, Colonel Buckmaster."

"OK. We can walk up the drive some if you like?"

"That will be fine. Excuse us young man," he says to Tommy "we won't be long."

We start walking. "How can I help then?"

"I can't say a lot I'm afraid. It's all very secret; but I understand you are a French speaker?"

"Yes."

"How so?"

"My mother's family was from France originally. My uncle moved back there and I lived at his house for eight years when I was growing up."

"You are obviously fit and Lord Horley tells me you are intelligent and well-liked. You could be just the sort of person we're looking for."

"Who are 'we', Sir, exactly? The army? There's no way I'm going to join any army, British or American, if that's what you're thinking."

"You're jumping to conclusions too quickly young man."

"Sorry, Sir, just don't want you wasting your time."

"Who are 'we'? Officially we don't exist. Despite my uniform I am only nominally part of the army, although ultimately we get our funding from the same place, which is why I came to see Lord Horley today."

"Does he know you're talking to me?"

"Not yet. But of course I will tell him if we can come to an agreement."

I'm sort of intrigued to tell the truth but I say nothing.

"My organization is composed of people such as you. Men and women who want to contribute to the war effort but don't want to join the armed forces. Individuals mainly; experts, ordinary citizens, school teachers, housewives, labourers… pretty much anyone as long as they are strong, both physically and mentally. And, in the case of my section, speak good French."

"What makes you think I want to contribute to the war effort, Sir?"

"You don't?"

"I know what war does to people. I've seen it. It stinks."

"Well I'm prepared to offer you the chance to help prevent that sort of war ever happening again. No need to decide now. Think it through. When you're ready to talk give me a call. Here's my card."

He opens a silver case and extracts a small card.

Colonel Maurice J. Buckmaster
Inter-Services Research Bureau
83 Baker Street
London
Telephone Welbeck 2929

I glance at the card and put it in my pocket. "OK, thanks. So long Colonel."

"Goodbye Joseph." He walks up the drive.

Tommy and I finish off the trees and call it a day.

Walking back to the cottage I think about what Colonel Buckmaster was saying.

Over the next two days I become broody and sullen. The sex with Lucy is perfunctory. She says she feels as though she could be anyone. We sleep together but we might as well sleep apart for all the good I do her.

"You're shutting me out Joey."

"I'm sorry, I don't mean to. I'm just thinking too much."

In the end she stops coming around. I can't blame her.

The war is killing tens of thousands and now, with Hitler's invasion of Russia, that's turning into millions. I still believe in my pacifist principles but I am finding it more and more uncomfortable living a quiet life while other guys are dying for the likes of me. The stories of Nazi atrocities make my blood boil. I need to find my own way of taking part in this. How can I face myself if I don't?

I come home from work, take off my boots and put them on an opened spread of the previous day's The Times in order to clean them.

I make myself a cup of coffee and put it down on the newspaper. As I pick up a boot to start polishing I uncover an article in the paper. The words 'Paray-le-Monial' catch my eye. I clear the newspaper of boots and coffee and read the short piece:

Following the explosion that destroyed the headquarters of the French police in Paray-le-Monial last week a house-to-house search was conducted to find the culprits. No one was found. As a result severe reprisals have been meted out by the local commander. Disregarding the 'border' Commander Philippe Morseau broadened his search to the unoccupied zone. Among those killed were five suspected terrorists, one of whom had a wooden leg, from the neighbouring village of Prizy. The house they shared was razed to the ground as an example to others.

I slump down in the chair and sense the emotion draining out of me. I stare straight ahead. Numbed. I feel helpless, then furious, then desperate. My best friend. Dead. If only I had gone to France, joined François, maybe I could have saved him… I am burning with anger. Anger at Philippe Morseau. At the Nazis. At myself.

I take the next day off, catch the Eridge train to Victoria and make my way to Soho and The French House Pub where I greet the bartender, buy a beer and ask to use the phone.

I pull the crumpled visiting card out of my pocket and dial the number.

"Inter-Services Research Bureau. How can I help?"

"I'd like to speak to Colonel Buckmaster please. Tell him Joey is calling."

"Joey? Just Joey?"

"Joey, yeah, or Joseph. He'll know."

"I see. Thank you, Sir. I'll come back to you shortly."

A series of clicks and silences follow.

"Hello. Joseph?"

"Yeah, is that Colonel Buckmaster?"

"It is. How are you Joseph?"

"OK thanks. You suggested we meet. I'd like to do that."

"Where are you Joseph?"

"The French House Pub in Soho."

"Good. I will come meet you and we can walk over and talk at my club. It's quieter there."

"OK. I'll wait here for you."

I go back to the bar to drink my beer.

Twenty minutes later a tall, beak-nosed man in a crumpled grey suit walks in. He looks out of place and yet quite a few people seem to know him. He speaks perfect French. It takes a few moments for me to recognize Colonel Buckmaster.

Moving through the bodies crowded around the bar, I make my way over to him, but he ignores me. I wait, unsure of what's going on. Then Buckmaster abruptly leaves the pub. I follow him. He is waiting at the street corner.

"Colonel?"

"Hello Joseph. Sorry not to speak to you in there. Too many people. Could be some who don't need to know that we are acquainted. Let's go to my club. It's not far."

Five minutes later we enter one of those 'Gentlemen's Clubs'. Buckmaster has a word with a man who guards the door. A tie materializes and I am asked, well told, to put it on. The first tie I've worn in years. The place is full of old men; rotting flesh.

I follow Buckmaster up the creaky grand staircase. Hundreds of dull-looking dead people stare self-importantly down from their picture frames. At the top of the stairs there is a writing room with small wooden shields on the wall. An overfed club member is asleep in an armchair, snoring. Who are these people?

Buckmaster beckons me into a little side room, rings a bell by the fireplace and then we sit down on matching red leather chairs. The bartender comes in to take our order.

"Joseph, what'll it be?"

"Beer, please." I say. Why does Buckmaster keep calling me Joseph instead of Joey? Maybe it's another one of their House Rules.

"One G&T and one beer, Harry, thank you. And Harry, please close the door."

We chat idly until Harry comes back with the drinks.

Harry leaves, closing the door behind him just as he was told. Buckmaster asks me why I've contacted him.

"I've had a change of heart. I've made up my mind. I want to be involved. I need to be involved. But I don't want anything to do with armies, or an Authority."

Buckmaster takes a sip of his G&T. I can see that he's pleased he's 'won'.

"I can't tell you exactly what it is that we do, Joseph, at least not until we're further down the line so to speak. But what I can tell you is that, if you pass muster, you will be in a responsible position;, responsible for recruiting and training others. You will be independent, to all intents and purposes. And the pay isn't bad, and it's tax free."

I don't care about the pay. It's not about the pay. But it's sounding better.

"Oh, and it's dangerous, very. There will be no one to support you except whoever you organize by yourself. There are roughly four hundred of us. There used to be more. Chances of survival are under fifty percent. Even less for the women."

I listen carefully. I'm trying to figure Buckmaster out. He doesn't give much away. He says I'd be helping to end the war early; save thousands of lives. Sounds like it could be true. We finish our drinks. I guess the interview is over.

"Let me know when you make your mind up, Joseph," says Buckmaster as he stands up to leave.

But he can tell that I already have.

3

Three weeks later

Captain Selwyn Jepson, civilised, meticulous, diminutive, prods thoughtfully at his pipe as he contemplates the young man sitting opposite him.

Joseph Quantock, 6'4" tall, striking looking, and very fit following his period of voluntary labour, is on the face of it an unlikely candidate for the role of secret agent where an ability to blend into the background is a virtual prerequisite.

Nevertheless Jepson, a popular novelist adept at understanding characters, senses something special about the young man. He decides to see how he fares at the SOE training school in Wanborough, near the Hog's Back in Surrey, and signs his approval for Joseph Quantock's attendance at the three-week course. From the moment he is accepted for training, Joey is given a code name. Henceforth he would be known only as Luke, or more accurately 'Luc'. No one, except Buckmaster, Selwyn Jepson and a very few members of the top staff at SOE's headquarters in London, would know his real identity.

I feel like a fool walking down Notting Hill in a prickly battle dress with a red pip on my shoulder and an odd side cap on my head. A young soldier passes me on the street and salutes. I think he's making fun for a moment but then I realize and I awkwardly salute back. I am now officially a Second Lieutenant on a salary of £500 a year, tax free as the man said, and on my way to a training camp at a manor house near Guildford in Surrey.

My train pass says "First Class to Guildford." Sitting in a first-class train carriage for the first time in my life feels even more awkward than this uniform. I'm beginning to think this is really not my scene, but I'm willing to give it a go.

At Guildford station a group of us wait around for someone from the camp. We stare at each other like dogs or cats sniffing tails with our eyes. A military vehicle draws up. We are all told to hop in. No clicking of heels or saluting. Training is about to start.

For the next three weeks we are hived off into groups for physical fitness and runs on the Hog's Back; we learn Morse code which we tap out on a simulated radio transmitter; we play at unarmed combat and learn about detonators, primers and various explosives. I almost end my military career, and everyone else's, by placing my charge on a piece of angle iron with the iron lying on top of the charge. Everything explodes as it should but three or four pounds of angle iron shoot up 50 feet or more into the air and seem to hover there as if selecting whose flesh to dive into. After what seems like three or four anxious minutes it buries itself in the quarry where we are standing.

The instructor understandably has a go at me. "You deserve a right bollocking, Luc. One more trick like that and you're out, for good!" I don't blame him. It was stupid.

We still don't know what's in store for us but it's clear that we are being sorted out and judged. Some visitors come down from London, two majors and a woman officer of some kind, and take a meal with us. We think that maybe one of them is a psychiatrist. Although officially none of us knows what we are being trained for it is pretty clear that it must be something to do with espionage. And as we are all French speakers, presumably in France. But no official is saying anything.

At the end of the three weeks we are given leave and told to expect a summons from HQ.

In the sparsely furnished bedroom number 238 of the Hotel Victoria, an enormous building in London's Northumberland Avenue that serves as his temporary office, Selwyn Jepson fingers the dossier that lies on the green baize-covered trestle table in front of him. Its contents are not encouraging.

The Wanborough reports state that Luc 'is a loner', 'taciturn', 'likely to be disruptive', 'enigmatic', 'would not take kindly to authority, even at a distance' and, albeit reluctantly, recommend failing him.

On the other hand, the Wanborough staff also remark that Luc is a man of 'considerable intelligence coupled with remarkable integrity', 'sensitive, with few illusions', and the report ends with 'very much his own man'.

'Quite so' thinks Jepson. After all, being 'very much his own man' was not a bad quality for an agent who would have to rely entirely on himself in the field, with only a dangerous, secret, radio link with headquarters…; if it worked.

"Cigarette?" Jepson opens a tin of Russian cigarettes. He offers me one.

"Thank you, Sir. I'll save it for later."

"Now I'll be honest with you, Luc" says Jepson, standing up "the team at Wanborough has serious reservations about your ability to serve in the field."

He pauses. I wait. I'm pretty sure I can hear a "But…" coming.

Jepson walks over to the window to see more clearly into the bowl of his pipe. Apparently satisfied with his tobacco packing he gazes down onto the street below.

"But," he continues, "I am willing to have them proven wrong. I am relying on you to do that. What do you say?" He turns sharply and looks directly at me.

"I say that's the right decision, Sir."

I can almost hear him thinking 'Cocky bastard' but he smiles and hands me a train pass. "Very well Luc. You're booked on the night sleeper to Glasgow. The train stops at Fort William. From there you will take the local train to Arisaig. You will be met at the station. The course you will be taking is very vigorous, both physically and mentally demanding, and designed to sort out the wheat from the chaff. Students learn a number of useful skills ranging from sabotage techniques to how to kill a man with their bare hands in a matter of seconds. It lasts three months."

Jepson sits down and takes a deep drag on his pipe.

"From the local inhabitants' point of view it is a military establishment and you will, I'm afraid, have to wear uniform at all times that you are in public view. If all goes well we will meet again briefly before you become operational. If it doesn't, we won't, and you will be detained at an isolated holding camp for an indefinite period before being released back into the outside world. Is that clear?"

"Perfectly, Sir."

"Well as you'll see, you have a return ticket so I'm taking a positive view. Off you go then Luc. You've a train to catch. Good luck."

I walk out of the front door and join the rush hour crowds on Northumberland Avenue. The dusk and fog cocoon the slow-moving cars. I take the Underground to my temporary digs in Notting Hill Gate. My heart is beating fast. Even if I may have doubts, my body is telling me that I've made the right decision. I always get conjunctivitis when I think I've made a wrong decision. A built-in safeguard. The adrenalin propels me forward.

A few minutes later Selwyn Jepson, looking like any other dapper little businessman in overcoat and hat, emerges from the Hotel Victoria to catch the bus. He gets off at Selfridges and walks down Baker Street to Number 83. The sign outside the nondescript building reads 'Inter-Services Research Bureau'. He shows his pass to Security, climbs to the third floor and knocks on the door of Room 113. Vera Atkins, elegantly groomed in her neatly-pressed, honorary FANY uniform (for reasons of disguise), is seated at her desk.

"Good evening Vera. What a welcome sight you are." *Jepson, like most people in 'the Firm', thinks the world of Vera Atkins. A former WAAF squadron officer, she is now Buckmaster's Intelligence Officer, Special Assistant, Friend to all Agents, Mother Confessor, Guardian Angel and the force to be reckoned with at the headquarters of 'F' Section, the French section of the Special Operations Executive. Jepson pulls up a chair and sits beside Vera's desk.*

"How did my boy do?" *she inquires.*

Vera had met Luc, without him being aware of her identity, during the Wanborough training session. She felt she recognised an unusually promising individual and hoped that Selwyn Jepson would feel the same way, despite reports from the training camp.

"Well I am backing my hunch, or should I say our hunch" *replies Jepson.*

"Good, I'm sure it's the right thing."

"Is that you, Jepson?" *Buckmaster's voice booms from the inner sanctum.*

"Yes Sir."

Vera stands up and the two of them walk through to Buckmaster's comfortably furnished office.

"Good to see you Jepson" *says Buckmaster. He motions to them to take a seat.* "What's the low-down on Luc?"

"I'll get straight to the point, Sir," *says Jepson, pulling out his ubiquitous pipe and lighting it between phrases;* "I think Luc has the right stuff… to become a first-class agent… but he needs to convince the people at Arisaig better than he did at Wanborough. I've read him the riot act and he is aware *of the consequences… if he fails."*

"What do you think his chances are?"

"Better than 50/50 … I'm prepared to bet on it. And, so I believe, is Vera" Jepson glances in her direction.

Buckmaster trusts Vera Atkins' instincts; her ability for talent spotting is legendary.

"He won't let us down Sir, I'm sure of it" adds Vera.

"Fine," says Buckmaster "we're all agreed then. We'll see how it goes in Arisaig and hope for the best. I think Arisaig will knock the rough edges off him. We've had an appalling time in France lately and we really need to send the best agents we can find if we're to have any hope of fulfilling the PM's remit there. The whole of the Prosper circuit has been compromised; we've lost many of our crack agents, not to mention the core of the French Resistance in the north-east of the country. We cannot entertain the idea of any more mistakes."

It's 8:00 p.m. The meeting over, Jepson bids farewell to the others, and steps out into the blacked-out street. He wraps a thick scarf around his neck against the cold November night.

The 10:00 p.m. night sleeper to Glasgow is shunting into its platform as I arrive at the main concourse of Euston station. Perfect timing. I buy a hot drink and a cheese sandwich and check the departures information. 10:00 p.m. Platform 3.

I mail a couple of letters and walk along the platform to find my reserved compartment. As I get onto the train I turn and just catch a glimpse of Selwyn Jepson, and his pipe, disappearing around the barrier at the end of the platform.

What's he doing here, I wonder?

I locate my compartment. Only one of the bunks is made up so it looks as though I'll be alone. Or maybe it's always what happens in first class? I stow my knapsack in the string baggage container above the bunk and settle into the seat to read the evening paper.

The hitherto unknown Lieutenant-General Bernard Montgomery has been knighted and promoted to General following his victory over Rommel "The Desert Fox" at El Alamein……. Hitler forces King Christian of Denmark to appoint the pro-Nazi Erik Scavenius as Prime Minister……… The Indian minesweeper Bengal sinks two Japanese merchant raiders despite being heavily outgunned….. American General Mark Clark almost drowns after being landed by canvas canoe off of Gibraltar.

I turn the page over:

German troops marched into Vichy France today, allegedly to save Vichy from invasion. The operation was carried out by German and Italian units. Within 24 hours they controlled the whole of the territory formerly ruled by Vichy except for a small enclave around the naval base at Toulon. Field Marshal von Runstedt said that "the attitude of the population is indifferent" except in Marseilles.

So, the charade has ended at last. No more 'unoccupied' France. The train takes a sudden jerk forward. I open the window to have a last look at London but close it quickly, my face is blackened by the sooty smoke billowing past the window from the coal car.

A few minutes later, a conductor knocks on the door to my carriage and pulls it back by the leather strap.

"Evenin' Sir. Ticket please." He glances down to check the destination on the ticket.

"Oh, Fort William" he looks me up and down. You must be headed up to that Special Training School I'd wager? Mysterious goings on there the locals say… mind you it's all in a good cause

I guess. Good night to you, Sir."

He pulls the door half-closed and then peers through again to throw in "and Good Luck!"

Not very secret after all, this secret training school. I take the saved cigarette out of my pocket and light it.

An hour or so later I undress, climb into my bunk and, some time after the water stop at Peterborough, I fall asleep.

"Cup of tea and a biscuit, Sir?" The same guard is back at 8:00 a.m. looking just as fresh as the night before. "You'll be needing to alight in fifteen minutes to catch your connection."

The Arisaig train (Queen Victoria's Special Railway, the guard proudly informs me) is already sitting at the station as our train pulls into Fort William. I have no difficulty finding a seat and within five minutes I'm on my way; one hour to Arisaig.

The Western Highlands of Scotland look unreal against the blue backdrop of the sky. I haven't seen a landscape as sharp and clear as this since Ethiopia.

We're yet to be given any information as to where we're going or what we'll be doing but it's clear that, in one way or another, we are going to be organizing some form of resistance in France or some French-speaking area. I need to prove to these people, and to myself, that I have the necessary physical and psychological resources. More than just revenge. I feel a fury for what has happened to François and millions like him.

Once I'm in the field I'll have to depend totally on myself. As the man says there will be no instructors; no Selwyn Jepsons or Colonel Buckmasters to stand between me and death. Only my own mental and physical strength, a familiarity with the methods of sabotage and self-defence, a willingness to kill, a network of hand-picked men and women, local knowledge, cunning and a sense of survival. I'm apprehensive but at the same time excited. I like the fact that everything will be my own responsibility. I'll only have myself to blame.

A screech of wheels signals our arrival at the Arisaig halt. A bitterly cold wind slaps me in the face as soon as I pull down the window and reach out to open the train door. I am the only passenger getting out. The platform appears empty. Then I notice an alarming-looking guy in a kilt. As I approach I see that his scarred and gnarled knees have turned grey in the cold.

"You'll be Luc, the new student. I am Willy Ferguson, Staff Sergeant William Ferguson for those that care for such things."

"Good to meet you, Sir" I say, with a half-hearted salute.

Ferguson explains that the outfit he's wearing is the uniform of the Argyll and Sutherland Highlanders. I follow him to the waiting army Jeep. I've never seen a man who wore so much of his life on his face. The sunken cheekbones are as grey and scarred as his knees in the cold.

"It's about a twenty-minute drive to the house. Hop in the back with the others."

I throw my knapsack in and climb into the back of the Jeep. There are four younger guys sitting on either side of the Jeep's rear compartment. They look like stable boys. Their boots are heavily clad in manure. We exchange nods. I stare out of the back window as the Jeep bumps its way along the track on the rugged terrain. Not a sign of civilization anywhere once the village disappears from sight. Just desolate terrain, no wildlife, not even a bird. I feel a pang of apprehension but I stamp it out.

We pass a noticeboard apparently put up by the War Office, PROHIBITED AREA.

Fifteen minutes later we slow down to a crawl. Two guards are manning a barrier to the entrance of what seems to be a sizeable estate. Ferguson flashes his ID and then drives through. A long winding drive leads to Arisaig House, a large, imposing, cold granite mansion. I imagine it was the home of some imposing, cold Victorian magnate. We pull up to the front door.

"Out you get Luc, I'm taking these lads to the stables. Just walk in the front door and declare yourself at reception. Our paths will cross later."

I jump down, grab my things and wave goodbye. The Jeep disappears in a shower of grit and I walk into the reception area.

"Good morning Lieutenant, you're right on time. That's unusual. I am Sergeant Turner, Mary Turner. It's good to meet you." The receptionist is a good-looking brunette in her mid-twenties. Even her FANY uniform is unable to conceal her firm and fit figure. She pulls out a folder with LUC marked in red on the cover.

"I see Willy Ferguson brought you up from the station."

"He's been through a few wars by the look of it" I say as I drop my knapsack on the floor and take the folder. It's full of forms: uniform requisition forms; arms forms; disclaimer forms, and a lengthy wad of papers containing the syllabus for the whole course.

"He's a man of few words, is Willy" Mary Turner says, absent-mindedly filing her nails,

"quite appropriate given his job."

"And what might that be?" I look up from the wad of papers, curious.

"Willy's our expert on silent killing."

"Figures. Should I read through these now?"

"You'll want to read the syllabus at your leisure but you need to sign the relevant forms right away. Better read the small print, you could be signing your life away," she adds with a sly smile, "in a way you are."

As I read the forms I realize she's not kidding. The 'army' was accepting no responsibility for any injury including accidental death; it would deny knowledge of your existence if anyone inquired after you. You were to reveal your true identity to no one, not even senior staff; there would be no communication with anyone in the outside world during the entire eight-to-twelve-week (depending on the individual agent's ultimate role) training course. Any failure to comply with these rules would result in immediate dismissal and posting to something called 'the Barrack' for such a period of time as you were no longer considered to have relevant sensitive information. Chilling stuff.

Formalities completed, Mary Turner issues me with a new Battle Dress. "We had to get this one in especially from HQ. We don't often get people as tall as you here. Usually they like agents to be inconspicuous. Guess they make them bigger in America?"

I smile and raise an eyebrow. She blushes.

She wraps up against the cold and together we amble over to the dormitory block, a dismal-looking Nissen hut situated behind the house.

"You may want to wash and unpack. The wash hut is next door, behind the dorm block. Most students want to familiarize themselves with the syllabus so why don't you sit down and read it. It will probably take you an hour or so. When you've finished come through to the mess hall, next to reception, and meet the other students before the meal, it's bully beef and tinned sardines today. Not too appetising I know. There are only twenty of you here at the moment. The classes used to be much larger but HQ in their wisdom decided to be more selective. Too many wrong calls in the past; people putting their colleagues at risk out in the field, that sort of thing. So now it's a smaller course and longer, twelve weeks, and much more intense. See you in a while."

Mary Turner wanders off and I settle down on the bed and open the folder entitled Syllabus of Lectures.

CAMP ARRANGEMENTS.
DRESS   A1.

On arrival in Camp you will be issued with Battle Dress (or Summer Drill) and the necessary accessories. This uniform will be worn during all working periods, for the following reasons:
Security. This is a military establishment. For the benefit of local inhabitants and visiting tradesmen, it is considered advisable for the military appearance of the Camp to be consistently maintained.
Wear and tear. Many of your activities on the course will be undertaken out of doors. By wearing your issued Battle Dress you will save your civilian clothes and/or uniform.
There is no objection to your wearing whatever clothes you please for relaxation in the evenings.
You are not required to render military compliments to the officers of the camp.

COMMUNICATIONS

No incoming or outgoing mail can be received/sent during the period of the course.
Telephone calls may only be made with the express permission of the Camp Officer Commanding.

MESSING AND BAR SERVICE

a)   Messing will be charged at the rate of 1/- per day. A service charge of 1/- per week will be made to cover gratuities to the staff.
b)   Bar. Within the limits of current rationing, beer,

spirits and cigarettes are obtainable from the bar which will be open only during the following hours:

1215–1245

1800–1900

1945–2230

c) Accounts. All messing and bar accounts will be rendered and paid on the day previous to final departure. Subsequent purchases will be paid for in cash.

d) Meal Times.

Breakfast	0815 Hours
Lunch	1245 Hours
Tea	1630 Hours
Supper	1900 Hours

Please observe these hours. Kitchen accommodation and staff is limited.

I was getting the picture. Regimented camp but relaxed in terms of officialdom which suited me just fine. Reasonably civilized regimen too. I turn over the page:

OBJECTS AND METHODS OF IRREGULAR WARFARE
OBJECTS   A2.

The enemy seek to obtain from their own, from satellite and from occupied territories, the maximum advantage:

a) Politically. For example, by:

Indoctrination

"Divide and Rule"

b) Economically. For example, by:

      Use of materials
      Use of factories
      Recruitment of foreign workers
      Financial swindles
c)   **Strategically. For example, by:**
      Use of communications
      Offensive and defensive bases
      Use of Quisling and Satellite manpower

But spontaneous resistance has occurred everywhere:
Politically. e.g. Norway's battle of Churches and Teachers
Economically. e.g. France's resistance to labour recruitment
Strategically. e.g. Mihailovic's guerrillas and abortive
Haute-Savoie rising
Sporadic risings are useless. Necessity to coordinate where
possible has produced tabulation of fundamental objectives
in the waging of Irregular Warfare.

And so it continued for 394 pages. I skimmed over courses on Security, developing Cover, constructing an alibi, disguise, methods of counter-espionage, responses to personal searches, stealing a car, surviving an interrogation, recruiting and managing agents, developing an organization, communication (internal and external), selection of targets, selection of dropping zones, detailed descriptions of the Nazi party and its affiliates, and of the German Army and police services, tactics of small raiding parties, ambushes, camouflage, concealment, street fighting, sabotage of railways and roads, demolition, weapon training and, of course, close combat and silent killing. Not to mention endless hours of physical training.

My head is reeling with the thought of learning all of this in three months. But the notion that a few weeks later I might actually be alone in Occupied France and living this new persona every minute of every day sure concentrates my mind.

My fellow 'students' are a motley crew.

Luc is not aware that his fellow students include two policemen, a French count, two prostitutes, four ex-cons (and one not so ex) a defrocked Catholic priest, a Russian émigré, two railwaymen, a telephonist, a school teacher from Sidcup, a Spanish anarchist, a florist (male) and a wrestler (female). But the emphasis at Arisaig is on paramilitary training rather than team-building. The students' first course is in small arms training.

The small arms training instructor was just that. A small, wiry Scot named Macpherson who, it turns out, used to be an officer in the Shanghai police, like Willy Ferguson.

"Right you bunch of pansies," he yells as we stand on the asphalt 'playground' having just completed a five-mile run. It's 5:30 a.m. "I'm going to introduce you to your weapon of choice, my choice not yours. You are going to learn all about the Sten. And when we finish with the Sten, you're going to learn all about the Bren and the Hotchkiss and the Fiat and the Vickers and the MG34 and MG42 and the Schmeisser MG38 and the tommy-gun. And when we're finished with those we'll go on to rifles, ours and theirs, and the Yanks' carbine too now that they've deigned to join the war."

He stares at me. I'm being singled out, again. The token American, 'the ones who didn't join the war on time.' OK.

"Luc, d'ya know how to strip a Sten?"

It takes me a second or two to decipher what he's saying. His accent is even stronger than Ferguson's.

"Sure, Sir" I say, not having any idea. All I know is that it breaks down into three parts.

"Typical Yank. All talk and no action."

I walk over and pick up the Sten. Thinking hard I pull off the magazine which sticks out at right angles to the barrel and looks like it's asking to be pulled out, then I undo the barrel, then the butt and lay all three pieces with the magazine in front of Macpherson.

"Right, that's made the Yank feel superior. But I know and you know that you all could have done that, right?"

"Right" they all shout.

"The Sten gun" Macpherson continues "has a .35-inch calibre which just happens to be the same as the Schmeisser MP 38. And why would we make a gun the same calibre as a popular German one?"

"Stolen from the same bloke? " "Made by the same man? " … and other wisecracks.

"Because the ammo is interchangeable. Clever, eh?"

"The Sten can be fired with single shots or in bursts. Single shots may well miss, either because you're a bunch of assholes or because the barrel is too short. We recommend two shots minimum. Don't forget, it's cheap so you'll see a lot of them. But beware, some of our friendly manufacturers are more used to making drainpipes than guns and you'll often find the barrels have burrs of metal inside. Check every time, if you don't, the shot would more than likely kill you and not the enemy. And we don't want to waste the government's money now, do we?"

Following small arms training the syllabus moves on to Willy Ferguson's course on silent killing.

Some of my fellow students seem to have almost as much experience in this area as Willy, although perhaps they've learned from ju-jitsu manuals. Willy's methods owed more to life on the Shanghai waterfront than to official training techniques. We benefit as a result.

"This course of instruction is going to teach you how to kill. The silent killing system of combat is designed for use when you have lost your firearms, which is something you should never do, or when the use of firearms is undesirable for fear of raising the alarm."

Willy has our undivided attention.

"Some of you at some time probably learned how to box according to the Queensbury Rules. We are not interested in what you can do under the Queensbury Rules here. We are interested only in what the Queensbury Rules considers 'Fouls'. It is the Fouls that you will be taught here."

Willy points to the straw dummies in front of us.

"My main objective is to make you attack-minded, and dangerous. You will learn how to attack your opponent's weakest points before he has a chance to attack yours. The only concession we make here in Arisaig is that you must observe the submission signal: two taps on your opponent's body, on your own body, or on the floor. You will get no credit for maiming or killing a fellow student."

He uses a dummy for demonstration.

"The most deadly blows are those with the side of the hand. Fingers together, thumb up, hand tensed and striking where your hand is broadest, half way between the base of your little finger and the wrist joint. The preferred points to strike are the back of the neck, on either side of the spine; from the bridge of the nose to the base of the throat; on either side of the head and the throat; on the upper arm; on the forearm and in the kidney region. Kick with the side of the foot below knee height. Once your opponent is down, go for the kill by kicking the side or the back of the head, never the top."

Over the next few weeks we practice open-hand chin jabs, knee, head and elbow attacks and finger-tip jabs to the solar plexus, the base of the throat or the eyes: only useful in temporarily maiming as a prelude to moving in for the kill, Willy emphasizes. Other delicacies involve spinal dislocation, knife fighting, survival in crowd fighting (by constant movement); Japanese strangles, rock-crushers, match-box blows, flying mares and gagging.

Willy's 'tutorials' give us a self-confidence and, dangerously, a sense of physical invulnerability. After the grueling course, which includes being attacked in the middle of the night by an instructor in a Gestapo uniform or by Willy himself, I begin to feel as though I can take on anyone, regardless of their strength or size. No matter how an opponent reacts I now know a dozen different alternatives to extricate myself and how to exact terrible pain and certain death.

Ironically, this produces a Buddhist-like feeling of calm.

Demolition practice incorporates midnight sorties using live explosives, railway sabotage on disused stock of the London, Midland and Scottish Railway, boarding and leaving a train travelling at speed and house storming. Daytimes are devoted to infantry tactical training, stalking deer, poaching salmon, laying ambushes and intensive map-reading and cross-country work. We also learn to sail small boats, presumably to aid our escape. But from whom? And where? We still haven't been told where we are going and what we are going to do if and when we get there.

The colours of the moors, the trees and the shore are brilliant and beautiful. The hideousness of war is thousands of miles away. But I feel it getting closer. The bars at Arisaig House are well stocked and we are all encouraged to drink whisky, and to drink a lot. I suspect, rightly I discover, that an instructor is observing how we deal with drink, how discreet or indiscreet we are.

'Mimi', a busty local, is sent in to seduce us, clearly employed to test our pillow talk, to see if we talk in our sleep and, if so, in what language.

4

By the time 'Taciturn Willy' Ferguson drives me back to Arisaig station twelve weeks later, I feel like a different person; older, obviously; wiser, maybe; but a lot more confident about my chances of survival.

As he hands me my knapsack, the unemotional master of silent killing says "Well done my boy. I never would have reckoned on it when first we met but you were a star, it just goes to show… aye," he scratches his head "it just goes to show." I feel embarrassingly proud. We salute, sort of, and I walk down the platform to wait for the train to Fort William where I transfer for the onward journey to Euston.

Only mildly aware of the north of England speeding by the window, I stare into the distance. I think I've put to rest any lingering doubts the guys in charge might have over my suitability and so I allow myself to think of the real possibility that I may be in France, a fully-fledged secret agent, within a month, if that's their plan. Which I think it is.

The train pulls into Euston exactly on time. And now I am Luc no more, but Second-Lieutenant Joey Quantock once again. I step on to the platform looking, I hope, every bit the army man I'm not. Glancing around I spot Lucy's unmistakable mass of red hair and head for the barrier. After weeks of dormancy, the old urges return. We kiss until we become aware that people are stopping and staring.

"You got my letter then" I say "that's good."

"That's why I'm here Joey," she says putting her arm through mine "you look a changed man. Your old self again. I like the uniform!"

"Glad you do. Let's get out of here. I've booked us a hotel, a fancy one too." We walk briskly through the cold, grey London streets to Durrants Hotel.

The concierge checks us in. "Lieutenant and Mrs Quantock. Yes, your reservation is right here. Double room with a bath. Please remember wartime restrictions: no more than five inches of bath water. Last orders for dinner are in five minutes so please move swiftly."

I carry our bags up to the room. No sooner do I open the door than Lucy's on top of me.

"Let's skip dinner Joey. Let's go right to bed. What do you say?"

"I see you haven't changed Lucy Price. I don't know about you but I'm famished. We can always eat quickly."

"All right, but let's hurry."

Just as I'm about to close the door I notice a bottle of wine sitting on the bedside table.

"Just a second Lucy. What's this?"

"Must be a gift from the hotel. Look there's a note too" says Lucy. She opens up the card and reads it out loud

"For Lucy and Joseph. Have a good evening. SJ"

"Who's SJ?" asks Lucy.

"Oh he's my commander. I told him I was taking you here tonight."

"Ahh, what a nice gentleman."

Not so damned nice. It could only be from Selwyn Jepson and the only way he could have known that we were going to be here tonight was if he'd opened the two letters that I mailed at Euston Station the night I left for Scotland: one to Lucy and the other to the hotel making the reservation.

As promised, the dinner is brief. We're upstairs again by half past nine. Lucy is a bit tipsy from the wine. She's not used to alcohol.

I go into the bathroom to have a pee.

"Let's open this bottle of wine Joey" she doesn't wait for an answer "I feel like celebrating."

By the time I emerge from the bathroom two glasses of wine have been poured and the blankets pulled back on the bed.

"Undress me, Joey."

I decide to play cool and postpone the moment. I let her lie there provocatively while I take off my jacket and tie, socks and shoes and unbutton my shirt. Then I walk over to the bed and start to undress her.

Lucy goes quiet and limp, her eyes glisten; a wicked smile. I pull down her skirt and undo her stockings. She moves her body gently in harmony as I slowly strip her, savouring the moment, retaining contact with each article of clothing to the bitter end to heighten the excitement of the impending nakedness. She wriggles, as I pull down her underwear, to ease my task now that the time is drawing closer.

And then she lies there, completely naked. Her hair, splayed out on the pillow, gives her a look of wantonness like in one of those Victorian paintings I remember seeing in some book. Irresistible. I pull off my shirt and then my trousers and underpants. Clearly there's no more pretending I'm playing it cool.

"Atten-shun!" says Lucy.

"Hussey" I say as I lie down next to her "you're asking for it."

"I certainly am."

That's Lucy alright. I pull back her hair and gently bite the lobe of her ear. She gasps, takes my hand and guides a finger into her mouth and plays with it with her tongue. I move down her body and, cupping a breast, give her nipple an Eskimo kiss with my nose, and then use my tongue. I explore her body with my tongue. She responds with her hands. It's been too long… for both of us I think.

We can't wait any longer. Lucy arches her back as I enter her "Oh, Joey, yes, Joey," she moans as I hit the spot that always drives her wild.

With each thrust she lets out little panting sounds that gradually grow louder and louder. I too am gasping now certain that I'm about to explode. Then, miraculously, we simultaneously reach a crescendo. I collapse without withdrawing.

Before I finally sleep I think I notice a few tears drop onto Lucy's pillow, but she seems to be asleep.

The following morning I have to tell her that I'm going away and won't be able to contact her for a very long time. It sounds like a brush off but it's not. I've got to hide my feelings. I've signed up for this. She kisses me goodbye and watches as I hail a taxi and ask the driver to take me to Victoria Station.

As soon as the taxi drives around Hertford House and turns right into Manchester Square I tell the driver to pull over; pay him off, and briskly walk the few hundred yards to 83 Baker Street, as instructed.

I knock on the door of Room 134. "Come in" responds the sharp staccato voice.

I enter the smoke-filled room. Selwyn Jepson is seated at his desk.

"Good to see you, Luc. Sit down. I've asked you to come in just for a brief chat before you head off."

No time for small talk today. Jepson's all business.

"You'll go for a one-week parachute training course at STS 33 in Altrincham then you'll be sent to the SOE 'finishing school' at Beaulieu. There is a moon at the end of March. I'd like you to be ready to go then. That suit you?"

They must already have made up their minds. "Yes Sir, I'm keen to get into the field. What is SOE, by the way?"

"Your employer, dear boy. Although you are never to mention it outside the Firm. It stands for Special Operations Executive, sometimes referred to as the Baker Street Irregulars or by other less complimentary names. Its purpose, with the occasional exception, is to conduct warfare by means other than direct military engagement. I've had a glowing report from Arisaig, by the way. You seem to have impressed them alright. Well done old chap."

I have a bone to pick with him. "Thank you, Sir. And thank you too for the wine. I presume that was you?"

"A mere token old boy, mere token."

"I presume you knew about it because you opened the letters I posted at Euston? I saw you there by the way."

"Capital, dear boy. Absolutely spot on. We lost an agent twixt Baker Street and Euston a year or so ago. Disappeared into thin air. We think he may have gone over to the other side. Never can be too careful, old fruit. Need to make sure our chaps are kosher. By the way, might be a good idea to say goodbye to Vera Atkins before you go. She's a fan of yours and it's best to stay on the right side of her. She's very influential. Room 113. Off you go then. Hope to see you in a couple of weeks, depending on the weather."

This new 'jolly' Jepson makes me wince. I preferred his old sour self.

I'm not sure how Vera Atkins can be a fan if I've never met her but I follow Jepson's advice and walk along the corridor and poke my head around the door of room 113.

"Vera Atkins?" I ask. Then I recognize her. She's the lady I thought was a psychiatrist who ate dinner with us on the Wanborough course. We exchange a few words, she wishes me luck and I head back to Euston Station again where I buy a ticket for Altrincham.

This one-week course is more straightforward. We leap onto mattresses and mats practicing each stage of parachuting; the jump out, the fall and the somersault landing to reduce the risk of damage to muscles or joints. We hang onto straps attached to the roof of a barn, then slide down high wooden slides before graduating to parachuting from a barrage balloon and finally the real thing, parachuting from Whitley aircraft onto the grounds of Tatton Park. My jump is through a hole in the floor of the plane and not out of an open door. At the end of the week I get my instructions to go to Brockenhurst in the New Forest.

A battered Austin Seven is waiting for me at Brockenhurst Railway Station. The driver, an army corporal, apologizes for the state of the vehicle explaining that the regular car is being serviced so he has to make do with his own. We drive through the New Forest, avoiding the ponies, and pull up in front of Beaulieu House; "The peace time home of Lord Montagu" the corporal explains, "you can see why people's nickname for the SOE is Stately 'Omes of England."

Beaulieu is the SOE's finishing school. Finally we get to learn in more detail what SOE does. There are 12 finishing schools in the Beaulieu area. Our syllabus is divided into five sections.

Department A covers aspects of agent technique and clandestine life.

Department B conducts practical exercises to test agents'

aptitude for lessons taught in A.

Department C deals with the organization of enemy forces, overt and covert, focusing mainly on the Wehrmacht, Abwehr, SD and Gestapo.

Department D handles clandestine distribution of propaganda, known as 'moral warfare'.

Department E teaches the use of codes, ciphers and secret inks.

I settle into this last round of training quite easily. I recognize a few familiar faces from Arisaig and Wanborough. It's a strange sensation to be taught how to burgle a house by a well-spoken university professor. We have 'specialist courses' in forgery, sabotage, blackmail, slander and murder. We learn how to send and receive coded messages; to recognize all ranks of the German services; how the BBC sends personal messages during the French news; about the organization of the Gestapo; how to choose landing zones and to organize reception committees, and to undertake acts of industrial sabotage.

After supper one evening at the start of the third week of training, a thick-glassed, intellectual looking Armenian instructor gives me forged British identity cards and papers authorizing a weapons factory in nearby Southampton to give me a job. My mission is to make a copy of the secret plans of the factory. I'm going to be dropped off the next day. Half an hour after I am dropped off near the factory gates, all the police services in the area will be warned that a German agent has just been parachuted into the vicinity.

This is more like it. I take the papers and instead of going back to my room at Boarmans, 'F' Section's house in the Beaulieu grounds, I go in search of a fellow 'student', Billy Bowles. He has a reputation as a master forger.

At 6:00 a.m. the following morning I'm picked up by my friend the corporal to be driven into Southampton. Another 'student', a manly blonde code-named 'Paulette' who is reputed to be a first-class shot, accompanies me. The corporal drops me at the factory gates with my knapsack of sandwiches, a bottle of Lucozade and the identity papers. Then he and Paulette drive off.

Instead of reporting for duty as instructed, I start walking towards the town, or what's left of it after incessant Nazi bombing. Certain that I'm going to be followed, I stop in front of a shop window to light a cigarette. Clearly outlined in the window's reflection is the unappealing sight of Paulette, twenty yards or so behind me on the other side of the street. I continue walking, keeping an eye out for an opportunity to lose her.

A few minutes later I see my chance; a Working Man's Club. I abruptly turn into the entrance.

"Hello mate" I say to the old man at reception "is Ronnie here?"

"Dunno him mate" says the old man "'ave a look inside". I walk into the club room where a group of men are having their morning tea. They take no notice of me as I walk through the room towards the sign marked 'Toilet'.

Looking out of the toilet window I can see what they call the 'Garden', a small area covered in asphalt. Beyond it is an overgrown path alongside a neglected open space which must once have been some sort of park. I locate the back door and head for a thicket in the park. I take out a jacket and tie from my knapsack and a thin leather briefcase which I borrowed from a guy at Beaulieu. Then I ditch the knapsack along with the sandwiches and drink and make for a denser part of the wood.

Several minutes later, with a new moustache, an off-the-peg jacket and tie and carrying a small briefcase, I stride purposefully along the road to the factory. Paulette is nowhere to be seen.

"Your Identity Papers, Sir" says the burly security guard at the

factory gates. I hand over a National Registry ID Card and a folded sheet of paper. The guard opens up the
official-looking document.

WAR OFFICE

Whitehall, London

This is to certify that Jeremy Westmorland is an Inspector with the War Office Factory Contingency Department

I would be grateful if you would accord him all possible courtesies in the line of his official duties on behalf of the War Department.

Viscount Chandos

Minister of Production

"Who do you wish to see, Sir?"

Relieved that Billy Bowles' forgery seems to have done the job, I say "The Managing Director" in my best posh English accent. It hurts my throat but it seems to work.

"I'll notify his secretary."

Within ten minutes I am sitting in the secretary's office sipping a cup of coffee and explaining my need to see the detailed factory plans, including the areas assigned to the manufacture of secret weapons, in order to make contingency preparations in case the factory is bombed.

The secretary explains that the Managing Director won't be back until 4:00 p.m. as he is on his way down from Manchester.

I say I can't wait that long and that I need to get the plans back to Lord Chandos in London by early afternoon. Overawed by this visitation from the War Office, the secretary walks over to the safe and pulls out a fat document labeled TOP SECRET.

Twenty minutes later I walk out of the factory gates with a crisp new copy of the factory's secret plans in my briefcase. I hadn't needed the War Office telephone number that I was given as a last resort, in case I was picked up and interrogated by the police.

I ditch the itchy moustache at the earliest opportunity and catch the bus back to Beaulieu. The secret plans are on the instructor's desk by 2:00 p.m. Paulette, frustrated by her continuing failure to locate me, doesn't return until 6:00 p.m. I can't resist giving her a little wave as she walks into the reception area where I'm pretending to read a book. She's not happy.

Five days later, on Tuesday 23 March, at 5:45 a.m., unable to sleep with the adrenalin running through my body, I pull open the blinds of my attic bedroom and look up at the reassuringly clear sky.

The duty officer knocked on my bedroom door at 10:00 p.m. last night to give me my orders. "You're on for tomorrow, Luc, best get a good night's sleep."

I get dressed and walk downstairs to the cafeteria for an early breakfast.

"Are you flying tonight sir?" asks the waitress.

"I sure am."

"Then you are allowed eggs and toast."

Two hours later I'm being driven swiftly through the early-morning countryside on my way to RAF Tangmere, an airfield in Sussex.

5

Several hundred kilometres away in north-eastern France, two groups of people are making their way independently towards Mme. Sainte-Beauve's hop farm on the outskirts of the little village of Estrées-St.Denis, a few kilometres west of the German concentration camp in Compiègne.

At a little past midnight on the previous evening, 22 March, Roger Chamberlain, an English aristocrat and well-known SOE agent who has been in France for two years, current alias Paul Chaboux, quietly closed the front door of the Hotel de la Poste in the Haute-Savoie village of St. Jorioz on the shores of Lake Annecy.

He made his cautious way through the dark streets to the barn at the edge of the village for his rendezvous with Henri Clabaud, 'Georges', the head of the local Resistance organization. Both men had been ordered to travel to London for debriefing. 'Paul' is concerned about leaving St. Jorioz with a new guy standing in, particularly one as fresh from training as Luc. However he has left his courier, Mathilde Chambrun, 'Claudine' in charge. He worked with her in Cannes following her arrival by felucca the previous December. His trusty wireless operator, Marc Weinberger, 'Arnaud', is also based nearby. He feels reassured, particularly as there are so many seasoned Resistance members in the area.

At the edge of the village, where St Jorioz gives way to open farmland, he approached the barn and recognised the outline of 'Georges' smoking a cigarette, framed against the door.

He shook his friend's hand, "Bon soir Georges. Everything is set for tomorrow night but unfortunately the pick-up location has changed. We need to get to Compiègne, it's about 90 km north-east of Paris."

Georges was understandably sceptical. "We'll see Paul, I bet it will be another wrong call." he replied, picking up his knapsack and strapping it onto his back.

They've tried three times to get to London but each time the Lysander dispatched from London was unable to land. The first time it couldn't find the landing strip; another time there was so much enemy activity in the air that the plane had to return to base; and the third time the reception group had been betrayed and the two of them had made a narrow escape.

"No, I think this time it will work." Paul reassured him as they started out towards Annecy "Arnaud gave me this message this afternoon:

LYSANDER BRINGING LUC YOUR REPLACEMENT STOP PLEASE HAVE HIM MET AND ALL LAID ON STOP"

The two men decided to take the first train out of Annecy that morning, due to depart at 5:00 a.m.

As they made their way to Annecy, sticking to the back roads, Georges asked "How does Arnaud feel about a new chap coming to replace you? He's not very happy I suspect?"

"No he's not; and nor is Claudine, but I've told them they have to be good to him. Anyhow we'll be back in a few weeks and Luc can head off down south, poor sucker."

They arrive mid-morning this same day, 23 March. They take rooms in the tiny Hotel de la Gare and then set off to look for a way to get to the hamlet of Estrées-St.Denis where they hope to find Mme. Sainte-Beauve's hop farm and the landing strip which London has assured them will be perfect for a Lysander.

As no bicycles can be found, they borrow a horse and trap and set off, looking just like two peasants on their way to the farm. Within minutes they pass by the Compiègne Concentration Camp where many Resistance members, including some of their own friends, are being held before the final trip to Germany, to work-camps, or to death. Both men feel a chill as they pass by the walls… "There but for the grace of God…"

It takes them about an hour to get to Estrées-St.Denis and to locate Mme. Sainte-Beauve's farm. It is enormous, surrounded by high walls. Paul yanks the bell by the gate. Moments later a distinguished-looking, grey-haired lady walks out of the front door and approaches them.

"Good afternoon, Madame" says Paul "Do you have a copy of 'Madame Bovary'?"

"No, but I do have Salammbô, also by Flaubert"

"Ah, I prefer La Comedie Humaine"

Passwords confirmed, Mme. Sainte-Beauve opens the gate. Paul and Georges introduce themselves and all three climb up onto the horse and trap and set off for the proposed landing field. London is right, it's ideal for a Lysander: a firm, flattish, clear space of at least 200 metres.

On their way back to the farmhouse, Paul asks "Would it be alright with you if we stay here and wait for the radio message from London confirming the flight?"

"I am sorry but that will not be possible" Mme. Sainte-Beauve replies as she climbs down from the cart "however much I should like to let you."

They understand. She is risking everything by letting them use the field. If her own workers discover what's going on, she risks being betrayed.

"D'accord, Madame" says Paul. "We will be back tonight and will not disturb you."

"I hope you are successful tonight" replies Mme. Sainte-Beauve as she bids them goodbye "for tomorrow the field will be ploughed."

The two men return to Compiègne in darkness. They wait in the hotel restaurant for word from Jean Besson, a local member of the Resistance, who has agreed to monitor the BBC broadcast in the home of the town's vet.

The remote, secret section of the 11 Group fighter airfield at RAF Tangmere is under heavy security. Our car is stopped several times on the way into the main airfield compound. I recognize the clandestine aircraft by the descriptions and illustrations used in the Beaulieu course; three Hudsons, and a little Lysander. We head towards a 16th-century manor house sitting awkwardly in the centre of all this twentieth-century activity.

After a brutal cup of black coffee and a Russian cigarette, some guy escorts me to the equipment room to get my supplies. He makes me strip and then re-dress, article by article, ensuring that any label indicating an origin other than France has been removed. My cover is that of a school teacher recovering from tuberculosis. They give me supplies; a pack of Gauloises, several hundred French francs in used notes, an identity document with my cover name, Christophe Martin, clearly printed at the top, a driving licence stating that, because I am to teach school in outlying areas, I am allowed use of a motorcycle. Secreted in the lapel of my jacket collar is a cyanide pill, standard issue for all SOE agents.

Dressed and ready for the flight, I chat with several agents who've just returned from France and are staying on at Tangmere for a debriefing. Charles Decosse, head of the Lyon réseau, or Resistance network, introduces himself to me. He is going to be my fellow passenger on the flight to France. A few minutes later we are both taken into the Operations Room. A large map of France is pinned to the wall. The many red marks, mainly along the coastline, indicate high-risk areas for flak. Even though the 'Moon Squadron' pilots are adept at avoiding these areas, they tell us that several planes have been lost lately to German ack-ack guns.

The squadron leader, a genial, chain-smoking ex-public school boy in his mid-twenties, starts his briefing.

"Welcome Gentlemen to RAF Tangmere. My name is Hugh Verity and I will be your pilot on tonight's run. This will be my one-hundredth run so it's something of a special night for me too. The Met report for our flight to Compiègne has just come in. The weather is fine with occasional cloud and a slight risk of mist in the landing area. Nothing unusual there."

Verity indicates the flight path and pulls out a photograph of a field.

"This photograph, taken by our reconnaissance people yesterday afternoon, shows our landing site in Département 60 near a hop farm 5.5km north of the little village of Estrées-St. Denis, WNW of Compiègne. It belongs to a charming French lady named Madame Sainte-Beauve. Air Ops are sending out a message via the BBC announcing your arrival to ensure that the reception committee is in place."

Verity is impressive and calm. It's reassuring to know that he's a veteran of so many flights. He takes us out to see our plane. "As you can see, even in the moonlight, the Lysander is a single-engined, high-winged monoplane. This one is my personal favourite. I've christened her 'Jiminy Cricket'. At 870 horsepower she has a cruising speed of 165 m.p.h. and a radius of action of roughly 450 miles. She weighs four-and-a-half tons. 'Lizzy', as she is affectionately known, was first developed by Westland in 1936 but suffered an ignominious infancy in the first year of the war. Of 180 Lysanders sent on observation missions in support of the Belgians in 1940, only 40 returned. She was dismissed as being unsuited for the task."

Not very reassuring. Verity continues as he walks us around the plane "However, they soon found a new role for Lizzy, and one at which she excels. With her ability to take off and land in very short distances, on roughish terrain, a Lysander is ideally suited for picking up messages etcetera (you attach a hook to the bottom of the fuselage); photographic missions, ground attack (she can carry two Browning machine guns and twelve small bombs fitted to the wheel bearings) and of course for picking up and dropping off 'Joes', you chaps. She is painted matt black to make her invisible to searchlights but we found that the view from above makes the silhouette positive against low cloud so I've had the upper surfaces recamouflaged in dark green and pale grey."

Verity is wearing a mixture of civilian clothes and uniform so if we have to abandon the Lysander in France for some reason, such as getting stuck in the mud, he can ditch or burn his uniform and hang on to his dark roll-neck sweater. He says he also has an escape kit with a wad of French francs, passport photographs for ID cards, a map of France printed on silk, compass, fishing hook and line and some concentrated food tablets.

We walk back to the house where Selwyn Jepson has just arrived from London. He's here to debrief the returned agents but he takes the opportunity to wish us well and share a bottle of wine.

Shortly before 11:30 p.m. Verity, Decosse and I get into a big American Ford station wagon and are driven out to our Lysander. Verity helps us stow our luggage under our hinged wooden seat and on the shelf in front as we face the tail. We fit our parachute harnesses on and climb into the back cockpit of the Lysander, just large enough to hold two agents; three at a pinch; four in a crisis. I plug my flying helmet into the intercom and test the microphone to make sure all is in working order.

Verity talks to me through the intercom, explaining everything he is doing. I pass on the information to Decosse. Verity then straps himself into the cockpit, slides the roof shut, completes his final checks, primes the engine and starts up. He lets the engine tick over for a few minutes until the oil temperature is 5°C, tests the flying controls and the brake pressure. Satisfied, he opens her up to 1,800 rpm, changes the propeller to coarse pitch, notes the large drop in rpm, and returns it to fine pitch. At cruising throttle he checks the alternate magneto switches. Everything appears to be OK. He waves away the chocks, and we await clearance for take-off.

At precisely 11:46 p.m. Verity turns on to the long flarepath, eases the throttle fully open as we taxi along, and then we take off. I can't remember ever feeling so exhilarated. There's so much to see and listen for and think about that there's little room for fear. Once we reach the safety speed of 80 mph, Verity eases the stick back and climbs away turning onto his first course for the coast of France.

6

In a small studio in the basement of London's Bush House a BBC announcer is reading out the following, to him meaningless, message. He repeats it twice.

MOTHER GOOSE WILL LAY A GOLDEN EGG

To Jean Besson, listening to the wireless set at the local vet's house in Compiègne, however, the message is confirming that the Lysander is on its way. He jumps onto his bicycle and pedals as fast as he can to the Hotel de la Gare. Paul and Georges are just finishing off their meal.

"Ah, Jean" says Georges on seeing his friend come through the door "come join us for a drink."

"No I can't. I need to get to my aunt's house and would like you to give me a ride."

Neither Paul nor Georges need an explanation. Clearly Besson has received the message and the mission is on.

They pay their bill, make their apologies, fetch their bags and leave the hotel. Jean Besson escorts them through the blacked-out train station and opens the door of a darkened train. They sit inside and wait. The train for

Paris pulls away from the adjoining platform and shortly thereafter their own train shunts its way out of the station.

Twenty minutes later, at the halt before St. Just en Chaussée, the three men get off the train. As with every crossing and bridge throughout the country, it is manned by two Frenchmen who guard it from dusk to dawn against sabotage. If anything occurs during their watch they are taken as hostages, or shot. The three men mutter a "Bon soir" to the guards and disappear into the night. Jean Besson has memorised the directions.

"After about 300 metres we fork right, getting into wooded country. Then we travel for about three km until we reach the brow of a hill and we see the Route de Flandré, N 17, at right angles to us, about one kilometre away. There we turn sharp right and we'll see the field over the brow of another slight rise. In the distance we'll see Madame Sainte-Beauve's farm."

By 9:45 p.m. they have cleared the brow of the hill. The railway line separates them from the farm. They avoid crossing at the level crossing for fear of alerting the guards so close to the landing field.

"I hope they don't get into trouble for what happens tonight" says Paul.

"C'est la vie" replies Besson.

They continue quietly and cautiously along a path and through the woods. As they approach the landing field they stop dead in their tracks.

"Attention" whispers Besson grabbing the others' arms to still them, "we are not alone. There's someone in the trees over there." He points towards a copse on the right, just at the edge of the landing field.

Are they Germans? Have they been betrayed?

They stand stock-still. There are dry leaves underfoot. The trees sway gently in the wind. For what seems like three or four minutes they stay there, listening.

And then they hear someone whistling. It's the V-sign – the dot, dot, dot dash of Beethoven's Fifth; the BBC's call sign to Europe.

"That's Marchais" says Paul "what the hell is he doing here?" They walk out into the open and over to the copse where the moon now casts its light on two figures, and then two more. Marchais, the man who organized the Marseille Resistance réseau, is visiting Paris to find more recruits as replacements for those who have so recently been betrayed.

Marchais walks over to greet Paul and the others; a broad grin on his face and a bottle of wine in his hand.

"You frightened us out of our wits, you great French toad" says Paul.

"Wrong animal" exclaims Marchais, laughing, "Good to see you, mes amis. You must join us for dinner. The chef has laid on something special for tonight."

As they walk over to join the others, Marchais explains his presence to Paul.

"I've come to pick up your replacement, my dear Paul. I thought I would drive him to Paris for a few days and let him get accustomed to our ways before he goes to St Jorioz. It is better for him than the alternative, a haystack here in Compiègne, don't you agree? Your lady from Baker Street asked me to meet him."

"What about the curfew? How are you going to get through all those checkpoints around Paris?"

"We are being driven by a doctor, so that's helpful. Plus our papers are good for the whole night. We have German permits and Ausweises and an excellent forgery of the Kommandant's signature" he grins.

Paul laughs, admiring the cheek.

Marchais introduces him to the others. Two men from the village who are known to Jean Besson; Guy, a doctor friend of Marchais' from Paris, and two other men from the Lyon Resistance group who have come to meet Charles Decosse.

Paul decides to organize the landing lights before they settle down for 'dinner'.

The Lysander pilot will look for the well-known inverted L shape formed by a group of torches to indicate the landing area.

"It's good we have all these men here" says Paul, "it means we won't have to attach the lamps to sticks like we usually do."

Paul and Marchais determine the exact dimensions of the field necessary for the landing and lay out handkerchiefs to mark where the torch bearers should stand. They then give the others their instructions and, satisfied that all is in order, the motley group settles down in the cold moonlit forest to an impromptu meal of cold rabbit and wine. And they wait.

The night wears on. They hear the distant coughing of one of the men at the level crossing, and lower their voices.

Next, they hear the drone of a plane approaching. Three men run to their posts and hold bicycle lamps out in a row, along the direction of the wind. Paul stands with another torch and flashes the agreed Morse code letter for the day, B. The pilot pays no attention and roars overhead. They wait for it to return.

There it comes, back again. Paul flashes up the code, visible to 7,000 metres. Each man tense with anticipation. But once again the pilot ignores him and flies right on by.

It's just as well. The pilot is a German and the plane is a Junkers 88.

Half an hour passes. They start to get disillusioned. "Do you think they will come?" asks Marchais.

"The BBC message has gone out, so it should be OK. But who knows what problems they might be having up there with all this activity in the sky."

And he is right.

The din of the Lysander's propeller is deafening. But the moon is bright and the sky clear as we approach the French coast, flying very low to avoid the German radar. Verity heads for a gap in flak defences that he knows well and then banks swiftly to avoid being spotted by a fighter base. A searchlight flashes by several times and then fixes on us. Suddenly I feel so vulnerable, helpless. But this is Verity's 100th flight I tell myself. He knows what to do.

A flak gun suddenly opens up, a Roman candle of bright balls of fire come drifting up and Verity takes evasive action. None of them succeeds in scorching the plane. Zigzagging away, we disappear behind one of the few clouds and breathe more easily.

As we approach the area around Compiègne, we are chased by a night fighter and shot at with tracers. We have to fly off course and for fifteen minutes or so we're hopelessly lost.

It's only trust in our 25-year-old pilot that stops us from panicking. I hate being a passenger in any vehicle but I've never felt as helpless as this – a piece of flotsam being tossed around by the waves.

Just as all appears hopeless, Verity's voice comes through the microphone. "Five minutes till landing, mates."

I tap Decosse on the shoulder and signal "Cinq minutes." Decosse and I check and double-check our gear.

The landing ground is only a few kilometres from the German camp at Compiègne. Verity drops the Lysander down to 30 metres and searches the horizon for the tell-tale torches which will illuminate the 'runway' and indicate the direction of the wind. He sees the ground signal flicker on with the code letter, B. He flashes the response code in recognition from a small lamp below the fuselage and circles round again, sees the inverted L sign formed by torches perfectly lit below, throttles back his engine and comes in to land pulling up just six metres from two men, whom we hope are not Germans.

It's 1:58 a.m.

I pull back the sliding roof of the cockpit and jump out onto French soil. Decosse hands down the bags before jumping out himself.

Now starts the next chapter in my life. I smile, almost laugh.

The two men on the ground are friends of Decosse and greet him briefly. One of them says to me "Welcome Luc, we're not half glad to see you. I'm Paul and this is Georges. We are the return package to England."

"Good luck" I reply "have a good trip home."

"We'll see you in a few weeks. Lots of excitement here. Terrible lack of loo paper though," with that, Paul and Georges climb up the small ladder attached to the fuselage, settle themselves into the Lysander's rear cockpit, pull the sliding roof closed and lock it with the safety catch. Verity revs up the engine and 200 metres later they're airborne.

Within moments the Lysander disappears from sight, the landing lights are extinguished and Mme. Sainte-Beauve's field is returned to bucolic tranquility.

Decosse says good luck, hugs me goodbye, exchanges a few words with members of the reception group and disappears in the direction of the N 17 with his comrades from Lyon.

Two days later one of them, a double agent, betrays him to the Gestapo. Decosse is shot dead trying to escape.

The leader of the remaining members of the reception group introduces himself to me as Marchais. His two friends, Besson and Guy, shake my hand and we all bundle into a horse and trap. I sit in the back leaning against some bags of manure. The night is cold and the moonlight casts an eerie glow on the surrounding landscape. We take cart tracks across fields and occasionally pass silhouetted houses and ghoulish woods. I huddle against the manure, too cold to stink; both me and the manure.

The scene becomes even more macabre when we pass the Nazi detention camp on the outskirts of Compiègne. It's a relief to pull up at the inn where two of the reception committee have left their bikes. I jump down and brush muck off my clothes. Besson and two other local guys return the horse and cart to their rightful owner, say goodbye, pick up their bikes from outside the bar and return to their wives and families.

"Our plan, Monsieur Luc" explains Marchais, as Guy, the doctor from Paris, and I walk with him along the main street "is to take you by car to my apartment in the rue de Babylone where you can stay until you are ready to leave. Even though there is a curfew, we have arranged for the necessary papers. You will be perfectly safe there for a few days, they are used to me having relatives from the countryside coming to stay in the big city. My friends and I can get you anything you need, just let us know."

I thank Marchais and say I will stay for a couple of days to acclimatize myself and to test out my cover as a schoolmaster.

Marchais beckons Guy and me towards a garage of one of the larger houses just off the main street. He quietly opens the garage door so as not to alert the neighbours and reveals an ancient Citroën. "Courtesy of the local deputy mayor M. Jean-Louis Grenier."

Marchais explains that M. Grenier will insist the car has been stolen when he reports it to the police in the morning. The doctor takes the wheel while Marchais masks the headlights (a requirement for driving through Paris, although not in the countryside apparently) then we push the car into the street, close the garage door, jump in and only then does the doctor turn on the ignition. To no avail. Three, four times he urges the Citroën into action but it's useless, the battery is dead. We give it a push. We clamber out of the car and push it as fast as we can down the moonlit street until it finally jump-starts.

Someone opens their bedroom shutters.

The Citroën, still operating on petrol instead of gazogène, like most cars in France, is now purring along responsively as we head south-west to Paris along the deserted roads, only occasionally encountering other vehicles. Once we get close to the outskirts of Paris everything changes. Germans are all over the place, or at least their vehicles are. But we aren't stopped and questioned. I know my own papers are in order but I can't vouch for my companions. They talk as though this were all a great game.

We find our way to the rue de Babylone without incident. I am surprised to find that it's in the heart of the 7th arrondisement, smack opposite German military barracks. The doctor dumps the car in a side street, throws the keys into a household garbage can, says goodbye to us and disappears into the night. Marchais and I pretend to be two late-night drunkards returning home as we wend our way, arm in arm, across the street to his apartment building. We enter a small courtyard, passing by the concierge's office.

"Bon soir M. Gotin" says the bleary-eyed concierge, sitting at the window, "your neighbours are away tonight. Sleep well."

Marchais replies "Merci René." We take the elevator up to the fourth floor.

"René is one of ours" he tells me on the way up to his apartment "he's letting me know that the Nazi officer that lives in the next door apartment is out tonight." The elevator comes to an abrupt stop. Marchais opens the old-fashioned gates and we step out into a clean-looking hall, high ceilings, carpeted floors and dull wallpapered walls.

Marchais' apartment is surprisingly spartan given the relative luxury of the apartment block. "I don't usually stay here" he explains "just use it as my HQ and keep it as a safe house for visiting agents. There are Germans on the doorstep but what safer place to be, n'est-ce pas? You can sleep on the sofa. I'm sure you're tired and tomorrow you'll want to familiarize yourself with France. It's been a few years since you were last here, hasn't it? You'll like St Jorioz. It's a pretty place. My wife lives there." Marchais calls through from the kitchen. "Will you have a whisky before you turn in?"

"Love one" I say, settling down on the sofa while registering that Marchais must have been briefed about my previous life in France.

Marchais hands me a whisky and then slumps down into a badly-sprung armchair with his own glass. "Tomorrow I leave early" he says as he twiddles the ice cube in his glass "I have things to do and an appointment for lunch. I suggest you sleep until you feel like waking. There is some reasonable black-market coffee and some bread in the kitchen. Help yourself, yes? I propose we meet at the Pont Neuf, south side, at 3:00. We can then go for a coffee and I will introduce you to a friend who will see to anything you need before you move on. I'll leave an old suitcase for you to use; borrow anything you want."

I thank him for his hospitality and drain the whisky glass. It's 3:30 a.m. "I think I'll turn in' I say.

"D'accord, M. Luc, moi aussi" says Marchais "See you tomorrow at the Pont Neuf."

7

The lights are still burning at 3:30 a.m. in the Hotel Lutetia, the Left Bank Headquarters of the German Military Intelligence, the Abwehr.

Sitting at his desk on the third floor, Colonel Hans Froehling picks up the phone and dials a number in the 16th arrondissement.

Sleeping fitfully as always, Sergeant Karl Metzger is nonetheless startled by the phone. Always the good soldier, he immediately jumps out of bed and, standing to attention, picks up the receiver. He knows it will be HQ.

"Ja?"

"Metzger, how soon can you be here?"

"I'll leave at once, Herr Oberst, I can be with you in 25 minutes."

"Good, I've got a complicated case here, Metzger, and I want you to take it over. There is someone here I want you to meet. See you soon. Heil Hitler."

"Heil............." but Froehling has already hung up the phone. Metzger, his carefully-pressed uniform hanging in readiness on the back of the bedroom door, quickly dresses, smoothes down his remaining hair, dons the blue beret and dark glasses he considers an essential part of his uniform, his 'mystique', salutes himself in the mirror and, satisfied, walks determinedly out of the apartment house to the garage,

commandeered from the publisher living in the top-floor apartment, and jumps onto his motorcycle.

Karl Metzger has long been one of life's misfits, and recognises himself as such. As a young man with a misshapen physique (giving him the appearance of the numeral seven) he took refuge in foreign languages which he mastered effortlessly, and the piano which, he feels, he could have pursued to concert performance level had it not been for the wall-papering corporal who has taken control of his beloved Germany.

He has few friends and a frustratingly high level of testosterone. This he blames for his not infrequent outbursts of uncontrollable anger and his all too frequent demands for instant gratification by the opposite sex. Plenty of accommodating French girls are readily available, for a token price.

An uninspiring clerk for a Hamburg export firm before the war, he was recruited in August 1939 by the German Army as a translator in recognition of his fluency in French. Or so he understood.

In fact he, along with dozens like him, found himself part of the Abwehr. The most important of the German Military Intelligence services, the Abwehr is controlled by Admiral Canaris and, interestingly, includes a substantial number of opponents of Hitler. Of whom Metzger likes to consider himself one. He dislikes the Nazi ideology. He dislikes the hierarchy of the Abwehr. He feels himself superior to the oafs above him and he feels he has proven it time and time again.

By carefully infiltrating Resistance groups, Metzger has already taken a key role in destroying several of the largest and most successful circuits in France. The British consider him, with good reason, a sinister and dangerous man who has already done more damage than 'Cicero' did in Alexandria. And yet Metzger is still only a sergeant and seemingly destined to remain so. He is a bitter man. But he's determined to show 'them', the Abwehr brass, what a 'little man' can do.

As he leaves his bourgeois apartment and speeds, like a black widow spider astride a BMW, through the deserted streets of Paris at 3:55 a.m.

on 24 March,, 1943, he senses that another opportunity to show his superiority is about to present itself.

The Hotel Lutetia is a 300-room Art Deco hotel built in 1910. One of the grand Paris hotels in its heyday, and ironically the place where General Charles de Gaulle and his wife spent their honeymoon, it sits staunchly on the corner of Boulevard Raspail and the rue de Sevres in the heart of St Germain des Prés. Since being requisitioned as the Abwehr HQ, it has turned into an ominous, forbidding building, even to the Nazis. It is permanently staffed by 50 officers and men, supported by 20 female assistants. The bedroom that serves as Colonel Froehling's office is not one of the choice ones but is comfortable enough. Metzger knocks on the door.

"Enter... ah Metzger. Sit down. Have a cigarette" Metzger is momentarily caught off guard, unused to being treated in such a familiar way by a superior officer. "Meet Monsieur Gaston, a friend of the Fatherland."

Gaston, a balding, swollen-bellied Nazi collaborator has, it transpires, a female agent named 'Alice' in his employ. Alice has a Russian friend who belongs to a dangerous Resistance group with an HQ in southern France. He had informed her that a senior Resistance agent would be coming to Paris on 23 March but will only be in the city for a few days.

"Do everything necessary for his arrest Metzger" demands Froehling, "be cautious. Ask for the support you need. But be successful, Metzger! M Gaston will bring you up to date."

Gaston, apparently French, turns out to be a consummate linguist speaking five languages without the trace of an accent. He summarises the investigation so far.

"The man we must arrest is named Marchais. He has formed a very effective terrorist group in the south of France. They have been responsible for destroying trains, killing German officers, blowing up factories... we know this all from my agent, 'Alice', a French lady formerly in the employ of British Intelligence. She has convinced her Russian contact to suggest to

Marchais that she should be the replacement for Marchais' chief man in Paris whom we arrested last month.*"*

Gaston is interrupted when Colonel Froehling's phone rings.

It's 'Alice'. She reports that Marchais will be at Café Maurice off the Champs Elysées at 1:00 p.m.

Gaston and Metzger spend twenty minutes discussing tactics. Deciding they won't need extra support, they arrange to meet at the café at 12:30 p.m.

Metzger is dismissed. He leaves the Lutetia and on the way home he considers his position. Always suspicious of being set up by his superiors, he resolves that two of his own trusted agents will be at the café. He has his future to think of. He wants to ensure that nothing will go wrong. On returning home he telephones each of them and gives them their instructions.

The following day, at 12:30 p.m. precisely, Metzger meets Gaston at the door of the Café Maurice. Together they enter, point to a table, and are immediately seated in the gallery. Gaston's agent, Alice, is sitting at the front of the café reading an out-of-date fashion journal. Metzger's two agents are having a conversation a few metres away from her. And two lovers sit whispering sweet nothings to each other at a table in the corner. The male half of the loving couple is Gaston's man, Jean-Paul, playing his role rather too convincingly Gaston observes.

They wait. 1:00; 1:15; 1:30 and still no Marchais. Metzger starts to get suspicious. In his experience, women agents are always apt to embroider things. Perhaps this Alice is just another one who thinks that clandestine behaviour is a romantic game.

Gaston and Metzger almost decide to give up when Gaston grabs Metzger's arm. Alice's Russian contact comes in with two other people, a man and a woman.

The man is tall, thin and about thirty. The woman is younger, slim and elegant. Metzger and Gaston can see everything from their vantage point. The Russian waves to 'Alice' and the three of them walk over to her table and sit down. They enter into a lively conversation.

Gaston leans over to Metzger and whispers "That is Marchais and his secretary, Suzanne, with Alice's Russian contact."

Fifteen minutes later 'Alice' pulls out her handkerchief and blows her nose; the signal that the conversation is drawing to a close.

Metzger and Gaston pay their bill and walk downstairs towards the door, a route that takes them past Alice's table where she and Marchais are just saying their goodbyes. Metzger's two agents also head in the same direction.

Metzger moves in. "Monsieur, Madame. German police. You are under arrest. If you behave and come quietly you will have no trouble."

Marchais makes a run for the door but Metzger's men grab him. He relaxes his muscles, accepting the inevitable, turns to 'Alice' and spits in her face.

Metzger slaps him.

Suzanne yells "Leave him alone you pigs."

Metzger slaps her, hard.

Metzger's two agents then leave the restaurant and a minute later pull up in a large Citroën. Metzger leads Marchais and Suzanne out of the café and bundles them into the back of the Citroën.

They drive off at high speed in the direction of Fresnes prison.

8

I wake up at 9:00 a.m. No sign of Marchais. He must have gone already. I munch on a piece of bread, down a cup of coffee and take a weak but refreshing shower. I lay out my schoolmasterly clothes; dark shirt and tie, corduroy jacket, dark trousers and brown lace-up shoes, and get dressed. Making certain I have my identity papers, I extract enough money to buy some lunch and to cover any travel expenses. The rest of the money I stash with my other clothes in the old suitcase that Marchais gave me and stand it next to the couch.

After checking that I've left nothing incriminating around, in case the flat is raided, I borrow a hat from among several hanging on Marchais' hatstand, pocket the spare set of keys left for me on the hall table, and mentally run through everything I am wearing, taking with me, and leaving behind. Satisfied that everything is in order, I open the door, pull it firmly closed behind me and, avoiding the elevator and possible close encounters, head down the stairs.

René, the concierge, is at his window.

"Bonjour René."

He barely looks up from his newspaper, "Monsieur" he responds, not sure of me yet.

I walk out into the brilliant sunshine and take a deep breath. Braced with nostalgia, I'm in Paris for the first time in almost ten years. I can't help but smile.

It's quarter to ten. I plan to get my bearings, observe the Occupation first-hand, and then stop for a glass of wine and a meal at the Left Bank brasserie, Balzar, if it's still there. Located on the rue des Ecoles, it was a favourite haunt of François and my French friends before the war. It's also a stone's throw from Boulevard Raspail and the Hotel Lutetia, now the Gestapo or Abwehr HQ.

This is a smart section of Paris. You don't see too many people poorly fed or clothed around here. German officers walk in groups down the rue de Bellechasse looking strangely anxious. I cross over the Seine and walk through the Tuileries to the rue de Rivoli.

Great red and black oversized Nazi banners hang at regular intervals all the way down the rue de Rivoli. A bus carrying German troops drives slowly down the street, watched over by guards in front, on either side of the road and behind, all with automatic pistols drawn. The Resistance must be making serious inroads for the Germans to be so nervous. I half expected them still to be goose-stepping down the middle of the road and for Nazi officers to be swaggering along the pavements flashing their medals at the populace as we were told they did a couple of years ago.

I stop in front of W.H.Smith, the English-language bookstore now renamed Frontbuchhandlung. The window is full of posters and pages of the colour illustrated bi-monthly German propaganda magazine, Signal, now translated into French, of course.

A German officer emerges from the shop, sees me and demands my papers. My first chance encounter with a German and he immediately suspects me. I fumble in my pockets. I show him my ID as the schoolmaster Christophe Martin. He peruses the document. All seems in order. He stares condescendingly at me. I try to look blank. He returns my documents.

I cross the rue de Rivoli and climb the steps to the Tuileries on my way back to the Left Bank. My heart is beating faster than usual. It would be all too easy for some officer, like the one who has just demanded my papers, to recognize me should my description be circulated. It's a warning.

Someone once said that Paris was a sentient being and I used to agree, but there is little sign of it today. It's more like a city on hold. As if Lot's wife has cast a backward glance. The remains of a once-lively Paris form a forlorn backdrop for this sickening Nazi spectacle.

I find my way to the rue des Ecoles. The Brasserie Balzar is still there, and open. I go in. It still has that old world feel about it (except for the single ladies lunching alone, which you wouldn't have seen before the war). Moustachioed waiters in their long white aprons stand around joking among themselves. Three Nazi officers are sitting at a table with three female companions, presumably French.

I choose a table in the corner, near the kitchen. It offers a good vantage point for the door and doesn't attract undue attention, I hope. The waiter is a gruff, well-fed man in his late sixties with a lazy left eye and a moustache that tapers off into two upturned, waxed interrogation points on either side of his mouth. When he speaks, they wobble comically.

I order a steak-frites and a glass of Burgundy. Marchais mentioned that Balzar is one of the favoured black-market lunch places that doesn't require food tickets so I can pay with francs. Looking around the room it's hard to believe there's a war going on; that rationing is in full swing.

The waiter seems quite happy to discuss the clientele out of earshot of the Nazi officers. He tells me that the Boche dine there every day and that it's considered one of the safest places for foreign agents to come as the Germans are 'off duty' when they're here and only have eyes for their whores "and for the wonderful food, mais bien sur."

Alarmed at the revelation that Balzar is a favourite watering hole for agents, I resolve not to come here again. I finish the steak (stopping myself just in time from leaving my knife and fork at 'half past six' in the English manner), order a large espresso and the bill.

The waiter brings coffee and the bill and explains to me with a wink and in English that the wine is 'on the house'. I look up at him quizzically. He says, with a conspiratorial grin, "Mai oui, Monsieur, your French is impeccable but the accent is that of Mr Franklin Roosevelt, not that the Boche will notice."

I shrug, explain in French that I've never been to England or America, thank him for the service, leave a modest tip, and head for the exit. Once outside, I turn left and walk purposefully towards the Boulevard St Michel. For the second time today my disguise has been questioned.

It's 2:20 p.m. Plenty of time for a leisurely stroll to get to the Pont Neuf for my 3:00 p.m. appointment with Marchais.

I wander over, stopping here and there, enjoying the spring day. I pass by a billboard for a movie *'Les aventures fantastique de Baron Munchhausen'*. Someone has scrawled over it in large letters FILM BOCHE-N'Y ALLEZ PAS. When I get to the south side of the Pont Neuf I notice a second-hand bookstore. I stop to glance through the reduced price offerings. A street boy, he could be no older than ten, comes up and pulls at my jacket.

"Please Monsieur, my mother is starving. I need to talk to you."

I am irritated, for sure, but there's something unusual in the boy's use of language. Why would he 'need to talk to me'?

"Un moment," I say dismissively as I pick up a paperback volume of de Maupassant that I remember from Uncle Sam's library and take it to the cash register. The street boy waits, sullenly, by the book stall. I pay for my purchase, pocket the book and walk out of the shop. The boy follows. As we approach the Pont Neuf, I turn to him and say "So talk to me…"

"The rose is in bloom," he replies. Marchais' code. "Monsieur Marchais has been arrested at the Café Maurice. You must leave Paris immediately and not go back to the apartment. They have also arrested Monsieur Marchais' secretary. They have been taken to Fresnes." The boy shouts convincing abuse at me and runs off into the back streets of the Left Bank.

Merde. If Marchais has been arrested I've no time to lose. I know that very few agents, even the best, are able to keep secrets while being subjected to Gestapo torturers.

Most of my money is back at Marchais' apartment. I have just enough to get to Annecy where I am due to make contact with the SOE agent, Claudine. She too is in danger of being compromised now that Marchais is being held by the Gestapo. Marchais said that his wife also lives near Annecy, in St Jorioz.

I decide to lie low for a day or two and to find my way to another safe house in Paris belonging to Mme. Carmen Dupré, a contact given to me by Selwyn Jepson. She is a professor at the Sorbonne and, more importantly, unknown to Marchais.

All of my papers are with me. I've left no incriminating material at Marchais' apartment. There's nothing there that can be traced back to me but I'm annoyed at not having my money or suitcase of clothes.

Twenty-five minutes later I catch the train from Montparnasse station to Montrouge, a suburb on the south-western outskirts of Paris. I've committed the address to memory.

20 rue des Mauvais Garçons.

I find the house easily. It's protected from the road by a high wall in which is set a blue door. The name by the bell, written in an elegant script, is Dupré. I ring the bell and wait. No answer. I ring again holding the button down for longer. Soon I hear the sound of an inner door opening and a woman's voice.

"Oui, qui est là?"

"Un ami de la rue de Boulanger" I say, quoting the code that identifies me as a Baker Street agent.

"Un moment." The door opens. An elderly woman emerges. She must be in her mid-eighties, her lined face is lightly rouged. She has intelligent eyes, deeply set, already appraising me.

"Follow me Monsieur… ?"

"Luc."

"Monsieur Luc it is a pleasure to meet you. I am Carmen Dupré."

We cross the enclosed patio and go through the living room of the house to the kitchen. There's an easel set up by the window with a canvas of a still life lying on a small table beside it.

"Make youself comfortable Monsieur Luc. You are travelling very light."

"I will explain Madame." I sit down in a large armchair. "I see you're an artist Madame."

"It is my hobby. I paint little works of great detail to forget the horrors going on around me."

She has a slight Spanish accent.

"It is time for a drink, n'est ce pas?" she says, shuffling over to the corner cupboard. "What will you take? I am very fortunate to have cousins in the countryside who send me food parcels from time to time including whisky and various home-made wines. Unless of course you would like a soft drink?" she looks over her shoulder at me "but I think you are not the type."

There is a twinkle in her eyes. I like her already. "A whisky would be great."

"Very well, I'll get us some drinks and then you must tell me all. It doesn't look as though you are planning on staying. Are you on the run?" she pauses, her arm reaching out for the whisky bottle, "I suspect you are?"

"I am now it seems, yes."

"Ah, then it will be the good whisky. I only offer that to people on the run. Most of you are if you find your way here."

She pours me a generous whisky and herself a small glass of home-made wine. She brings them over and sits down next to me. We talk. She doesn't probe and I find myself liking her more and more as I fill her in on the events of the past 24 hours. She nods wisely on occasion, asks the odd question to get a clearer picture, but lets me talk.

When I finish, she puts down her glass of wine and, in full professorial mode now, says "You must leave Paris tomorrow morning. There is no question about that. It is far too dangerous for you to stay here any longer. Sleep here tonight and then leave at 7:00 a.m. with the rest of the workers so there is less of a chance that you will be noticed. Despite the renewed activity of late, the Paris Resistance group is largely decimated. Double agents and collaborators are everywhere. Denunciations are rife. You will not be safe even here. If they have been able to get M. Marchais to talk, your identity will already be known to the Gestapo. And you are not an easy person to disguise."

I agree. After all, the 'beggar boy' had no difficulty in recognizing me at the Pont Neuf.

She gets up and shuffles over to fetch the bottle of wine from the counter. "Do you have a place to go to?" she says, pouring herself another half glass of wine.

"I have to go to St Jorioz in the Haute-Savoie. I am due to replace an agent who is normally based there. He's now in England. His courier is still there and I need to be briefed by her."

"Well that means you will only have to go to the Gare de Lyon which isn't too bad. There are pretty regular trains from there to Lyon and the Haute-Savoie. Unfortunately it's also a very popular route with the Germans, so you must be careful."

I accept her offer to spend the night. She says she will arrange for spare clothes to be brought to the house by her friend the laundress. We stand at the kitchen counter as I help her to prepare a meal from the sausages and beans sent by her country cousins. We talk together like old friends, despite the sixty years that divide us.

It transpires that Carmen Dupré, for many years a professor of Spanish Literature at the Sorbonne, fought with the partisans in the Spanish Civil War. She was badly wounded but has all but recovered, the only evidence remaining being her slight shuffle when she walks. While in Barcelona she befriended an Englishman, a novelist named Selwyn Jepson, with whom she has remained in contact.

"Have you read his books?" she asks.

"I didn't even know he was a writer."

"Oh yes, quite a successful one. A novelist. I have one of his books here, it is called The Death Gong. It is not to my taste but I understand it is very popular. It was he who persuaded me to provide a safe house for his agents. I have seen many of you come and go through this house. Alas quite a few are gone forever."

She is aware that she risks being betrayed by a captured agent but she is old, she says, and 'somewhat infirm'. Yet she still burns with the passion for freedom that drew her to Spain, birthplace of her mother, in 1936.

She tells me about what life has been like in Paris in details that never reach the English papers, or indeed the 'classrooms' of SOE training camps.

"Ever since Paris opened her legs to the enemy, the whole city has been consumed with fear. It started in May when we heard the news that the Belgian army had surrendered. Then your Winston Churchill urged us all to resist. But he gave us nothing with which to resist, except hope. And hope has been dashed for most of us.

Then in June they came. At first the Germans tried to gain our confidence by mingling like tourists, the drole de guerre. Many people pretended as though nothing had happened, including many of our famous artists, writers and intellectuals who should have known better. Both Jean Cocteau and Colette have written for the Collaborationist Press. Picasso, Derain, Sartre, Simone de Beauvoir all live and work as usual. Others fled, like Peggy Guggenheim, who drove her Talbot out of Paris carrying her diamonds, paintings and her Spanish maid. At least she departed with panache!" she smiles.

"Paris has changed from a city of five million before the war to more like one million today, mainly the workers and the poor have been left to face the enemy. And of course several hundred thousand Jews. Many have committed suicide."

I listen hard and drink slowly.

"The Germans are omnipresent, their tentacles spreading like an octopus into every side street in Paris. They started stealing our food while our poor had to sell their cooking pots for bread. Rationing is everywhere. Housewives queue from four o'clock in the morning for five hours and often return empty-handed. Bread, if you can get it, is made partly of bran and partly of some inferior rye.

Our milk is watered down, often by the shopkeepers themselves of course. The napkins that we can buy dissolve when you try to wash them in hot water; the ersatz soap scratches anything that it washes; the coal substitute is famous for its ability to put out any fire, glass bends like rubber, jam smells of floor polish and as for chocolate, well it is a substance that defies description in polite society.

Some of us are lucky. We have relatives in the countryside who send us food and clothing when they can."

She pours me another drink, and continues.

"The Germans talk to us of cooperation. Bah! They steal our potatoes and patronise the most expensive brothels in Paris. Many women become collaborators, 'horizontal collaborators' we call them, and all the time the despicable Pétain and his Vichy flunkies preach to us that we are only atoning for past sins; that the Nazis are our saviours; that collaboration with the enemy is the sign of a true patriot. And so our young people join up, responding to the marshal's call, thinking he is a new Talleyrand destined to outwit Hitler instead of the stupid old man he really is, compos mentis for three hours a day.

The intellectuals and the aristocracy, well-known people whom the English entertained and admired before the war, you can see them at Les Deux Magots, or at each other's houses giving dinner parties, and what parties! Gorging themselves on caviar and foie gras while the poor of Paris are starving. Some of the poor are even eating their cats. I heard yesterday that a father bludgeoned his daughter to death because she used his food stamps for God's sake."

She pauses, takes a sip of her wine, and continues.

"And as for the Jews. They are only allowed to go to the shops between three and four in the afternoon when the shelves are depleted and most of the shops are closed. They have been rounded up in their thousands, six or seven thousand of them, and taken to the Velodrome d'Hiver in the 15th. arrondisement. No food for five days. One water tap. Ten latrines. Women giving birth. Can you imagine? Of course they could not have done that without the help of the Milice, the French militia whose actions and methods are many times worse than their Nazi masters. We have done our best to help the Jews, they were our neighbours, our friends, we've known them all our lives. And yet there were, are, some of us who want to ingratiate ourselves with the Nazis and so turn them in. Many concierges, hairdressers and waiters wanting a few extra francs have turned traitor. Of course they know pretty well everyone's secrets and will tell lies about them. The people of Paris turning on the people of Paris.

And still they come in the night and whisk them off to the Velodrome d'Hiver where the collaborators, wearing their Nazi uniforms with a Tricolor badge, denounce them to their Nazi superiors with an enthusiasm that makes even the Germans cringe."

The old lady pauses again. I am worried that the anguish of all this is wearing her out.

"But spirits seem not too low; there must be some light on the horizon?" I say.

She brightens up a little. "Yes, yes, there is hope and as long as there is still hope you will find determination and a will to live. We get hope every time we hear the BBC broadcasting their nonsensical messages. No one knows what they mean, these messages "The cat will jump over the moon tonight" or "Rosa loves the tulips in springtime" but we know it means something and that is enough for us. And you. You give us hope. As for our valiant Resistance fighters, the average life expectancy for a member of the Resistance this year is shorter than it has ever been."

"Some say the life expectancy for a British agent in France is now about 18 days instead of the usual 18 weeks. And after the last 24 hours I believe that." I interject.

"Eh…" responds Carmen Dupré with a shrug. "The problem for the Resistance, as I am sure you appreciate, is that, unlike you, they cannot just catch a plane home when their job is done. They live here, as do their families and friends and neighbours. They have their livelihood and livestock to think of. All these things are not at threat for you, only your own life. When an act of Resistance is committed there are always reprisals, especially in the countryside but also here in Paris. They will take a Resistance member's sister out and rape and kill her for revenge. They have forced husbands to look while they have murdered their wives and thrown their babies into ravines. They will then round up all the young men over the age of 18 in the area and send them to work in Germany to make weapons to kill their own countrymen, or they send them to the concentration camps. The entire population of one village was massacred. And all the time that geriatric marshal, Pétain, sits down there in Vichy sucking up to the Nazis. They fool themselves that they are 'saving France', that Pétain is 'l'homme providentiel'. What a bunch of old socks!"

She pauses, looks at me and says, "You must be aware of this. It is important, as you will find collaborators and potential collaborators everywhere. Trust your own instincts. I sense your instincts are good. Too many of your friends have been caught because they have trusted the wrong people."

"I'll be careful."

She smiles. "The wonderful thing about the Resistance is that it has united all different sorts of people, communists with Royalists, old with young, intellectual with anti-intellectual, Catholic with Protestant and foreigner with Frenchman. People who wouldn't even speak to each other before the war are now living, sleeping and fighting together all because it is an ideological struggle for the dignity of man. Politically they are not fighting for the same future but they are fighting the same enemy. Even some of the rich have been selfless enough to join, although most of them support the Vichy in order to protect their businesses from the 'communist tendencies of the working classes'. They fear the return of the front populaire more than they do the Germans."

I am grateful for this private tutorial. It's humbling. We continue to talk long after dinner is over, after the last drop is drained from the bottle of whisky. And after the laundress has come and gone.

It's past midnight when Mme. Dupré finally says good night. Before going up to bed she gives me one name, that of her cousins, the Turrels. They live near the town of Seyne-les-Alpes in the Basses-Alpes region of the south of France.

"If ever you are in trouble they will help you. I will see to it."

With that she shuffles along the corridor and up the stairs to her bed.

I settle down on the sofa to spend my second night in France.

Promptly at 6:30 a.m. I wake up, shave, shower and get dressed in my 'new' clothes. At Mme. Dupré's request the laundress has left a small suitcase into which I put my dirty clothes and my copy of de Maupassant. Leaving her to sleep I let myself out of the house and find my way back to the train station, falling in with the rush hour passengers.

At Montparnasse I leave the train and board the Métro.

Looking at the reflection in the window as the Métro passes through stations on its way to the Gare de Lyon I notice a middle-aged man, dressed in a green raincoat, sitting in a nearby seat. He too is staring at the window. At my reflection. Or am I getting paranoid?

Instead of getting out at the Gare de Lyon I decide to get out at Châtelet. The crowded streets and numerous cafés will offer me the chance to lose this man if he is following me. The train pulls into the station. Just as the doors are about to close I leap up as if I suddenly remember that this is my stop. I just make it through the doors.

As I run up the stairs, momentarily forgetting my 'tuberculosis recovery' I glance behind me. There he is. The little man in the raincoat. Barely five steps behind.

It's almost 8:00 a.m. and the bustling streets are heaving with people. I dart into a café, then exit through the alternative entrance. I cross the street and enter a cavernous warehouse. There's no time to spare. I'm clearly being followed and I need to make it to the Gare de Lyon in good time to catch the 9:30 a.m. train to Annecy.

Out on to the boulevard I once again lose myself in the crowd and decide to walk, only switching to a back street just before I get to the station. I leave the main street, take the little road parallel to it and, checking in the window of a patisserie, make certain that I'm not being followed. I go into the patisserie and buy what passes for a demi-baguette. Then, seeing that the coast is still clear, I take the fastest route to the station.

A good proportion of the German Army seems to be in the station this morning. Troops arriving, troops departing, and troops standing around and staring.

At the ticket window, hoping that my voice doesn't betray my nervousness, I ask for a one-way ticket for the 9:30 a.m. train to Annecy.

"All trains to Annecy are reserved until 9:00 p.m. Germans only" states the clerk. I buy a ticket for the 9:00 p.m. train.

Deciding that it's too risky so soon after Marchais' arrest to stay on the streets for the next 12 hours, I go in search of a nondescript café.

9

Two Italian soldiers occupy the seats opposite me on the train to Annecy. Across the aisle, a couple of talkative teenage girls are on their way to meet their Italian boyfriends.

Facing them is a young, bespectacled German officer reading de Maupassant, in French. In different times we could well have struck up a conversation, I'm thinking.

Within half an hour, lulled by the semblance of security and the numbing noise of the night train, I fall asleep.

Twice during the ten-hour journey to Annecy I am prodded awake by the overzealous conductor with a demand to inspect my papers, conscious no doubt of the German officer's presence. At Chalons sur Saône, the old border between the 'Occupied' and 'Unoccupied' zones, everyone's papers are half-heartedly checked.

At 6:00 a.m., an hour outside Annecy, the train comes to a sudden halt. The two Italian soldiers opposite me pull up the blackout blind.

"Che c'è?" they yell to their colleague already standing outside, a cigarette in his mouth and rifle at the ready.

"I terroristi."

Someone has cut down the telephone poles and laid them across the line. A group of prisoners are marched by the window presumably to help clear the obstruction. The Italian soldiers, noticing my interest, pull down the blind.

The German officer continues to read his book without so much as a curious glance. Does he think he's a member of a superior race? Or is he just absorbed in a fictional world, and who can blame him?

At 7:30 a.m., half-an-hour late, the train pulls into Annecy's soot-blackened station. Its drab appearance contrasts strongly with the faded grandeur of the Paris gares.

A couple of soldiers are leaning against the ticket barrier chatting. Their rifles, slung over their shoulders, face backwards. No one checks my ticket, let alone my papers. I'm clearly in the Italian sector now.

Outside it's eerily tranquil on this crisp March morning. Walking towards the lake, shimmering in the early light, I note poignant reminders of calmer times; disused souvenir stalls, a rotting bandstand, piles of torn deckchairs from days when French, and Swiss, Germans and Italians from across the nearby borders, descended on this picturesque town to frolic.

Towering above is the desolate Glières massif reaching into the clouds and dominating everything for as far as the eye can see. The sort of place Bluebeard would have as his domain in a children's story. A haunting mixture of foreboding and mystery.

The Albertville bus stops on the western side of the lake. Venice-like water laps at the doors of the houses along the canal. A young couple are sitting on a little porch, sipping coffee between amorous cuddles, oblivious of the world around them. People seem cheerful and robust in stark contrast to the grey-skinned, hungry Parisians.

But the Fascist flag flying above the Mairie, the jackbooted guards and the growing tension on the streets as they gradually fill with people, are signs enough of where and when we are living.

Oppressed by the number of uniforms, I locate the bus stop. Discovering that the next bus for St Jorioz is due to leave in ten minutes' time, I sit down on my suitcase and observe the locals. Cyclists on their way to work, truckloads of Italian soldiers pass by and German officers, accompanied by their wives or mistresses and pet dogs, amble along the lakeside for their morning stroll.

Right on time, the Albertville bus pulls up. Three people are waiting with me and another three are already on the bus. I guess that most of the traffic at this time of day is coming in to Annecy as opposed to leaving. I choose a window seat on the left-hand side of the bus so I can see the lake.

As the bus passes through various small villages, a few souls get on and off. In twenty minutes or so we arrive at the crossroads in the village of St Jorioz.

We stop opposite the Hotel de la Poste where the two SOE agents Claudine and Paul are staying. I get off, walk across the street and, leaving the hotel on my left, keep my eye out for Les Tilleuls, the 'safe house' where I was instructed to meet Claudine and Mme. Marchais. Twenty metres down the street I turn right onto the rue de la Gare. Les Tilleuls, set a little back from the road, is a three-storey villa. I can just make out the large faded letters across the front of the house, HOTEL DE LA GARE which it must have been not too long ago. Marchais has rented it, under an assumed name, for as long as the war lasts.

I knock on the door.

A red-cheeked young man, about my age, answers. I give the password and introduce myself.

"Good to meet you. We have been expecting you. I am Robert. Robert Bardot. Come and follow me, Monsieur."

Bardot leads me into a large smoke-filled room with a long refectory table in the centre.

He identifies the others around the table.

First, Claudine, a pretty, young woman in her late-twenties with a mass of auburn hair, large dark eyes and a determined mouth.

Then, Mme. Marchais, a slim strawberry blonde.

In the hall are two young men, twins it seems, who seem to be at Bardot's beck and call.

But it's Claudine who is in charge.

"Luc, it's good to see you" says Claudine stubbing out her cigarette. She brushes some ash off of her sweater and walks over to shake hands with me. I shake hands all round and sit down at the table.

"Tell me Luc, what news is there of my husband?" said Mme. Marchais, pouring me a cup from the still warm coffee pot. "We know he is in Fresnes, but we know nothing more."

"That is as much as I know, Madame. They also took his secretary."

Claudine's grimace at this last piece of information suggests that this is perhaps a bone of contention for Mme. Marchais.

"Luc," says Claudine " I have reserved a room for you at the Hotel de la Poste. It is a meeting place for the local Resistance and you will be in the thick of things there. The Cottet family run it. They are very resourceful people. We are very fortunate."

A Resistance cell and foreign agents living openly in a village of no more than 150 inhabitants. I don't like the sound of this. Seems crazy. I remember Carmen Dupré's advice to trust my instincts.

"I'd prefer to stay somewhere else. I passed a small hotel on the way in from Annecy, a few kilometres away, the Hotel de la Plage.

I'd rather stay there."

"Please yourself," says Claudine "why don't you go and settle in then and we can meet for lunch at the Hotel de la Poste?"

"OK, I'll meet you at 12:30?"

"We'll be there" replies Claudine. I ask where I can get hold of some cash.

"We have plenty," Claudine walks over to a safe, extracts an envelope and hands it to me "that should be enough for getting on with. Paul is bringing back some more."

Bardot loans me a bike and together we ride to the Hotel de la Plage. Bardot explains that he is Marchais' Number Two. Marchais had been in Paris, he said, trying to reconstitute a réseau that had recently been decimated through the treachery of a double agent. He was only just beginning to repair the damage that had been done.

"And Claudine" I ask, "what is her role?"

"Claudine is in charge now that Paul is in England. He went to England a few days ago with Georges who is head of the Resistance here in the Haute-Savoie."

"Ah yes." I remember, there was a guy named Georges boarding my Lysander with Paul.

"Claudine is Paul's courier, but her job assisting him doesn't stop at nightfall if you know what I mean" says Bardot pressing his right forefinger to his nose. I smile, having suspected as much. Claudine's quite a looker. We turn off the road into a short driveway.

"Right, here you are. The Hotel de la Plage. They have vacancies I am sure. Do you want me to wait and see?"

"No, I'll be fine. Will I see you at lunch?"

"Bien sur" says Bardot as he heads out of the drive.

I check in at the reception. Mme. Guibal, the proprietress, a petite lady in her late fifties, takes down the details from my identity card. She is meticulous, slow and inquisitive. She lets me leave my bike in the front hall. She assigns me a first-floor room with a view across the lake, as I requested. I pay a week in advance and go to my room.

The room is sparsely furnished. I unpack what little I have with me and lie down on the bed. It's as hard as a plank. I think through my meeting at Les Tilleuls. It worries me. It seems mad to have a 'safe house' so close to the Hotel de la Poste. It's all too open, too lax for comfort. Maybe I'm just the new boy being extra cautious. Maybe.

Mme. Guibal is once again at reception, gearing up for a chat. I explain I am late and must join my friends for lunch. I get on the bike and head up the driveway to the main road. Then, another error, I ride off on the left instead of the right and get sworn at by a farmer in his cart.

As it turns out, Bardot is not at lunch. Only Claudine and a big young man with dark hair, thick eyebrows and an imposing nose whom Claudine introduces as Arnaud, the wireless operator. "Pleased to meet you" I say as I sit down to join them.

"Hmm," replies Arnaud viewing me with undisguised contempt.

"Don't mind Arnaud" says Claudine, "he doesn't like the idea of anyone replacing Paul, even temporarily. But he'll settle down. He's like a bad-tempered dog. He's quite a good chap normally, except for when he is homicidal, which is too often these days."

Arnaud shrugs. We settle down to a lunch of bread, sausage and cheese. The hotel proprietor has even produced apples and wine. Claudine is as pretty and flirtatious as Arnaud is solemn and taciturn.

Claudine describes the situation in Cannes where she, Paul and Arnaud had operated a very successful réseau. The whole circuit had been blown; just how, they are still not sure. Virtually all their agents were rounded up and carted off to concentration camps. She and Paul managed to get out by train. A few days later they sent for Arnaud. Mme. Marchais, a native of St Jorioz, met them when they arrived and introduced them to Jean and Simone Cottet, managers of the Hotel de la Poste.

They found a safe house for Arnaud in the hamlet of Les Tissots, four kilometres up in the mountains above the village of Faverges, 12 km south of St Jorioz. It's a clear and safer place for him to operate his transmitter.

Claudine and Paul met up with Georges, the local Resistance leader. His base is in a village on the other side of the lake. They are now in the process of finding new recruits, developing new contacts, finding new landing fields and dropping zones; in effect starting all over again. They chose the Haute-Savoie for its perfect location, its sparsely inhabited mountains and relative inaccessibility to vehicles. The mountains are ideal for the dropping of agents, weapons and supplies, and for hiding in. Plus the whole area is in the more relaxed Italian occupied sector and close to neutral Switzerland.

I get the impression Claudine is a bit naïve. Time will tell. People come up to greet us, conspiratorially, and then sit down at tables nearby. I recognize the waiters. The twins I saw in the hall at Les Tilleuls earlier on. The place seems more of a private club than a hotel open to the public.

Arnaud, the grumpy one, does impress me. Clearly a professional, he has a great hatred of the Nazis and an equally great capacity for turning that hatred into violence. He is also Jewish I guess, which of course puts him even more at risk than the rest of us.

"Why don't you spend tomorrow with Arnaud?" suggests Claudine, "I have to go into Annecy and do some errands. I'll get the bus back here about midday but we can meet up again the following day. Let's say at Les Tilleuls at 10:30 a.m.?"

"OK," I say "I'm keen to see Arnaud's set-up. It'll be good to see the area too."

Arnaud is predictably unenthusiastic.

"Go on Arnaud, you may even learn to like him." says Claudine.

Grudgingly Arnaud turns to me and says "I'll pick you up at Hotel de la Plage at 8:00 a.m. tomorrow. I won't wait around if you're not ready."

I smile.

Arnaud glares back.

We finish our coffees and Claudine has the meal put on her bill.

"I'll have a look around, get acquainted with St Jorioz and see you tomorrow Arnaud."

No response.

10

Metzger, the little man whose big moment has finally arrived, sits opposite Marchais in his cell. He's been sitting opposite him for five hours. He needs all his wits and cunning to extract information from the man who runs one of the most effective Resistance réseaux in all of France. He's already decided that it would be a waste of time to talk to Suzanne.

He probes, analyses, tries one tactic after another; never the threat of torture just gentle persistent questioning. But Marchais is resolute, saying very little. He too is analysing the situation. Sizing up his interrogator; assessing his chances of escape.

He feels certain that the owner of the café, one of Marchais' few remaining agents in Paris, will have sent someone to warn Luc.

Metzger doesn't let up. His questions, presented in a monotonic voice that makes Marchais feel as though he's slowly being driven mad by a dripping tap, continue well into the night and throughout the next day. Marchais reveals only the banal. He confirms he is a former French officer, that he has friends in Germany (indeed he lived there briefly, several years before the war) and that he has a passionate hatred for the Nazi regime.

Which gives Metzger a notion that is to prove more successful than he could ever have hoped.

They begin to talk about the Nazi regime in Germany. Whenever the conversation nears the topic of his own organization, Marchais clams up. But when discussing the Nazi regime he talks freely and persuasively.

Metzger, already very experienced in ingratiating himself with agents, decides to present himself as a disaffected German who hates both Hitler and the Nazi regime but loves the Fatherland. All of which is actually true. He has no respect, he says, for his masters in the Abwehr but they are far preferable to the Gestapo, who stop at nothing to extract information by torturing their prisoners. And it's well known that Admiral Canaris, head of the Abwehr, is anti-Nazi. In fact, unbeknownst to Metzger of course, Canaris is at that very moment in Smolensk, with his fellow conspirators, planning Hitler's assassination.

Metzger makes it clear to Marchais that if he cooperates he will not be handed over to the Gestapo, but that the opposite is equally true. In fact, Metzger simperingly explains, he has no choice but to hand him over unless Marchais comes up with the goods.

The next day Metzger meets Marchais, not in his cell, but in the interrogation room. The room is empty but for two chairs and a table. The walls are splattered with blood.

Almost immediately Marchais, clearly rattled, starts to talk. "Can we settle this case without involving the Gestapo?" he asks.

"Yes, certainly. All we need to do is to come to an agreement. At present I am in sole charge of your case. I hate the Gestapo as much as you do. But we need an agreement."

"All right" says Marchais, "Go to the Hotel Bergerac in the Quartier Latin and tell the concierge that you have come from me. Suzanne and I keep a room there. The guards here have the keys to my room, Number 13. If you go there you will find a suitcase in which there is one million French francs and four crystals for secret transmitters. Throw the crystals into the Seine and keep the money. I give it to you."

Metzger tries hard not to show his astonishment and delight that

Marchais has so willingly delivered himself into his hands. He has just proven beyond doubt that he is an enemy agent. Colonel Froehling will be proud. Perhaps proud enough to award him a promotion.

Metzger wastes no time in going to the Hotel Bergerac. There, underneath Suzanne's lingerie in the suitcase by the bed, is a wad of notes and the crystals, just as Marchais promised. Within an hour one million francs, and four crystals, are lying on Colonel Froehling's desk at the Hotel Lutetia.

"Well done Metzger. I am giving you full powers of investigation into Marchais' organization from now on. You are to concentrate on this alone until you penetrate the organization fully."

Metzger gets what he wants, except for the promotion.

He feels certain that Marchais is the key to the trail leading to a big organization. Perhaps the most important network still operating in France? Perhaps the driving force behind the entire French so-called Resistance?

Metzger, keyed up, is raring to go. As he walks back to his apartment from the garage he talks to himself, out loud. He is so animated that he literally foams at the mouth. It is time to provide proof of his friendship to Marchais.

At 7:00 a.m. the following morning he sits opposite Marchais once again, in the interrogation room.

"OK, Monsieur Marchais, I have done what you asked. Now what do you want from me? Call me Jean, that is what my friends call me."

"OK Jean, I want you to help me escape from here. Smuggle me out of here as your agent."

"That is not impossible, Monsieur Marchais, but first I must convince my chief that I have turned you and that you are prepared to work for us in the future."

"Excellent, I will pretend to work for you for a few weeks and then you can send me to do something for you in the south of France and I won't come back."

Metzger is not to be so easily persuaded. "Something along those lines, yes, but it is not as simple as you make out. My chief is convinced that you belong to a large organization. As proof that you are cooperating with us I must get some information on your organization."

"You must be mad, Monsieur Jean. I would never turn over to you those people who have risked their lives for me!"

"You need not do that. It could be dead material," Metzger pauses, then continues "you had crystals with you so you must have wireless transmitters. My people have great interest in wireless transmitters. Why would you care if one of them was discovered? You could send the operator off on some pretext or another and then we raid the place in his absence. No one need be lost to you."

"It can't be done," replies Marchais, "all of our transmitters are in the south of France where we have a strong organization."

Metzger absorbs this information.

"Well you must instruct someone to set up a transmitter in Paris."

"I need to think about this, Monsieur Jean. I will need your help of course. Can we discuss it tomorrow?"

Metzger is getting anxious. His chief is getting anxious and the Gestapo are getting impatient. It is now five days since the arrest and still Metzger has not broken Marchais' resolve.

"Alright Monsieur Marchais, but you must understand that getting you out of Fresnes is not an easy job. The Gestapo watch me every minute of the day. I must have one of your men in here to discuss the next move for us both."

The following morning Metzger walks into Marchais' cell and, to his surprise, finds him eager and ready to talk.

"Jean, if you bring me some writing paper and a pen I will give you two letters."

Metzger tells a guard to provide the paper and pen and leaves.

An hour later Metzger returns. Marchais has written two letters, he explains, one to his wife and one to Claudine, a British agent. He has told them that he has spent five days in Fresnes prison and that he has found a good friend there, a Monsieur Jean, who is going to help him escape. He says that in order to prepare a successful strategy, Robert Bardot, number two in his organization, should return with Monsieur Jean, the bearer of these letters, and meet him in prison. Marchais incorporates his personal code words in the letter to prove that they are really from him. He hands them to Metzger.

"Now, Jean, you must take these two letters to the village of St Jorioz on the banks of Lake Annecy in the Haute-Savoie. Once in the centre of the village you will see the main hotel, Hotel de la Poste. Don't go in as that will cause suspicion. The hotel is a popular meeting place for the Resistance."

Metzger, processing the information once more, lets Marchais continue.

"Facing towards the lake, take the road on the right of the hotel and walk down about 20 metres, follow the road around to the right and you will see my house, set somewhat back from the road. It is called Les Tilleuls. In it you will find my wife and Robert Bardot. They will look after you and Robert will return with you, I'll make certain."

Metzger catches the 9:00 p.m. train for Annecy due to arrive at 7:00 a.m. on Friday morning. From Annecy he will then travel by the Abbeville bus to the little village of St Jorioz.

11

I'm sitting in the small dining room of the Hotel de la Plage finishing a disgusting cup of 'coffee' and answering a stream of questions from Mme. Guibal who, uninvited, has joined me at my table, when a battered Renault pulls up at the entrance. A horn beeps three times, impatiently. Arnaud.

Mme. Guibal is already at the window, not wanting to miss a thing, as I leave.

"Will you join us for dinner Monsieur Martin? Friday night is especially good," she asks, still staring out of the window.

"I am not certain yet, my friend may have plans. If you have food left over and I've not eaten then I'll join you. But don't worry, I may even stay with my friend."

"D'accord, Monsieur, au revoir."

"Au revoir."

Arnaud is sitting in the driver's seat drumming his fingers on the steering wheel.

"Bonjour, Arnaud… sorry to keep you waiting," I say jauntily. Arnaud nods his head, "Get in…."

Mme. Guibal is watching us as I knew she would be. Nothing

sinister I don't think, just a lonely woman with little enough to entertain her in wartime France.

We head out of the driveway onto the Albertville road, swerving at the last minute to avoid hitting the 7:00 a.m. bus from Annecy. I am worried about ending my secret agent career in a humiliating local car crash. We follow the signs to Albertville. Fifteen silent kilometres later we turn off the main road and head away from the lake towards the wooded Semnoz mountain until we reach the village of Faverges.

We pass several medieval chapels and sanctuaries on our way through the countryside. I studiously ignore Arnaud's silence. Instead of stopping in Faverges, as I expected, we drive right through. Is he kidnapping me?

"I thought your place was in Faverges?" I say.

"C'est pas loin."

And then I remember, it's in a hamlet called Les Tissots near to Faverges. Five kilometres later we arrive at a small villa, seemingly a forest warden's, which overlooks a north-west gap in the mountains. Must be ideal for radio communication with London.

"Claudine has asked me to show you around so I will," says Arnaud. We walk through the villa, a living room–cum–dining room–cum–kitchen with two small bedrooms in the back. Arnaud pulls out an old brown leather suitcase from under his bed.

"Et voila. This is the radio transmitter. Since early last year it has been the instant death penalty for anyone found in possession of a transmitter," says Arnaud with, I am relieved to see, a mischievous grin.

"How often can you communicate with London?"

"Let's have a cup of coffee. Then I'll show you how it works."

Seizing on this unexpected display of civility I ask a leading question, "Tell me, Arnaud, how did you get involved in this business?"

"Anger" replies Arnaud as he puts the kettle on the small stove. "Anger at what the bloody Boche are doing to my country; to my people. I am Jewish. They took my father and mother and my young sister away to Germany… and you know what that means." He slices his neck with his forefinger. "My motive is revenge. I am determined to do as much damage to the Boche as I can and fuck anyone who tries to stop me. Anyone," he emphasises, handing me a mug of coffee and taking a seat, "and you, my American friend. What brings you here?" he says, more from suspicion than fellowship.

"Similar reasons, sort of. They murdered my best friend, or at least the collaborating French did, which is even worse."

"Bastards. How? Why?"

"In a way it was revenge too. My friend François and I were at school together, in Burgundy. One day I got into a fight with the school bully. Knocked him out. He's never forgotten. A few years ago he fell in with the Milice and they made him Chief of Police in the local town. I'm not around so he took it out on my best friend."

"Sounds a bit extreme."

"Well he found out that François was involved with the local Resistance, which gave him the perfect excuse. They discovered some incriminating newspapers and leaflets at his house, well it's my house actually, or was. They burned it down when they killed François."

Arnaud waits, expecting more.

"I'd more or less been a pacifist until then, even though I felt increasingly uncomfortable with other people fighting 'my' war, so to speak. François' murder was the trigger. Then I knew what to do. I was in no doubt."

Arnaud sips his coffee while digesting all this. His face muscles relax. I sense a thawing in our relationship.

"Bon, I understand better now. You're a man of deep convictions I think. That is good. Without those we are not men at all, n'est ce-pas?"

"So, what do you think of the set-up here in the Haute-Savoie?" I ask "Is it going to be as successful as Cannes?"

"Certainly, with Paul and Claudine it is bound to succeed. They are both excellent people although Paul puts Claudine in danger unnecessarily. She manages though. She is bright and courageous. We're doing fine. Why do you ask?"

"It makes me nervous." I say, even though I know he'll take it as a criticism, which it is of course. "It seems too relaxed; too many people coming to and fro between the Hotel and Les Tilleuls. It puts everyone at risk. It's not the way I'd run a réseau."

"And you've got lots of experience I suppose?"

"I haven't, as you know. But even so I think the set-up in St Jorioz is wide open, waiting for an accident which could endanger us all, including you."

Arnaud leans back in his chair and sighs. "Well, if you must know, one of the reasons I made my base up here is that I feel uncomfortable about it too. The devastation that occurred in the Cannes réseau was due to loose talk as well as sheer stupidity. But still, you're too quick to judge. You've been in France for a few days. Our group, or what is left of it, has been here for two years."

I change tack. "What happened in Cannes exactly? Why did things go wrong?"

He takes a deep breath. "The réseau was infiltrated, we don't know how or by whom. We had a large number of good people in the réseau. Most of them knew to be careful but we obviously had a rotten apple in the crate. Someone tipped off the Gestapo that we were going to blow up a viaduct; one of our biggest jobs. When we finished laying the explosives in preparation for the ammunition train to come, suddenly the fucking Boche appeared from every direction. They machine-gunned ten of our people and defused the charges.

They arrested a boy, aged 16, who was wounded. They took him to the square in the village near the viaduct, found out who his parents were, took them from their beds and brought them to the square too. Then they cut the boy's tongue out, in front of his parents. And when he was writhing with pain they gouged out both of his eyes. His mother fainted, his father screamed and full of rage he attacked the Gestapo officer who then shot him and finally shot the boy, leaving the mother on the ground with instructions that no one should touch her. By morning she too was dead. A broken heart I think."

This sort of thing was glossed over in training, the inevitability of reprisals following any of our successful, or even unsuccessful, actions against the enemy. The realization that my own actions, however just they might be, could cause such tragedies, such terror and loss to good people… somehow I must come to terms with this, I suppose.

It must show in my face. Arnaud is staring at me. I raise a questioning eyebrow.

He smiles. "You're not such a cocky Yankee bastard after all my friend."

I gesture gratefully.

"Yes, this is what people have to bear and it is we who are causing them to suffer like this," he continues "but the alternative is too terrible to contemplate. To leave them to live like pigs sucking the entrails of their culture through the Vichy teat, that is no life. And what else? To go to the land of the fucking Boche and manufacture bombs to kill our own people. Give me an honourable death first. What we're doing is right, we know it but we must sacrifice and part of that sacrifice is accepting that innocent people will be killed. Even more innocent people will be killed if we don't do it. But anyone who says he's not anxious or scared is lying. It takes a miserable bastard like me to see these things. So many times I've had my finger on the trigger of my Colt.38 ready to shoot and Paul or someone has stopped me. Each time I swear and scream at them, but they're right. My time will come and I must wait until the right moment. Meanwhile I'll do as much damage as I possibly can and use my talent which is knowing how, when and where to use this transmitting set. That's what I do best and that's how I shall help to win this war."

Then and there I decide two things.

One, that I will set up my own réseau with people I hand-pick to prevent anything like the mess in Cannes happening again.

Two, that I want Arnaud to be with me.

"Arnaud, thanks for this. You're a good man."

He laughs and goes over to the kitchen area to prepare something to eat. "You don't know what you are letting yourself in for."

While he assembles bits and pieces of food he talks and talks; about his love of music, of lost loves, of hatred for the Nazis, of the tribulations of the Jews, of Belgian poets and French painters. "My passion, apart from killing Germans, is the opera" he says "ever since I first saw La Traviata which brought me to tears at the age of ten. And as for Don Giovanni, only last week I was shaving with the window open. It was a beautiful spring morning. I was singing, quite loudly, Don Giovanni's part in the duet during the third scene of the second act, the one everyone knows of course."

I don't, of course.

"The one that goes…

'Là ci darem la mano,
là ci dirai di si
Vedi, non è lontano;

partiam, ben mio, da qui.'
And then all of a sudden I hear the response coming from outside
'Vorrei e non vorrei;
mi trema un poco il cor.
Felice, è ver sarei,
ma può burlarmi ancor'

I thought I had lost my mind. It was a man's voice singing the part of Zerlina, the peasant girl. I looked out of the window. It was the forester, another Mozart fan.

'Vieni, mio bel diletto!'

I shouted in my best 'come-hither' voice.

'Forget it,' he laughed, and walked off into the woods."

Uncouth in language; violent in his reactions; uncontrollable in his hatreds; there are nevertheless surprising attributes deep in Arnaud's hinterland.

He puts a selection of bread, fruit and cheese on the table. "We've got about half an hour before I need to check in with London." he says, "I'm waiting for an answer to a message I sent yesterday."

Arnaud stands up to get two glasses of water. "How much do you know about the Maquis?"

"Only what we were taught in training. It's a Corsican word meaning shrub or undergrowth because that's where a lot of young men, mainly young men, are living to avoid being conscripted for the service du travail obligatoire and sent to work in munitions factories in Germany. It also has a criminal element. Some Maquis groups are no better than armed gangs. Others are well-trained fighting men. That's about the extent of it."

"That's part of the story but let me tell you more, especially about our local Maquis here on the Glières plateau."

I pick at the cheese and listen.

"Until last month the groups of young men who went into hiding to avoid, as you say, being conscripted into the STO were known as refractaires. They were not just young men but included groups of atheists, communists, Catholics, Muslims, Jews, Protestants, radicals, socialists, royalists and veterans of the Spanish Civil War whose only common aim was avoiding the STO. Initially, here in the unoccupied zone sud or zone libre it was much less problematic to avoid the STO as the so-called 'Vichy Government' wasn't under great pressure to supply manpower to the Germans. In the northern zone occupée, it was a very different matter.

By the end of last year the zone occupée had sent 130,000 of its skilled workers off to German factories. The zone sud had only sent 2,500. Many of the zone sud's young men were able to stay in their home towns, simply going to ground when the conscriptors came to town. But since November, when the Germans occupied the south, Vichy were required to supply 500,000 young men from the south to make up for the disparity.

Five weeks ago, Pétain issued a new law requiring all young men aged 20 or 21 to register immediately for the STO. The gendarmerie took on their powerful new role with relish, corralling young men wherever they found them. They divided them into three groups: those who were exempt (agricultural workers, miners, railway workers, doctors and postmen, for example); those who were to be sent to compulsory service in Germany; and those who were to work for German factories in France. There was panic and protest, fuelled by the communists and Spaniards in particular. The towns no longer offered safe havens and the young men left in droves. Some formed suddenly intimate relationships with long-ignored rural relatives; others discovered farmers who would provide them with shelter in return for labour. But the majority simply took to the hills. There they joined up with groups of resisters and refugees from the zone occupée and Spanish Republican refugees or they formed, as you have said, loose and ill-disciplined, and thus dangerous, gangs of bored, frightened marauders. A few assembled well-fed and reasonably equipped, quasi-military units with a strict line of command and clear Resistance objectives. These formed the core of the Maquis.

Before long, joining the Maquis, becoming a maquisard, held romantic resonances for the disillusioned and angry young men that being a refractaire lacked. That single word Maquis united all those disparate types under one single inspiring umbrella. The Yanks and others just call anyone in the Resistance, at least anyone in any way military, the Maquis now and it has become sort of common parlance for an armed Resistance fighter.

You, Luc my friend, are now the Maquis, whether you like it or not. And we are proud to have you among us."

I felt as though I'd just been given a badge of honour, "I will wear the Maquis badge with pride, Arnaud."

Arnaud nods and continues "Under the strong command of a charismatic leader these individuals can be moulded into very effective fighting units. All they need is training, arms and equipment.

One of the most celebrated of these units is the one here, the Glières Maquis. 450 or so men are, so we've been told, living on the Glières plateau under the inspired command of a 27-year-old lieutenant named Tom Morel. He is highly decorated (including the Croix de Guerre and the Legion d'Honneur at the age of 24) and was an inspector at Saint-Cyr Military School in Aix-en-Provence before the war. When the French army was demobilised in November 1941 many of Tom Morel's fellow officers joined Vichy. Morel went into hiding and set about developing his secret army of resisters. A few other officers also escaped and set up Resistance networks.

Until the Germans occupied the whole of France, there were few military targets in the zone non-occupée. Thus the main enemy had not been the Germans but the Milice Française. As you know their ardent desire to please their masters results in a devotion to duty and acts of cruelty that the Germans themselves would hardly dare contemplate. Prospective Miliciens take an oath to Pétain, after a night's vigil, as if they were Crusaders. Perhaps they believe they are? They wear a uniform of khaki shirt, black beret and black tie. But of course many of them are in plain clothes. High ranking within the Milice are former Saint-Cyr colleagues of Tom Morel.

My message to London resulted from information we got from Jean Cottet, manager of the Hotel de la Poste. He is close to Tom Morel and the Maquis and told us that they are under threat from the Milice and desperately need arms. We've asked London to supply them, urgently. Today I should have an answer one way or the other."

"Very clear Arnaud, you should have been a schoolmaster."

"Actually I was, for a few years before the war."

"Me too."

"Doesn't surprise me, you have that harassed look about you. It's time to set up the transmitter. Prepare yourself for another lesson."

We walk into the bedroom. Arnaud removes the transmitter from the suitcase.

"You won't have seen this one yet Luc, it's the latest in a series of lightweight transceivers that London has sent over to us. It weighs about three-and-a-half kilos, which is not too bad, but when you've got the battery pack and the spares box which weigh twice as much it's a fucking load to carry around, and bury, hide or whatever else you may have to do with it."

He places the set on the small table ready for operation.

"We have to think of creative ways of disguising it, especially when moving around. I put mine in a suitcase. If I get searched though there's no possible explanation that would save my neck. It's curtains for us W/T operators. Life expectancy is currently running at five to six weeks. That's about one-third that of a regular operative like you." He obviously relishes his role at the sharp end. "The transmitter enables me to send up to 200 words per minute. My frequency is marked by two crystals inserted in the set. If I need to change my frequency I need to get new crystals sent out from London. This metre on the front makes it easy to tune in and match up to the aerial."

"Where's the aerial?"

"Come with me." We walk out the front door. Someone is walking down the path towards us. I grab Arnaud's arm. "It's fine, it's the forest warden doing his rounds." We approach the warden, "Well if it's not my little Zerlina…!" Arnaud says. The warden laughs. "Allow me to introduce my friend, Luc."

We shake hands, mutter a few pleasantries and, leaving the warden, head towards a clearing in the woods. "At the moment that is the aerial," he points at a clothes line attached from the roof of the cabin to a pine tree. "If there's no current then I have to use the batteries. They're just like car batteries."

"How often do you check for messages?"

"On a good day I try to check in twice. My QRX or schedule is 0700 hours and 1530 hours, which…" he checks his watch "is in about five minutes' time. But if Paul or Claudine want to relay a special message then I have an emergency QRX at 1200 hours but it's tempting fate to be on as much as that. It takes the Boche about twenty minutes to get a rough location fix with their detection equipment, even up here."

"How accurate are their detecting machines?"

"Well, I hate these bloody mountains but at least it's pretty secluded here. The woods give ideal protection. The Boche would have to be based directly north-west to be able to pinpoint where I am with any accuracy. It's getting close to 1530. Let's see if we've got an answer to my message."

"What did your message say?"

"I always memorise the messages, safer that way. It said:

MOST URGENT 2000 DETERMINED WELL OFFICERED MAQUISARDS STATIONED ANNECY M16 EXPECTING LARGE VICHY ATTACK MARCH/APRIL STOP BESEECH YOU ARM THESE MEN SOONEST STOP RESISTANCE INCENTIVE TO OTHER MAQUIS THROUGH THEIR VICTORY WITH OUR ARMS INCALCULABLE ENDS

I've exaggerated the numbers for effect. By the way, as you probably know if those guys taught you anything, when I send a message I include security codes to let London know that it's me, although they know my 'fist', my natural speed and style of communication, by now."

"Do you just use one security code? I seem to recall that W/T operators use two?"

"That's right. We use a 'bluff' code, the one we give to the Boche if we're arrested and tortured, and then another 'true' one which we should never reveal, although the Boche have caught on to the fact that we use two."

"Is London pretty efficient?"

Arnaud answers as he twists and twizzles the knobs. "They can be. But they can be idiots too. Dangerous idiots. If a W/T operator is under German control, and many of us have been, we try and alert London by missing out a code or by using different sign-off language. Not long ago an operator outside Paris was arrested by the Gestapo after they discovered him transmitting. They forced him to send messages to London with various requests. He did everything he could to alert London; missed out his bluff code, ended his message "Love and Kisses" instead of his usual "Adieu." When London received the message they refused to believe he had been 'turned'. Buckmaster sent a message back saying "You've forgotten your code be more careful next time." The W/T operator was never heard of again.

"Christ, how stupid."

"Well, it's pride I think. Not wanting to admit that anything was wrong with 'the Firm'. Sometimes they are just plain unprofessional. When I sent this message two days ago, London in their wisdom put some new girl on to receive it. All she could manage was 12 fucking words a minute. I sat there shitting bricks. To avoid being detected I really should limit my transmitting time to six consecutive minutes. Not one of the 46 people whose houses I have used has ever been apprehended. And I'm not about to let that happen because London has some incompetent on the other end of the line. I was so angry that yesterday I sent another message saying:

IF YOU PUT THAT BITCH ON AGAIN NEXT SUNDAY I QUIT ENDS

...and I will."

Arnaud locates his frequency "It could well be we won't have an answer yet. The bloody British seem to take days off even during war."

I laugh "But I thought you were British?"

"I am, I am, but of a different breed!" Almost immediately a message starts coming through. We both stare intently. Arnaud quickly deciphers it.

FROM: BUCKMASTER

WELL DONE STOP THIS IS WHAT WE HAVE BEEN WAITING FOR STOP WARN MAQUISARDS PREPARE THREE LARGE BONFIRES AT HUNDRED YARD INTERVALS IN STRAIGHT LINES OF WIND AND LIGHT THESE ONLY AT SOUND OF SQUADRONS APROACH STOP EXPECT DELIVERY OF ONE HUNDRED AND TWENTY-SIX REPEAT ONE HUNDRED AND TWENTY-SIX CONTAINERS BETWEEN MIDNIGHT AND 0200 HOURS FROM TOMORROW NIGHT STOP NO BBC MESSAGE STOP TALLY HO STOP ENDS

We grin and instinctively stand and punch the air, aware that a whole new chapter of our war is opening up.

"Mon Dieu, at bloody last. We're in business. We must warn the Maquis as quickly as possible."

"Let's go" I say.

"We can't do it by ourselves, we need help and I know where we can get it" says Arnaud. Moments later we are out of the villa and into the car.

"What's your plan?" I ask once I reassemble myself in the suicide seat of the Renault.

"We're going to Annecy, to the hospital. Why? To get a message to my friend who is one of the ambulance drivers. He knows where the Maquis are, as does Monsieur Cottet at the Hotel de la Poste, and he has a perfect alibi to be out and about at all times of the day and night driving his ambulance. We'll find my friend and then we'll go with him to find the Maquis, d'accord?"

"D'accord" I echo. Adrenalin is flowing through my veins at last.

12

Metzger waits half an hour for the bus to St Jorioz. The trip along the lake goes smoothly apart from a near accident outside the Hotel de la Plage when the bus veers into the opposite side of the road to avoid hitting two men in a Renault.

He arrives at St Jorioz about ten past eight and realizes that the stop is very close to his destination. Rather than go immediately to Les Tilleuls he decides to explore the village of St Jorioz. For two hours he walks the village, up and down every road and side street. He notes the cow paths winding up the steep slopes of the Semnoz and walks the bridle path down to the lake. He calculates the time it would take to sail to the opposite shore.

For days after, people would speak worriedly to each other about the odd-looking stranger in dark glasses and a beret who had been spotted all over town.

By 10:30 Metzger completes his reconnaissance. He walks by the Hotel de la Poste, a large Bavarian-style building that reminds him of the mountain holiday hotels of his youth, and heads for Les Tilleuls as instructed by Marchais.

A young, slim, well-built blonde aged about thirty opens the door.

"Madame Marchais?"

"Who wants to know?" inquires the blonde, looking distrustfully at the stranger.

"I am from Paris, Madame, and I have a letter from your husband." Metzger hands her the letter. She holds the door ajar with her foot, unwilling to let him in until she has established whether or not he's telling the truth. She opens the letter and as soon as she recognises her husband's writing she opens the door fully.

"I apologise Monsieur...?"

"Jean" replies Metzger

"I am sorry Monsieur Jean but one cannot be too careful. Please come in and join us."

Metzger walks through the hall, noting two identical young men packing up trunks and boxes. Planning a getaway, he wonders? He walks into the sitting room.

"Please, have a seat" says Mme. Marchais. Then she sits down and reads the note. It's short. Marchais was in Fresnes prison, he was well but hungry, he had not been ill-treated and since his arrest he had had several conversations with Monsieur Jean, the bearer of this letter. Although Jean was in the German Army he believes him to be trustworthy. Monsieu Jean also has an important matter to discuss with her and with Robert Bardot. Marchais also requests that Bardot return to Paris with Monsieur Jean and come to meet him in his cell.

Mme. Marchais folds the letter up and puts it in her bag. Her face reddens with the thought of having to be polite to a German Army officer but if her husband said he was OK, and the codes embedded in the letter guaranteed that he was the author, then she must trust him.

"Thank you Monsieu Jean. Please tell me what you have to say."

"I will happily do that, Madame, but it would be easier for me if Claudine and Monsieur Bardot were here as well."

"I'm afraid they both had to go to Annecy. Claudine by bus and M. Bardot on his bicycle. He will be back soon. I'm not sure how long Claudine will be."

But Metzger was lucky. Just at that moment Robert Bardot appeared at the door; slim, late twenties, wiry physique. A cool customer was Metzger's instant summation.

"Who is he?" says Bardot as he wheels his bicycle into the hall.

"He is from my husband, Robert. He is a German officer but we are to trust him."

"He's a what?" Bardot slowly removes the bicycle clips and pulls his trouser legs down over his socks.

"Let me introduce myself" says Metzger "I know it must be very confusing. I am in the German Army indeed I am in the Intelligence service, the Abwehr. In fact it was I who arrested M. Marchais."

Both Mme. Marchais and Bardot stare at him, then at each other, with their mouths open wondering what on earth they are doing allowing this German officer into the local Resistance headquarters. Bardot reaches for his gun.

"No need for that M.Bardot, I am not armed. You can search me if you like. You must appreciate I am putting myself at terrible risk by coming here, unarmed, into a village which is known to be full of Resistance members any one of whom would happily shoot me dead on sight."

"Go on…" says Bardot.

"Thank you. May I offer you a cigarette?"

"No" they both say in chorus.

"Well do you mind if I do, I need it to calm my nerves" lies Metzger.

"Go ahead" says Bardot "but explain what you are doing here or that bullet may come sooner than you anticipate."

"I have brought two letters, M. Bardot. One for Mme. Marchais and one for the English woman, Claudine." Bardot's expression does not soften; nor does his hand move away from the revolver.

"Here mon ami" says Mme. Marchais holding out the letter for Bardot "perhaps you had better read it before you get too excited?"

Bardot grabs the note from Mme. Marchais' hand and walks over to the window standing with his back to the German. He pulls out the letter from the envelope and begins to read.

When he finishes he looks over at Metzger who's been talking to Madame Marchais but anticipating his stare "Yes, Monsieur Bardot, we are expecting big things of you. Can you handle it?"

"Perhaps" says Bardot, piqued by the German's condescension but reassured by the letter from his chief. "First of all tell us what you have to say…"

"May I sit down?"

Bardot motions to one of the chairs by the table.

He and Mme. Marchais also sit down.

Metzger slowly explains his plan. He's a German, a proud German, he says, but one who hates Nazism and above all hates Hitler. He is doing all he can to keep Marchais out of the hands of the Gestapo but time is limited. Before long the Gestapo are sure to lose patience and would demand that he hand Marchais over. However, his boss, Colonel Froehling, is willing to let him keep Marchais at Fresnes prison for a while longer but he needs to prove he's getting important information from him, and he needs Bardot's help. Then, if all goes well, Metzger will arrange for his release having convinced the Germans that he had 'turned' Marchais into a counter-spy working for the Abwehr.

Bardot's expression is one of disbelief. How could anyone be taken in by this. He would be putting his own life at risk if he returned with Metzger to Paris. Their whole réseau was in danger of being blown, indeed it looked as though it already had been. And yet, Marchais, the chief that he admired more than anyone except for Georges Clabaud, had sent Metzger into the heart of the Resistance. He would have to go if only to stop his chief being handed over to the Gestapo.

"OK, I will accompany you to Paris as requested. When shall we go?"

"I am leaving on the night sleeper tonight as I have to be in Paris first thing in the morning, but I do not think it is wise for us to travel together. Come on the same train by all means but do not acknowledge me. The

Gestapo are everywhere, even here in the Italian sector of course, and if they see us together it would put everything at risk."

"Very well, where shall we meet?"

"I would like to come too." says Mme. Marchais. "We can meet at my apartment on the rue de Babylone."

"Fine" replies Metzger quickly, pleased at the prospect of discovering a Resistance rendezvous in Paris and momentarily wondering why Marchais and his secretary Suzanne had been staying at the Hotel Bergerac in Paris and not at his own apartment. Although he had his suspicions. "Let's meet at 2:00 p.m. tomorrow."

"D'accord" responds Mme. Marchais taking a piece of paper out of her handbag and scribbling down her address, "we will be there."

Metzger looks at his watch. It's already noon. "And now perhaps you could tell me where I could find a bite of lunch while I wait for Mme. Claudine?" he says, addressing himself to Mme. Marchais and deliberately ignoring Bardot.

"The Hotel de la Poste" she replies pointing out of the window "it's just over there."

"Thank you. Until tomorrow at 2:00."

"Yes, yes" they both reply and with that Metzger walks out into the bright sun and refreshing lakeside air and ambles over to the Hotel de la Poste.

The hotel is almost empty. There's one large table of people having a lively discussion, six men and two women. As Metzger takes his seat the conversation dies down. All eyes are on the newcomer.

Metzger has chosen a table near to the others but with his back to them, not wanting his face to be studied. He buries his head in the menu. Moments later the waiter comes over. Metzger recognizes him as one of the twins who had been packing up cases in the hallway of Les Tilleuls.

"Hello, again" says Metzger.

"Welcome, can I get you something to drink?"

He has an Italian accent which Metzger finds incongruous; an Italian Resistance member in the heart of Italian occupied France. But then he remembers his agents telling him that the hills around Annecy are full of Spanish Republicans and Italian partisans trying to form some sort of pathetic secret army.

"Just a glass of water and a sweet omelette please" says Metzger, picking up a newspaper.

The large group resumes talking but in a much reduced register. Within five minutes Metzger's food arrives. He drinks his water, eats his omelette and then beckons the waiter over to ask for another.

Ten minutes later the cook himself appears sporting a chef's white apron and a high cap, carrying the omelette. He turns out to be the other, more talkative, twin.

"We saw you at Les Tilleuls so we know you are a friend" he says, hardly managing to hide his suspicion nonetheless. "Do you live in Paris?"

"Yes," Metzger says.

"Whereabouts?"

"In the 16th"

"Ah, I was in Paris a few weeks ago. I expect I will go there again when Paul gets back. I could look you up!"

Metzger was just about to say what an excellent idea that was when a short, dark-haired lady from the large table turns around and says to the chef "Don't you know you are not to talk to the guests! Get on with your work."

"Can you get me a coffee" says Metzger "and the bill, please. And who is that?" he asks the chastised chef in a lowered voice.

"Oh that's Claudine."

Seizing the moment, Metzger walks over and asks Claudine to join him for coffee.

"Who are you?" demands the English woman imperiously.

"My name is Jean and I have a letter for you from M. Marchais who is in Fresnes prison. I have something important to tell you, for your ears only" he says glancing around the table at the suspicious faces.

"Very well, I will have coffee with you" says Claudine getting up and walking over to Metzger's table.

The waiter returns with a cup of coffee. "And another for Madame Claudine" says Metzger.

They sit down, an incongruous couple, the Abwehr sergeant and the English not-so-secret agent.

"Madame Claudine, may I hand you this letter from M.Marchais? Then I will give you the circumstances of M. Marchais' arrest and tell you of my plan to free him from prison. I also need to give you some very confidential information."

Claudine takes the envelope that Metzger proffers across the table and tears open the envelope. The waiter brings her coffee, which she ignores.

She reads silently, with no hint of emotion, very aware that her every movement is being scrutinized by Monsieur Jean. The letter was almost identical to that sent to Mme. Marchais except that it also discloses that Monsieur Jean will explain a plan to her personally.

Marchais assures her, in carefully-coded language, that Jean is to be trusted completely.

'We'll see', thinks Claudine. "OK, talk" she says.

"I am an officer in the German Army and a member of the military Abwehr, the counter-espionage staff with allegiance to the General Staff."

Claudine gulps, surreptitiously, showing no discernible emotion.

"We of the military Abwehr are a race apart. We are nationalists who believe in the Fatherland. We are watched by the Gestapo whose allegiance is to the Nazi party. I arrested Marchais to save him from the Gestapo and to make a proposal to this brave man. Within certain limitations Marchais is prepared to further my plans" he pauses.

"I am listening" says Claudine

"Germany is split. On the one hand you have Adolf Hitler and his blood-thirsty satellites, on the other you have the High Command of the

German Army. It was not the High Command that made war, Madame Claudine, but Adolf Hitler. It is long and complicated but suffice it to say that there are many of us who love our country and realize that Hitler is destroying it."

"I agree" interjects Claudine, "Germany is heading unstoppably for destruction."

"There you are wrong. If Germany is destroyed, Europe is destroyed. With Adolf Hitler out of the way, Germany could sue honourably for peace with the West. You, Madame Claudine, could be the intermediary between those who think as I do and London. It is not an unimportant role, Madame."

"And what do you want of me, Monsieur?"

He draws his chair closer.

"I want you to give me a transmitting set and code so I can get in direct touch with the British."

Claudine looks at Metzger with detachment. She knows she will have to play for time. This was much too big a deal for her to handle alone, she would need Buckmaster to make sense of all this. Only he could make it possible.

"I cannot give you a transmitting set, Monsieur, because I do not have one. Without that a code will not be of much use to you. On the other hand I have ways of communicating with London and I am prepared to do that, subject to certain conditions."

"Which would be?"

"I want to send one of my men with you to Paris to verify your story and to speak, alone, to Marchais. He will then come back here and report to me. If all is well I will decide what to do."

"I have already arranged for that Madame. Your man Robert Bardot will come with me to Paris tonight and I will take him to see Marchais tomorrow."

"You are very organized Monsieur, I congratulate you."

Metzger thanks Claudine and says he will await word. Bardot would bring her information on how to get in touch with him in Paris. He bids her good day, pays his bill and walks over to the bus stop. He decides to return to Annecy and, as he has time to spare, he will spend the rest of the afternoon watching a movie.

Despite the excitement of the day, Metzger falls asleep in the cinema and only awakes twenty minutes before his train is due to depart for Paris. He hurries to the station, increasingly conscious that there are two men following him. At the station he notices Mme. Marchais walking up and down agitatedly on the platform but within moments she is joined by Bardot and the two of them get onto the train.

Metzger settles himself into his sleeping compartment aware that the two men following him are probably on the train but doubting they would try anything before he gets to Paris. In Paris he will lose them.

13

The ambulance driver, Thierry de Rome, a former fishmonger in his late forties, enthusiastically responds to Arnaud's request. We jump into his old boxy van, converted into an 'ambulance'. With bells ringing, we pass through Annecy. Then, with bells silenced, we take to the side roads, pass over farm tracks, wind up on the Thônes road and, twenty minutes later, arrive at the end of a dirt track high up on the massif near the plateau of Glières. Thierry assures us that even though we've seen no one, our every move has been watched by the Maquis since we turned off the Thônes road and started up the track. But the ambulance is well-known as is the blond-headed, snub-nosed Thierry de Rome sitting in the driver's seat; so we pass unimpeded.

We park by another vehicle just off the track.

Having been warned of the ambulance's imminent arrival, a smart young guy, clearly an important figure, perhaps even Tom Morel himself, is waiting for us. As he walks towards the ambulance Thierry tells us to stay put, jumps out and grasps the man's hands in a familiar shake. The maquisard throws his arm around Thierry and they walk away, deep in conversation for a minute or two.

Arnaud and I wait in the ambulance until we are given the all-clear. Unlike our friends in St Jorioz, these guys aren't taking any chances.

"Come on out," Thierry beckons to us.

"Welcome to the Glières plateau, mes amis" says the maquisard, "I am Tom Morel. Come with us to our 'HQ' and we will talk, yes?"

We walk up the track together passing groups of men, some are well-dressed, others haggard and poorly clothed. At the 'HQ' Tom Morel offers us cigarettes and coffee while Arnaud reveals the contents of the message from Buckmaster and explains exactly what is needed from the Maquis.

Tom Morel can barely hide his excitement. Rumours have been circulating that the plateau is to be surrounded by a strong force of the paramilitary Garde Mobile any day now. He has been deeply concerned as to how he could possibly muster enough support to counter the expected attack. The Maquis will need all the help they can get. With the weapons from London, Morel will at last be able to properly equip and arm his several thousand men, many of whom are new recruits having joined within the last few weeks as a result of the new STO law coming into effect.

Arnaud tells me that Morel's excellent cover for his work is that, somewhat ironically, he holds the position of Director of the Annecy Office of Voluntary Recruitment for Labour in Germany.

Relaying his precise requirements to Arnaud, Morel orders his men to prepare the drop site. Arnaud and I join in to help hack away branches to form the beacons. I decide that I can be of much more use here for the time being. Before I head back to the hotel tonight, I'll ask Tom if I can join him for a week or so.

Metzger is fast asleep on the night sleeper to Paris by the time the drone of aircraft gradually turns into a roar over the skies of the sleepy town of Annecy.

Claudine is lying awake when, shortly after midnight, she hears the R.A.F. squadrons fly overhead. She jumps out of bed and flings open the windows. There are tears in her eyes as she sees twenty, no thirty, bombers flying over St Jorioz in the direction of the maquisards in the mountains. She knows that her message to London must have been received and that Arnaud would have ensured that the news reached the Maquis. She goes back to bed and sleeps, soundly.

Moments later the R.A.F. squadrons approach the mountains of the Haute-Savoie where they drop precisely one hundred and twenty-six containers of weapons between three blazing beacons that have been lit by men who slipped into the bush and prepared cans of paraffin several hours before.

Punctually at 2:00 that afternoon Metzger arrives at 50 rue de Babylone. He quickly surveys the area and notices his two shadows from St Jorioz sitting on a bench opposite the apartment. Metzger knows he lost them in the crowd by the station but is reasssured that they must be Bardot's men, not Gestapo, for they know the address.

He walks into the foyer of the building and is stopped by an insistent little concierge who asks him his business. Careful not to antagonise anyone lest things should go wrong, Metzger treats the man politely and explains that he is a friend of Mme. Marchais and has come to pick up a colleague who is staying with her.

"And your name?" says René, the bleary-eyed concierge.

"Jean, Monsieur Jean" says Metzger.

René, his face resembling a pickled onion, picks up the receiver and mumbles into the intercom "Madame Marchais, there is a suspicious, bespectacled, shady looking character in a beret down here asking for you. He claims his name is Jean."

René feels very protective of Mme. Marchais.

"Send him up, René. We have been expecting him."

Reluctantly, his eyes never leaving Metzger's face, he escorts the visitor to the elevator and presses the button for the fourth floor.

"Number 213" he adds as he shuts the elevator doors. Metzger withdraws his fingers just in time.

Touching the side of his jacket where he feels the reassuring lump of the revolver he picked up from the office, Metzger isn't sure what to expect inside the apartment, although he's pretty certain that Bardot would want to see Marchais before trying anything.

He presses the button to number 213 and instantly Mme. Marchais opens the door. Several men are seated at a table; Bardot and three others.

"Right on time, Monsieur Jean" says Bardot "are you ready to go?"

"Of course" says Metzger.

"I will see you later, Madame" says Bardot as he gathers up his coat and briefcase.

He turns to the two men and says, in front of Metzger, "If I am not back here in three hours give the alarm to the whole organization." The men nod and say 'salut'.

Bardot and Metzger walk out of the building. The two men who had been tailing Metzger are now sitting in the front seat of an old Citroën. Bardot and Metzger get in the back.

On arriving at Fresnes prison, Metzger shows his pass and explains to the guards that he is taking a witness to confront one of the prisoners. A guard orders the driver to park the car outside the gates. Only Metzger and Bardot are allowed inside.

Marchais is ecstatic to see his number two again. And relieved that he can trust Monsieur Jean. He embraces both men and they all three sit down in Marchais' cell.

"Now I know I can trust you" he says to Metzger. "See, didn't I tell you that he was a good man" he says to Bardot, who nevertheless

remains unconvinced.

Marchais and Bardot talk about domestic matters for a few minutes and then Marchais outlines his plan to Bardot.

"Robert, I want you to return to St Jorioz and get Arnaud to ask London to send a plane. Monsieur Jean, accompanied by Claudine and Paul, needs to go to London so Monsieur Jean can present his peace plan to the British. Monsieur Jean will arrange for my release, I will pretend to be a man who has become an agent for the Nazis. In return, and because we know we are going to win the war, I have guaranteed Monsieur Jean's safety in London but first we need to convince his higher-ups of our willingness to 'betray' our colleagues so our story is believable. Can you arrange for a dummy transmitter to be planted somewhere in Paris and let me know where so I can 'betray' it to the Germans?"

"Well, of course, if that's what you want me to do" replies Bardot.

Metzger eyes Bardot carefully, sizing him up. Perhaps this man will be a good agent for the Abwehr, he thinks to himself. But he realizes he will have to stall; things are moving too fast.

"My dear friend" Metzger begins "I trust you implicitly but how do I know that your name carries any weight in London? It could be that the minute we arrive, I am arrested?"

Marchais, a little upset at his word being doubted, says Metzger will have nothing to fear. If necessary he, Marchais, would put his life on the line to save him. Metzger mock bows approvingly but says "I need a form of protection. What I propose is that you give me a list with names of your agents on it. I will then give it to a friend of mine here and he will keep it as security should something happen to me. If all goes well I will arrange for a message to be sent via the BBC and my friend will destroy the list. If anything happens to me your agents will be arrested but they will be treated as prisoners of war and not as spies, that much I promise. What do you say?"

Marchais hesitates.

"*My dear Marchais, do you really think that it will be possible for your men to escape the clutches of the Gestapo? Most of your comrades are under observation already. As you know, I'm sure, many agents that you think are working for you are really working for us. If I am not double-crossed, they will come to no harm. If I am double-crossed at least their lives will be saved. I can be no fairer than that.*"

Marchais looks at Bardot for some sort of reassurance. Bardot shrugs his shoulders as if to say 'we have no choice'.

Marchais sits down and writes the names of twenty people in Bordeaux, Marseilles, Strasbourg, Nancy and the Haute-Savoie.

The last name on the list is 'Luc, a British Agent'. The address, provided by Bardot, is Hotel de la Plage, St Jorioz.

Bardot and Metzger leave Fresnes and drive to a café in the Marais where they can discuss arrangements.

An hour later Bardot returns to Mme. Marchais' apartment to inform her of the outcome of the meeting.

He reassures his own men that all is OK. He will return to St Jorioz on the night sleeper, report to Claudine and ask Arnaud to request the aircraft. He instructs his men to stay in Paris pending his own return in a few days with news of the plane.

Bardot arrives back in St Jorioz shortly after 8:00 the following morning. He goes straight to Les Tilleuls and finds Claudine talking excitedly to several members of the group about the successful arms drop the night before.

"*Ah Robert, welcome back. What news?*" Claudine offers him a cup of coffee. "*Everything seems to be going well at the moment, n'est ce pas?*"

"*Oui, I met with Marchais and we have hatched a plan. Where is Arnaud? I need to contact him urgently.*"

"*He is still up in the hills with Luc, the new man. We had an enormous drop of weapons the night you left for Paris. The whole Haute-Savoie Maquis are now an armed force thanks to the R.A.F.*"

"*When are Arnaud and Luc due back?*"

"Maybe tonight, yes… I think tonight. Thierry de Rome is going to pick them up this evening."

Bardot is reassured.

"So what was the outcome of the meeting? Does Jean still want a transmitter to send messages to London?"

"More than that. He will arrange for Marchais to be released if we organize an aircraft to come and pick up Monsieur Jean and you and Paul, if he's back, and take you all to London so he can present his peace plan personally to your Prime Minister."

Claudine takes it in. It tallies with her own discussion with Monsieur Jean. She feels that if Marchais is convinced of the story, which clearly he is, then there must be something to it. She's excited but she feels she needs higher authority before she gives the go-ahead.

"Robert, I need to get Arnaud to send a message to London before I request an aircraft. Can Monsieur Jean wait a few days?"

"Yes, I told him I would return to Paris next week. That is no problem."

Claudine checks the date. It's 12 April.

She returns to her room at the Hotel de la Poste and composes a message to London. She is sure Paul will know what to do.

Arnaud turns up at Les Tilleuls later that evening.

Claudine hands him a message for transmission as soon as possible to London.

Arnaud looks down at the piece of paper:

FROM CLAUDINE STOP ABWEHR OFFICER BY NAME JEAN CONTACTED ME ST JORIOZ SUGGESTED IF YOU PROVIDE HUDSON HE WILL RELEASE MARCHAIS AND SUZANNE RETURNING WITH PAUL AND ME TO LONDON AND THEN DISCUSS MEANS OF ENDING WAR STOP ENDS

Arnaud stares at the words in disbelief. "Claudine have you met this guy? You actually believe all this crap?"

"Yes I've met him and I'm not sure. We had a cup of coffee here in the hotel…"

"You had coffee with a Nazi officer. Here? In our hotel?" Arnaud asks incredulously.

"Yes, he approached me with a letter from Marchais, from prison, Fresnes."

"God alive I would have shot him on the spot."

"Yes, I suppose you would have and signed the death warrant for Marchais and Suzanne and destroyed any chance for peace in the process. Off with you Arnaud and send that message."

Arnaud leaves, wondering aloud about Claudine's mental health. How could she believe this guy? On the other hand she's been right so many times before. And he knows himself to be hot-headed, perhaps he's just overreacting?

He rides his bicycle back to his mountain hideout at Les Tissots.

At his 07:00 sked the following morning he duly transmits the message to London.

By chance, Buckmaster and Roger Chamberlain were visiting the Baker Street Signals Room when they heard the clacking of the teleprinter.

"Paul, look at this" Buckmaster mouths through his dropped jaw to Roger Chamberlain as he reads the message from Claudine.

Within minutes the answer is sent back to Arnaud:

JEAN HIGHLY DANGEROUS STOP YOU ARE TO HIDE ACROSS LAKE AND CUT CONTACTS WITH ALL SAVE ARNAUD WHO MUST REMAIN BY HIS MOUNTAIN SET STOP FIX DROPPING GROUND YOUR OWN CHOICE FOR PAUL WHO WILL LAND ANYWHERE SOONEST STOP ENDS

I feel better knowing that I can be of use to Tom Morel and his maquisards. He's agreed that I can go up and work with them. Given the lack of security in St Jorioz I decide not to let anyone know that I'm joining him, except Arnaud of course.

Partly psychological and partly having done some physical labour at last, I got the best night's sleep since I've been in France. I leave the Hotel de la Plage, under the ever watchful eye of Mme. Guibal, and walk to the Hotel de la Poste to have breakfast with Claudine, as promised.

The breakfast room is almost empty, just a few old men at the bar munching on some sort of brioche substitute and drinking what looks like rum. Jean Cottet mouths "Bonjour" from behind the bar. Claudine is already sitting at a table by the window, drinking coffee.

I join her. "Have a seat. I've already asked M. Cottet to bring us some bread and coffee, that OK?"

"Fine" I say, sitting down. She seems tetchy. Gone is her self-confident air. Before long I realize why.

She starts to talk about a meeting she's had with a German calling himself Monsieur Jean. I sense she is testing the waters to see what sort of reaction she might expect from Paul when he gets back from England. But if she expects approval from me she's not going to get it.

"I don't believe this guy's story for a moment and if you know what's good for you, you'll get out of here, along with the rest of us, as soon as possible. It's far too dangerous for any of us to stay here. We all ought to leave immediately. The whole réseau is at risk."

Her discomfort transforms into anger.

"If you can't stand the heat then I suggest you go. You'll never make a good agent if you run at the first sign of trouble. You have no right to tell me what to do."

"Stay if you must" I say "but I'm outta here. You're making a big mistake." I return to the Hotel de la Plage, hastily pack, make my apologies to Madame Guibal, tell her she can keep the money I've paid for the week and catch the bus to Albertville; making sure she knows I'm doing so.

Luc's bus passes Arnaud as he cycles back to St Jorioz to deliver Buckmaster's message to Claudine.

Having read the message, Claudine is now properly frightened for the first time since she left Cannes.

At 11:00 she and Arnaud set forth from the Hotel de la Poste along the road marked Col de Leschaux to find a dropping ground for Paul's imminent arrival. They cycle 11 km to the start of the stony mountain path, hide their bikes in the undergrowth and, buoyed with excitement at the prospect of Paul's return, climb the 800 metres to the summit. It doesn't take them long to locate the hog's back. Approximately 300 metres by 80; it will provide a good dropping zone. They yank branches from nearby trees and drag them over so they can set them alight later. They mark the spot with a hastily assembled cross and return to the Hotel de la Poste.

Claudine decides to stay at the Hotel instead of moving across the lake as instructed. She's certain, and has been reassured by Robert Bardot, that if Buckmaster is right and Jean really is dangerous, he won't make a move until the 18th.

She sets in train plans to move the following day.

Arnaud cycles back the 16 km to Faverges and then pushes his bicycle 1,000 metres up the mountain to the path leading to his radio hideout in Les Tissots. Exhausted, he eats a hunk of bread, a piece of garlic sausage, and collapses into bed.

At his 07:00 sked he sends the following message to London confirming the dropping zone:

STUDYING SEMNOZ ANNECY P 14 STAND BY ALL
NIGHT 14 AND 15 APRIL

*The new girl, his opposite number in the London Receiving Station,
responds immediately by sending him the BBC message that will alert them
to Paul's arrival:*

'Le carabe d'or fait sa toilette de printemps'.

*Arnaud re-stows his transmitting set, satisfied that London has listened to
his complaints about the 'bitch', and goes back to bed. It will be a long day.*

*At noon Arnaud gets on his bike and heads down the hill once again to
Faverges. He stops at the Café du Vin for a pastis, a leisurely bite of lunch
and flirtatious banter with the owner's daughter. All he has to do now is
to get to the Hotel de la Poste by 7:00 p.m. Then he can listen in to Jean
Cottet's hidden set to see if Paul is coming. If there is no message he will do
the same thing the following night.*

*At around 5:00 p.m. Robert Bardot stops in at the Hotel de la Poste to
see Claudine. He finds her having a cup of coffee in the bar.*

*"Claudine" says the worried-looking Bardot, "Luc has vanished; he is
no longer at the Hotel de la Plage. No one knows where he is."*

*"I know. I sent him away" she says, not wholly accurately, "it's getting
too hot for him here."*

*"Where has he gone? The manageress at the Hotel de la Plage says he's
gone to Albertville."*

"I don't know where he's gone" says Claudine, "what does it matter?"

"I just wondered," he says, and leaves.

*This brief encounter disturbs Claudine. Nothing she can put her finger
on, just Bardot's interest, the sheepish way he looked at her; how he phrased
the question, the keenness of his interest in Luc...*

*Arnaud's puffy red face appears around the door of the hotel bar
approximately ten minutes later. His smoking/cycling combination has him
panting like a retriever.*

"*Claudine*", he says "*I got the message from London, immediately. It was god-damned marvellous. They must have fired that 12-word-a-minute bitch just as I told them to. It looks like Paul is coming tonight if all goes well.*"

"*Wonderful*" replies Claudine "*do you want a coffee?*"

"*Sure.*"

Claudine drains her coffee cup, orders two more, pulls out a pack of cigarettes and offers one to the panting Arnaud. "Ah, nectar..." he says extracting one from the pack. As he does so, he notices something amiss in Claudine's expression.

"*You look a little preoccupied Claudine; thinking about Paul?*"

She smiles, "No, just worried about Bardot. I have a nasty feeling he may be working for that German."

"*What?" Arnaud splutters into his coffee "the little bastard. I'll kill him. What makes you think this?*"

"*Nothing specific but he's not himself. He seems nervous and is showing an abnormal interest in Luc's whereabouts.*"

"*Luc's whereabouts? He's at his hotel.*"

"*Not any more he isn't. I sent him away. I think his presence here now would only complicate things.*"

Arnaud, uncharacteristically, keeps quiet. He has a nagging fear that Luc is right and that a disaster is looming. Still he feels all will be right once Paul returns. Like Claudine, he has great faith in Paul.

The two of them agree not to involve Robert Bardot in anything sensitive for a while just in case Claudine's suspicions are confirmed.

Just before 7:00 p.m. Claudine goes up to her room to listen for the BBC messages on the portable set that she and Paul had used in the south. Arnaud goes down to the cellar where he finds Jean Cottet standing beside the 12-valve receiver that he keeps hidden beside the boiler.

At 7:30 the shrill, but perfectly enunciated, tones of the BBC broadcaster voice the daily announcement:

Voici maintenant quelques messages personels

And just as predictably the German jamming apparatus comes into play. Jean Cottet and Arnaud strain to hear. "Buggers" murmurs Arnaud.

"Patience, mon vieux" responds Jean Cottet. They hear bits and pieces of a variety of messages but there is no sign of theirs. They decide to celebrate not having to climb the Semnoz for the second time in 24 hours by having a pastis in the bar. Moments later Claudine comes downstairs wearing a heavy sweater and her walking boots.

"What are you doing? Let's go" she says.

"But there was no message" says Arnaud.

"Oh yes there was," replies Claudine "you just weren't listening carefully enough."

Arnaud looks chastised but quietly wonders if Claudine hasn't imagined it because she wants Paul back so much.

Ten minutes later Claudine, Arnaud, Jean and Simone Cottet set off on the road to Col de Leschaux.

It's 8:20 p.m. The plane could arrive any time between 12:00 p.m. and 2:00 a.m. They have no time to lose. If the Halifax pilot doesn't find the bonfire he will take Paul back to England. More than likely he won't be able to return until the May moon.

Three hours later the tired, sweaty group of four arrive at the spot that Claudine and Arnaud had marked on the top of the Semnoz. They are in time. They would have heard the four-engined bomber if it had already passed over.

Arnaud, still unsure that Claudine really had heard the wireless message, goes to the old chalet where they had hidden the makings of the bonfire. He and Jean Cottet assemble a substantial number of the branches on a foundation of straw, ready for a dousing of petrol as soon as the bomber is spotted.

The moon is so bright that they are pretty sure the pilot will be able to see them with his naked eye. They pass a flask of brandy around and wait.

"Here he comes!" cries Arnaud half an hour later. They all strain to listen and yes, it is definitely a plane, a large one. Arnaud runs to get the petrol; empties the entire bottle onto the branches and lights a match. The lit fire sends flames shooting into the night sky.

"There's no possibility they are going to miss this" says Arnaud. They stand peering into the sky. Then they see it, the deep dark underbelly of a 30-ton bomber, heading straight for them.

The plane passes right overhead and circles around to come in along the length of the hog's back so it has a better chance of safely dropping its six parachutes onto the 300 metre stretch.

And there they are, six beautiful chutes dancing in the moonlight as they gradually make their descent. Only one is carrying a man. Claudine strains her eyes to pick out Paul's chute. The bomber roars overhead, flames shooting out of the four engines' eight exhaust pipes, and disappears. Arnaud and Jean Cottet run to pick up the containers. Claudine waits while Paul, coming straight down onto his feet, narrowly avoids landing on her head.

Moments later they are in each others arms, their mouths connecting passionately, oblivious to the cold and to the other three waiting figures silhouetted in the moonlight.

They return to St Jorioz, reaching the hotel at 5:30 a.m. It has taken them over four hours to haul the steel containers, each weighing 115 kilos., and the other smaller parcels of arms and equipment back to the hotel. They hide the precious contents in the Cottets' basement to await collection by the Glières Maquis.

Claudine emerges from the hotel at 8:00 a.m. having washed and changed. She catches the 8:15 bus for Annecy where she hopes to find Tom Morel. He is staying in a safe house on rue Jean-Jacques Rousseau awaiting news of the previous night's drop of additional arms and equipment.

At 12:30 she returns to the Hotel de la Poste where she and Paul eat lunch.

At 2:00 p.m. Paul rows Claudine across the lake to Talloires to visit

Madame Clabaud, Henri 'Georges' Clabaud's Russian wife. While there, they take rooms in a small hotel confirming to the owner that they will check in the following day, about noon.

They have three days until 18 April, the day Claudine figures Jean will make his move, if indeed he plans to make one.

They row back across the lake before dusk. Arnaud joins them for dinner that evening. Claudine has told Paul about her suspicions of Bardot who has not been seen for two days now. Arnaud asks about Luc. Have they heard anything?

"No nothing" says Claudine "I think he was so alarmed that he got as far away as possible as quickly as possible. Not good that he runs at the slightest provocation" she comments. Paul smiles. Arnaud shrugs.

Paul warns Arnaud that it is about time they all obey the instructions from London. "Claudine and I are planning to move across the lake in the morning. We've already taken some rooms. And you, Arnaud, you must stay in your mountain hideaway until further notice."

"But, Paul," he remonstrates, "I want to be with you and Claudine. I will go crazy sitting on that mountaintop. I don't even like bloody mountains."

"Don't worry. It won't be for long, and to make sure you go tonight I want you to send this message to London."

Paul hands Arnaud the message. He opens it and reads:

RAF AND RECEPTION PERFECT STOP ALL UNDER CONTROL

"Pah" says Arnaud, "that can wait."

"No it can't" says Paul with just a hint of irritation in his voice, "they are waiting for it. It must go tonight."

"Alright, alright but don't leave me on that fucking mountaintop."

Arnaud says goodnight to Claudine and Paul, mounts his bicycle and rides the 20 kilometres back to his hideaway.

Paul takes his clothes off and lies on the bed in the semi-dark, watching Claudine undress by the light of the moon. Her firm breasts and prominent nipples are seductively silhouetted against the light through the open window. Her last piece of clothing thrown on the chair she walks, naked, towards the bed. Paul pulls her to him. Flesh meets flesh. They kiss, passionately, deeply. Quickly rediscovering the precise places that cause each other the most pleasure, they make love with animal-like abandon, revelling in their new-found energy. The moonlight plays on their naked bodies.

Fully satisfied and ready to abandon themselves to sleep, Paul puts his arm around Claudine as she snuggles close to him. As he strokes her hair, he talks to her quietly about his hopes for the future, of the life he wants them to share after the war. But she hears nothing. She is already fast asleep.

Only one light still shines in the silent hotel. Jean Cottet and Simone are in the office catching up on their accounts.

Simone looks up and cocks her ear to the window, "Did you hear something outside?"

"No" says Jean. He pushes back his chair and walks over to the window.

He opens the shutters wide. It's a bright night, the moon still large enough to cast a clear light on the street. Jean Cottet sees no one. "It's all quiet." He glances up at the mighty Semnoz rising so high above the village and a smile spreads across his face as he remembers their success the night before.

Seconds later there are three firm knocks on the locked front door.

"Strange" says Jean Cottet, "who could that be?" Simone walks over to the front door and, peering through the window, recognizes the profile of Louis le Belge, one of the couriers based at Les Tilleuls.

Simone opens the door. "Come in Louis. What's the problem?"

Louis, a plump beet-faced Belgian blurts out "I have an urgent message for Claudine."

"Can't it wait until the morning, Louis? I think she is sleeping."

"No, it cannot wait. I insist you wake her now."

"Very well, Louis. You wait here."

Realising this really must be important, Simone walks upstairs and knocks on the bedroom door. There is no sound. She quietly opens the door and sees the two sleeping figures entwined in each other's arms.

"Claudine, Claudine" she says bending down and whispering in her ear.

Claudine, startled, jumps up. Paul barely moves. "What is it Simone? What's wrong?"

"Louis is here. He has urgent news for you. He says it cannot wait."

"I'll be right there" says Claudine grabbing a bathrobe. The two women then start down the stairs. Halfway down they stop and stare in astonishment at the assembly in the downstairs hall.

Metzger is standing at the foot of the stairs aiming a gun at Claudine.

"Don't try and warn Paul, Claudine. If you do he is bound to try and jump out of the window. The hotel is surrounded by Alpini troops. They have orders to shoot."

Claudine looks around the room. She gives Louis and Robert Bardot looks of utter contempt as they stand, sheepishly, among their Gestapo friends.

"You have played the game well, Claudine. But now it is over so kindly lead me to Paul's room."

Realizing that she would put the Cottets and the others at risk, especially Paul, if she tries anything, she reluctantly turns around and leads 'Monsieur Jean' and two Gestapo men to the bedroom.

Claudine opens the door and Metzger walks in and turns on the light. As soon as Paul wakes he realizes the game is up.

"What is your name?" asks one of the Gestapo men.

"Chaboux" replies Paul.

"Chaboux?" queries the German. "Or perhaps it is Chauvet as it was in Marseilles? Whichever it is it means Captain Roger Chamberlain, saboteur and filthy spy. I am Sergeant Karl Metzger of the Abwehr. You are under arrest.

Two automatic weapons point in his face. "Get dressed" barks Metzger "and you too Claudine."

Calmly and casually, Paul climbs out of bed and pulls on the clothes he had thrown on the floor a few hours earlier.

The couple, now handcuffed, are escorted down the stairs and into a waiting car.

"We are in a territory under Italian control" says Metzger as the two Gestapo men push Paul and Claudine into the back seat, "would you rather be taken prisoner by the Italians or the Germans?"

"The Italians of course" replies Paul, knowing full well that it will make little difference as the Italians will be forced to hand them over to the Germans almost immediately.

"Very well" responds Metzger, beckoning an armed Alpino, one of the elite Italian mountain warfare troops, to get in the front seat.

"Take them to Annecy prison, driver."

The Citroën pulls away from the hotel, makes a U-turn and heads back down the road to Annecy.

14

As dawn breaks over Lake Annecy the following day, Tom Morel, armed with his new Colt .38 revolver and his legitimate ID identifying him as Director of the Annecy Office of Voluntary Recruitment for Labour in Germany, leaves his safe house near the train station and catches the first bus to St Jorioz.

Alerted by Claudine the previous day that a substantial arsenal of weapons and equipment had been dropped onto the summit of Semnoz early that morning and that it is now hidden in the basement of the Hotel de la Poste, his plan is to borrow Jean Cottet's V8 Ford and drive the booty up to the maquisards on the Glières plateau.

But as soon as his bus approaches the intersection at St Jorioz he realizes that something is very wrong. What looks like a Gestapo car is parked beside the hotel. Alpini are lingering around the hotel and the bus stop. It is clearly pointless to think about removing the cache of arms. But he is more concerned about his friend Jean Cottet, the man he has to thank for alerting the British agents to the Maquis presence and their need for arms. So he decides to get off at the St Jorioz stop anyway.

Alpini are searching everyone's papers as they climb off the bus. Most of the passengers are returning home after working night shifts in Annecy. Tom

Morel shows his ID and is waived through.

Momentarily giving thanks that the Italians and not the Germans are responsible for this region, he opens the door to the hotel restaurant and is immediately accosted by a German officer accompanied by two plain clothes men who appear to be French.

"Identity card" barks the German officer at Tom Morel. It is duly produced and seems to be in order.

"Do you recognize this man?" the German asks one of the plain clothes men.

"No, Herr Sergeant, I have never seen him before" replies Robert Bardot truthfully.

"And you?" he turns to the other man.

"No, Herr Sergeant, he is not from here" says Louis le Belge, also truthfully.

Tom Morel breathes a little more easily. But the German officer is not finished.

Clearly suspicious, he continues the interrogation.

"Why are you here?"

"I have stopped off to have some breakfast on my way to Albertville to collect an ambulance. I am diabetic and not suited to any other kind of work so I am employed in Annecy supplying Frenchmen to work in German factories," he replies, pointedly, second-guessing the German's suspicions.

At that instant the front door opens again and another would-be breakfaster walks in. The three men lose interest in Tom Morel and wave him through to the restaurant. Four tables are occupied. All lone men drinking coffee. Collaborators? Milice?

Tom Morel sits at the bar instead of at a table in the hopes of being able to have a quiet word with Jean Cottet. But there is no sign of him. His heart sinks, certain that his friend has been arrested. Why else all this interrogation of everyone in the hotel? And what of the arsenal that presumably lies underneath the very floor on which the German officer is standing? Have they already found it and removed it? If not what can he do to retrieve it?

The kitchen door opens. A waiter walks in with a tray of breakfasts which he distributes among the tables. Then he walks over to the bar and asks Tom Morel for his order. He appears to be nervous. It is his first day on the job. The two Italian waiters having fled the previous evening.

Tom orders coffee, with some bread for dipping, and quietly asks the waiter if he could tell Jean Cottet that his friend Tom is here. The waiter eyes him carefully as he cleans down the bar with a towel and, without responding, walks back into the kitchen.

Two minutes later the waiter returns with another tray. Behind him is Jean Cottet.

Cottet shows an exaggerated excitement on greeting his old friend, clearly for the benefit of the other guests, and invites him to have his coffee back in the office.

Once they are inside the office and the door is closed the blood drains from Jean Cottet's face.

"What is going on mon ami?" asks Morel.

"Terrible news, Tom. Early this morning this man who was here a few weeks ago calling himself Monsieur Jean turned up and arrested both Claudine and Paul and took them off to Annecy prison. His real name is Metzger, Sergeant Karl Metzger. They are now conducting house-to-house searches looking for Luc and Arnaud. There are posters up on the trees on the main street with both men's images on them. It cannot be long before one of our Pétainiste countrymen turns them in. They are offering rewards. And threatening reprisals if anyone is found sheltering them."

Tom Morel absorbs this as fast as he can, his mind racing to figure out how best to help.

"I know where Luc is." he says.

"You do? Good." says Jean, "Is he close? Can you warn him?"

"Yes. He has been training our men. I will warn him as soon as I get

back. I hate to lose him. He has become one of us. But he needs to get out of here fast."

"But how are we going to get word to Arnaud? I would go myself but I can't leave here without being followed. Arnaud is so hot-headed that he may well already be on his way down here."

"Leave it to me" replies Tom Morel "Luc and I will find a way of getting him out of danger."

Jean Cottet looks relieved. "Oh, and there is the little problem of your supplies which are sitting in my cellar waiting to be discovered by the Boche. What are we going to do about that?"

"Haven't the Gestapo searched the hotel?" asks Tom, amazed.

"No, as soon as they located Claudine and Paul they appeared to be satisfied. They don't seem to suspect our involvement. Paul made a point of apologising, in front of the Gestapo, for putting us all in harm's way. And Bardot and Louis, the two from Les Tilleuls who betrayed them to the Abwehr, never had proof that we were personally involved in any way. We have always been cautious."

"Well let's hope it stays that way. By the way I think those two you mentioned are at the front door now, helping the Gestapo conduct their searches."

"Pigs" says Jean Cottet "all the more reason to get to Arnaud quickly and stop him before he does something stupid."

"Leave it all to us, mon vieux. You have helped us enormously. We will find a way of removing the equipment as soon as possible. Meanwhile please be careful."

The two men embrace. "Give my love to Simone" says Tom Morel "we will be in touch very soon." He walks towards the door. As he is about to open it he turns and says "By the way, if you find your Ford van missing one night don't be alarmed. We will only be borrowing it."

Jean Cottet grins.

Tom Morel pays the waiter and walks past the 'reception party' without establishing eye contact and out into the morning sun to catch the next bus to Albertville. From there he will take the road on the other side of the lake to return to the Glières.

It is already noon when the rural bus stops at the junction of the Annecy-Marouse Road and the track to Glières. Tom Morel gets off. As the bus disappears, several of Morel's maquisards emerge from the woods to greet him.

In the forefront is Jacques Villaz, the brightest and keenest of the young maquisards.

"Is Luc here?" asks Tom.

"Yes, sure" Jacques says as they walk up the track towards the plateau "he's been showing us how to use the new equipment, and a few other tricks as well. The guys have nicknamed him 'Le Grand Diable Americain'. We're ready to take on the Milice at any minute now" he smiles.

"Bien Jacques, let's go and find him." Morel, his arm around Jacques as they start the climb up the hill, confides in him "Luc is in great danger. The Gestapo are looking everywhere for him. He needs to leave here as soon as possible for his sake and for ours."

"What's happened, Tom? Why are they suddenly on to Luc?"

"Paul and Claudine, the ones who arranged for our equipment to be dropped, were arrested by the Gestapo last night in St Jorioz. They were taken to Annecy early this morning. By now they may well be in Paris. The Gestapo are combing the area looking for Arnaud, the wireless operator, and for Luc."

"What the hell can we do?"

"Don't worry. We'll get Luc and Arnaud out of here safely. And we'll retrieve the rest of our arms and equipment" says Tom, patting him on the back.

"More arms?" asks Jacques expectantly. To the men of the Maquis arms

are the first essentials, followed at a safe distance by women and tobacco.

"Yes. They were dropped on Semnoz along with Paul. They are being hidden for us in the Hotel de la Poste but as it's surrounded by Gestapo, some of whom are also staying there, we will have to steal them back again."

Jacques' eyes light up. He relishes the thought of stealing weapons from under the Gestapo's noses.

"Can I be…" he doesn't finish the sentence before Tom Morel answers.

"Yes Jacques you can."

Jacques Villaz, aged 24, is just under two metres tall with an athletic build, intelligent piercing eyes, a mop of dark curly hair and the thick pouting lips of a French crooner. His infectious smile and dimpled cheeks, augmented by high cheekbones, light up a countenance that is reflected back by those around him. Lacking the arrogance that often accompanies such looks, he is very popular with his comrades.

While serving as Captain Henri Frenay's number two, before the French capitulation, he proved himself to be a first-rate soldier. Always rising to a challenge, he is also liked and respected by his superiors. He pushes himself to achieve, volunteers for dangerous missions, and is never satisfied unless he gives his all. A confident all-rounder.

But it hasn't always been like this. As a young child he was indeed super-confident and hyperactive. The eldest child of a romantic and irresponsible university history teacher and one of his more glamorous former students, young Jacques often had to fend for himself. His father would spend most nights cavorting in town with his communist cohorts, often not returning home until dawn, if at all. He rarely spent much time with his wife and son, preferring instead the camaraderie of his peers and the adulation, and comforting bodies, of his female students. As a result, Jacques' mother became angry and bitter and took out her frustration on her only son, who learned to keep out of her way.

Jacques would return home from his primary school, take bread and fruit from the kitchen and go out to the playground to kick a football around with his schoolmates. When he returned home he'd eat his supper alone, go into his mother's bedroom (for she spent most afternoons and every evening in bed) to kiss her good-night and go to his room where he would look at the books he had procured from his father's study. Picture books of buildings around the world he found particularly fascinating. Before dropping off to sleep he would imagine his future as a famous architect. Despite this somewhat unstimulating home life, Jacques was a normal, happy, bouncy self-possessed young boy.

When he was aged about seven, this all changed. One dinner time he returned home from his football game at the playground a different lad. Even his mother was concerned enough to get out of bed and sit with him while he ate his meal in unreachable silence. It would be many years before Jacques would comprehend what had happened that day in the playground. All he knew then was that he felt as though he had been cut loose somehow from the world he had known; as though his dinghy were attached to a fast moving ship by a strong rope and then suddenly, in a split second of realization, the rope had been severed and he had been left to drift, alone, in the sea of life.

Gradually, over a period of two to three years, Jacques learned to confront his sense of isolation. He hurled himself into every activity available not resting until he had mastered it, whatever it was, from climbing to shooting to fishing (on rare days his father would let Jacques accompany him) to fencing, to football and fighting.

By the age of twelve, when his father left for the Spanish Civil War never to return, Jacques had two young sisters. He would help his mother care for them and, although her days in bed were somewhat curtailed, he largely took responsibility for them, especially after his father's disappearance. His sisters depended on him, needed him and loved him. He had found new meaning to his life.

At the age of nineteen he joined the army, to further his own physical and psychological development and to help provide for his mother and his *young sisters. He was rapidly promoted, having attracted the attention of Henri Frenay, his captain, through his trustworthiness, his determination and bravado. When Armistice was declared on 22 June, 1940, Jacques returned to Annecy and the following year, armed with nothing more than Frenay's recommendation, joined Tom Morel and what eventually became the Glières Maquis.*

Jacques and Tom Morel approach the clearing now where many of the maquisards are assembled, close to a hundred of them. Some are gathering wood and stores of food and clothing donated, voluntarily or involuntarily, by the local populace. Others are resting. Luc is surrounded by thirty or so young men, mainly in their early twenties but quite a few in their teens, teaching them how to assemble their newly-acquired sten guns. He catches sight of Tom and the others and immediately hands over responsibility to one of the more experienced men.

Tom and his mates are staring at me. I wonder if something has gone badly wrong.

"Tom, everything OK?"

"No Luc. Bad news. Very bad. Claudine and Paul were arrested last night. They've been taken to Paris I think, probably to Fresnes."

"Shit! It was that German, Monsieur Jean, something like that?"

"Oui, his real name is Metzger, Karl Metzger. He's a sergeant in the Abwehr. Paul had just returned from London."

I think of how best to save my skin as we sit down together outside the tent where the food is being prepared.

"Paul and Claudine were spending one final night at the Hotel de la Poste before going into hiding across the lake but Metzger had been tipped off by one of the guys at Les Tilleuls, Robert somebody I think Jean Cottet said; or it could have been Louis, they were both there when I got to the hotel this morning."

"Robert Bardot and Louis le Belge?"

"Yes, that's right. Robert Bardot. Don't know about the Louis guy.

"I know them both."

"Yes, and they know you," responds Tom Morel.

I nod.

A maquisard brings us two cups of hot coffee.

"And you know what that means Luc?" says Tom.

"I do. I have to get out of here, and fast. But what about Arnaud?"

"He has not been arrested, yet. Nobody knows exactly where he is except for Jean Cottet and it isn't going to be easy for him to leave the hotel any time soon with all the Boche about, not to mention Robert Bardot and Louis."

"I know where he is. I'll find him, but I'll have to hurry."

"It won't be safe for you Luc. Every Gestapo and probably all the Milice in the area will have your picture by now. There is a price on your head. Quite a large one, actually. I was almost tempted myself."

"Merde" I say as I get up to return my coffee mug to the galley. "Anyhow I'm flattered. I won't take unnecessary risks. I'll keep to the back roads as far as possible. It will take me a while though. Is there any chance I can get a ride to Faverges? I can go on by foot from there."

"We'll find a way" said Tom "but I'd like to send someone else with you, though, to act as another pair of eyes and ears."

"Who?" I say, not liking the sound of this. Claudine's arrest has convinced me that in future I'd be better off travelling alone.

"One of my best men, Jacques Villaz. He knows the area well. His mother used to live in St Jorioz. She was killed by a Gestapo car last December. The bastard didn't even stop. Left her dying by the roadside."

"Is Villaz here?"

"Yes, he's the guy who gave you the coffee" says Tom beckoning Jacques over with a wave of his hand.

I recognize him now, close up.

"Ah yes, you were the expert on railway explosives, n'est ce pas?"

"That is kind of you."

"Well Jacques I hear you are to accompany me on a mission?"

"It would be an honour" he bows "if you'll take me? When do we leave?"

"As soon as we can arrange transport, if I take you."

He looks embarrassed. "Excuse me, but I'm very eager."

Tom Morel leaves us to get better acquainted and goes off to arrange our transport. I take the opportunity to quiz Jacques. Much as I trust Morel's judgment I want to make sure this guy is up to it. My life depends on it. So will his.

Jacques sits on the ground next to me.

"What made you join the Maquis, Jacques?"

"I was in the French army, serving with Captain Henri Frenay, when the Armistice was declared. After we were ordered to throw down our weapons without even a fight, the authorities assured us that we would be remobilised in France (we were on the north-eastern border) but Frenay and a few others convinced me that this was a lie. We would be taken as prisoners to Germany. So we agreed to escape. Frenay went to Lyon, his home town, where he has formed a Resistance group called Combat. He is now, for certain, one of the most powerful men in the French Resistance."

"Why didn't you join him?"

"My mother lived near Annecy, in St Jorioz actually. Also I have two young sisters here. My father was killed fighting in the Spanish Civil War, or that's what we think. We never had confirmation. I heard people talk of a Resistance group forming near to Annecy, on the Glières plateau, and so I came here. My mother is now dead and my sisters and their two baby daughters are staying with my aunt. I see them when I can, but it's very dangerous. There are many collaborators who would be happy to betray us."

"Why didn't you join the Armistice Army like 84,000 of your fellow countrymen? At least Hitler allowed you that. And you could have kept your rank and salary and looked after your sisters?"

Jacques' face hardened. "Do you need to ask? Do you think that any of us could work for the German puppet Pétain and, worse, Laval, the pathetic men who encourage us to be collaborators 'for the glory of France'? It would be better to die."

Jacques is a decent guy and beneath his toughness there's a sensitivity. I decide to trust my instincts, and Tom Morel's of course.

We shake hands. "I'm glad to have you with me, Jacques."

Tom Morel returns.

"We'd better be off. We don't have much time."

He tells us about the arms cache in the basement of the Hotel de la Poste. He says he'll send several of his men down to the hotel for lunch. They will be responsible for locating the weapons and equipment that Claudine and the others had brought back from the Semnoz and would load them into the back of Jean Cottet's van. With the hustle and bustle of the day, the noise they would make should go unnoticed. The load itself, however, would have to be removed at night. Preferably without alerting anyone.

Tom explained to Jacques and me his plan for stealing the van from the hotel garage, perhaps by creating some sort of diversion, and bringing the booty back to the Glières plateau.

I see an opportunity here. I want to do this myself, along with Jacques and maybe even Arnaud. "We'll handle that part Tom" I say "if that's OK with you Jacques? It will give Arnaud and me a good chance to get our own back, besides we know the hotel pretty well, at least Arnaud does and I'm sure he'll insist on being involved."

Jacques responds enthusiastically. Tom Morel less so.

"It doesn't make sense Luc to have the two most wanted men in the area undertaking this mission. We need those weapons but we also need you alive."

I press my case. "If all goes according to plan, Arnaud, Jacques and I will be in St Jorioz by late this evening, the right place and the right time to pick up the arms and bring them back here. There's no one better placed to do it."

Tom Morel reluctantly agrees.

"Alright, I suggest that we take you down the eastern side of the lake" says Tom "let's not take unnecessary risks. There's a maquisard who works as a fisherman living near the abbey on the outskirts of Talloires. He'll loan you a boat and you can row yourselves across the lake, it's not wide there, it should only take you ten minutes or so to reach Duingt. Obviously don't drift to the north-west or you'll find yourselves in St Jorioz. Once you're in Duingt you'll have another 18 kilometres to Faverges which you'll have to walk, unless you can somehow acquire some bicycles. That OK with you Luc?"

"Seems sensible to me. How about you Jacques?" Every minute we delay Arnaud is closer to arrest.

"D'accord, d'accord."

I check my watch. It's a quarter to two. "How soon can you get us down to the lake, Tom?"

"Right away. Look over there" he points at an aged, green Renault 9 hidden in the trees. "We keep it for emergencies. It's in excellent shape despite its appearance" he assures us "I'll drive you myself. I need to see Albert, the fisherman anyway."

Jacques and I gather together a few supplies; bread, cheese, a tin of horse meat and bid our comrades adieu before bundling into the Renault which Tom has already started up. No one else is aware of our mission. Another lesson from Arisaig: the fewer people who know where you are, what you are doing, the safer you tend to be.

On the verge of positive action at last, I feel that old surge of adrenalin as we motor down the rough track towards the main road. It brings with it a heightened sense of awareness of everyone and everything around. I don't find concentrating easy unless I am completely passionate about something, or someone. Now I am.

Tom offers around his pack of Gauloises. As we approach the N203, Tom acknowledges a signal from a lookout in the woods above us and motions us to be silent. He slows the Renault to a crawl and then pulls it off the track so we are invisible from the road. He switches off the engine. We all listen intently.

Thirty seconds later a convoy of six open trucks carrying Alpini troops goes by, followed a minute or so later by a voiture de la detection, its antennae for detecting transmitters on top. Taking up the rear is a black Gestapo Citroën.

"Looks like the Abwehr have handed over responsibility for this case to the Gestapo" says Tom, "not good news for any of us."

"It's inevitable with the capture of two such high-profile agents as Paul and Claudine" I suggest.

"There's a price on your head now Luc, don't forget. You'd better choose your friends carefully."

After a few minutes, Tom spurs the little Renault into action. We emerge from the ditch and, on reaching the road, turn left towards the Lake.

Tom nips up a side track one kilometre before we hit the main road into Annecy, drives through a run-down farm and out onto the road bordering the east side of the lake. Twenty uneventful minutes later we pull into the drive of the Abbaye in Talloires. Tom parks the car in a barn near to an old stone cottage by the lakeside and switches off the engine.

Albert, 56 years old, round, ruddy-faced with great big watery eyes and wearing blue overalls with the top flap undone to expose a chest matted with grey hair, emerges from the house wiping his mouth with an oversized napkin. "Ah ha" he says, recognizing his friend Tom coming out of the barn "you and your criminal friends are just in time for lunch. We are eating late today. Come on in."

"We are in a hurry Albert" says Tom apologetically "we need to borrow a boat right away so my friends here can make it across to Duingt. It's very urgent."

"Well they'll have to wait because the boat won't be back for half an hour so you might as well have a bite, n'est ce pas?"

I am keen to find Arnaud before it's too late, especially having seen the detection vehicle and Gestapo car heading along the Annecy road, but there's little choice but to wait for the boat to return.

The three of us enter the fisherman's house where we find Albert's wife Marie-Claire, stirring a big fish casserole and gossiping with an attractive young foreign lady. She looks to me as though she might come from the Balkans.

Marie-Claire, identically proportioned to her husband, stops stirring the pot, dries her hands on her apron, and welcomes us with a great big smile revealing her single remaining upright tooth.

"Bon jour, bon jour" she says "asseyez vous; buvez, mangez, bien, bien" and returns to fetch the warmed-up casserole which she places invitingly in the middle of the table.

"Du vin?" she enquires, pouring the wine from a jar into our glasses without waiting for an answer.

Tom and Albert discuss arrangements for the boat. Jacques and I help ourselves to the fish casserole pausing only to mouth our appreciation. I am quietly preoccupied with the foreign lady in front of whom Tom and Albert are discussing arrangements so openly.

"Oh by the way Luc," says Tom, sensing my unease from the other side of the table, "this is Madame Clabaud, the wife of Georges who runs the Resistance here. Well he does normally. Right now he's in England."

I nod and turn to Madame Clabaud "Good to meet you Madame. I think your husband and I met very briefly."

"And good to meet you, Sir" she replies "I have heard a lot about you and I am glad to see that you are safe, or at least as safe as any of us these days." Her accent is strong. Now I remember, 'Georges' has a Russian wife living on the east shore of Lake Annecy.

We chat for a few minutes. She's had no more news of her husband since he left for London with Paul. She has only just heard about Claudine and Paul's arrest from Albert who returned from St Jorioz to tell them the news this morning.

"Did Albert tell you about Robert Bardot?" interrupts Tom.

"No, is he OK?" says Mme. Clabaud.

"He's OK yes, in a manner of speaking, but he is working for the Germans. It was he who tipped off the Gestapo to arrest Claudine and Paul."

Mme. Clabaud turns white with shock. "But he's like a son to my husband, and to me. He would never do such a thing!"

"But he has" says Tom "I saw him with my own eyes when I went to the Hotel this morning. He's working with the Gestapo, and so is Louis something."

"Him I can believe" says Mme. Clabaud "but Robert Bardot, never... there must be an explanation!"

"I am sorry" says Tom "I think the explanation must be money.

Or maybe threatened deportation? It's hard to tell what it might have been. Maybe he was just frightened."

Once again I'm putting others in danger and they, me. Robert Bardot knows where Mme. Clabaud lives and the Gestapo might well come calling. And now she has met me and has probably heard Tom and Albert discussing the rescue plans for Arnaud. If the Gestapo want to get this information out of her they have their ways.

I'm relieved when a couple of middle-aged fishermen come in the door and announce that the boat is back.

Jacques and I thank Marie-Claire for the lunch, say goodbye to Mme. Clabaud and follow Albert and Tom out of the door and down to the lakeside where a fishing boat is waiting.

Albert points out the right route for us to take to Duingt to avoid being spotted from St Jorioz and tells us where to moor the boat. If the boat isn't back by nightfall he will arrange for his son to ride his bicycle to Duingt and bring it back tomorrow.

Tom assures us that if anything interferes with his plan to transfer the equipment from Jean Cottet's cellar to his van that afternoon he will arrange for a message to be delivered to the Café du Vin at Faverges by 6:00 p.m. If there is no message we are to assume that everything is safely in the van and ready for us.

The two of us board the boat. I take the wheel and Jacques unties the rope from the hitching post. The little engine, still hot, bursts into action and we are away. We wave au revoir to Tom and Albert who are already on their way back to the house.

"Luc, what is the plan?" says the eager Jacques sitting down on the stool in the cabin.

"Well I've been thinking it through…"

"I thought I could hear your brain churning during lunch."

"I was a bit preoccupied until I discovered who the Russian woman was."

"Oh yes, the wife of Georges. You need not worry, she's one of us."

"That may be true but Robert Bardot knows where she is, doesn't he? And it won't take the Gestapo long to put two and two together."

"Mon Dieu, you are right."

"Well, we won't go back there for a while. Once we've dropped the boat at its mooring let's find a couple of bicycles, it shouldn't be too difficult. We can 'borrow' those to ride up to Faverges, otherwise it's an 18-kilometre walk and then we have a climb of almost 1,000 metres before we reach the place where, I hope, we'll find Arnaud."

"Bicycles are a good idea" says Jacques "I will find some and bring them to the boat. You stay on board, out of sight… as Tom says, you are a marked man with a price on your head," Jacques pauses "by the way, how much are they offering for you?"

I smile "Not enough to interest you, I'm sure. Anyway, Robert Bardot is ahead of you in the line."

"Yes, I know" says Jacques "not all Frenchmen are like Robert Bardot."

"Let's hope."

The lake is not busy this afternoon. A few fishermen are out. A gendarmerie boat is bobbing up and down at its mooring as we skirt the lakeside château and pull into the rushes at Duingt. The trip across the lake only took us ten minutes or so and there's a good chance that nobody noticed us crossing let alone pulling into one of the twenty or so moorings hidden in the rushes.

"Alright, I'll lie low here until you return with the bicycles" I say as we secure the boat.

"Make sure you stay out of sight" Jacques cautions me, already playing protector, "we need you for a little while yet." And then he is off through the rushes and onto the path that runs down to the Albertville road.

I marvel at the startling differences between the various French people in my acquaintance. There are those who come up trumps; Carmen Dupré, Jean Cottet, from what I hear, Tom Morel, Albert the fisherman, and probably Jacques. And then there are those who turn or were turned at the drop of a pin, like Robert Bardot.

I've got to be able to judge if I'm to recruit the right sort of people into a new réseau. I wonder what would happen if England or the USA were occupied. Would the same thing be true? Would people collaborate? Sure they would. Maybe even I would? I hope not but it's human nature after all. I'm sure we all have, at a deeper level, the same psychological make-up. It's only with the superficial characteristics that we show our differences. Education, culture, sophistication may take people further away from the deeper level than others but basically I think we are all genetically programmed the same way. Enough philosophizing. I set my mind to planning our next moves.

Twenty minutes later a beaming if slightly dishevelled Jacques walks along the jetty wheeling two bicycles. "Eh voila!" he says.

"Great. Women's bicycles. Good move Jacques."

"Better than nothing" he replies.

"How on earth did you get them so quickly?" I ask.

"I did them a favour" he says, winking.

"What, both of them?… in twenty minutes!"

"Remember, I am French, Luc" he says with a smug expression on his face "I promised I would leave the bicycles by the mooring before 8:00 tonight."

"By which time you'll be ready for a recharge I suppose?" I say with a smirk as I mount the bicycle.

We look a little incongruous as we ride along the road to Faverges. The freshly-cut flowers in the baskets don't help and we ditch them as we hit the outskirts of Duingt.

An hour later, approaching 6:00 p.m., we pass the Café du Vin at the intersection of the roads to Laroche and Faverges. We take our bicycles around to the back of the café. I wait while Jacques goes inside to have a word with the patron.

A few minutes later he returns. "It's OK to put the bicycles in the garden shed, Luc. We can collect them when we come down."

"No word from Tom then? I guess it's still a little early" I say as we push the bicycles into the back of the shed.

"The patron has heard nothing but he says that barely twenty minutes ago a voiture de la detection passed the café at high speed and headed up the road to Faverges."

"Merde"

It's a ten minute walk into the village of Faverges. Our plan is to pass by the forest warden's house and then take the path through the woods that will lead us up to Arnaud's hideout in Les Tissots, about a twenty-minute brisk walk to the outskirts of the hamlet. We'll keep out of sight as much as possible in case my face is recognised. Tom Morel says there are Gestapo posters of Arnaud and me on walls in Annecy and St Jorioz.

We are reasonably confident of our plan. It's just past 6:00. If we can find Arnaud and get back down to the café by 7:30 that will give us enough time to see if there is a message from the patron, pick up the bicycles and ride back to Duingt. It will be dark by then and we can walk the few kilometres to St Jorioz.

The road turns sharply to the right as it enters the outskirts of Faverges. The forest warden's house lies a little back from the road. A low wall surrounds a front garden enclosing a parking space for several vehicles. The path into the woods lies just beyond.

As we approach the warden's house I grab Jacques' arm. Clearly visible over the top of the wall are the aerials of a voiture de la detection.

Have they found Arnaud? It's the forest warden's cabin that he's staying in, after all.

Passing the house, we take the raised path beyond the garden wall from where we can observe the house and garden. We wait and listen. We hear occasional noises from within. There seem to be four or five people there. One is a woman. One is definitely German. To our relief none of them sounds like Arnaud. His booming voice would have raised the general decibel level considerably. Perhaps he's had the good sense, uncharacteristically, to stay in his hideout as instructed.

After a few minutes the woman's voice rises higher and higher, pleading desperately, interspersed with quick, sharp retorts in German. The front door is flung open. Two Gestapo officers appear dragging a boy, he can be no older than 16. They bundle him into the voiture de la detection, climb in and start the engine. The woman clings to the car and cries out. The forest warden tries to console her, to no avail. The car spews gravel onto the couple and takes off down the hill towards the café.

And not up the hill to Arnaud, I note with relief. Clearly the forest warden's family hasn't betrayed him. But it has cost them dear.

"Pigs!" says Jacques as he watches the grieving couple return to the house.

We both know that if the trail hadn't led the Gestapo to Faverges, the Boche would have suspected nothing.

"I think we'd better have a quick word with them to find out what's going on before we go up to Arnaud's."

"It's not a great time for them" says Jacques, "… but I guess you're right."

We knock loudly twice on the front door. An upstairs curtain is pulled back and the frightened face of the forest warden looks down.

He recognizes me.

He nods and closes the curtain.

Jacques and I glance at each other, uncomfortably.

The warden opens the door. Tears well up in his eyes as he peers around outside and lets us in.

"You saw what happened?" he asks, his voice still jittery with fear and anger.

"Yes."

"The Boche took my son. He's 15 years old. They say they will send him to Germany with the STO."

"I am so sorry" we both say.

Jacques puts his arm around the warden's shoulder. "He'll be OK. Don't worry. They took my brother too. They are treating him well."

The warden smiles a reluctant smile. His wife's sobs maintain a steady rhythm upstairs.

"Do you have any news of Arnaud?" I ask "I'm sorry to ask you this now but we need to get to him before the Gestapo do."

"If they haven't already" says the warden "we told them nothing but they know that someone is transmitting from this area. They were asking me all sorts of questions about Arnaud. They are certain it is him. They asked me where the springs are in the forest. They think he's probably based near one of them. I gave them a list but I made some of it up. Nothing near Arnaud's place. I haven't seen him for two days."

I tell the warden what's happened to Claudine and Paul and

reassure him that, as a result, we would have Arnaud out of the cabin by nightfall. I thank him for the help he's given to the Resistance and to the British agents in particular. We try to comfort him, but I'm in a hurry. We assure him that there will be no sign of Arnaud ever having been in the cabin. I'm pretty certain the Gestapo will track the place down at some point soon and wreak vengeance on the warden if they find any indication that Arnaud has been there.

We take our leave of the distraught man.

Relieved at the news that Arnaud has probably stayed in the cabin as instructed, we start up the mountain path with renewed vigour. But both of us know that voitures de la detection almost always travel in pairs.

"I didn't know that you had a brother?" I say.

"I don't" says Jacques.

We pass no one else on our way up the hill to Arnaud's hideout but our hearts are in our boots and we exchange few words.

Twenty minutes later the track ends in the little hamlet of Les Tissots. Arnaud's hideout is directly in front of us. There's no sign of any detection vehicle. No evidence of recent car tracks at all along the path. Indeed no visible signs of life.

Then, simultaneously, we both stop. "Do you hear that noise?" asks Jacques. We listen intently.

"Definitely human" I say.

"Yes, but was it pain or pleasure?"

I strain to hear more clearly. Grunts and murmurs and occasional sighs emerge from the cabin at heightening decibels.

"Pleasure I'd say, Jacques…yes, definitely pleasure." The two of us laugh in amusement and relief. "It seems our friend Arnaud is alive and well."

"Shall we break the door down and surprise him in flagrante?" suggests Jacques.

"Unwise, I think, an Arnaud aroused, so to speak, would be a very dangerous animal. He is likely to have one hand on his pistol even now."

"Tricky" sniggers Jacques. We approach the cabin. I knock twice loudly on the door and call out for Arnaud.

Grunts and sighs cease instantly.

"Un moment, un moment, Mon Dieu" comes his deep unmistakable voice.

Betowelled, sweaty and unamused Arnaud opens the door. A buxom blonde hides behind him hurriedly putting on her clothes.

"For Christ's sake Luc, I've heard of coitus interruptus but this is bloody vindictive. I suppose you've been waiting and watching you dirty Toms. Merde." He turns around and walks back inside. The towel, being of insufficient size, does little to preserve his dignity.

Uninvited, we let ourselves in.

"Au revoir et excusez-moi Dominique" yells Arnaud as the flush-faced blonde smiles coyly skipping past us on her way out the door, pulling on her shoes as she goes.

"If you don't mind I'll get dressed. Help yourselves to coffee, vermin," Arnaud says as he walks into the bedroom, slamming the door. He instantly opens it again and points at Jacques "Who's the Boy Scout?"

"He's one of Tom Morel's most valuable soldiers, Arnaud." The door closes.

Jacques organizes the coffee as I sit down on a broken chair and survey the room. It won't be difficult to remove any trace of Arnaud, there's not much here anyway.

Various inaudible expletives emanate intermittently from behind the closed bedroom door. Outside it's getting dark but there's a good moon. Jacques pours three coffees. We are going to have to move quickly if we are to accomplish the evening's objectives.

A fully clothed Arnaud emerges from the room "To what do I owe this dubious pleasure?" he enquires as he finishes buttoning his shirt.

As he looks up his eyes focus on mine for the first time. "Oh God…what's happened?" He pulls up a chair.

I tell him of the arrests of Claudine and Paul; of their removal first to Annecy and then, we suspect to Fresnes; of the arrest of the forest warden's son a hundred metres down the mountain, and of our need to extract Tom Morel's arms and equipment from the garage of the Hotel de la Poste. I emphasise to Arnaud the grave danger he is in; that the Gestapo were in town precisely because they think Arnaud and I are still in the area.

Arnaud, his big face wet with tears, sits silently nodding until I finish. He stares at Jacques, stares at me and then lays his head down on the table. I knew that he would take this news very hard. But I also knew he would emerge with a fresh determination… it was just a matter of time.

And it doesn't take long. Arnaud bangs his head on the table. His hands, lying on either side, gradually form themselves into clenched fists.

"Fuckers! Fuckers! Fuckers!" he says sitting up straight and staring furiously at me.

"What's the plan?"

Jacques and I pull our chairs up closer to the table. "First we have to get you out of here immediately. Is your transmitter packed and ready to go?"

"It's next door. I can be ready in five minutes."

"Good. Be careful not to leave anything here that can be traced to you for the warden's sake. He's suffered enough. It won't take the Gestapo long to find this cabin. They're already quizzing people in Faverges."

Arnaud moves restlessly on his chair. "And what next? When do we make a move on the fucking Boche?"

"Why don't you collect your things together and we can talk about the details as we go down to the café. We have to stop off there to see if there's a message from Tom Morel."

Arnaud, clearly trusting me now, goes to extract his transmitting equipment from its hiding place. Jacques washes up the coffee cups.

"If there is no message then we need to find a way of liberating the arms and equipment tonight."

"Pray God there's no message" yells Arnaud from the bedroom.

"We've got to think of some way of distracting the Gestapo and the Alpini so we can open the garage door and get Jean Cottet's van down the road without them hearing or seeing anything" I say, hoping to encourage Arnaud to come up with an idea.

"I'll distract them alright," Arnaud walks into the room with his jacket on, his backpack secured and carrying the suitcase containing his wireless transmitter.

"We don't want bloodshed, Arnaud. Not yet anyway" I caution as we walk out of the cabin and close the door "just a bit of ingenuity."

Arnaud stops to get his bicycle out of the shed, loads his suitcase onto the back and the three of us walk down the hill.

"We have to go to Duingt to return our bikes" I explain, "we left them at the café. And then we go on from there by foot if the plan goes ahead. I really don't think it's wise for you to risk going to St Jorioz, Arnaud. You'd better stay in Duingt until tomorrow and then we'll find a way of getting you out of the area, preferably back to England."

"Have you lost your marbles? Are you completely mad? Not only am I not going back to England before I exact my revenge on the Boche but I am not staying like a frightened chicken in

Duingt. It's been bad enough staying on the mountain for the past few days. And see what happens when I'm not there. You obviously can't manage without me."

I could have predicted his reaction virtually word for word.

"Bon. It's your life at risk mon ami."

Ten minutes later we pass the forest warden's house. Only the light in the bedroom is still on. "I'd like to go and speak to them" says Arnaud.

"Another time my friend. We're running out of time."

The three of us walk up to the café. A van is parked outside. Arnaud puts his bike in the shed next to ours and throws a blanket over the top. We walk inside. There are only two men at the bar. Arnaud recognizes both of them. One is an electrician. He owns the general shop in St Jorioz and helped Arnaud fix a component in his transmitter a few weeks back. The other is the electrician's cousin, a fisherman who lives in Faverges.

They greet each other and the electrician offers us all a Calvados. "No time right now" says Arnaud "but thank you." A corner door opens and the patron's daughter Dominique, refreshed from her recent exertions, comes in to see who the new customers are.

"Bon soir gentlemen" she says, barely suppressing a giggle, "can I be of service?"

"Provocative hussy" says Arnaud, adding, as an aside to the rest of us, "as pretty as a peach and stupid as a cabbage." Dominique flicks a towel at him. "Yes, you can get your father toute de suite." He glares at his recent conquest.

"Hmph…" she turns heel and walks back inside.

The owner emerges. "Ah mes amis, I have nothing for you. I am sorry."

"We aren't" says Arnaud.

We say goodbye and go to pick up the bicycles from the shed.

"I guess that means everything is fine?" says Jacques.

"Looks that way" I say "as long as there hasn't been some cock-up."

It is now 9:30. If, for some reason, Tom's messenger didn't arrive I'm pretty certain Tom would have found another way of getting a message to the café. After all it's been three-and-a-half hours since the 6:00 message deadline. We reassure ourselves that the mission is on and concentrate our minds on just how we can rescue the equipment as we cycle down the darkened road to Duingt.

After riding for fifteen minutes Arnaud yells "Stop! I know how to distract the Gestapo. You two go on. I have to ride back to Faverges." He turns his bicycle around. "What time do you want the distraction?"

"Midnight" I yell back.

"OK, midnight. It is now 10:00 exactly." We synchronize our watches.

"Pick me up when you have the vehicle. I'll wait for you at the end of the driveway of the Hotel de la Plage. You remember it Luc" shouts Arnaud. And he is gone.

God knows what Arnaud has in mind but I'm not going to worry about that now. I trust him. Jacques and I ride the rest of the way into Duingt in silence. We drop the bicycles off by the empty mooring.

It's 10:30. Farmhouses are silhouetted against the mountains by the light of the still substantial moon. The chill evening air refreshes us as we walk the short distance to St Jorioz.

On approaching the first village house we take a right down the path that leads past the station. We cross over the tracks to keep out of sight of the two villagers who were commandeered to guard the station, even though it has long been out of use, and join the road on the far side. It should take us up to the back entrance of the Hotel de la Poste, close to the garage.

I indicate a mound on the bank of the stream, parallel to the road, that should give us a good vantage point from which to see if there are still guards at the hotel. We climb up to the top and watch and listen. Nothing.

"Jacques, you go along the east side of the stream. You'll be able to see what's going on in the front of the hotel. I'll check out the garage and then meet you back here in a few minutes."

"D'accord, Luc."

Once Jacques disappears I creep up to the garage at the back of the hotel, peer through the window and, aided by the moon, just manage to make out the shape of Jean Cottet's van. The handle of the door gives. Looks like Tom's men have done their job. I pull the garage door ajar and step in. I take a few quiet steps forward. There are voices in the room above. They sound relaxed and end-of-the-dayish. The keys are in the ignition. A large blanket is covering the contents of the back of the van. Cautiously I lift up the blanket just enough to expose the gleaming barrels of sten guns. Deep breath. I close the van door and stand stock still. Noises outside. Inching my way to the front of the garage I see Jacques returning and disappearing behind the trees.

I open the garage door, quietly close it behind me, creep into the bushes and make my way back to the mound where Jacques is waiting.

"Is it all there Luc?"

"Yup, everything. What's it looking like out front? Were you able to see?"

"Yes. There's a Gestapo Citroën parked in front of the hotel. Two Alpini are sitting on the steps, smoking. Another man is standing in the dark, just beyond the entrance. I couldn't see whether he was

Gestapo or not. A third Alpino came outside and said something in Italian to the others. I could hear voices inside. They were speaking German. I think there must be seven or eight men altogether but there could be more."

I check my watch. It's quarter to twelve.

"What about Arnaud?" whispers Jacques "Do you think he's here?"

"We won't know until midnight but I'm sure he's planning something. God knows what. All we can do is to get ready and wait until we see or hear something."

It's eerily quiet. There's a slight breeze. The moonlight darting in and out of the trees and reflecting off the stream adds to the general spookiness.

"OK, Jacques" I whisper "let's go to the van. At exactly half a minute to midnight you open the garage doors wide. I'll get into the van. As soon as the diversion occurs we'll roll the van down the hill towards the station. You push. Once we get to the station, I'll start the engine, you jump in and we'll drive along the same track that we walked down to get here. We're going to have to drive in front of the hotel but let's hope we'll have enough of a head start to get out of St Jorioz before the Gestapo come after us. Let's go."

We silently walk back to the garage, creep in and open the doors of the ageing V8. I get into the driver's seat. Jacques waits by the garage door. It's now five minutes to midnight. Even louder than the beating of my own heart, I can still hear voices from the room above. The wait is interminable. Would the van start? Would Arnaud be there? Would we be shot at by the guards? Would the French guards at the station sound the alarm? Would the Cottets be shot in reprisal?

I give Jacques the thumbs up. That's better. Only thirty seconds to go now before he opens the doors.

And then it happens. The most God-awful racket. The sound of the outlawed Marsellaise being broadcast at ear-piercing levels throughout the village of St Jorioz. There must be loudspeakers on every street corner. I imagine confused and startled inhabitants sitting bolt upright in their beds asking themselves: Has General de Gaulle returned in triumph? How curious that he would have chosen the little village of St Jorioz to make his grand re-entry!

Trying hard to control our laughter we manoeuvre the V8 down to the station and start the engine. Then we swing up onto the main road. I urge the ancient vehicle on with encouraging words and a heavy foot. Gestapo officers in various states of undress are running up and down the main street brandishing their pistols. We see Alpini shooting at the tree tops. The village has taken on the appearance of a Marx Brothers comedy. As we pass the Hotel de la Poste an Alpino, returning down the main street fresh from his tree-shooting exercise, just manages to fire a shot at us before we disappear from sight. The bullet rips through the canvas covering of the van, shoots out the other side and shatters the windscreen of the parked Gestapo Citroën.

A few minutes later we come to a stop at the entrance to the Hotel de la Plage driveway. Sitting on a boulder, smoking a cigarette, is the unmistakable figure of Arnaud.

"Enfin!" he says by way of a greeting. He yanks his bicycle (complete with wireless transmitter still tied on the back) out of the bushes and wheels it over to the van. Jacques helps him lift it on top of the hidden arms and then both men squeeze into the front seat alongside me.

I put my foot down and the heavily laden van lurches back onto the road and speeds, in its manner, towards Annecy. I turn to Arnaud and slap him on the back. "Bravo my friend... a true touch of genius!"

"Oh" says Arnaud "a little glimmer perhaps?"

We all laugh.

I keep an eye on the rear-view mirror. "How the hell did you do it?" I ask Arnaud.

"Well" replies Arnaud, clearly relishing the retelling "when we were riding our bicycles down the road from Faverges back to Duingt I was trying to think of what we could possibly do to create a suitable diversion. I thought of starting a fire or blowing up the train station or creating some sort of deafening sound. Then I remembered seeing the electrician at the Café du Vin in Faverges. I knew he would have the answer. So I rode back to the café and had a little talk with my friend. He told me that he had a whole loudspeaker system in his shed that they used to string up along the streets when they had village festivals before the war.

We put my bicycle into his van and drove back into St Jorioz."

"Back into St Jorioz? Tonight! You're nuts" I say.

"The only recording he had was the Marsellaise" he continued "and what could be more appropriate, I thought. Eh voila… the electrician's two sons helped us to throw the wires up into the trees. We just balanced the loudspeakers between the branches. Nobody saw us. The Boche were all at the Hotel de la Poste."

Jacques and I listen, full of admiration. I keep my eye on the rear-view mirror. I can't figure out why we're not being chased.

"I don't think we will be followed, Luc, not for a while anyway."

"I don't think a shattered windscreen will stop them."

"Their car also has two flat tyres" adds Arnaud. We both glance at him. "Just a precaution."

"You're a one-off Arnaud" I say. He beams. I slow the van down as we approach Annecy.

"Take the first left beyond that barn on the corner" instructs Arnaud "it will give us a longer route but keep us out of Annecy.

I'm sure the Gestapo will have warned the fucking Milice and local gendarmerie by now."

I take the first left and we find ourselves on a dirt track that crosses over a field of newly-planted wheat. "Don't imagine the farmer will like this much" I remark.

"He won't mind. He's the mayor" says Arnaud "and he needs to win re-election after the war." We drive on for several kilometres. All is clear. I think how excited Tom Morel and his men will be to see us, allowing myself to believe that we'll make it back unscathed. We drive down the N230 until it meets the Annecy road, turn left and follow it along until the crossroads where we turn onto the track leading up to the Glières plateau.

The maquisards des Glières are assembled en masse at the parking place at the foot of the path up to the plateau. I stop the van. And give them the thumbs up. Smiling faces greet us as we climb out of the V8. Tom Morel hugs all three of us.

"Congratulations, mes amis! We are all in your debt." The men cheer. Morel organizes the unloading of the arms and equipment into carts that they can drag up to the plateau more easily.

It's been a great week for the arming of the Maquis, although a heavy price has been paid. It's now time for Arnaud and me to move on.

"Stay tonight, of course, and we will ensure that you are transported safely in the morning, Luc" says Tom as we climb up the path. "But I have one request…"

"Anything" I say.

"That Arnaud stays with us for ten days or so. Is that OK?"

I frown "Arnaud is a hunted man, even more than I am for they may think that I am out of the area. They know that Arnaud is still close to St Jorioz. He will be in grave danger."

"We'll look after him, Luc. We are strong now, thanks to the

British. He'll be alright with us. Just ten days. We have no means of communicating and we have wireless transmitters that need repairing. Just ten days."

"Well, you'll have to ask Arnaud. Officially he's been told to clear out of this area but if he wants to take his time doing it then that's up to him… I'm only afraid he'll agree."

He does of course.

Jacques asks Tom Morel to allow him to go with me to help form the new réseau in Cannes. Tom agrees. I'm delighted.

The following morning Tom Morel drives Jacques and me over mountain tracks to the railway station at Albertville where we buy tickets for the train to Cannes.

15

Almost a month after their capture, Paul, now known to be Roger Chamberlain and thought to be a nephew of the former prime minister, and Claudine, now known to be Mathilde and thought to be Mrs Roger Chamberlain, were taken from prison in Marseilles.

The Italians had moved them from Annecy where they were interrogated by the OVRA, (the Italian Secret Police) to Grenoble and then Turin, then Nice, Toulon and Marseilles. After lengthy negotiations, the Gestapo finally took over responsibility for them on 7 May and immediately put them on the night train to Paris. They sat up all night between two uniformed Gestapo officers.

At 10:30 a.m. their train pulled into the Gare de Lyon. Chamberlain and Mathilde were bundled out and marched along the platform. At the barrier they were greeted warmly, with a low bow, by the ever punctual, ever courteous, Monsieur Jean.

"Welcome Mr and Mrs Chamberlain. Sergeant Karl Metzger of the Abwehr at your disposal" he said.

Metzger ordered Chamberlain to be handcuffed. Three Gestapo cars waited outside the station. Metzger got in the front car; Chamberlain and his minder in the second and Mathilde and her minder in the third. They were driven at high speed through the sunny streets of Paris, watching the people go about their daily business. They headed south towards the Porte d'Italie.

Fresnes Prison was the biggest criminal prison in Europe. Situated a mere 14 km from the Place de la Concorde, it had been commandeered by the Gestapo as soon as France fell. A forbidding, grey, Victorian monstrosity, it had housed hundreds of thousands of men and women in its time. Not a few had jumped to their death from the high balconies that run along the inside of the building. Others had been taken at dawn to the execution wall.

Lately a sizeable number had been transported to concentration camps in Germany.

The iron gates swung open. Fluff from the ash trees that give the prison its name fluttered down onto the cars as they entered. The gates shut. The passengers disgorged. The nightmare worsened.

Chamberlain and Mathilde were taken through the main hall to an ante-room which housed a group of erect wooden coffins. Chamberlain was locked into one. Mathilde into another. Two hours later a male guard unlocked Chamberlain's coffin and took him to a bare room where he was stripped naked. An S.S. woman with short cropped hair and a scowling face unlocked Mathilde's coffin and she too was taken to a bare room and stripped naked. The humiliating prison admission procedure was once again in full swing.

They were prodded and poked, insulted, and ridiculed and asked their identities by the guard and a uniformed officer.

"Paul Chaboux, aged thirty-one, married, French."

"No. Roger Chamberlain, English spy" came the officer's sharp retort.

"Mathilde Chambrun, aged thirty-one, married, Roman Catholic, French, born at Dunkirk, 1912."

"Mathilde Chamberlain, English spy."

An hour later, they were allowed to dress and were given a blanket and a dirty grey sheet.

"Cell two hundred, Second Division. No concessions by order of the Gestapo" came the command. Roger Chamberlain was marched along the corridor and down to an underground passage.

"Cell one hundred and eighteen, Third Division. No concessions by order of the Gestapo."

"Schnell, schnell" barked the S.S. woman, ordering Mathilde to walk down the steps to a different, darker underground passage. She was escorted to a dingy cell. She dropped her blanket and sheet onto the bed. And waited.

The determinedly masculine S.S. woman returned to Mathilde's cell an hour later and ordered her to follow.

Metzger was waiting in a little room at the end of the landing of Third Division cell block.

"I am truly sorry to see you in a place like this" he said as she entered and sat down on a wooden chair opposite him. "You deserve better. I was forced to arrest you as you know, to keep you from the Gestapo. It is we, the Abwehr, who are in charge of this case. I have seen to that. But only if you cooperate. If not they will take you."

"That is what you told Marchais. The end result appears to be the same."

"There is no need for you to stay here Madame Chamberlain, only you are not really Madame Chamberlain I now know, are you? I know a good deal about you. For instance I know that you have three young daughters; that you are a member of the French Section of the War Office, that your headquarters is in Baker Street and that your chief is Colonel Maurice Buckmaster, a tall man with an overhanging lip who was educated at Eton and Oxford and speaks fluent French and German."

"I have nothing to say."

"Do you think self-sacrifice is noble, Mathilde? You are a mother. Your duty is to your children. Why protect Arnaud and Luc? They would not do the same for you. How naïve you are."

"I have every reason to believe that they would do exactly the same for me. In any case I am only responsible for my own conscience."

"What would you say if I told you that I am arranging for Roger Chamberlain to be traded for a German prisoner held in England and that he is eager to go, leaving you here to rot."

"I would say that you were a liar, Monsieur."

Metzger, showing no emotion, continued. "I know you are fond of music. The night before last I went to a concert where they played Mozart's Divertimenti for String Quartet and Two Horns. It was enchanting, with two minuets in the French manner. There is another concert in two weeks. I could arrange for you to come with me."

"I cannot be bought, Monsieur."

Metzger stood up. "It grieves me to see you here, Mathilde."

She stared back, unmoved.

Metzger walked out of the room.

The S.S. woman took Mathilde roughly by the arm and led her back to her cell.

Three days later Metzger tried again.

As Mathilde was brought into the interrogation room, Metzger stood up and offered her a cigarette. She accepted, took one drag and stubbed it out.

"Roger Chamberlain is well and sends you his love" said Metzger, pretending not to notice, "I have given him some cigarettes. He enjoyed them. We talk often. He is much more forthcoming than you."

"Really?" said Mathilde.

"You know that if you choose not to cooperate with me the Gestapo will take you to 84 Avenue Foch. They want to know the whereabouts of Arnaud, your wireless operator, and of the British officer called Luc who stayed at the Hotel de la Plage. They are not as patient as I am, Mathilde."

"Are you about to offer to save me from the Gestapo again?"

"Yes, I am" said Metzger.

"I have nothing to say," came the response.

"Then there is no point in my coming any more" said Metzger. He stubbed his cigarette out; turned heel and walked out the door.

The following day they came for her.

On arrival at Avenue Foch she was taken up to the fifth floor and shown into a large, book-lined office. A well- dressed young man sat behind a mahogany partners' desk. He was the civilian interrogator.

Smiling, he offered Mathilde a cigarette. And then, oozing charm, he began to ask the questions.

"What is your name, Madame?"

"Are you an English spy?"

"Where is Arnaud?"

"Where is Luc?"

"Do you have radio crystals?"

"Name the people in your terrorist network."

For two hours the questioning continued and for two hours Mathilde refused to answer a single question.

His patience worn out, the interrogator's expression turned sour. He pressed the button concealed beneath his desk.

Mathilde heard the door open but did not look around. She noticed a distinct smell of eau-de-cologne. She saw the interrogator nod at someone behind her and then felt her dress being torn. A moment later she screamed in agony as a red-hot poker was placed on her third vertebra.

"It's not much fun is it, Mathilde. And so easily avoided. Where is Luc?"

"I have nothing to say."

"Where is Arnaud?"

"I have nothing to say."

The dapper, sweet-smelling interrogator bent down.

"Would you like to take your shoes and stockings off or shall I do it for you. I can assure you I am very adept at it."

"I will do it myself" replied Mathilde. She carefully pulled off her shoes and stockings.

"Mathilde, my colleague here is going to pull out your toenails one by one, starting at the little toe of your left foot. In between each evulsion, to

use the correct medical term, I propose to repeat my questions. You can bring the ceremony to an end at any moment by answering those questions. There are those who faint after the third or fourth toenail. If you do faint, we can always revive you with brandy and the ceremony will continue. Now, before we begin… where is Luc?"

"I have nothing to say."

A handsome young man, aged less than thirty, took her left foot in his left hand and applied the steel jaws of the pincers tightly around the tip of her nail. Slowly he pulled the nail. Mathilde screamed but no words came out of her mouth. Blood oozed all round as the nail gradually tore away from her foot. Her torturer dropped the nail on the floor.

"Now would you care to tell me Luc's address?"

Mathilde could not reply. She shook her head.

The interrogator sat on top of his desk, between framed photographs of his two rosy-cheeked young daughters, swinging his legs.

The young man knelt down again, looked up at her with his dark brown eyes, and took hold of her left foot. Once again Mathilde felt the agonising pain and watched with horror as the nail came away from its bloody stub.

Again the question. Again the refusal.

After what seemed like an eternity, there were no toenails left to pull. Her torturer stood up and awaited his orders. The interrogator looked at Mathilde.

"You are a remarkably resilient woman Mathilde. As you have shown no willingness to answer my questions I have no alternative but to start on your finger nails." He turned around, walked back to his desk and picked up a cigarette.

Mathilde heard the door open. The interrogator dropped the unlit cigarette and jumped to attention.

"Is this Frau Chamberlain?" a voice behind her enquired.

"Yes Major" replied the interrogator. They spoke rapidly in German to each other.

The interrogator turned to Mathilde and said "The Major tells me I am wasting my time and that you will never talk. He has ordered that you be taken upstairs. I, however, know that I could make you talk, given time. I think we will meet again Madame."

He gave an order and the young torturer laid the pincers on the table, walked over to the door and held it open for Mathilde.

"Permettez-moi, Madame" he said, in his native French.

Metzger lost interest in Mathilde, just as he'd lost interest in Marchais who, having served his purpose, had now been dispatched to the Compiègne concentration camp.

Roger Chamberlain was a different matter altogether. Metzger saw Roger Chamberlain as his ticket to promotion, fame even. If his superiors weren't suitably impressed that he had arrested the nephew of a British prime minister, they were certain to be if he could persuade Chamberlain, in the same way he had Marchais, to arrange for a flight to England. That way he could also capture an aircraft.

Metzger spent many hours in Chamberlain's cell. He didn't try to elicit information from him, believing it to be a lost cause for the time being. Instead he wanted to befriend him. First he would make friends. Then they would socialise together (he could always get him out on a day pass) and finally the trust between them would be so great that an aircraft would be arranged.

And who knows, he might even be able to get him drunk enough to reveal the whereabouts of Luc and Arnaud.

What Metzger hadn't reckoned with, however, was the German High Command. Rumours had reached their ears that a member of the Abwehr was spouting anti-Nazi sentiments. There was talk too of a flight to England and treachery of the highest order.

It did not take long to identify the offending Abwehr member as Sergeant Karl Metzger. Only the intervention of his superior officer, Colonel Froehling, saved him from arrest, and worse.

Metzger was reprimanded. His excessive zeal had not endeared him to his superiors.

He was given new orders. As a precaution, he was removed from the case involving Chamberlain and Mathilde.

Shortly thereafter, Roger Chamberlain and Mathilde Chambrun were transported to Germany. Chamberlain was put in special internment and given beneficial treatment in deference to his supposed illustrious relation. Mathilde was taken to the notorious Ravensbruck Concentration Camp for Women.

Metzger, however, was not to be deterred. His superiors had made no mention of Arnaud and Luc. An arrest would soon regain him their confidence, he decided.

As he rode his motorcycle home that night to his bourgeois apartment; his grand piano and his French mistress, Metzger formulated plans for trapping his prey.

16

This morning, Albertville station is host to an alarming array of gendarmes, gardes des voies and Milice. Gestapo too. Jacques returns from the men's room. He's seen a Gestapo officer with a sketch of Arnaud. Clearly they are on the lookout for him. My likeness too has been posted in St Jorioz. God knows where else.

I try to stay out of sight until the train comes. The platform is crowded, which helps. I stand with a group outside the waiting room. A man bends down to pick up something he's dropped. He reveals two posters on the wall behind him. Arnaud and one of me.

Instinctively, I turn away. But even I find it difficult to recognize myself. The drawing has me wearing glasses and a thick moustache.

Gradually I make my way down the platform to where Jacques is standing.

The train approaches. Jacques and I wait to board. He gets on first. As I'm about to climb onto the train someone shouts:

"Halt!"

I pretend I haven't heard. Two Milice grab hold of me and pull me back onto the platform.

"Papers!" yells a Gestapo officer. I cough, a resounding tubercular cough. The officer turns away, fearing infection. I produce my papers and explain that I'm returning to Cannes to recover from tuberculosis. The officer glances at me, then at my papers.

"You are a professor, yes?"

"No" I say "a secondary school teacher." And then I bite my tongue, hard.

The officer looks up at me, about to question me further when he sees the trickle of blood oozing out of the left hand corner of my mouth.

"Go, go" he says, taking a step backwards "and take your foul disease with you."

I pull myself up onto the train.

Jacques meets me in the corridor. He has seen the whole procedure through the window.

"I was worried there. That was very clever… the blood and all," he says as we walk to our compartment.

"And it damned well hurt" I say, just managing a grin.

We settle into our seats; the tubercular teacher returning home to the Cote d'Azur accompanied by his friend the farm labourer who's been visiting relatives in Annecy. The train pulls out of the station and we settle down for the trip to Lyon, and on to Cannes, via Vienne, Valence, Montèlimar, Avignon, Marseille, Toulon and St. Raphael. An uncomfortable number of stops with their inevitable searches.

Surprisingly we are alone in the carriage. This is unusual in wartime France but the train is sure to fill up at Lyon. Jacques and I discuss our next steps. Cannes is bound to be a hotbed of secret police, possibly even on the lookout for me, as well as disillusioned and possibly angry former members of Paul's réseau. The only contacts I have there are a wireless operator, recommended by Arnaud, and the address of a safe house belonging to a Baron de Malval.

We agree to book into a hotel near the station for a few days. I plan to locate the wireless operator to see if any useful members of Paul's old réseau are still around and operable and then decide whether to resuscitate it or to start from scratch. My instinct is to start from scratch.

As the train approaches Lyon we immerse ourselves in the newspapers – copies of the collaborationist press' Signal which we found on the shelf of our compartment. Jacques keeps an eye on the platform. There doesn't seem to be any unusual Gestapo or gendarmerie presence. An elderly couple open the door of our compartment and ask Jacques if the empty seats are reserved.

"No" says Jacques "but my friend is very sick with TB. You might do better sitting somewhere else." They are gone in a flash.

Jacques settles back down to his newspaper, keeping a watchful eye on the platform when he sees a small man go by the window.

"C'est pas possible!" says Jacques "One moment," and he disappears out the door.

The small man gets on to the train via the door of their same carriage. The train pulls out of the station as Jacques casually walks along and peers into the different compartments. Just before he reaches the end of the carriage he sees the elderly couple who had vacated his own compartment so rapidly. The only other person in the compartment is the man whose gait he had recognized.

Once he mentally removed the man's beard and dark glasses he revealed the sharp nose, jutting chin and deep-set eyes of his old commander, Henri Frenay.

What luck! But how to get a chance to talk to him in private?

Jacques opens the door to the compartment where the three people are sitting.

"Monsieur le Docteur, please will you come and see to my friend, he has

tuberculosis and is spitting blood!" The old couple grab each other's hands, mentally urging the 'doctor' to leave and to not come back.

Frenay, instantly recognizing his former colleague, collects his large briefcase which, although it could just pass as a doctor's medical kit, is in fact full of the latest edition of Combat!, his Resistance newspaper, and follows Jacques out of the door.

Wordlessly they walk along the corridor. Jacques opens the door to his compartment.

Jacques and a small man walk into the compartment, close the door and sit down next to me. It's unlike Jacques to be so lax about security.

"Luc" says Jacques "this is my old commander, Henri Frenay, the head of Combat and leader of the most important Resistance movement in the south of France."

"Mon Capitaine, this is Luc. He is a British agent and has been helping the Maquis in Glières."

"Enchanté."

"Enchanté."

We shake hands.

"Jacques, it is good to see you. I must be more careful with my disguise from now on" says Frenay.

"Your disguise is very good, but your gait is unmistakable."

"Ah well, it seems to have done me a favour this time. I see that you have not been lazy these past two years, Jacques. But what takes you down to Cannes, and in the company of a British agent?" he says, nodding at me, somewhat suspiciously.

Briefly, Jacques recounts the story of the dropping of arms, brings Frenay up to date on the Glières organization of Tom Morel, the arrest of Paul and Claudine, and of my mission to reassemble the Cannes réseau.

Frenay listens attentively. He knows and admires Tom Morel and his organization in the Glières, he says. He has mixed feelings about British agents. He remains to be convinced, preferring the home-grown variety.

He has also had little success in getting British cooperation for the arming and funding of his own organization.

Now living in Cluny under one of his ten cover-names (for he is a hunted man, not only in Lyon) he is not in an especially ebullient mood. He says it is dangerous for us to be together on the train. He suggests that we meet the following day for lunch at the Café Belvedere, not far from the station in Cannes. It's owned by a friend.

As he leaves the compartment, Frenay turns to me and says "I suppose you know that you are walking into a viper's nest? Every member of Paul's réseau left in Cannes was compromised by a double agent. We eventually found him. He died a slow and painful death. You will find nothing but enemies in Cannes or, even more dangerous, frightened former friends."

"Thank you for the warning" I say "We'll see you tomorrow at 1:00 p.m."

"D'accord."

So that was Henri Frenay. Could be a great help to us. And perhaps even vice versa. We settle back to reading Signal.

Jacques stares out of the window at the passing Provençal countryside. "I remember when I was almost 12 years old, before the Spanish Civil War separated us forever, my father brought me fishing here at about this time of year. I'd love to recreate that trip one day. The mayflies will soon be hatched."

The sight of one of the omnipresent gendarmes opening the compartment door jolts us back to reality.

No fault is found with our exquisitely-forged documents.

Cannes, at first glance, seems bright and festive. There is much less evidence of the occupiers. Perhaps it's the barely detectable remains of a sunny day that give this impression?

I identify a possible hotel from an old guidebook attached by a string to the station ticket office counter. The Hotel de Paris is, apparently, fairly small; quite comfortable with 'le charme d'un manoir' and quite close to the station, and thus close to the Café Belvedere.

So the 'tubercular teacher and his farmer friend' amble along the Boulevard d'Alsace to number 34. The Mimosa is flourishing. Shrubs and flowers I've never seen before line the street.

The receptionist welcomes us in the friendly manner forecast by the guidebook and offers to bring a sandwich and a glass of wine to our room. Within minutes we are settled in.

After a short while, bathed, fed, seemingly safe and dead tired, we take to real beds and are soon asleep.

Had they known, as they succumbed to a well-earned sleep, that at that very moment Karl Metzger was supping with Robert Bardot in a restaurant a few hundred metres from the Hotel de Paris, they might not have slept so soundly.

But they didn't. So they did.

Bardot had told Metzger about a conversation between Claudine and Luc in St Jorioz. Claudine said something to Luc along the lines of "You might as well go to Cannes because there is nothing for you to do in St Jorioz."

Metzger was obsessed with finding Luc. He felt certain that the arrest of Luc, the new head of the SOE in south-eastern France, for that is what Marchais had led him to suspect, would gain promotion and recognition.

He and Bardot had taken the Paris-Lyon-Cannes train four days earlier. They had interrogated jailed Resistance members who had served with Paul; questioned collaborators and gendarmerie and pored over reports from Abwehr intelligence agents based in Cannes, all to no avail.

Satisfied that no one in Cannes had seen Luc or even knew what he looked like, they were having a final meal before taking the night train back to Paris.

The following morning we awake to find the room bathed in brilliant sunshine. The French doors open onto a little balcony from where it's possible to catch a glimpse of the sea beyond the twin cupolas of the Hotel Carlton.

"Did you know that the cupolas on top of the Hotel Carlton were modelled on the breasts of the famous courtesan, La Belle Otéro?" says Jacques leaning out of the window to soak in the morning sun.

"Where do you get these tit-bits of information, Jacques? I bet it's all made up."

"No, no it's true. The architect Marcellin Mayère was so enamoured of her breasts that he tried to recreate them for posterity."

"So you studied architecture as well as sexology?"

"No, I didn't study architecture. I am just interested and have read a few books about it.

The sexology doesn't need studying. It comes naturally to a Frenchman!"

"Touché."

We shower, who knows when the next opportunity might be, and dress for breakfast.

There are only two other people in the breakfast room. Overheard conversation reveals them to be a husband and wife who have travelled from Perpignan with a food parcel for their son who is in prison for refusing to work in a factory commandeered by the Germans. They seem nervous but Jacques' humorous quips soon put them at their ease.

Back in our room we plan the day. I send Jacques to check out the address of Xavier, the 'pianist' recommended by Arnaud

I give Jacques clear instructions that he is not to contact Xavier until he is fully satisfied that neither he nor Xavier have been followed; that Xavier is trustworthy and has not been compromised since the collapse of Paul's réseau. Jacques is to follow Xavier, possibly for several days, to see how he spends his day; who he sees; how he behaves. Only then should he make a plan to meet.

For my part I go to check out Villa Isabel in the Route de Fréjus, the safe house of Baron de Malval. Arnaud has stayed there on several occasions. If all seems in order we'll stay for a few nights until we're satisfied that either the réseau is worth resuscitating or that it's too dangerous and unproductive to remain in Cannes in which case we'll move elsewhere.

We pack our modest suitcases, agree to meet at the Café Belvedere at 1:00 p.m. and check out of the hotel.

Jacques doesn't have to wait long at the bus stop. At least the buses are running on time he notes. He buys a ticket and, the bus being full, stands at the back with four or five others. Gradually it dawns on him that the bright, bustling city of Cannes is actually full of fear. Everyone on the bus stares at the ground or straight ahead, avoiding eye contact at all costs. They look tired, worried and hungry. There are not many fat people riding buses in Cannes in 1943.

No one speaks. When the bus comes to a stop, several people cautiously edge their way to the door and step on to the pavement as if relieved to have survived the ride. Then a new kind of fear takes over. The fear of being accosted; of seeing someone who might possibly get them into some sort of indefinable trouble. The German Occupation is still relatively new to

Cannes. The Parisians had been putting up with it for three years.

The gloom is infectious. Jacques, who normally would have engaged a neighbour in conversation, feels himself strangely subdued. Partly he is just reflecting the mood of the bus and partly he is furious at his countrymen's apathy. All they seem to care about is toeing the line; keeping out of trouble. As long as they have enough to eat and don't talk to anyone they don't trust, they should avoid trouble, they reason. They are the 'attentistes', for they mind their own business and wait to see what is going to happen.

Long Live Pétain, Long Live our Beloved Marshal... Jacques imagines he can hear the refrain mouthed in unison by the mass of seemingly spectral passengers as the bus pulls up to the market bus stop. Almost everyone gets off.

The market itself is depleted of almost everything but some obscure relative of the turnip called 'rutabagas' which is normally fed to cattle but now dominates everyone's diet and every café menu. Still, it was food.

Jacques crosses the marketplace and heads north-east, away from the city centre, until he finds the rue Marcelin Berthelot. He walks along the tree-lined street until he comes to No. 16, a modest, clean, two-storey house just like all the others on the street. Its only distinction is a palm tree smack bang in the centre of the garden, its base surrounded by white pebbles that somebody had cleaned and painstakingly placed in an accurate, if unnatural, circle.

Conveniently, there is a run-down bus shelter across the street from No. 16. Jacques sits down on the bench, resting his small suitcase beside him. Partially obscured by the side of the shelter, it is a good position for surveillance.

Half an hour passes and there is no sign of life in No. 16. The curtains in what Jacques presumes to be the bedroom are still closed. He looks at his watch, 9:20. Perhaps M. Xavier is just a late riser?

A bus comes by. Opens its doors. No one gets out. Jacques remains seated where he is. The bus doors close.

Forty more minutes go by. No change.

Just as Jacques was thinking that this could all get quite dull, a short, moustachioed, middle-aged man wearing a blue overall and a beret stubs his cigarette out on the pavement in front of No. 16 and looks briefly about. Jacques feels momentary eye contact, or is he just being over-sensitive? The man takes his key out of his overall pocket, opens the door, walks inside and turns back for another glance across the street as he closes the door.

Moments later another bus comes by. This time Jacques gets on, pays for his ticket and takes a seat behind the driver. A couple of minutes later he asks the driver to stop to let him out as he has forgotten his keys. The driver obliges and Jacques finds himself a quarter of a mile further up the rue Marcelin Berthelot.

He hopes that the man from No. 16 will have spotted him getting on the bus and been reassured that he was not being followed.

Jacques makes his way casually back down the street on the same side of the road as No 16. As he draws close, he ponders how to place himself to see and not be seen when the man in the blue overalls emerges from the house and starts to walk down the street towards Jacques.

He mustn't do anything to arouse suspicion. He can't cross over to the other side of the road. It would look too obvious. His mind is racing as his prey closes in on him. There is nothing for it, he would have to be direct.

"Excuse me, Monsieur."

The man in the blue overalls stops. His back to the fence. He says nothing.

"I wonder if you could help me. I am lost. I am looking for the house of my aunt. Do you know a Mme. Duras who lives on this street?"

"No, I do not know her" comes the reply. The voice is curt, abrupt, to the point. The eyes are bright, wary. "Bonjour" and he walks off.

"Bonjour" replies Jacques. He continues to walk slowly away down the street for two or three minutes until the man turns down a side road. Then Jacques turns around and retraces his steps.

The man is 50 metres or so ahead of him as Jacques turns down the side road. Jacques picks up his pace a bit and gains just enough ground to see clearly when the man, walking in front of a parade of shops, turns into a shop with a bright blue awning. It looks, to Jacques, like a café.

Jacques continues down the street and walks by the shop with the blue awning. It turns out to be a shoe shop, a small shop selling shoes with wooden heels. There is only a salesman inside.

He wonders if he could have been mistaken as to which shop the man had entered? But next door is a baker's shop, all boarded up. Beyond that is a disused flower shop.

Walking past the flower shop and seeing an alleyway just beyond it that would afford some cover, Jacques ducks into it. He puts down his case and, pretending to look for a cigarette, starts fumbling in his jacket. He's hardly got his hands into his pocket before he is seized from behind, a large hand grabs his throat and another twists his arm and pulls him back into a doorway.

"Who the fuck are you and why are you following me?" says the man in the blue overalls, his intelligent face turned evil by his seething fury. "Answer me before I slit your throat."

Jacques, reeling from the excruciating pain, decides that now is probably as good a time as any to discover if this really is Xavier, code name of the former 'pianist' to Paul's réseau.

"M. Xavier, I am a friend of Paul's" he splutters. The hold is only very slightly loosened.

"Paul who?"

"Paul and Claudine from England. I don't know what last name he was using when he was here."

Still gripping Jacques in a loggerhold the man in the blue overalls starts asking him questions. Why are you here? Who are you with? Why do you want to contact me? Who do you work for?

Despite the intense pain, Jacques refuses to answer any of his questions. Was this really Xavier? Had he turned traitor? He suspects the man is carrying a weapon of some sort. Is this to be his end? An ignominious death in a deserted alleyway, for nothing?

Thoughts go racing through his brain as the man tightens his hold, preliminary to... to what?

"OK Jacques, you can relax now."

Jacques, gasping for air in relief as well as disbelief, manages to garble "How do you know my name?"

"I am sorry, mon ami. This has been a little test. I met with Luc last night."

"Bastards, both of you!" Jacques says as he tries to regain his breath "I'll kill him!"

Xavier laughs. "It's as well you should learn the fine art of surveillance now rather than when it's too late. You've passed the trustworthiness test but failed the surveillance test miserably. You have a lot to learn, mon ami. Tell Luc I will meet him at 3:00."

Jacques takes a few moments to regain his composure. Then he starts back down the road to the market to wait for the bus back into town. The emotional rollercoaster he has just experienced - fear turning to anger turning to relief and back to anger – settles down to an acceptance, almost gratitude, for what he's just been through.

Life on the run in a city was very different from life on the Glières plateau. Here there's a settled fear. You had to have your wits about you all the time.

It's a few minutes after 1:00 by the time Jacques gets back to the centre of town and locates the inappropriately named Café Belvedere tucked down a side street behind the station.

The only people in the café are two young girls sitting at a table in the corner playing with some boxes.

"Is the patron here?" asks Jacques, assuming them to be members of the owner's family.

"Papa" both girls shout in unison.

A man in his thirties appears at the door, on crutches. He is tall, tanned, with a boxer's build, a broken nose and only one leg.

"Bonjour, Monsieur. Can I help?" he says, standing at the open door.

"I am looking for a friend, Henri… I think you know him?"

"You must be Jacques… yes?"

"Yes"

"Henri is upstairs and expecting you… follow me".

Jacques follows the one-legged owner up the stairs and into a room the same size as the café downstairs. It has four tables.

Henri Frenay and I are sitting, talking and smoking alone in the upstairs room of the café when the owner comes upstairs with Jacques.

"Henri, here is your friend."

We both look up. I smile at Jacques. Jacques does not smile back.

"I am sorry, Jacques… it was a necessary precaution."

"Thank you for your trust" he replies, clearly upset.

"Come on pull up a chair and sit with us. It's a lesson worth learning, no? It may well save your life one day. In any case I have to be absolutely certain of how you react under pressure. No offence?"

Jacques turns to his old boss Henri Frenay "I'm beginning to regret introducing you to this unscrupulous Yank, Henri."

Frenay smiles. "Mon ami, some wine please to nurse our wounds."

The owner brings three glasses of wine and some bread to the table, "Shout if you need anything else, Henri."

Frenay nods and waves him away.

For several years now Henri Frenay has been a hunted man. He has changed his code name and domicile often. His own mother even threatened to denounce him to "our beloved Marshal." Many of his closest colleagues involved in the Combat group or working on his newspaper have been arrested, tortured and killed. He has been telling me of interminable fraternal battles with other Resistance groups. Former army colleagues have tried to hunt him down; others, now working for the Vichy, have secretly provided him with funds. He has made a Lysander trip to England and met with de Gaulle on his estate north of London, mainly to plead for funds and materiel with which to arm the thousands of Resistance fighters he has painstakingly assembled since he and Jacques escaped. Precious little was forthcoming from de Gaulle or the British. Recently he met with Allen Dulles, head of the American Intelligence Corps, based in Switzerland. Dulles, much to the fury of the British, gave handsome financial and materiel support. But British pressure ultimately forced Dulles to curtail his activities in support of Combat!.

In a few days' time Frenay says he will meet de Gaulle again, this time in Algiers. Meanwhile he's agreed to impart what advice and help he can to Jacques and me.

"First of all, Luc, you must know that every Abwehr, Gestapo, Gendarme and Milice functionary has your picture, no matter how bad a likeness, and is on the lookout for you, having been warned by Abwehr HQ that you are rumoured to be in Cannes."

"I figured as much, how do you know?"

"I have good contacts in the Gendarmerie. I checked you out after we met on the train. I wanted to make sure that my friend Jacques, who sometimes lets his heart rule his head, was going to be OK."

I nod. Jacques rolls his eyes.

"I am afraid that your friend Marchais and his cohorts have given the Abwehr every detail of information they had on you, not that there was an awful lot to tell. Apparently, though, your work with the Maquis in Glières earned you quite a reputation.

They figured you would be a dangerous man down here. I hope they are right."

I want some hard facts. "What do you know of the Cannes réseau? Is it worth resuscitating? We were planning on moving into the Baron's house today hoping that it would be a safe house for us to stay in for a few days but Xavier tells me the Baron has fled to Paris and the Gestapo have taken over his house."

"That was a big blow. In fact he has been arrested. Our information is that he has been sent to Germany which probably means execution in his case." Frenay takes a sip of his wine. I notice that he seems to do everything with military precision including sipping his wine and marshalling his thoughts.

"Luc, I advise you that if you want to be of any use to anyone, indeed if you want to stay alive beyond next week, you should leave Cannes as soon as possible. There is virtually no one left in Cannes from Paul's réseau who would be willing to stick his neck out.

They are far too frightened; those that have not yet been betrayed. Xavier is still here, as you know, but I think his days are numbered."

My frustration is beginning to show. I've been sent here to reorganize the Cannes réseau in preparation for an Allied landing. I've got to do that somehow.

"I understand what you're saying Henri. I need to create a new réseau in this area as quickly as possible. When the Allies land we need to have secured the coast and the road north as far as we can. Just to cut the Allied advance short by a few days will save thousands of French and Allied lives. If I am not able to stay in Cannes, a vital location for us to secure, my mission will have failed."

"Mais non, Luc. I think it is perfectly possible for you to organize from a distance. Why don't you set up your headquarters in a safer place, say up in the mountains. I have done something similar, basing myself in Cluny because it would be suicide for me now to be based in Lyon."

I mull the idea over in my head.

"What about Xavier?" Jacques asks me; the first words he's directed at me so far "I understand you had an assignation with him last night although how without me knowing I do not understand."

"You're a sound sleeper, Jacques."

To Frenay, I say "In fact Xavier maintains that the transmission is so weak from Cannes that he is thinking of moving to Montèlimar if there is any chance of the réseau being resuscitated. Apparently through his membership of the Freemasons he has many useful contacts there. Perhaps we should do the same?"

"Excellent idea." agrees Frenay "The French Freemasons have good contacts with the trade unions and Socialist Party ties, very different from the English version. They could prove to be very helpful to you, and not just in Montèlimar. This place is even more dangerous now that the Baron is no longer here. There is an eccentric Englishman named Sawyer who has a spectacular house beside the sea. He's been of great help to our people but I think you'd be pushing your luck, and his, by contacting him. You should make for Montèlimar without delay. You, Jacques and Xavier. I will give you the contact information for three individuals who'll be able to be of great service to you. I know I need not tell you how careful to be with this information."

"Of course."

"Firstly, there is a man near Marseilles who works in a factory making aircraft parts for the Luftwaffe. People who work in these factories can pinch stuff, dynamite cartridges, detonators, delayed action fuses. He is a bit of a loose cannon, sometimes mad but can be very effective. His name is Jean-Paul Cassis.

Secondly, in Beaurepaire, there is a Dominican monastery. The prior, Father David, has been most helpful in sheltering Maquis, Jews and Allied airmen and smuggling them on to the escape route through Spain. He has his own cell, one might say, of six other monks. I propose to you he might be good at locating dropping zones, for he knows the area like the back of his hand.

Et enfin, and most remarkably, there is an American lady, I think that, like you, she has French ancestry, I'm not sure. She is the only vet in Digne. She has performed many valuable services for the Resistance and has built her own network in Provençe and the Basses Alpes. She also has funds. Where they come from she will not say, I suspect they are private but she puts them to good use for the cause.

I think these three people will be a help to you and once they know and trust you, they can put you in contact with others so you can build up your own réseau. Mais, not here in Cannes, d'accord?"

I thank Henri Frenay for the contacts. We relax over the ersatz coffee. The café is an oasis of calm.

"One final question, Henri. You have a very successful organization. How have you saved yours from being penetrated and why did Paul's fail so badly?" I ask.

Frenay, flattered by the question, answers immediately. He breathes deeply, I can almost see him organizing his response so as not to use any unnecessary words.

"I have cardinal rules which I insist that I, and all those who work with me, follow."

He stares into my eyes, assuring himself of my complete concentration.

"One. I discovered early on that there is a big difference between the sort of men that you need for daring hit-and-run and sabotage and those that you need for the long-term liberation struggle. I hire different individuals for each and create the cells with the former and what I have called a Secret Army with a one-time general in charge, for the latter. The two types are usually in conflict with one another. It is best to keep them apart.

Two. I have no cells larger than six men. Although I know who each man is, they do not know me, only the leader of the cell knows how to contact me. And he does that through one of my three postboxes. My postmen always know how to contact me and they leave messages in the appropriate postbox for me when they can.

Three. I change my house regularly. It is a mistake to stay too long in one place. People get to know you, your habits, your routine, your comings and goings, the way you walk, as I have learned, and so on. Sometimes it is inevitable, but as a rule I try never to stay longer than three nights in one place.

Four. My recruiting style is meticulous. I never recruit anyone without having them carefully followed and noting down who they see, where they go, what they spend their money on and being careful to note such things as whether they suddenly have more money than usual, in which case where does it come from? At the end of the day it comes down to instinct. Experience has taught me that a man's look hardly ever plays false.

Paul, on the other hand, was in my view very careless about such things. He had that English belief that he was invincible. There was not much discipline in the réseau and I believe that the recruitment process was slipshod."

Jacques and I take it all in. I agree with what Frenay has said. I need to mould my own réseau with a careful blend of chemistry between recruits and a religious devotion to discipline.

"I must go." says Henri Frenay, looking at his watch. It's quarter to three. He stands up, at parade-ground attenion, and lights another cigarette. "If I can be of any help just leave a message for me with the vet in Digne, her name is Marianne by the way." Frenay embraces both of us with a final "Bonne chance" and disappears down the stairs.

Jacques and I finish off our coffee. He is now back to his old self, I think. We decide we will leave tonight for Montèlimar. We'll need to arrange transport and to see if Xavier will be willing to join us, for we'll need a 'pianist'.

Voices downstairs. Adult voices. They sound calm enough and moments later Xavier appears at the door.

"Ah, mes amis… I hope you have left some lunch for me?" he says, pulling up a chair. It's only now that it dawns on me that we haven't eaten anything but stale bread, so engrossed were we in our conversation with Frenay.

I call down to the owner for three plats du jour. As soon as Xavier sits down, the meal arrives. More stale bread, an unidentifiable better-not-to-ask soup, hunks of cheese and a fresh pot of ersatz coffee.

As we eat, I fill Xavier in on the meeting with Frenay and sound him out on the idea of going to Montèlimar.

Xavier, between slurps, agrees. "After last night's BBC broadcast my own life is in more danger than ever."

"How come?"

"Following the arrest of everyone involved in Paul's réseau, and once the Baron had fled to Paris, I made it my business to find out who had betrayed us, apart of course from the double agent that Frenay's men had already dealt with. Fortunately, as the wireless operator I had to spend a lot of my time in the hills because the reception is so bad around here, and no one except for Paul and Claudine, and Arnaud of course, knew who or where I was. So I have been able to move around in relative safety."

"But what happened last night to put you in danger?" asks Jacques.

The soup, and thus the slurping, finished, Xavier explains that, to discover who the collaborators were, he concentrated first on the few members of the réseau who had not been arrested. Ironically the ringleader turned out to be one of Paul's réseau who had been arrested. The Gestapo had done a deal with him in prison. They promised to let him go free if he agreed to work for them.

"Jean Marie le Jeune was the man. I assembled a list of names of the collaborators, headed by le Jeune, and asked the BBC to broadcast them. The broadcast went out last night. It has already had an effect. On my way here I passed by the house of one of Paul's couriers who was also working for the Milice. There was a big sign painted on the front of his house for all to see saying 'TRAITOR LIVES HERE'. I don't think he will be living there for long or anywhere else for that matter." Xavier says with relish, downing the last of the coffee. "It may take them a while to trace the broadcast to me but it is best not to hang around." He wipes his mouth on a corner of the paper tablecloth.

"Jacques my friend, how are you after our little encounter?"

"He's fine" I say, smiling. Jacques shrugs.

"Well, yes he's fine but he could do with a few lessons in the art of surveillance, n'est-ce-pas?"

"We'll see to that" I say "but apart from that he passed muster, yes?"

"Certainly, without doubt."

"Thought so." I say "Let's make our plans for relocating. How can we get to Montèlimar tonight?"

"OK" said Xavier, keeping an avuncular eye on Jacques "I have a friend in the highway commission who regularly drives to Avignon and points north. I can ask him to take us if he is here in

Cannes. Of course he may not be, in which case we can always try to hitch a ride."

"How long will it take you to see if he can take us?"

"No time at all. I just have to walk downstairs. My friend Hervé is married to the sister of the owner. Give me a few minutes."

Hervé, as it happens, was at that moment downstairs talking with his brother-in-law. Xavier joins them and puts the suggestion to Hervé.

"I'm due to make an inspection of the N7 for my Vichy controllers within the week. I've already warned my men. But I could always bring the inspection period forward. The element of surprise, no?"

And so it's agreed, without even having to leave the café. Hervé will leave this evening for Montèlimar with Xavier, Jacques and me as his passengers.

Xavier arranges to meet us at the café at 10:00 p.m. He says he has to go home to collect his belongings and to send a final message before carefully packing his transmitting set.

17

The run-down but deceptively productive farm of Roger and Sylvie Bidou lies 5 km to the east of Montèlimar near the medieval village of Montboucher sur Jabron.

Snuggled in the corner of a 75-hectare park surrounding the château of the Marquis d'Arlande, the Bidou farm has 20 hectares of its own. Before the Occupation it was an arable farm. Following the fall of France the Bidous, with the help of their 22-year-old son Alain and several of his friends from the village, still managed to grow everything from maize and wheat to a wide variety of vegetables. Even now they manage to keep pigs, chickens and a few head of cattle.

Those of Alain's friends fortunate enough to work on the farm, thereby avoiding serving with the STO, are able to feed themselves and their families quite well, especially by wartime standards. They are also able to supply care packages to relatives in Paris.

At the end of November 1942, young Alain Bidou was arrested, along with three of his friends, for anti-German behaviour. Their crime was to have altered the slogan, painted on the wall of the Hotel de Ville in Montèlimar, Deutschland siegt an allen Fronten (Germany is victorious on all Fronts) so that it read Deutschland liegt an allen Fronten (Germany is prostrate *on all Fronts). Handed over to the Gestapo by the Vichy prefecture, all four were badly beaten. Under torture they admitted to being communists. The Germans had vowed to make an example of anyone committing anti-German acts, especially if they were communists.*

At dawn on 2 December 1942 the four young men, all aged in their early twenties, were taken to the square in their village of Montboucher sur Jabron, and shot. Their bodies were displayed for all to see until the following day when the families were permitted to remove them for burial.

In Nazi-occupied France there is little inclination for the ordered, peacetime mode of mourning espoused by Catholics, good and bad. That would have to wait. On the other hand more compelling and galvanising alternatives present themselves. As soon as the Bidous had buried Alain's disfigured body in the snow-dusted graveyard of the d'Arlande chapel, they returned home and set about transforming their farm into a formidable centre of resistance.

Roger Bidou forged links with like-minded socialists, well-connected deserters and communist school teachers, one of whom had been his son's political mentor.

In the sub-cellar of a farm outbuilding, Roger Bidou set up an office and installed a BBC receiver, the news bulletins of which he would copy and print out on a roneo printing press. He quickly became recognized as an ace forger, a reputation reinforced when Jean Jacques Fournier, generally acknowledged as supreme in his craft, was murdered by Milice in his hospital bed in Lyon.

Within a matter of weeks the Bidous' farm became a hive of resistance activity. In addition to forging and printing, Roger Bidou provided support for the families of arrested communists; acted as a postbox for local Resistance organizations; and operated a safe house for British agents, the most memorable of whom was a young Jewish wireless operator with the SOE code name Arnaud. He had worked in the Cannes réseau run by two British agents known only as Paul and Claudine. Arnaud stayed with the Bidous for several days at a time, when transmitting from Cannes became difficult or dangerous or when he was in want of a good meal.

The Bidous had not heard of, or from, Arnaud for several months until the following message was hand-delivered to them on the night of 19 April, 1943:

MES AMIS FOUR FRIENDS NEED SAFE HOUSE ARRIVE TOMORROW MORNING EARLY BY CAR PLEASE TAKE CARE OF YOURSELVES AND THEM LOVE AS ALWAYS ARNAUD STOP

Consequently, when they hear an official car from the Highway Department coming up the winding drive to their farmhouse at 4:00 a.m. the following morning, the Bidous are already prepared with made-up beds, food and plentiful supplies of tea and coffee.

Our ride from Cannes is uneventful. We don't see a single patrol, German or otherwise. But what the journey lacks in excitement it makes up for in discomfort. Xavier is short and not thin. At 193 cm I am significantly taller than the average Frenchman, and Jacques at 185 cm is not small either. Hervé, the driver, complements his considerable bulk with silent flatulence that pollutes the Highway Department's ageing Renault.

Nevertheless we arrive safely at our destination. And safely before the start of the working day.

Hervé drops the three of us off at the farm gate, turns the car around and speeds back in the direction of Montèlimar to avoid arousing suspicion so far from a highway.

As dawn is breaking, our bedraggled threesome makes its way up the garden path to the farmhouse. A welcoming light shows through the crack under the front door.

The Bidous, both in their mid-50s and still, despite the years of privation, with the healthy, weathered features of the hardworking farming family, are at the door. They sleepily greet us and encourage us to sit down and eat the porridge and coffee that Sylvie Bidou is preparing.

It takes us no time at all to finish off the porridge and down the coffee. All we think of is sleep.

"We have made up cots in the barn for you. Just come over when you wake up in the morning and we will have a proper breakfast" says Roger "and don't worry about the farmhands. They were all friends of our son, Alain, and are used to seeing occasional strangers emerging from the barn."

Within twenty minutes all three of us are asleep in the room at the top of the barn.

It is already noon by the time we emerge into the bright sunshine. Three young men are in the farmyard, breaking for lunch. They wave to us as we walk over to the main house.

Roger and Sylvie are sitting and talking at the table in their meticulously clean kitchen. Ten minutes later we are gorging ourselves on a sumptuous breakfast of oranges, eggs and barley 'coffee'. While Sylvie bustles about serving us, Roger asks what help we need.

"Apart from your advice, what we need as soon as possible are Passes for our different cover identities. Jacques and I already have documents certifying us as a teacher and farmer but we should have our districts altered to this area as we hope to stay around here for a while. If possible we should change Jacques' profession to teacher as well, with, like me, permission to use a motorcycle. And Xavier urgently needs something that will explain why he is exploring the countryside for a suitable place to set up his transmitter without fear of arrest."

"Why not a water engineer?" suggests Roger Bidou, "It will

give Xavier the perfect alibi. He can say he is exploring elevated areas looking for new sources of water."

"Excellent."

"I will set to work immediately." He gets up from the table and asks Xavier what colour his eyes are, "Brown" and his last name, "Rioux." Xavier hands over his current ID so Roger can reuse the photograph.

"Do you want to see my 'studio'?" he asks.

"Of course."

We cross over to the barn and close the heavy barn doors behind us. We help move several pieces of equipment to reveal a trapdoor. Roger lights two oil lamps and we climb down a makeshift ladder to his workroom.

"Preparing false identity cards is no easy task." explains Roger as he settles down among his stocks of blank and prepared documents, rubbers, India inks, stamps and zinc plates.

"Normally the real Christian name is kept to lessen the chance of a blunder. The first letter of the last name is often kept and a new name created, taking care to avoid overused names like Dupont." He pulls out a stock of prepared ID cards and talks as he works. "We never use birthplaces like Paris or any large city where records are more likely to be kept and accessible. Ideally we use a town where the mayor's office or the records office has been destroyed by bombing. We have to limit descriptive terms to the ones currently in use. Eyes can no longer be black, for example, but they can be chestnut or blue-grey. We take great care to use the accepted abbreviations and of course the accurate signature of the relevant authority granting the permit, usually the mayor."

Roger removes the photograph from Xavier's old ID and painstakingly writes, using black ink, the new name Xavier Roche.

"Then there are new certificates with their own peculiar

requirements. A demobilization certificate requires the use of some twenty stamps for example. The other problem for us is that stamps are frequently withdrawn and requirements altered. Depending on an individual's circumstances additional cards may be required such as ration cards and coupons, work or residence permits, civil status certificates, movement permits, passes for restricted areas and so forth. All these are also subject to continuous changes which we need to be constantly aware of. Fortunately I have enough contacts in various mayors' offices to keep me up to date."

Five minutes later, Roger shows me the finished document confirming that Xavier Roche is a Water Engineer attached to the Compagnie de l'Eau at Montèlimar. It looks perfect.

"But it is not yet complete." he announces with a flourish. He walks over to a cupboard and takes out one shoe. In letters a centimetre or two high he has etched an official emblem into the heel. He takes a small brush, dips it into the India ink and paints it onto the heel. He then presses the heel into a blank piece of paper, testing the impression. It is slightly inky but he says that the second impression should be just right.

He takes Xavier's document and asks me to hold it steady on the table. He then presses the heel firmly onto the page with Xavier's photograph and the 'mayor's' signature.

"Eh voila!"

Within an hour Xavier rides off down the track to the main road on a borrowed bicycle and in possession of his new dog-eared identification document. He heads for the heights of Allan, the closest high ground above the plains of Montèlimar, where he hopes to find a suitable dwelling amongst the ruins of the old village.

Meanwhile, over coffee, Jacques and I talk through the priorities for our new réseau.

The first step is to check out potential recruits. Roger Bidou urges me to consider three of his young employees "My two nephews, Benoit and Laurent, are young and inexperienced but they are absolutely trustworthy and I'm certain they would be quick learners. The third young man is their friend, Marc. All three of them live and work here on the farm. They were close to our son, Alain, who was murdered by the Gestapo. I know they are keen to find some way of avenging his murder."

"Your son's murder gives us an added incentive too. Can Jacques and I meet with these boys soon, say this evening?"

"I'll arrange for them to come over after supper."

Roger leaves to start his chores while Jacques and I map out our plans.

After supper, huddled together in a semicircle in front of the fire in the Bidous' front room, Marc and the two cousins Benoit and Laurent drink coffee and listen silently as Jacques recounts the story of his life among the Glières Maquis. He emphasises the hardship and danger, lest the three young men (six years younger than me) should be seduced by any perceptions that life as a Resistance fighter is glamorous.

I take over from Jacques. I try to be calm and professional and to treat our potential recruits as equals. I talk about the hard work, the need for fitness, the need for unquestioning loyalty and discretion and, of course, the dangers involved in joining the réseau. I underline the requirement for absolute discipline and explain how one careless mistake can jeopardize the whole group and many other people as well. I hope I gain their respect.

Marc, a sinewy 20-year-old with a broken nose and a generous mouth, seems the brightest of the three. There's a fire in his eyes that speaks of something else, I'm not sure of what. But it's clear that joining the réseau is a matter of great personal importance. He is the natural leader and speaks first.

"Luc, Jacques, we've been waiting a long time for you. We've listened carefully to what you've been telling us. We're not going into this with our eyes closed but please understand we're dying of frustration here. We've been working, if you can call it that, with groups of so-called resisters for over a year but we feel emasculated. We've got no weapons. All we've really done is schoolboy pranks. We are men. We want to fight like men. But we are isolated and impotent without help. If you can give us training and provide us with weapons we promise to support you and to persuade others to join."

I'm impressed with this guy; old, like so many now, beyond his years.

"Good, Marc. I can see that you're enthusiastic and bright, all three of you. But you've got to agree absolutely to abide by certain rules of action."

They're listening carefully.

"The formerly successful réseaux in Cannes and most of those in the north of France have been infiltrated by German or Milice spies and collaborators. That was down to poor recruitment. Just as Jacques and I have to be convinced that you are made of the right stuff, so must you be convinced about anyone you would recommend joining the group. Careless talk, whether naively on a bus or after one too many drinks in a bar, has caused the murder or deportation of hundreds of Frenchmen and of some of our best agents who came here to arm and organize groups of resisters.

I am determined that our réseau will be completely secure. Always. I may sound like a boring school teacher but believe me I have seen the terrible price paid by careless people and I don't want to lose anyone that way. If you feel you can't cope with this, don't join. We won't think the worse of you."

"We understand what you're saying. We won't let you down."

Marc speaks on behalf of all three men. Although the cousins Benoit and Laurent are quiet they seem to have taken it all in. I try and get them to talk.

"Benoit and Laurent, what about you two? You're very quiet."

"Marc is a good talker" says blond-headed blue-eyed Benoit, who still has the truculent teenager look about him, "and he likes to talk, so we let him. But that doesn't mean he's any more committed than we are. Just more talkative."

We all laugh. He's the joker of the three. His younger cousin Laurent lives in his shadow a bit I suspect. He has the same colouring as Benoit but seems more introspective. Maybe brighter.

"And you, Laurent?"

"I'm very serious about joining Luc. Alain was my best friend. I know that this is about more than revenge but I want to join for Alain. I will not let him, or you, down. You can trust me, trust all of us, on that."

And I do. I feel as though I may actually be making headway. Indeed, we may already have half of our first six-man cell right in this room. Ironically, of course, it will break one of Henri Frenay's cardinal rules, that only the cell leader should know how to contact me, but I'm sure it won't be the last time I'll have to do that.

I tell the guys that I will be in touch soon to let them know when our first meeting will take place and we break for the evening.

I'll take Jacques on a surveillance expedition to Montèlimar tomorrow morning. Then I'll obtain some sort of transport and go in search of a potential dropping zone so that we can organize our first delivery of arms and ammunition.

After a good night's sleep Jacques and I walk to the village square and catch the first bus to Montèlimar. As in Cannes, eye contact is avoided. There's a palpable sense of fear and suspicion, even if almost everyone thinks that an invasion is imminent and that the Americans are about to land.

Jacques and I stop for a coffee. We listen unobtrusively to the chatter of the early-morning workers assembled in the café. We learn very little. Only banalities make safe conversation, that's clear. We move to a corner of the café where we can't be overheard and I quietly teach what I have learned about the fundamentals of surveillance to Jacques.

"Once again there are certain basic rules, some they taught us in training, others I learned on the streets of Paris."

"Go slowly," cautions Jacques "I am not able to take notes."

"First and foremost, when you are following someone, the important thing, as you now know, is to be inconspicuous. Ideally you should be under average height, so that's one strike against us two for a start."

I take out a pack of cigarettes, offer one to Jacques, take one myself and light both.

"In a perfect world, you'd have several people following the target with you, each with a different cover. Say a tradesman in his van; a lady pushing a pram; a man with his girlfriend, or a shopper. Here too it will be more difficult for us until we get a larger group together, but we can make a start. If possible always wear everyday dark clothes appropriate for the locale and the weather of course; quiet shoes, and wear a watch to give you a reason to stop for a moment or two. A pack of cigarettes or a pipe is also useful if you suddenly need to stop without apparent reason. Plenty of small change is a must so that you can run into a shop or use a telephone or buy any small item off the street. It's also a good idea to vary your appearance during the day by taking off a hat or coat for example. These points may seem small but they could save your life."

Jacques listens attentively, while trying to look nonchalant, in this public place. He is having to learn the ways of an actor quickly. It doesn't come naturally to him, which speaks well of him as a person, but he needs to try if he's going to stay out of trouble.

"Most of your surveillance will take place on the street or in a café, therefore it's important to remember never to get too unnaturally close or too far away from the person you're following; keep other people or objects between you insofar as possible; never mimic the other person's gait and always, if you're by yourself, follow on the other side of the street as this gives you more protection and also a better vantage point. And never make eye contact. Observe him or her through the reflection in a window instead. And if you're in a café, always sit where the other person has his back to you, order short meals and drinks and pay the bill straightaway so you can leave in a hurry if needs be."

Jacques says he feels confident he can handle things ok. Before leaving the café, I ask him to memorize the names of three individuals recommended by Roger Bidou, along with their places of work. Jacques is to seek them out, mentally record their movements, note their habits and characteristics; where they go, who they see, what they do, what they eat and drink and how they behave generally. Then he'll report back on their suitability as potential recruits.

I pay the bill, say goodbye to Jacques and walk to the home of Raymond Daujat, a 35-year-old corn merchant who operates a local safe house for the Resistance. I borrow one of Daujat's vans which comes complete with German permit and take off immediately in the direction of Avignon.

Three days later I return to the Bidou farm having located and negotiated the use of a potential dropping zone. Over the next few weeks I'll have to find several more but at least now, once contact with London has been re-established, I can arrange for the dropping of much-needed supplies.

Every day for ten days, Jacques, carefully adopting the routine of a man going to work, goes in to Montèlimar armed with more names and each individual's place of work or residence. Following my rules, he tracks likely recruits; some he dismisses almost immediately for being too young; too quick-tempered; too fond of pastis; too talkative. Others he follows but becomes suspicious of their routines; of the people they visit. One young man, also a former friend of Alain Bidou's, is clearly a member of the Milice. He visits the local Milice HQ with what looks like a file of reports at the same time each day.

On Thursday 29 April, Jacques hands me a list of 15 people; 10 young men, 4 young women and a priest. These are our potential recruits.

Xavier too arrives back from the hills. Having found a deserted shepherd's cottage, Xavier persuaded some friendly neighbours to help him make it waterproof. They have also loaned him a bed, table and chairs. What's more, he explains, he's been able to set up his transmitter and has already sent the message that I gave him, requesting supplies.

"Fantastic," I say "we have recruits or potential recruits at any rate; a dropping zone and we've made contact. It looks as though we're finally in business."

"Not quite" says Xavier, handing me a message just received from Baker Street:

IN NO POSITION SUPPLY ARMS ETC FOR SEVERAL WEEKS STOP OTHER PRIORITIES IN NORTH STOP REGARDS TO LUC STOP END

The buggers. But I have to hide my disappointment. Not only am I being pursued by the Abwehr and quite probably by the

Gestapo and the Milice, and potentially the German Army, but we are always in danger of being betrayed by collaborators, and now it appears that I have another 'foe' to contend with. Baker Street.

"But I do also have some good news" continues Xavier "a mutual friend of ours will be stopping by tonight for dinner."

"That could only mean one thing" I say "Arnaud."

"Oui, c'est lui."

Despite the disappointments, I am elated to be seeing my new 'old' friend again. He will make the embryonic team complete and provide masses of experience, good humour and practical help.

An hour or so later there comes a loud banging on the Bidous' front door. Mme. Bidou opens it cautiously only to be swept up bodily into the massive arms of Arnaud.

"Sylvie… the prodigal son has returned!" He kisses her loudly on the mouth much to the astonishment of the diminutive Mme. Bidou and much to the amusement of her husband who is embraced only marginally less warmly himself.

"Luc you old dog, what a treat for the eyes" another bear hug for me and for Xavier. "Xavier, it was good to get your message. I hope the Diable Yankee is treating you well?"

"No complaints Arnaud."

"Diable Yankee indeed" says Jacques.

"And Jacques, mon frère, you've grown older in these few weeks." Arnaud envelops Jacques in a semi-embrace, semi-shake.

The calm, not to say austere, living room is thus electrified by the presence of Arnaud.

The Bidous open two bottles of their pre-war wine that have been hidden in a cave, its whereabouts known only to Roger. There is a carnival atmosphere to the place; I try to forget the bad news from Baker Street.

The six of us sit down to one of those long, lazy relaxed

dinners that have become only a memory. We drink and eat and talk and talk.

"Any news of Paul and Claudine?" I ask at one point.

"Not good I'm afraid. Our contacts in Paris say that Claudine was tortured, they don't know about Paul, but she clearly didn't say anything. They are both being sent to Germany, to Ravensbruck I think. We know no more than that."

"Jesus, I'm so sorry. She's a brave girl. I can just imagine what those bastards did to her." A gloom falls over the table.

"And Robert Bardot and Louis?"

"Both working with the Abwehr. In fact Bardot was down in Cannes not too long ago with Karl Metzger, 'Monsieur Jean', the fucker who caught Paul and Claudine. Rumour has it they were looking for you."

I'm not surprised. Metzger is the kind of trumped-up petty bureaucrat that I dislike most of all. But a more persistent, resilient type you're not likely to meet.

Arnaud speaks excitedly about the Glières Maquis and their gathering strength. They have arms and ammunition sufficient to last them several months. Tom Morel is gaining increased recognition from the Resistance, from de Gaulle's Free French organization in London and from the SOE. He is also, inevitably, attracting the increased attention of the German Army and the Milice, whose numbers have recently swelled following a recruitment drive by the Vichy.

"And you, my friend, we've a lot to tell you now that you've come to join us," I say.

"Sadly, mon cher, I can't join you. Not now anyway. Apparently our chiefs back home cannot do without me. They want me back to go on some course. I resisted; told them I was indispensable to you. But they wouldn't listen. I have to go but I'm bloody well going to come back on the next plane if I can. I'm taking the Spanish escape route and catching the felucca. I aim to be back within a week. Any messages for home?"

Disappointed and suspicious that Baker Street may not allow him to return I answer "Yes one. And use your most colourful, characteristic language. Tell them that they will have a revolt on their hands if they don't get arms and ammunition to our new dropping zone near Avignon, fast. Tell them, thanks to the Bidous and Jacques here, that we have organized a Resistance réseau of several hundred men already and that if they know what's good for them the arms will come tomorrow, at the latest."

"Several hundred? Really?"

"Well, several anyway."

"Ah ha, will do" says Arnaud, beaming. "I'll particularly enjoy telling the bird-nosed man himself exactly where to go if he doesn't come through for you. I'll insist."

"And make sure they send us another radio operator and a courier. Female" I add.

"Mais oui, mon ami, to look after all your needs."

At the crack of dawn the following morning Arnaud leaves for Spain.

18

Jacques has discovered a run-down barn in a forgotten field outside the tiny farming village of Charols on the banks of the Rubiron, east of Montèlimar. It will do nicely as our headquarters.

Over the next two weeks Jacques and I, meeting as discreetly as possible in various cafés in and around Montèlimar, interview 15 people selected as potential recruits. We speak to each person separately and informally. Anyone with a criminal past we deselect. Even though they're more likely to have the appropriate knowledge they are also more likely to lack the trust, loyalty and reliability that characterize the ideal cell member. One rotten apple can infect an entire cell. We question everyone's motives. We're meticulous. We are weeding out the 'adventurers', we hope. It's imperative that each cell member puts the group's overall objective above his or her own self-interest.

During the course of the interviews, two of the young men tell self-serving stories, clearly concocted, and are discounted. I feel instinctively that one of the others, a school teacher, is a likely plant by the Milice. Just a gut feeling. All three men are warned that if word gets out about the formation of Resistance cells in the area, they will be tracked down and summarily executed. That should put the fear of God into them but also reassure everyone that this is a serious organization where we protect our own.

Later on, the twelve successful recruits meet together, for the first time, with Jacques, Xavier and me at our barn HQ. A motley crew, they vary in age from 19 to 49, but if we do our job properly it won't be long before we develop that bond so critical for people whose lives depend on one another.

Sitting on a tree stump in the centre of the old cow shed, with the new recruits sitting in a semicircle on the floor in front of me, I describe the planned organization. I sound worryingly like those authoritarian figures I so despise.

"Welcome to the first-ever meeting of what we will now officially call the Rugby circuit. With your help, we plan to grow this circuit, from these modest beginnings, to the largest and most successful Resistance network in southern France. Over the next few weeks we are going to put you through some gruelling training. It's essential stuff and I've no doubt at all that you'll be able to handle it. Before we go into the specifics, however, we want to tell you a little about ourselves. Jacques will start."

Jacques takes my place on the tree stump. "Welcome. Apologies to Marc, Benoit and Laurent who have heard most of this before. As you now know my name is Jacques. I used to be in the army but when Pétain declared an armistice I joined the Glières Maquis rather than work for a traitor. Living with the Maquis was not a glamorous life. Not only did we have to live through freezing cold winters with little to keep ourselves warm but we were reliant on the goodwill of the villagers. Sometimes the maquisards were little better than bandits, forced to steal and even to resort to violence on occasion. Young people with nowhere to go and people on the run from the STO had no choice but to take to the hills. However, you can be just as effective, in many ways even more effective, by remaining at home, at a job and working steadily but quietly. Plus you have a better chance of keeping fed and warm. Given the choice, I would much rather be a sedentaire than a maquisard. But one day you may not have the choice and then the hills will be your only refuge. When Luc arrived in the Glières to help us I asked to come with him to set up a new réseau. And that's why I am here with you today."

There is shuffling on the floor, lighting of cigarettes, as Jacques' words sink in. I can tell they like and admire him and feel he is one of them. I have a way to go before I can instil that same feeling, I think.

"I know that some of you have had some experience of sabotage already," he continues, "two of you blew up the kiosks selling collaborationist newspapers in Avignon last month, I hear. And you may or may not know that Marc here and one of his friends persuaded girls in an Avignon brothel popular with German soldiers to put itching powder in their clients' underwear."

A ripple of laughter.

"I understand that there were no reprisals, but keep checking your underwear Marc."

Marc turns beet red.

My turn on the stump. "Thanks Jacques, I can tell you a few stories about Jacques that would turn his face the same colour, Marc. Maybe later." The recruits are feeling more at ease now. "Meanwhile, to let you know a little about me, I'm an American as you can probably tell. And a pacifist you may be surprised to hear. But the Nazi and Fascist dogma and the atrocities committed in their name made my blood boil. I didn't want to serve in a regular, uniformed army but when the opportunity to help stop the Nazi onslaught, without joining the army, came along I volunteered enthusiastically. The Milice also killed my closest friend and I know that some of you, particularly those of you who were friends of Alain Bidou, have suffered the same loss. Revenge is a powerful motivator but it must only be part of the mix. We are here because we believe, first and foremost, in saving France and the rest of the Free World, from the Nazis. Our specific objective, and this you must always bear in mind, is to do everything we can to smooth the way for an Allied invasion from the south."

I pause to light a cigarette. The only movement in the room.

"I am officially an enemy agent as far as the Germans and their servants the Pétainists are concerned and therefore will be immediately shot if I fall into their hands. My original objective was to take over the Carte circuit operating out of Cannes but that was compromised and almost everyone in the organization, save Xavier here, our wireless operator, was either arrested or shot. One of the fundamental problems in that circuit was the sloppy recruitment, I think Xavier will agree. Many of those joining were simply enthusiastic students but it takes more than that to make a successful operator. Some of the arrested Carte people have been released and have become collaborators. But here we have the opportunity to select only the best people for this new Rugby circuit."

The enormity of the task is not so great that it outweighs a feeling of pride among the recruits. They seem to feel good about it.

"First off" I continue "I am going to appoint three leaders of the three cells. I know we aren't quite up to the maximum number of six yet but it won't be long. Marc, you are to lead Cell 1."

Recovered from his embarrassment now, young Marc raises his hand in acknowledgement.

"Father Thibault, you will lead Cell 2."

The 49-year-old Catholic priest is known to all, churchgoers and non-churchgoers alike. He smiles, "Merci."

"And Anne-Marie, will you be the leader of Cell 3?"

"Of course" says the young lady from the telephone exchange.

"In future cells the leaders, and only the leaders, will know how to contact Jacques. But these cells are special because you all know where Jacques and I are living, some of you live there too. But that will not always be the case, even with these cells, as one day in the not-too-distant future, Jacques and I will have to leave you in charge. No one, except our 'pianist' Xavier and Jacques will know how to contact me. But you will always be able to get me through Jacques and rest assured I will always know what you are up to.

The plan is simple and affords maximum security, for yourselves as well as for the rest of us. Whenever a cell member needs to contact Jacques or me they should leave a message in the postbox. Jacques will tell you more about this later. He will arrange for the messages to be picked up regularly and will also contact cell leaders with information and instructions whenever necessary. He will always know how to contact me.

Finally I must reiterate what I've said about security. We need to be absolutely certain of your total dedication and blind obedience to the Resistance cause and to the demands of the Rugby circuit in particular. If you aren't happy with that, you must leave now. If you stay, and collaborate, you will be shot."

A few of them seem uneasy, naturally. No one leaves.

"From this moment on you're no longer recruits, you are fully fledged members. Our lives depend on one another. We'll go through the training schedule with you now and if you have any questions we can deal with them at the end."

Over the next two weeks Jacques and I put the new members through a rigorous daily physical routine involving a regular fitness regimen plus exercises designed for their particular jobs in the types of the terrain they are likely to encounter.

Cycling, for instance, not only requires the necessary physical ability, but each recruit has to learn how to travel avoiding the skyline when cycling. When walking they have to learn how to move silently through the undergrowth. We teach them how to melt into the background in town and country alike and generally how to avoid attracting attention or, worse, suspicion.

With the small arsenal of weapons the corn merchant in Montèlimar has managed to secrete in his hayloft, Jacques and I teach the teams how to use Sten guns, Bren guns, rifles, and how to camouflage them.

Restless and eager, they are quick learners.

Having taught the basics, we graduate to sabotage techniques, concentrating first on the railways. I explain how emery powder, a fine carborundum powder, when mixed with a lubricating oil and put into the axels of railway trucks, will cause them to burn out, suddenly, once the trains are travelling at full speed, hundreds of kilometres away, forcing the wheels to jam and the train to crash. I tell them how to switch the destination labels on railway trucks so that propeller parts destined for the Front can end up, after a two days' journey, in Marseilles and spare parts destined for a French factory in Marseille can end up, uselessly, back in Berlin.

They love this.

We follow this with 'attack and kill' methods; communication and surveillance techniques, reception committee practice; weapon use and care; shooting practice (without actually firing); disguise and the rudiments of sabotage from cutting telephone wires to blowing up railway trains.

The following week, Jacques puts the teams through a trial run for their first mission, to blow up a train from the factory where Henri Frenay's friend works. Marc, the leader, is to be responsible for making up and placing the actual dummy charge on the stretch of track. So as to minimise the chance of reprisals they choose a piece of track as distant as possible from any house. Fortunately there's an extensive stretch of unguarded track through the forest near Charols, and here, one Wednesday night, Jacques gives the men their dress rehearsal.

Marc's team make their way independently to the site not far from our HQ. Each person has been allocated a specific job. Marc is to lay the charge. Two armed men are to guard either end of the track; one is to stand near to Marc and keep his eye out for warnings from the track guards. The fifth person, the telephonist and cell leader Anne-Marie, will guard the getaway vehicles (in this case bicycles) under cover in the woods and keep her eye on the approach road.

The dummy charge is laid, warnings are given and heeded and the midnight train from Marseille passes by without incident.

Crucially, however, it has sprung the dummy charge.

Back at the farm, Marc and his team report their success to Jacques, unnecessarily as it happens as Jacques observed the whole scene from his vantage point on the other side of the track. He congratulates them on a textbook performance, but warns them about being more cautious in future as no one has observed him standing metres away.

Marc smiles, admiringly. He had suspected as much.

It's the middle of May. We've already recruited and trained a further fifty resisters, primarily from the Avignon and Montèlimar region but also from further afield. I decide it's time for me to head for Isère and locate dropping zones for the eastern sector.

Word is spreading, apparently, quietly but effectively, that there is a serious réseau being formed which has the potential to be well-armed and effective, and that it is rumoured to be run by a mysterious American named Luc. Our recruitment strategy is gaining pace.

But it's not only friendly ears that hear of our success.

19

Word of this mysterious American has also reached a dozy little 15th-century town in the Isère named Beaurepaire. Specifically it has reached the ears of Father David, friend of Henri Frenay and prior of the Dominican monastery perched on the hill overlooking the town.

Ever vigilant and ever curious, Father David has always kept an eye out, as he did his morning rounds in the village and outlying areas, for 'Le Grand Diable Americain'.

Father David had a friend in Montèlimar, Monsignor Pierrot, from a local Catholic church. Monsignor Pierrot had just informed him that one of his parishioners, a young school teacher originally from the Isère, had confessed to having informed on a local Resistance group being organized by an American named Luc. The school teacher said that he had tried to join Luc's réseau but that for some reason he had been deselected early on.

As Monsignor Pierrot related it to Father David, Luc had told the school teacher that he was glad to have someone from the Isère in the group and had asked him if he knew Beaurepaire. The teacher said no. But the fact that Luc was interested in Beaurepaire had clearly registered with the teacher.

Father David was aware that his friend Henri Frenay had given his name to Luc. He felt certain that one day soon Luc would show up in

Beaurepaire. Meanwhile Father David pondered on how to get word to Luc that he had been betrayed by the school teacher.

Early one Monday morning towards the end of May, Father David was driving his horse and trap north of the town on the road to Champs Martin. He was on his way to visit the Comtessse de Julienne who lived, with her 35-year-old son, in some vestiges of style at the Château de Julienne. Widowed just before the war, she devoted her energies to tending her once grand and beautiful garden; embroidery, reading and urging her lazy son into some sort of action. Every Monday morning it was her habit to take breakfast with Father David. Not through any religious conviction. They simply enjoyed each other's company.

Father David would update her, over steaming black coffee and fresh baguettes, butter and jam ('the rich had their sources') on all the local gossip, carefully avoiding revealing any confidences of the Confessional (unless unavoidable in the greater cause of liberating France of course). This Monday was no exception and Father David involuntarily licked his lips as he urged his ageing mare along the road to Champs Martin. His imaginings of freshly baked croissants and lively conversation were interrupted when he noticed, out of the corner of his eye, a stranger riding a bicycle that was too small for him down the track from les Varilles towards the Champs Martin road.

'Ah ha' he thought 'Le Grand Diable Americain' if I'm not mistaken. He pulled on the reins tightly and brought the old grey mare to an unexpected standstill. She looked back quizzically at Father David as if to ask if there were some mistake. The prior shrugged his shoulders and smiled complicitly.

I am staying, outside Beaurepaire, in a hamlet named les Varilles with Guillaume, a cousin of Jacques. He is a 'coquetier' and he says he can introduce me to a network of good ordinary people who will be only too willing to help me recruit new members for the

Rugby circuit. His job is to gather poultry, ducks, game, rabbits and eggs from local farms and to sell them on. He also collects rabbit skins. These skins he sends to a guy in Chazelles-sur-Lyon who makes felt hats out of them. The man in Chazelles has a friend who is a hatter in Lyon. Over a period of five or six days Guillaume makes it possible for me to meet all these people and so our network grows.

One especially warm summer's day I borrow Guillaume's bicycle. It is too small for me and I keep having trouble with it, but it's faster than walking. Just as I'm coming up to the Champs Martin road I notice a priest in a horse and carriage who seem to be waiting for something. I wonder vaguely if this could be Father David when the priest shouts over to me "Monsieur, are you from around these parts? I am lost. I wonder if you could tell me how to find the Château de Julienne?"

I am immediately suspicious, of course. How come a priest, clearly from the local Dominican monastery, can be lost looking for a local château? I go up to the horse and carriage, or rather cart, and notice the priest has a mischievous smile.

"Bonjour, mon ami" I say "No I'm not from here. But on the other hand I'm not lost and yet you, who live here, are?"

"Ah" said the priest, clearly enjoying himself, "you must be Le Grand Diable Americain."

"You, uh, seem to be surprisingly well-informed Father."

"Ah" said Father David looking heavenwards, "we have our sources. Let us just say it is a fortuitous meeting between God and the devil on the road to Champs Martin."

"Yeah, let's. I guess you must be Father David."

"Bien sur. Why don't you put your bicycle in the cart and join me for breakfast. I am going to the Château de Julienne."

"If you can find it."

Father David lets out an unpriestly guffaw.

I'm going to enjoy this I decide as I lift my bicycle into the back of the cart and jump up beside the priest who urges his old grey mare into action.

"Henri Frenay told me that you might be in touch. I have been half expecting you."

"I was planning on contacting you once I had had a good look around, Father."

We move quite swiftly now towards Champs Martin.

"I think you will be most interested to meet my hostess and she will certainly be interested to meet you. She has been a great help to the Resistance, financially, or so my friends in Lyon tell me."

"But first you must tell me how you recognised me, leaving out the divine intervention bit if you don't mind" I say.

Father David gives the mare some gentle physical encouragement. "Actually it was divine intervention in a way. My friend Monsignor Pierrot in Montèlimar heard the confession, Hail Mary, Mother of God forgive me etcetera, etcetera, but all is fair in times like this, n'est ce pas? My friend heard the confession of a young school teacher whom you most wisely, it seems, deselected from your little band of resisters."

A refreshing breeze blows across the plain as we enter into the village of Champs Martin. Father David and I talk animatedly, like old friends, as he explains that not only had the school teacher told of my plan to come to the Isère in his confessional but that he had confessed to betraying me to the Milice.

"Who will by now have informed the Abwehr" I add.

"More than likely" says Father David as the mare pulls the cart through the gates to the château. "I think you would be wise not to remain in Montèlimar, or stay too long here for that matter. And perhaps it was a mistake to give the school teacher the information that you were interested in Beaurepaire? "

There's priestly admonishment in his look.

"You're right. It was stupid of me." I had broken another of my own rules.

Château de Julienne is an impressive building. A classic 18th-century Palladian structure I would guess. Large shuttered windows with painted frames in a faded ochre colour. The gardens show signs of neglect that seem to enhance their beauty. We pull up to the open front door.

Having secured the mare and cart, Father David and I walk up the steps into the house. No sign of life. We walk through the elegantly furnished living room and out of the French doors which open onto an old brick terrace with a view across the fields to the forest that lies west of the house. Perfect for a dropping zone.

"Bonjour Father. You have brought a friend I see" says a casually but expensively dressed man in his thirties as he emerges from a pergola under which is a beautifully laid breakfast table. "Bonjour Monsieur… ?"

"Luc"

"Claude"

"Enchanté." We shake hands.

"Claude is the son and heir" explains Father David as we walk through to the pergola "we are hoping one day that he will find his calling but so far it has eluded him."

Claude laughs. "I'm afraid I am a great disappointment to my mother and to her spiritual advisor here" he remarks in an aside to me "but my time will come."

Claude hurriedly organizes another place at the table. No sooner had we all settled down than another French door opens and out steps a sprightly lady in her mid-seventies. The first thing that strikes me as the three of us stand up is how distinguished she looks despite the fact that she lists to the left, probably due to a spinal deformation. She starts talking as soon as she comes out of the door. Her personality dominates the space instantly; which explains the son, I think.

"My dear Father. I see you have not only brought news but a giant to breakfast this morning. To what do we owe this honour?"

"Bonjour M. Géant" says the diminutive lady extending her hand to me.

"This is my new friend, Luc" interjects Father David by way of explanation, "we have known each other for approximately twenty minutes but I am sure you will find his company both entertaining and illuminating."

I shake the Comtesse's hand cautiously "Bonjour Madame la Comtesse."

Without letting go of my hand, the Comtesse turns to Father David and says "Well Father, I had no idea you were so impetuous. There is hope for you yet. A little impetuosity never did any harm. Especially to a priest. Isn't that right, Monsieur Luc? I am sure it is good for the soul."

Introductions over, we are served breakfast by an ageing retainer, a haughty looking woman who could pass for a duchess herself had it not been for her maid's uniform.

She eyes me suspiciously, to my discomfort, until I notice that she eyes everyone suspiciously, including the Comtesse.

"Bien Monsieur Luc," says the Comtesse, who drinks tea not coffee and barely touches her food "Father David says you are entertaining and illuminating. So entertain and illuminate."

Father David looks at me with an expression that says "What can I do? This is the way she is."

Realizing that I'm in an awkward position, Father David explains the situation.

"Madame, Luc is a very important British secret agent, or rather American secret agent who works for the British. He is over here organizing, training and supplying the Resistance in preparation for the Allied liberation of France. I believe, although I do not know for certain, that he is here to find recruits and to find places where arms could be landed and stored." He looks to me for confirmation.

"That is correct Madame. I understand from Father David that there is a possibility that you might be able to help us in this endeavour?"

"Us?" the Comtesse says in surprise "Is Father David in cahoots with the British Secret Service? My goodness Father, what would the bishop or whatever he's called say?"

"Well he's called the Master and he is not to know. In any event I have not yet offered my services to Luc although I am considering it…"

"Good for you!" says the Comtesse.

I consume the real coffee and buttered croissants with gusto.

"Tell me, Monsieur Luc, what can a frail old lady with a bad back and an under-employed son do to help your cause?"

Claude ignores his mother's ill-concealed digs.

"First and foremost we need a good dropping zone where we can land supplies, arms and occasionally agents. Secondly we need a safe house where agents can stay without attracting attention. And thirdly we need to build up a Resistance réseau here in the Isère as it's vitally located near the Route Napoleon and the German garrison in Grenoble.

The old lady listens attentively.

"Monsieur Luc, I suggest we go for a little walk and I will talk over your requirements with you," she says as she stands, indicating breakfast is over.

The Comtesse and I walk down the steps to the garden leaving the others to speculate.

As we walk, the Comtesse talks. She explains that her husband was a wealthy industrialist and amateur philosopher who inherited the château twenty years ago. He died of a heart ailment shortly before the invasion of France. Since then she has maintained the household as was his wish, except that several of the staff have left.

"I think they found me a little difficult" she says with a twinkle.

She tells me how she provided a safe house for members of the Lyon réseau run by M. Frenay and on several occasions has given refuge to British airmen on their way to the Spanish escape route. Even that route, relatively easy before November 1942, is now dangerous. "Only about half the escapes are successful. If people are caught on the French side they are dispatched to a concentration camp; if on the Spanish side they are interned in Miranda Camp on the banks of the Ebro where they have a better chance of surviving, particularly if they are British or Canadian because of their embassies in Madrid. The others are left to rot and to fight each other with knives for the meagre rations of food. I want to do more, of course, but we are surrounded by collaborators or would-be collaborators. Many are jealous of our lifestyle and would gladly deliver us into the hands of the Gestapo on some sort of trumped-up charge, let alone a real charge."

"Can your maid be trusted?" I ask.

"I trust no one more" replies the Comtesse. "She has worked with us for thirty years and is as fiercely devoted and protective as a Yorkshire Terrier, whom she somewhat resembles don't you think?"

I like this lady. "I know it means you'll be taking an enormous risk but I could really use your help. Your fields would make perfect dropping zones and I can't think of a better safe house, there must be a hundred rooms here?"

"I don't know. I've never counted. I do know however that there are more windows on the outside than on the inside which is mysterious, is it not? There must be a secret room somewhere."

"See, it's designed for the purpose."

"D'accord" responds the Comtesse "I will provide you with what you want under these circumstances. Your people may use the field but there is to be no sign of their having done so by the following morning. My house will be available for them to use but all arrangements are to be made with Lucille, the maid. I do not want to know about it or to see any signs of anyone. It is much easier and safer for me if I remain aloof. Thirdly I want you to take my son into your réseau. It is high time he did something for France and I believe he would respond well to your character. Finally, do give a job to Father David. He is a very good and brave man and I am sure he can be of help, after all what better cover for someone than a priest's cassock? Besides it will give him something to talk about other than religion which bores me to tears."

In one fell swoop the Comtesse has countered all my prejudices about the French aristocracy. I place my hand on her shoulder, gently; the 26-year-old congratulating the 74-year-old for her courage and conviction.

"You're quite a lady, Comtesse."

"That" she beams "is a compliment indeed, from an American." We walk back up the garden path and join the others. "Well I must be off now" says the Comtesse "I have an embroidery class. I will see you again M. Luc?"

"Bien sur, Madame. I will be in touch shortly."

"I look forward to it. And do not forget our little pact," with that she disappears through the French doors leaving us to finish our coffee. Father David and I prepare to depart.

"We'll meet again soon" I say to Claude.

"Ah, I see mother must have put in a good word for me?"

"That she did." He's alright, this man a decade my senior. I think we may be able to use him.

"Good, I look forward to it."

Father David takes me back to the crossroads where we met.

"Thank you for that, Father. It was a real help. That's quite some character, that Comtesse. I'm sure Claude could be useful. He's bright and I don't think his mother gives him enough credit."

"Bien Luc. If I can be of service to you just let me know. You can contact me at the monastery."

"Thank you Father. It's good to know that not all Dominicans are like Savanorola."

Father David winces.

"If I need to contact you urgently I will use a different code name; let's say Ignatius? Yes, Ignatius, that seems appropriate under the circumstances. And many thanks for all you have done." I repeat as I pull my bicycle down from the cart.

"A bientot, Ignatius" the priest shouts as he starts back down the road to Beaurepaire.

I mount the bicycle and head back up the track to les Varilles where I plan to stay another night at the home of Jacques' cousin Guillaume.

20

Late that same Monday night Xavier the 'pianist' leaves his mountain hideout and makes his way by bicycle through the blacked-out countryside to the Bidous' farm. He creeps into the barn, shakes Jacques awake and hands him an urgent message, just received from London.

At 4:00 a.m. on Tuesday morning there is a loud rapping at the front door of Guillaume's house here in les Varilles. I grab my pistol and creep to the top of the stairs. Guillaume is already at the door. He uses the code; a voice responds with the password and Guillaume lets him in.

Little more than a boy, he explains that he is working as a courier for one of the Resistance cells and that he has a message from Montèlimar for a man named Luc which he has been asked to deliver to this address urgently. Guillaume says fine we'll see that Luc gets it, takes the message, offers the guy some food and a drink, and lets him go.

Recognizing Xavier's handwriting I open up the message:

WILL DROP SUFFICIENT SUPPLIES MONTY 02:00 MAY

27 CONFIRM OK CONFIRM YOUR USE CHEERS STOP ARNAUD SENDS LOVE ENDS

At last Baker Street is waking up. I waste no time. Guillaume loans me his motorbike and by 4:20 a.m. I am already speeding down the road and heading back to Montèlimar.

At 7:00 a.m. I pull into the Bidous' drive. Jacques is awake and taking a bath in the outdoor tub that serves as our bath during the summer. He jumps up, secures a towel around his waist and comes over to greet me.

"Fancy dress?" I enquire.

"No just a celebration so I'm cleaning up my act."

Half an hour later we join Roger Bidou in the kitchen to agree how best to organize the reception of our first arms drop. We alert the Montèlimar cells. Excitement, almost audible, ripples around the Resistance community. Morale is at its highest for a long time, perhaps ever.

By a quarter to midnight that evening a field belonging to a local farmer just off the Route N7 between Montèlimar and Avignon has been transformed into a dropping zone. The men have planted their flares at the prerequisite distances to form the upturned L that the pilot will be looking for. The night is clear so we anticipate little difficulty with the drop. The Germans are not yet prone to scouring this area as so far there has been no record of drops around Montèlimar. All that is bound to change after tonight.

It's ten minutes until 01:00. Marc assembles his team to stand by their flares and to await his signal. 01:15, 01:30 comes and goes, the guys are growing restless with anticipation but lose none of their fervour. This is the night they have been waiting three years for. The first tangible step towards erasing the shame of what they feel is their national humiliation.

At 01:45 Marc, with Jacques and me standing by, gives the signal for everyone to be quiet. We all listen intently. In the distance they hear the unmistakable drone of an aircraft. To my ears it's the unmistakable drone of the throttled-down engines of a Hudson. Good news.

Marc looks to me for the signal. I give it. Marc tells his men to light their torches. The field is instantly transformed into an easily recognisable dropping zone.

Now everything relies upon the pilot's accuracy.

And the absence of Germans.

Always at these moments SOE operatives are very aware that many, if not most, of the circuits have been infiltrated and that all too often this has resulted in the arrest, and often murder, of agents dropping from the skies and/or the slaughter of the reception party and confiscation of the supplies on the ground. So far tonight seems calm, though I did insist that Marc leave valuable men to guard all four tracks having access to the field.

At precisely 02:00, as the Hudson flies overhead, Marc flashes the code letter B that we've been assigned for this drop. The Hudson is assigned the code letter J.

Using the specially mounted searchlight on the undercarriage, the pilot signals dot dash dash dash, the letter J. We're in business.

The Hudson circles around and disappears out of sight. Then it returns twice as low and seemingly twice as large as before. Suddenly the night sky is punctuated with parachutes glistening in the moonlight gently bobbing their way towards the ground. The guys with their torches gawk at the sight in amazement.

Great cylinders land one after the other on the farmer's field. One or two fall among the trees and have to be disentangled from the branches. I silently praise the efficiency of the RAF pilots who volunteer for these missions. They are not always popular with their superiors who view the SOE and its band of 'uncontrollable amateurs with a license to kill' with suspicion. This one knows his stuff. He circles once more, drops another twenty glittering gifts and then disappears back to England, with any luck.

Most of the cylinders survive the fall intact. Some had been inexpertly packed and their contents broken and useless. The others contain explosives, 50 Sten guns, 55 Bren guns, several mortars, rounds of ammunition, 60 rifles, 5 pistols, 15 grenades, time pencils, cigarettes and bars of chocolate.

Marc organizes half of his men to gather up the supplies and to distribute them among the various modes of transport. The farmer's hay cart bears most of the weight. The remaining men retrieve the broken canisters and their unusable contents, bury them and cover up all traces of their having been there.

The group disperses making their separate ways back to their homes or, in the case of the hay cart, to the barn where the weapons and supplies will be stored pending their use, which we all hope will be imminent.

For the next couple of days Jacques and I plan our first major act of sabotage. Despite having sufficient arms and ammunition to mount an assault on the hydroelectric station at L'Argentière, I decide that our first objective should be to blow up the train transporting propeller parts and aluminium refined from bauxite in the factory managed by Henri Frenay's friend, Jean-Paul Cassis, in Toulouse. The Germans are desperately short of metal needed to transmit electricity. Copper is non-existent and the alternative is aluminium, shipped to Norway where hydroelectric power is still available in large quantities. I dispatch Jacques to Toulouse to find out what time the train with the largest load is scheduled to depart for Germany. He takes with him a box of emery powder as a gift for M. Cassis.

Meanwhile Xavier arrives with a second message from London. I think Arnaud must be behind all this sudden activity and silently thank him.

AS PER REQUEST ALAIN AND MONIQUE ARRIVE 18 JUNE YOUR NEW DROPPING ZONE STOP ARNAUD PROVIDED GRID REFERENCES STOP USUAL TIME ENDS

"As long as these two are up to the mark" I comment to Xavier "we should be in pretty good shape. I presume Alain is the 'pianist' in which case I'll send him to the Digne area, we can use someone good there given the number of new recruits we've got. Not to mention the growing number of Maquis on the Vercors plateau. He could prove really useful. Unless you'd rather go of course, Xavier?"

"Not at the moment. I don't want to leave just as things are heating up" replies the taciturn Frenchman.

"Fine, that's decided then. And Monique will be the courier, based here. We've got to have someone here who is able to roam free and women are much less likely to attract unwanted attention, at least of that kind."

Three days later Marc and I and two men from the farm wait at the dropping zone near Avignon. At 12:03 a.m. precisely, we spot the by now familiar shape of the Hudson flying in low from the north. We exchange recognition signals and after a perfect circle, two silken parachutes burst forth into the moonlit sky and carry their human cargoes safely to earth.

"This bodes well," I say on reaching the two while they are still unbuckling themselves and preparing to bury their chutes "a perfect drop. Well done."

Alain is your stereotypical Frenchman. Short, round-faced, wide-eyed, full lips (if not quite pouting like Jacques' crooner lips).

He looks as though he'd been born in a pair of blue overalls with a beret on his head. Turns out he escaped from France to England and was then trained by the SOE as a wireless operator. Monique is an attractive Irish brunette who somehow manages to look smart even in a jump suit. She looks both fit and able.

"Welcome to France" says Marc "we've got about a half hour or so to walk. Did you have a good trip?"

"Perfect" says Monique.

"Oui, no problems at all" says Alain. Marc helps him reassemble his wireless set, bits of which have come loose in the fall.

We split up and walk in pairs back to the farm. I walk with Monique. It turns out she is married to a Frenchman and is a skilled yachtswoman.

After several days at the Bidou farm to acquaint themselves with our methods and with the objectives of the Rugby circuit, I send Alain to Digne where he is to contact Marianne, the American veterinary surgeon recommended by Frenay. She will put him in touch with the leader of the local Resistance, a former Carte member named Theo Gautier.

Monique, posing as a Red Cross nurse, finds digs in Montèlimar with one of Marc's aunts. Her cover gives her access to whatever mode of transport is available, usually a bicycle.

On 25 June, Jacques returns from Toulouse. Frenay's contact at the aircraft parts factory, Jean-Paul Cassis, has given him invaluable information, plus an insight into the sabotage they are carrying out in the factory.

Last night, before Jacques left Toulouse, he and Jean-Paul had lingered around the railway yard, chatting and smoking and surreptitiously ensuring that the emery powder they were inserting into the axels of two departing engines was well and truly embedded. It was unlikely the trains would get much beyond

Grenoble before they seized up.

Jacques explains all this to me, barely able to conceal his excitement. He also produces the train schedule with the departure time of 8:40 p.m., 7 July 1943 underlined.

"Why this particular train?" I ask.

"Jean-Paul tells me that a consignment of tank parts and spares has been brought forward by three weeks 'on personal orders of the Führer'. Jean-Paul and his men have had to work throughout the night in order to meet the target. The 7 July trainload is likely to be the most important ever to leave the factory. There will be extra security; extra troops and every inch of track is due to be inspected by scout cars 24 hours prior to departure."

"I'd have preferred something a little less ambitious for our first mission but this is too good an opportunity to pass up. What's going on to require Hitler's personal intervention?"

"Apparently they are urgently required for the Russian front where a major attack is imminent. The Russians are proving formidable enemies, it seems, and the German Army is in trouble. Will our guys be ready by then?" asks Jacques.

"They're ready now. Marc's team certainly is. And the others will be too. I'm pretty confident but this will be the real test."

The following ten days we do almost nothing but practice for the derailment. Day after day I talk the teams through even the smallest detail. Jacques and I monitor them as they put what they've learned into practice. Rapt attention. Lots of questions. Not a stone unturned.

The evening of 7 July is uncommonly warm, even for this time of year. As dusk descends it makes little impact on the heat. Four of us are cycling, separately, towards the forest some twenty kilometres south of Montélimar. My ride is draining and slow despite the surge of adrenalin. We have timed our rendezvous, near a section of track that we reconnoitered last week, for 9:00. Train number 211 from Toulouse, destination Bremerhaven, with its freight of tank parts; propeller parts, essential spares, ammunition and God knows what else is due to pass through the Lesieux tunnel dissecting the forest of Montchamp at precisely 9:43 p.m.

I've chosen the Lesieux tunnel both for its relative isolation and in order to maximise the damage and delay that a derailment could cause to the German military machine. The tank and propeller parts were identified by Jean-Paul Cassis as being placed in the third to seventh cars. With any luck the derailment will cause the ammunition carriage spontaneously to combust. The resulting damage will be irreparable.

Jacques and Marc leave the Bidou farm on my borrowed motorcycle at 8:30 p.m. We decided that they should take the motorcycle and then leave it for the last two men to enable them to get away from the scene of the anticipated explosion as quickly as possible. Anne-Marie and I arrive at the rendezvous, a derelict shed some 80 metres from the tunnel, more or less simultaneously at the allotted time of 9:00. There is no sign of the others. Anne-Marie stows the bikes and I go for a quick recce of the tunnel. There are certain to be guards posted this evening, given the importance of the cargo.

By the time I return, Jacques, Marc and the cousins Benoit and Laurent are all waiting at the rendezvous, expectantly. We settle down in the woods, beyond earshot of the German guards. A slight breeze brings momentary relief from the heat. The group, their faces blackened with burnt cork, listen carefully.

"Two guards at both ends of the tunnel," I tell them, "there's no way we can eliminate all four guards and lay the explosive before the train gets here, but we shouldn't have to.

Laurent and Benoit, you two need to eliminate the two guards at the tunnel entrance. We can forget about the tunnel exit guards for the time being. You need to wait until the guards are standing and chatting together which they're likely to be doing during this boring wait, and then attack them silently from behind, just as we've planned. Once you've killed them, put on whatever outer clothing they are wearing. The engine driver will doubtless be on the lookout for trouble and so will any guard on the train. Let's hope they're not waiting for any particular signal. Once your mission is accomplished, cough three times loudly in quick succession. That'll be the signal for Marc and Jacques to enter the tunnel and place the charges. Chances are the other guards won't be inspecting the track again before the train comes. That all OK?''

The two cousins look at each other and then at me, signalling their assent. Although they have practiced many times it would be the first time that either of them has killed a man.

I wish them 'Bonne chance'.

Benoit and Laurent move quietly off towards the undergrowth that covers much of the distance to the tunnel.

Marc and Jacques unpack the two charges, each of which is designed to remove a metre or two of track. One should do the job, if properly triggered, but just to be sure they are going to place two. Meanwhile they'll wait for the cousins' signal.

Anne-Marie goes to the exit end of the tunnel to keep the two guards under surveillance and to alert me should there be any unexpected developments. I am going to keep close to the young cousins. I want this to be the group's responsibility and the group's achievement. It will do wonders for morale if it all comes off successfully. But I need to stay close by in case there's trouble.

The night is virtually moonless. I follow Benoit and Laurent as they move cautiously through the undergrowth and approach the southern end of the tunnel. I can just make out the silhouettes of the two guards. One of them is holding a torch which he half-heartedly uses to illuminate the surrounding area once or twice. They are standing next to each other, talking.

The cousins quietly leave the cover of the undergrowth and approach the track. Laurent pulls his knife out in readiness. Benoit goes to do the same, but apparently his shackle is empty. He must have dropped his knife. "Merde" he mouths to Laurent, pointing at the empty shackle. Laurent indicates to Benoit that he will have to kill the guard with his bare hands. It's essential that neither guard has the chance to respond, or even cry out, before they are killed.

They are now about two metres away from, and more or less directly behind, the guards.

Poised to pounce, they suddenly hear a voice echoing through the tunnel yelling something in German.

The cousins slink back under the protection of the trees, just as we practiced in training.

One of the German guards walks into the tunnel a few metres and yells back

"Ja, alles ist …." and the cousins couldn't make out the last word…

I assume the guard is just confirming that there are no problems.

The two guards resume their positions. Time is running out. Laurent, knife at the ready, gives the thumbs up sign to Benoit. As they silently creep up behind the Germans the soldier on the right pulls a cigarette out of his pocket and goes to light it. The other one, opposite Benoit, sits down on the milestone.

They hardly have time to move before the cousins attack. Laurent strikes a violent blow on the standing guard's neck with the side of his right hand, the most deadly blow of all. In the same movement he clasps his left hand over the guard's mouth and nostrils, dragging him back and down as he does so. Then, in one great orchestrated movement, he brings his right arm around and thrusts his knife deep into the man's kidneys.

Benoit, simultaneously attacking from the rear, strikes a violent blow on the right side of the other guard's neck, goes immediately into the head-hold position and takes the German down onto his thigh. Holding his forearm between the guard's jaw and temple, he grabs his right wrist with his left hand. A quick snap upwards and backwards neatly dislocates the spine and breaks the neck with a reassuring crack.

As they pull the guards' bodies back into the undergrowth, Laurent coughs three times loudly. They quickly remove the guards' uniforms and put them on.

I give the go-ahead to Marc and Jacques and then go down to the tunnel entrance. I give the thumbs up sign to the cousins. No sign from Anne-Marie at the north end of the tunnel. So far so good.

Marc and Jacques creep quickly up the bank towards the tunnel entrance. The cousins have already taken up their positions.

Cautiously carrying their charges, fog signals and detonators, Marc and Jacques enter the tunnel. They need to go far enough in to do maximum damage to the tunnel without going so far that they alert the guards at the other end.

Marc stops first, about 12 metres in. He sets down his two charges ready to assemble as he has done many times, blindfolded, in training. Jacques moves on another eight metres. All is quiet.

Each man inserts two No.8 detonators into the fog signal initiators and then tapes them to long double cordex tails about three or four inches from the ends. Then they strap the charges to the right side of the railway line, northbound, with the fog signals at the southern end, the end from which the engine will approach. If all goes according to plan the engine will crush the fog signals which will then initiate the detonators. The charges should remove several metres of rail and derail the train.

If all goes according to plan.

Just as Marc and Jacques are completing their tasks a voice from the north end of the tunnel booms

"Halt!"

We all freeze.

"Ja" comes the answer from the south tunnel entrance, taking me by surprise. It's Benoit.

"Alles ist gut Walt?"

Christ, I realize it's 'Walt' not 'Halt'. What will Benoit answer?

"Ja, ja, alles ist blitzsauber!"

I remember that Benoit knows two phrases in German, taught to him by a German speaking girlfriend before the war. One was about how beautiful she looked wearing a "Rote Geranie", the other was "Alles ist blitzsauber" or "Everything is spic and span".

"Ha ha" comes the shouted response from the other end, then something unintelligible but from the sound of his voice it was a good enough reply.

This is something we didn't practice in training and I am bloody impressed with Benoit. I also know that he has used up almost all of his German vocabulary.

While not fully understanding the implications, Marc and Jacques must have realized that the exchange was between the cousins and the guards and they make their way cautiously back to the entrance.

Relief all around, but no time for congratulations. It's 9:31. Marc and Jacques disappear with me into the woods where we are joined by Anne-Marie.

At 9:33 the three of them climb onto their bicycles and make their getaway as quickly and quietly as possible, leaving the motorcycle for Benoit and Laurent who will have to be quicker but will be less concerned about being quiet, if all goes well. I take my bicycle and leave it in readiness for my getaway but I stay to see that everything goes OK.

All remains quiet back at the tunnel. Benoit and Laurent slowly move down the line so that they'll be 15 metres or so away from the tunnel entrance as the train approaches. There is a danger that being so far from their position might alert the train driver that something is wrong but I figure he won't have time to stop. In any case they have no choice if they want to save their lives. After the engine passes they'll run for it. Heading into the forest as fast as possible. They'll only have a matter of seconds before they too risk being blown apart by the explosion.

9:38. No sound of an approaching train. A breeze is finally cooling the evening down. The cousins, finding cigarettes in the borrowed uniforms, smoke and wait. If the train is delayed then it's likely the tunnel guards will walk through and want to discuss what they should do; whether they should radio for advice. I see Laurent lean down with his ear to the track. He must hear the vibration as he jumps up quickly and signals to Benoit. The train is coming. It's two minutes early.

Gradually the ghostly, noisy, blacked-out engine becomes more and more visible as it gets closer to the tunnel. It's as eerie a sight as I've ever seen. Against normal procedure, Benoit and Laurent stand on the same side of the track, Laurent holds the torch. The train is going faster than usual which is a good sign. Less chance he can stop before hitting the charges. Louder and louder the train comes towards them, spewing smoke into the clear night sky. Pray God the charges are triggered.

Only moments now.

Even at the speed it's travelling the train's side draft almost knocks the cousins over. They turn and run scrambling down the bank towards the forest. They hardly have time to think before two enormous explosions force them onto their stomachs.

Deafening explosions and groans of twisted metal so deep and cavernous that they seem to be coming from the bowels of hell. The cousins scramble up the hill, run towards the shed, jump onto the motorcycle and speed off down the woodland track. I follow, pedaling as fast as I can.

The force of the explosion combined with the four or five metres of displaced track and the speed of the train resulted in the entire train being derailed inside the tunnel with what was left of the engine appearing out of the northern tunnel exit while the last carriage blocked the entrance on the southern end. The fires inside the tunnel ignited the explosives in carriage four of the train which destroyed the entire consignment of arms and ammunition; killing everyone on that carriage and leaving the guards at the tunnel exit mute with fear. Within two weeks, charged with dereliction of duty, the guards would be transported to Hamburg on their way to the Russian Front. Perhaps fortunately for them they would never make it. On the night of 24 July the British dropped 2,300 tonnes of high explosives and incendiary bombs on Hamburg killing more than 1,300 Germans, including the two guards.

The following day we celebrate our first major coup with a slap-up meal at the Bidou farm. The team's success in destroying the train will, I explain, not only do serious damage to Germany's immediate plans on the Russian front but it will also serve the longer-term objectives. By making the rail link impassable for weeks to come it will force more German soldiers to be deployed down in the south of France instead of in the north where they are needed to prevent any Allied invasion. The men are justifiably proud. At last they have made a serious inroad on the enemy's capability.

We are not in quite such a festive mood when we hear, two days later, that on the orders of the Gestapo chief in Marseilles, every man, woman and child, born and unborn, in the village of Les Deux Eglises, the closest village to the tunnel where the train was destroyed, had been taken into the village square and systematically mown down by machine guns fired by a contingent of the Montélimar Milice. 150 deaths, ten for every German who died on the train.

At the headquarters of the Abwehr in Paris, Sergeant Karl Metzger, sweating profusely in his basement office on an uncomfortably hot August afternoon, pored over a second batch of notes from the young school teacher in Montélimar. It made for disturbing reading. When Metzger had read the teacher's first report the previous month he wasn't convinced that the man identified as Luc in the report was the same British agent he had been searching for since the arrest of Chamberlain and Mathilde in St Jorioz. Even when the physical description was confirmed he was not 100% certain. He knew he would not therefore be able to convince his superiors to allow him to go on another of his 'pointless' sorties in search of Luc.

But now everything had changed. The derailment of a major consignment of weapons destined for the Russian front, and the total destruction of its cargo, warranted the highest priority, of that he was certain. And, whereas heretofore no major activity on the part of the so-called Montélimar réseau had been detected, now that too had changed. And Metzger for one was finally convinced that Luc was at the root of it all.

He had found his prey. Henceforth he would pursue Luc with all the single-minded obsession of Ahab pursuing his whale. No obstacle would impede his mission. It was time to pay the young school teacher turned informer a visit. A visit that Metzger fervently hoped would result in the arrest of Luc and his own longed-for promotion.

He would depart for Montélimar within the week.

21

On this same hot August afternoon Monique and I are sitting at the cast iron table under an olive tree behind the Bidous' farmhouse. Monique is looking even prettier than usual, her hair pulled back, gathered and secured by a long, thin paintbrush. A touch of rosiness, thanks to the heat, adds warmth to her cheeks. She is dressed only in a light cotton smock pulled tight under her breasts. It's hard to concentrate. Looking, I'm sure, like a courting couple enjoying respite from the summer heat we discuss how to respond to a 'request' from London that I should return as soon as possible for debriefing.

I suspect they plan to use me as some kind of pawn in an interdepartmental match of wits back in the UK. Because I've lasted five months and have had some success, they want to trot me out as an example of why they need more funding. Bureaucracy again. I don't want to waste time in London and am going to resist.

Dictating my reply to Monique (she has a pencil, too, in her hair) I explain to Baker Street that we are at a crucial juncture in the organization of the new réseau and that to leave now would be to risk undoing much of what has been achieved. Over the past weeks and particularly since the spectacular train success, we've recruited several hundred more people into cells as far away as Lyon to the north, Montpellier in the south-west and Cannes in the south-east.

Jean-Paul Cassis has started a Rugby circuit cell in Toulouse. Begun shortly after Jacques' visit to the factory, they have already put out of action twenty locomotives, twenty tankers and 150 grease-boxes. In the east, the Lyon cells have cut all lines to Italy for 4–7 days seriously impeding Italian troop movements. Thanks to the work of cell leaders there are now upwards of two thousand cell members on whom the Rugby circuit are relying, and vice versa. It was counter-productive, I say tersely to London, to consider leaving them at this delicate stage. I end the message by offering to send Monique back instead, knowing they are unlikely to agree.

Monique is not amused. Having spent several years waiting to get to France she isn't about to volunteer to go back.

"It won't be necessary, Monique. You haven't been here long enough to provide them with the information they think they need. They can damned well wait." She is not reassured. "In any event we've both got to get out of Montèlimar soon. Ever since the train project I've been expecting an increased Gestapo presence. So far there doesn't seem to have been any, at least not that we have noticed. I half expect to see Karl Metzger here."

"Perhaps they're all preoccupied elsewhere" suggests Monique "I hear rumours that the Paris réseau has been decimated once again."

"Yup. London suspects a double-agent is involved. Too many agents have been killed upon, or shortly after, their arrival in France. And this is only happening in the Paris area."

Monique finishes transcribing the message. It's been two months since she and Alain were dropped into France. The courier's job is one of the most dangerous jobs in the Resistance, partly because people tend to discover a courier's habits; to know where they live but also because they invariably have incriminating letters on them and have to be present in many dangerous places. Most of them are female because of the relative ease with which young women can get around and charm their way past guards. Despite all this, Monique clearly finds the day-to-day drudgery of the job boring. She yearns for something more exciting to do. I don't want to lose her now. I am impressed by her resourcefulness. And I have an important mission for her to undertake.

"Can you get that message to Xavier and have it transmitted to London? Then I need you to engage in a little subterfuge of your own."

"I'm all ears" says Monique, stuffing the message into the toe of her shoe.

"There's a school teacher in Montèlimar who lives very close to your digs. We were keen to recruit him initially but I became convinced that he was a Milice plant. In the event we let him go. Then, on my first trip to Beaurepaire, my suspicions were confirmed. He is a collaborator. He must also have good contacts in the Abwehr as he's channelled information through to Paris. I suspect he's still doing that. We need to have him eliminated."

Monique baulks at the implication. "Surely this is way beyond a courier's remit. Although I've been trained to kill if attacked, premeditated murder was not something I have been trained for, either physically or psychologically" she says.

"Don't worry. I'm not asking you to kill him. Just to set him up for us. I want you to make him think that you're keen to go to bed with him. He's got quite a reputation in town so I'm certain he'll be amenable."

Monique doesn't know whether to be relieved or concerned.

Flattered or insulted. She listens, suspiciously.

"OK, this is the deal, let me know if you're uneasy about anything. Ideally you'll befriend him at the Café de la Place where we know he always takes morning coffee. Try and get him to propose meeting up with you somewhere more private but don't take him back to your place. On no account should he know where you live. OK?"

"Assuming he doesn't already. All he has to do is check with the gendarmerie. I've had to register my address."

She's right of course.

"Once he's gained confidence in you and you feel he might be willing to meet you in some more private place, let me know. We can then talk about a good location for a rendezvous. You can leave the nasty bit to me."

"OK, but I really don't want to go to bed with the man unless I absolutely have to."

"I hope that won't be necessary but if it is then you'll have to grit your teeth and think of France. You don't relish sleeping with him and I don't relish killing him but if needs be, we must. He's a real danger, not just to us but to the whole réseau here. He may know many of the new recruits and it's at least possible that one of them is continuing to feed him information. I do know that he's betrayed us to the Abwehr."

"What if he doesn't fancy me?"

"He's not blind, Monique, just an asshole."

Blushing, she agrees to sit near to the teacher at the café the following morning. And to take it from there.

"What's his name by the way? How will I recognize him, Luc?"

"His name is Philippe. He looks just like a school teacher. 30 years old; tousled dark hair, glasses, maybe."

"A bit young for me, don't you think?"

"We know that he likes women of all ages; anything between, if the rumours are right, 12 and 60."

"Delightful!"

"He'll probably be wearing a corduroy jacket if it's at all cool outside, otherwise a short-sleeved shirt and tie. He wears reading glasses and may well have them on, reading a book or a newspaper. Jacques noticed that he also has a slight nervous twitch. His left shoulder I think."

"Irresistible" says Monique, and departs on her bicycle to find Xavier.

The following day at 9:00 Monique goes to the Café de la Place to take her morning coffee. She easily spots the school teacher, twitch or no, and sits down at a table within sight but not too close.

She orders a black coffee. Drinks it quickly, pays her bill and, on the way out she establishes momentary eye contact with the teacher. Nothing more.

At the same time the following day she sits two tables away. The school teacher nods hello. Glances are exchanged but no move is made. Monique begins to think that maybe her fears are well founded. The man doesn't find her attractive. As she gets up to leave, he gives her a quick goodbye wave.

"So much for my sex appeal" Monique says to me when we meet briefly back at the farm.

"He's probably being cautious, maybe even having you checked out. He's probably more wary now that he's in communication with the Germans. You've just got to be patient."

On the following day, Thursday, Monique picks up messages to be left at the postbox (the corn merchant's house in Montélimar) and departs for the café. She is surprised to see that the school teacher is not alone. She sits at the same table as she had on the previous day so as not to arouse any suspicion.

She nods hello. The school teacher looks up and smiles. His companion, a man aged about forty wearing a blue beret and dark glasses despite the sunless morning, turns around and glances at her. Monique thinks there is something vaguely sinister about this fellow but then gives it little thought, resigning herself to the fact that another day would go by and she was no closer to achieving her objective.

The two men speak so quietly that their conversation is barely audible. Monique can't make out what they are saying. The older man seems to be giving the school teacher instructions and then, without warning, he stands up. They shake hands and, pausing to bow slightly and mouth the word "Madame" at Monique, he leaves the café.

No sooner has the man disappeared than the school teacher stands up and, bringing his coffee with him, walks over and asks Monique if he can join her.

"Pourquoi pas?"

He sits down.

"I've noticed that you have the same habit as I, coming here for coffee each morning. Are you new in town?"

"Yes, I'm from Paris. I was just sent here to work with the Red Cross for a month or so to replace a colleague who is having a baby."

"Ah, today is Paris day. My friend is also from Paris. He hates to be away from it. He's going back tomorrow."

"What does he do in Paris?" asks Monique feigning slight interest.

"I'm not sure. He's a bit secretive. He's a very good musician though. That's how we know each other. I don't ask much about his work."

Monique decides to let the school teacher do all the talking.

"My name is Philippe by the way. I teach school here in Montèlimar."

"I am Helene" says Monique, using the name she had registered with at the gendarmerie.

"What a lovely name. It's my mother's name. Perhaps, Helene, as you don't know Montèlimar I could show you around? I have the day off tomorrow and it would be a great privilege for me if I could take you out. Perhaps we could have lunch tomorrow? I have to meet Jean, the guy from Paris, in the afternoon but I am free until then. What do you say?"

"Well I could. I am free for lunch. I don't start work until the afternoon."

"Fine, do you by any chance like to fish?"

"To fish? Uh… I don't know, yet. I've never been fishing."

"Well it's time you learned. Shall we meet here at 9:30? I will bring a packed lunch. You have a bicycle I see and so do I."

"OK, tomorrow at 9:30 it is." She then excuses herself saying she has to go and visit the hospital.

"I will pay for the coffees" says Philippe.

"You're very kind, Monsieur"

"A demain"

"A demain"

Monique gets on her bike and heads down the road out of town. At the first crossroads she notices that the sign saying 'Hospital' is pointing in the direction from which she has just come. She stops at a tabac, buys a newspaper, then gets back on her bicycle and rides past the café in the direction of the hospital.

Philippe is still sitting at the table.

As is the man from Paris.

Monique rides her bicycle through the back roads to the Bidou farm. She finds Luc at the kitchen table talking to Jacques.

"Ah, Monique, how'd it go?"

"Well, Luc, enfin!" Monique says pulling out a chair and sitting down at the refectory table "I do believe so. We are going fishing tomorrow," she grimaces.

I laugh "Well, it may be a strange first date but it's ideal for our purposes. You'll be alone in a relatively deserted place I imagine, excellent."

Jacques and I talk Monique through the proposed scenario for the next day. I'll tail them as they leave the café. There are only so many possible fishing spots. I am unlikely to lose them. Forty minutes or so after they are settled, Monique will say she needs to have a pee and will leave Philippe and walk off into the bushes. I'll handle it from there.

Satisfied that she is in sight of fulfilling her objective without having to sleep with the man, Monique gets ready to leave. "Oh, by the way, I don't know if it's important but it struck me as a bit strange."

"What's that?"

"When I got to the café this morning Philippe wasn't alone. He had a strange looking man from Paris with him. They talked briefly but quietly and then the other man shook hands, said goodbye and left. Philippe told me that he didn't know what exactly the man did for work because he was very secretive about it, but apparently he is some sort of musician. Anyway, what struck me as odd was that I drove my bike past the café a few minutes after I left because I realized I had told Philippe that I was going to the hospital and I had started off in the wrong direction. When I rode past the café again the guy from Paris had returned and was back sitting down with Philippe."

Jacques and I exchange glances. "What did he look like?" asks Jacques.

"About 40. He was wearing pretty nondescript clothing, a beret and dark glasses."

Metzger!

I have a quick flashback to St. Jorioz and Mathilde's description of Karl Metzger, a.k.a. Monsieur Jean. "Did you find out his name?" I ask.

"Jean I think. Yes, definitely, Jean. They are going to have a meeting, apparently, tomorrow afternoon before Jean returns to Paris."

I thank Monique, congratulate her on doing a good job and reassure her that I will follow her very closely tomorrow.

After she leaves, I turn to Jacques.

"We've got trouble. Jean is obviously our friend Karl Metzger, the Abwehr agent who arrested Paul and Claudine in St. Jorioz."

"And searched for us in Cannes with Robert Bardot" interjects Jacques.

"Exactly. I don't think Monique will be in any danger, not yet anyway, but we need to eliminate Philippe as soon as we can. If they are going to have a meeting tomorrow the timing of this fishing trip is perfect. I think I'll borrow Roger Bidou's fishing pole and put an end to this man."

"What if it's a set-up, Luc? Maybe Philippe suspects Monique. Or maybe Metzger does. Won't she be in great danger?"

"She may."

True to his word Philippe is waiting for Monique at the Café de la Place at 9:30. Fishing pole and picnic bag to hand.

They leave right away rather than take coffee at the café.

Ten minutes later Philippe and Monique are cycling in the direction of the forest of Montchamp, scene of the previous month's successful railway explosion. A minute or so behind them is a lone cyclist, a home-made disassembled fishing pole visibly protruding from the long bag slung over his back. At the bottom of the fishing bag is a simple but highly effective pistol, designed by SOE's scientists and technicians, known as a Welrod. A compact tubular weapon, it's unusual in that it's used in a two-handed grip, one hand gripping the magazine which acts as a pistol grip and the other hand gripping the barrel of the silencer. The recommended operational range is three metres.

Four kilometres down the road to Montchamp, Monique and

Philippe turn off onto a track leading east. From studying my map when searching for dropping zones I recall that there is a small lake lying not too far from the road. As though I've had a sudden puncture I stop, get off my bike and examine my tyre. I'm not being followed. The spectre of Metzger is haunting my thoughts now. Making me a little paranoid. I get back on the bicycle and continue down the road and up the track. Knowing the lake is not far, I ditch the bicycle, retrieve my 'fishing' bag and continue on foot.

Twenty minutes later I spot two figures sitting close to each other by the lake, a fishing pole leant against a tree trunk. In another twenty minutes or so Monique should, according to our agreement, excuse herself and walk to the nearby undergrowth to pee.

I move slowly up some thirty metres to the east of the couple where the trees afford more protection. I remove the fishing pole and retrieve the Welrod, charge it with three cartridges, and stealthily make my way through the woods until I'm ten or so metres behind them. And I wait.

Philippe wastes little time in making his first amorous moves. Monique responds somewhat unconvincingly. Ten minutes later, as the petting looks as though it is about to take a more serious turn, Monique excuses herself, stands up and walks casually towards some bushes.

Philippe also stands up, stretches and preens himself, no doubt relishing the thought of what is about to come.

But it is I who cock my weapon.

Slowly moving down towards the bank of the lake until I'm less than five metres away I aim the Welrod precisely. Whether Philippe hears me driving the bolt home or not I'm not sure but in any event he turns and stares directly at me. He has just enough time to register who I am before the bullet hits him in the chest.

The force of the impact throws him back into the lake.

Monique emerges from her hiding place. The two of us pull Philippe's body to a deeper part of the lake where we weigh it down with stones so it will rest, temporarily, on the lakebed.

Monique retrieves her bicycle. I hurl Philippe's into a deeper part of the undergrowth for some lucky picnicker to find, and we head back to the road where I collect my bike and we ride together back to the farm.

When Monique gets home she finds Marc's aunt in a terrible state, shaking with fear. Monique manages to calm her down enough to discover that the house had been searched by the Milice. Marc's aunt has been threatened. Monique's room has been ransacked.

Sergeant Karl Metzger sat seething at the Café de la Place. It was 4:30. The wretched school teacher was already forty minutes late. He had found nothing at the girl's room and now it was likely he'd have to return to Paris empty-handed. Or almost.

At 6:00 he left for the station to catch his train back to Paris. Although he had not had a chance for a full debriefing from the school teacher or the opportunity to give him the new instructions; to take him to Luc alive and receive immunity from prosecution for his indiscretions with a 12-year-old girl, he had received one potentially invaluable lead. His trip had not been entirely futile although it looked like the promotion would have to wait.

Despite the dispatch of the school teacher, I'm keenly aware that the Gestapo are now on to me. For the sake of my teams, the Bidou family in particular, as well as for myself, I must get out of here. I spend the next three weeks in discussion with Jacques and the leaders of each of the Montèlimar, Avignon, Marseille and Toulouse cells going over plans to attack the hydroelectric station at L'Argentière. They will have to do this without me. I can't put off the trip back to England much longer.

On 12 September I leave for Digne because the town, famous for its baths, is strategically placed on the Route Napoleon between Cannes and the Vercors plateau. My plan is to contact Marianne, the American vet whose house was the postbox for the local Resistance; Alain, the 'pianist' who was dropped with Monique, and Theo Gautier, the local Resistance leader. The Basses Alpes cells of the Rugby circuit are already 100 men strong. They will need to grow to ten times that size, maybe more, over the next few months. I'm also thinking of making Digne my new HQ and therefore I need to familiarize myself with the area as best I can.

I book into a small hotel on the outskirts of Digne. Tomorrow I'll explore the town and perhaps contact Alain. In any event I'll have to check in with Marianne to see if I have any messages.

It's midday and there is one message, it reads:

MONIQUE ARRESTED GESTAPO STOP JACQUES END

By dusk I am back in Montèlimar once more sitting at the Bidou kitchen table with Roger Bidou, Jacques and Xavier.

Xavier tells the story, in so far as he knows it.

"Monique came to the house of the corn merchant, M. Daujat, at around five o'clock yesterday afternoon. She left a message with Daujat for the Avignon réseau.

I was talking in the garden with Daujat when his wife came out to say that Monique had just arrived with a message and did we have anything for her to take back for Luc.

As I stood up to go into the house we heard the screech of tyres as several cars drew up in front. It could only have been the Gestapo. Daujat and his wife immediately took refuge in the cellar of the adjoining house. I leaped over the wall and made my way through the back gardens of the other houses before coming out onto the street.

After a while I wandered back along the street towards Daujat's house. The Gestapo were escorting Monique out of the front door. She looked completely calm, as though they had come to collect her for a tea party. Then they drove off towards the prison."

I say nothing for a minute or two, then "Do you think there is any chance we can spring her from the prison?"

"She'll have been taken to Lyon by now" says Jacques "the Gestapo wouldn't leave her here for a moment longer than necessary, it's over 24 hours since her arrest. She'll be long gone."

I am sure he's right. "Xavier, were the Gestapo all in uniform when they arrested Monique?" I ask.

"Oui, Luc except for one man, I guess French, in civilian clothes and wearing a beret."

"And dark glasses?" I say.

"Yes" replies Xavier, quizzically.

"I thought so. I think you'll find he's not French but an Abwehr agent named Sergeant Karl Metzger. Our late school teacher friend must have been behind this."

Metzger is getting on my nerves. The next day, 17 September, we discover that Jacques was right. Monique was already in Lyon undergoing interrogation at the Gestapo HQ after which Metzger accompanied her to Fresnes prison in Paris. Montèlimar has been 'burnt'. It's time to get out. At noon I call my team and the local cell leaders together for a final briefing at our original hideaway in the woods which Monique didn't know about, just as a precaution. Xavier, Jacques, Marc and the Bidous plus Anne-Marie, on her lunch break from the telephone exchange, and Father Thibault are all here.

"Mes amis, following Monique's arrest the time has come for

us to move quickly. The Gestapo have their methods of extracting information and while Monique is one tough lady and we have pretty watertight security we would be irresponsible not to protect our circuit as best we can."

The people around the table shift uneasily. But they have already acted professionally. They immediately closed down the Daujat postbox and ceased using it as a safe house. I feel pretty secure that nothing Monique was forced to reveal could endanger those who weren't at the Bidou farm. But the rest of us are all at risk if she talks. And when an agent is captured you must always assume they will talk.

I can sense the tension in the room.

"I must leave as soon as possible. The cells for which you're responsible are fast reaching their maturity. You're well armed and equipped and thoroughly trained. It's time for you to take personal charge of your cells. I'll still be contactable and will still visit as and when I can.

Xavier will remain here as the wireless operator for the time being. All messages to and from Xavier will now be left at a new location which Jacques will reveal to you. We are removing everything compromising from the Bidou farm just to be safe. Jacques has found alternative accommodation for Marc, Benoit and Laurent. We don't want any evidence here which may put the Bidous at risk.

Jacques will stay here for the next few weeks to ensure there are no problems. Once Jacques leaves to join me he'll hand over responsibility to Marc. Jacques will also be responsible for contacting all the other cell leaders in the Rugby circuit and for ensuring that lines and means of communication are clarified, working and secure.

Marc, Anne-Marie and Father Thibault, along with all other

cell leaders, you will maintain constant contact with Jacques in order to transmit requests, receive instructions and to get agreement for action. It's imperative that all subversive actions are approved and carefully controlled. The powers that be say that our existence will be justified if we can shorten the war by just a few days. I think we can do better than that looking at the team we've got."

They relax now, perhaps welcoming the increased responsibility.

One final request, I know I don't need to tell you, of all people, how important the Resistance families of France are to the success of our mission. People like Monique and myself have only our own lives to lose but you in the Resistance risk your own lives and those of your families and friends, your homes and your livelihoods, on a daily basis. We must try at all costs to avoid putting them, and ordinary French people, in danger. Sometimes it will be inevitable, but by keeping to the rules of security and by exercising extreme caution and consideration we can limit the danger." The room is dead quiet. "I must leave you now but I do so in the certain knowledge that Jacques will stand in for me here. I love him as a brother. I know you do too. He will deal with any problems you may have. A bientot, mes amis. Bon courage et bonne chance."

There are few dry eyes in the room as we say goodbye.

Five minutes later I ride down the track to join the road to Beaurepaire. Once I return the borrowed motorcycle I'll get a ride down to Digne.

22

Digne-les-Bains, chief town of the department of the Basses Alpes, is an agreeable summer resort lying along the left bank of the Bléone. Before the war its hot springs attracted rheumatic Germans by the coachload. In the fall and winter it was a popular base for Italian climbers of the Provençal Alps.

The 15th-century cathedral of St-Jérôme, built on the highest point of the hill, dominates the town of some 13,000 souls. Uncomfortably close to the cathedral stands its nearest neighbour, the fortress-like prison, now Gestapo headquarters. Its Nazi flags have been clearly visible through the plain glass cathedral windows ever since the stained glass was removed by prudent vergers.

Opposite the prison, in the top-floor apartment of a four-storey wooden building, sandwiched between two elegant stone houses on the Rue de la Mère de Dieu, Alain the 'pianist' is waiting to meet with Luc. It's 9:30 p.m. The streets outside are dead quiet save for the starlings, ducking and diving in and out of the prison courtyard.

Alain has chosen this seemingly vulnerable apartment for his base precisely because it is so close to Gestapo HQ. He is banking on the fact that his transmitting equipment is less likely to be detected amongst the Gestapo's own devices.

I'd been here in Digne for two weeks before my first call on Alain. I booked into the unassuming Hotel Square Monge without alerting anyone in the local Resistance, except for Henri Frenay's friend, the American vet, Marianne. We are using her house as a postbox. I've used the last two weeks to explore Digne and the surrounding area, thinking about its suitability as a headquarters. I've also taken the opportunity to follow Alain to learn his habits as I'd not had a chance to get to know him before I sent him to Digne shortly after his arrival with Monique. He is likely to be of pivotal importance in the future.

Marianne is a tough, no-nonsense, can-do lady of about thirty. A Vassar girl. She exudes efficiency and self-confidence and is refreshingly direct. At the outbreak of war she left the then neutral US to come to her mother's hometown, Digne, to offer services that went beyond those of the typical vet.

I explained to her that, whereas it was likely I'd be returning to England for a week or two in the near future, I was planning on setting up a Rugby circuit HQ in the area and would need to rely on her facility. She immediately offered to help. I left a message for Alain saying "Will come to your place tomorrow 9:30 p.m. please leave door open. L."

I feel reassured by Alain and Marianne and I am convinced that the Digne area, with its proximity to the coast; to the Route Napoleon; to the gathering Maquis presence on the Vercors plateau and to the major German Army presence in Grenoble, has all the makings of an important base. But I don't want to be in the town itself. I need a place secure for my own and others' comings and goings. I also need to be near convenient dropping zones.

Having taken the precaution of selecting a room with a window providing access to the street, I quietly climb out of my bedroom window, close it behind me and move silently through the darkened streets of Digne to the Rue de la Mère de Dieu.

I climb the four storeys, apparently without being seen by the neighbours, and find Alain waiting for me; a pot of coffee on the gas stove.

We talk by candlelight. One of the reasons I've come to see Alain is to get him to recommend a convenient village in the surrounding area that will meet my requirements for an HQ.

I tell Alain about the Turrel family, Carmen Dupré's cousins. He promises he will explore the area where they live and report back to me by the time I return from England.

I still hope that I might be able to postpone or even cancel altogether any trip to the UK but at noon the following morning, when I go to Marianne's postbox, I find a message from Baker Street:

GO TO PARIS NOVEMBER 12 STOP MEET BISTRO PLACE CLICHY EIGHT THIRTY SUNDAY MORNING MAN WITH FIGARO NEWSPAPER END

No request this time. An order. I go back to my hotel room and start to pack my bags.

Ever since my arrival in Cannes I've been in sole control of my own, and my people's, destiny. I've hand-picked the best people available. All close-knit, loyal and secure teams relying upon each other, and ultimately upon me. Now I'm being ordered to leave them to return to Baker Street and its desk-bound bureaucrats. Why can't they leave me to get on with the job? I've grown used to this covert world. It's become a drug to me and by leaving it, even temporarily, I know I will have withdrawal pangs. Worse, I am bound to forget some small but vital element in maintaining my security, and my life, by being lulled into another, safer, world back in the UK. I belong here with these people. They've become my family, the only family I have.

Reluctantly I finish packing, check out of the hotel, go to the station and buy a ticket to Cannes where I can catch the train for Paris.

The night train from Cannes pulls into the Gare d'Orsay early on Saturday 13 November. Rather than stay in a hotel I decide to go to see Carmen Dupré in Montrouge.

Just before lunch I arrive at the little house on the rue des Mauvais Garçons. I'm about to ring the bell when I notice that the name Dupré is no longer written in Carmen's elegant handwriting but is printed in ostentatious black and gold block letters. This is not like Carmen Dupré. I walk along the street to find the laundress' shop. I'm pretty sure I will recognize her from the time I stayed with Carmen after Marchais' arrest and pretty sure that she will know if anything has happened to Carmen Dupré.

As soon as I walk into the lavanderie the laundress recognizes me. She looks suddenly flustered. She is attending to an elegantly-dressed lady, an unusual sight in austere Paris suburbs.

"Bonjour Monsieur, your laundry is not quite ready. I am having a little difficulty with a stubborn stain. Can you come back in half an hour?"

I say "Of course" and leave quickly.

Once the 'stubborn stain' departs I return to the lavanderie, now empty. The laundress welcomes me in, locks the door and turns the sign over. Closed for Lunch.

"Oh, Monsieur, it is good to see you. Obviously you did not ring the bell of Mme Dupré's house; it is now occupied by a German colonel. That was his mistress who just left."

She ushers me into a small work room. I sit down while she boils some water for tea.

"What has happened to Carmen Dupré, Madame?"

"Je ne sais pas, Monsieur. Je ne sais pas. I wish I knew. The house was stormed one night by the Gestapo. They ransacked it and then left. The following day the colonel and his mistress moved in. No one has heard a word from Mme. Dupré since. That was just over two weeks ago. Unfortunately three Resistance members have come to seek refuge and each one has been arrested. Mon Dieu, when will this nightmare end?"

We talk, or rather she talks, as we drink the weak tea.

I tell the laundress I'll stop by next time I'm in Paris and leave for the station. I spend the night at a hotel near to Clichy.

At precisely 8:30 the following morning I walk into the only open bistro in the Place Clichy. There are just a few people in there. I sit at a table next to a square-built man with a shock of dark hair, roughly my own age. He is reading Le Figaro.

The man ignores me. A waitress takes my order. While waiting for the coffee I initiate the communication.

"Can you tell me what the weather forecast is for tomorrow?"

"It's fine" replies the man, now looking me straight in the eye, "how is the weather down south?"

"Much the same" I say "but getting hotter in certain areas."

There's something not quite right about this guy. I can't put my finger on it. Perhaps it's my paranoia, but I remember Henri Frenay's comment "a man's look hardly ever plays false." I make a mental note to check him out when I get to London.

"You are to take the 4:15 train to Angers this afternoon. You will be met. There will be a black Citroën outside the station entrance, the driver will be smoking a cigarette."

The man stands up, offers me his copy of Le Figaro and leaves.

At 0800 the following morning the Hudson bomber Angers deposits me and my fellow passengers, François Mitterand and Pierre du Passage, at RAF Tangmere. I change into my Second

Lieutenant's uniform, get in the back of a black saloon and pick up the copy of The Times thoughtfully procured for me by the SOE driver.

As the car approaches south London and moves sedately through the dismal, grey, rainy streets, I feel suspended in no-man's land. Just one short airplane flight has lifted me from a world where I have to be ever vigilant, secretive, constantly in fear of my life and in charge of my destiny, and deposited me in the relative safety of these London streets. Jacques, Xavier and the others are far removed.

But it's London that seems foreign to me.

The car moves silently along the Purley Way, past Croydon Aerodrome as I skim the newspaper.

Harrods advertises Beaver and Lamb Coats, they have four of the former in stock at £38 and five of the latter at £49.

The King and Queen entertained the Regent of Iraq, Emir Abdullah, at Buckingham Palace, the King having conferred the GCVO on the Emir that morning.

Mr Michael Tippett will lead a group of madrigal singers at the National Gallery later today to coincide with the unveiling of Holbein's portrait of Christina of Denmark.

Sotheby's are holding an auction of Lace, Fans, Ceramics and Glass while Christie's are disposing of the late Mrs Harry McCalmond's casket of fine jewels.

Surreal. Fucking surreal.

Over in the West End, Oscar Wilde's Ideal Husband is receiving mixed reviews; Miss Peggy Ashcroft, fresh from her movie success in Quiet Wedding, is treading the boards in Dark Room at the Whitehall Theatre while Sybil Thorndike is performing in Lottie Dundas at the Cambridge and the non-stop revue is still not stopping at the Windmill.

Smetana's opera, The Bartered Bride, is being revived at Sadler's Wells. The Market is up and 1,600,000 turkeys are expected to be sold by Christmas.

I fold the paper and place it on the seat beside me. I feel sick to my stomach.

Luc would feel still sicker if he knew that his erstwhile courier Monique was even now on her way to Ravensbruck (where she would be gassed in April 1945); Claudine, already at Ravensbruck, was close to madness with pain from her torture at the hands of the Gestapo; and, as Luc's car was pulling into Baker Street, Sergeant Karl Metzger was a few hundred kilometres away in Paris badgering his superiors to allow him to travel to Digne where his informers had spotted his prey the previous week.

The driver, having been detoured by bomb damage to the Marylebone Road, passes by the SOE HQ at 64 Baker Street and the French Section Offices at Number 83 before pulling up in front of Orchard Court, a Federal-style block of flats on the corner of Portman Square and Baker Street.

I enter Orchard Court and take the elevator up to the fifth floor. The door is opened by Park, formerly the doorman at the Paris branch of the Westminster Bank, and now the all-seeing, all-knowing, guardian of the SOE's apartment in the building.

"Good morning Sir. Trust you had a good journey?"

"Fine thanks. Everything OK here?"

"As well as can be expected, Sir." Park is a man of few words, and those few very carefully chosen. I catch a glimpse of another agent leaving as the lift doors close.

"Busy day today, huh?" I say to Park

"About usual, Sir." There's not much point in talking to him. Lips sealed tight.

We walk down the hall of the spacious apartment (renowned among agents for its black-tiled bathroom and onyx bidet) and knock on the door of the 'sitting' room. The British sit; the Americans live.

"Enter" Maurice Buckmaster is, indeed sitting, in one of the armchairs.

"It's good to see you back here in one piece Luc," he says, calling me by my nom de guerre and motioning me to a chair "I'm afraid you are the exception lately. We've had a terrible time in the Paris area. The whole circuit has been decimated yet again. Damned if I know how this time. That Alice woman is now working for us again, or so we hope. But that's not what you're here for. We need to know how things are going for you. Vera is going to join us. Cuppa tea?"

Park brings in tea. Vera Atkins arrives as elegant as ever. Buckmaster, obviously delighted to have some real first-hand information at last, asks me to bring them up to date on what is happening in the south of France. I'm tempted to say that if he had read the reports I'd been sending he would know, but I hold my tongue.

For the next few hours I paint a picture of thousands of courageous and restless men, women and children who risk their lives in the hope, so far pretty much in vain, that they would be well armed with the promised weapons and provisions from Britain.

Vera Atkins looks faintly bored.

Buckmaster speaks. "My dear Luc…"

I wince.

"…you must think of this period as preparation for the big day, not as a period of intense activity itself."

Impatiently I reply "You can't keep thousands of men up in the hills doing nothing but training and waiting. These people are in constant danger. They need to see tangible results or they will become disillusioned and dangerous very quickly."

"It's their country, Luc. We are helping them" interjects Vera. I wonder if she would be so blasé if they had been English. I get the feeling that Vera is a tad xenophobic.

Buckmaster smiles his supercilious smile. He clearly fears I've 'gone native'; he's right.

I check my temper and continue "If we are truly to make a difference to the Allies' chances of success we need to cause as much angst to the enemy as possible. Now. We cannot do that unless we have support. We have promised them support. We cannot retain their loyalty unless we provide that support. So far our efforts have been pathetic."

"I understand your frustration" says Buckmaster, offering cigarettes around and lighting one for himself, "and it's not for want of trying. We are up against all sorts of barriers here. It's very much a chicken and egg situation. The paymasters don't want to divert supplies from other fronts unless they see results but I'm afraid France just isn't the priority at the moment."

I emerge several hours later, cynical and angry. "Not a priority" for fuck's sake!

I hail a taxi to take me to my hotel. Durrants again but without Lucy Price this time. They have forbidden me to contact her.

Not that he could have even if he'd wanted to. Lucy Price had been dead for two months. Killed by a German bomber offloading its unwanted bombs onto the Kent countryside following a raid on London.

Best he didn't know she was dead, they'd decided. Might have had a demotivating effect.

For the next two weeks, I've been interviewed endlessly by SOE staff desperately in need of first-hand information to boost their chances for getting increased appreciation, and funding, from the top brass. First the Chief of Operations (France) then the Head of Planning followed by the man responsible for briefing the agents.

Word gets around. Apparently my pacifist past and subsequent conversion has made an impression on the top brass. They promote me to Captain. Then I am summoned to Intelligence HQ, the first SOE agent to be accorded this 'privilege'.

I must have played my cards right because the flow of weapons increases accordingly. Both the Beaurepaire, where Father David's Brothers had rallied to the cause, and the Montèlimar dropping zones are now receiving regular supplies of arms and ammunition. Jacques reports that Resistance numbers are increasing in proportion to the arms supply but emphasises everyone's frustration at being Resistance mainly on paper. They are growing restless. They want action. They want me back. I can't get the image out of my mind: young men dressed in sandals and 'bleus' in unheated mountain huts at 3,000 to 4,000 feet in the freezing cold waiting for our supplies. And here I am in cosy Baker Street. I want to return.

The December moon period comes and goes. More meetings. More frustration.

It's now one boring day in mid-January. I am sitting in the small office allocated to me temporarily at 83 Baker Street reading through the reports on the Carte and Prosper circuits, the ones that had been so devastatingly infiltrated by Abwehr agents. The reports have been given to me by a guy called Nigel Miller. He's in charge of agent coordination.

One item in particular catches my eye. A Lysander pilot notes that "although losses so far have been pleasantly low" (very British terminology that) "one disturbing development has been the number of recent losses to agents dropped into the Angers area. On five separate occasions agents have been arrested on landing, or soon thereafter. Twice, recently, agents were machine gunned before they had even hit French soil."

I throw the report onto the table and pick up the phone. I want to call Martin Bettinson. Bettinson is Buckmaster's number two and, in Buckmaster's temporary absence, should be able to give me the answer. I start to dial the number and then think better of it. Instead I call Nigel Miller.

"Nigel Miller?"

"Yes"

"Luc here, Nigel. I've come across something in these reports. Can I stop in and have a word?"

"Certainly Luc. Second floor room 124."

Nigel Miller was a psychiatrist in civilian life. A short, skinny man with a mop of curly dark hair, he's a sort of male version of Vera Atkins. Calm, helpful and firm. His job is to keep all the agents happy.

"Nigel, I've come across a disturbing comment in one of the pilot's reports that you gave me and I am wondering if you've got any thoughts about it?"

"Shoot, Luc."

"Well this Angers dropping zone has a pretty bad record recently for losing agents. Is anyone here concerned about it?"

"I think so, yes. I've told Buckmaster. He agrees it sounds very fishy. Ten agents have been lost within the past six months."

"And what's he doing about it?"

"He's told Bettinson to get it sorted out. They've all been organized by D'Ancourt. He's one of our best men in the field. You met him in Paris. He was the guy in the Clichy Bistro who organized your pick-up. He's arranged 110 pick-ups himself. No one has done more. I'm sure he'd know if his circuit had been infiltrated. He's been there from the start. I did wonder if maybe that Alice woman had turned into a triple agent? She's been involved in two of the bad drops but Buckmaster is satisfied she's firmly on our side now that it looks as though the tide is turning in our favour."

"Well I'm glad it's being sorted out. Still, I think I'll warn my friends not to volunteer to be dropped at Angers."

"Don't blame you" said Nigel.

Interesting comment. I go back to my office.

23

One week later, on 4 February, I finally get the okay to return to the field. It's been almost three months that I've been stuck here in London. I am going to be taken out by Lancaster (I wonder how they got hold of that? SOE are hardly ever given the right to use such big bombers) captained by Squadron-Leader Cook with a crew of six, and dropped in Beaurepaire next Wednesday 9 February.

I've been taken off the shelf and allowed to start living again. I send a message to Jacques giving him the news and telling him to go to the Château de Julienne on Wednesday to ask Claude, son of the Comtesse, to join him in the reception committee. Usual dropping zone.

I spend the next two days gathering supplies, money and forged documents to take with me. I also arrange with Nigel Miller, 'the fixer', for several canisters of weapons to be dropped at the same time. It will be Christmas in February for the Rugby circuit!

On Monday 7 February Nigel Miller knocks on the door of my office.

"Come on in."

He looks worried.

"Hey, what's up. You alright?"

"I've just received an order direct from Bettinson telling me that you are to be dropped in Angers and not Beaurepaire." He sits down. He's shaking.

"No fucking way."

"But it's an order" says Miller, nervously. He's clearly afraid that I might try to make him do something he shouldn't.

I offer him a cigarette to calm his nerves. I'm not wholly surprised by this development but I thought there was only about a 30% chance it would come to this. Nevertheless it does give me time to think up a contingency plan.

"Nigel, what if the pilot does make a drop at Angers as requested and then flies on to Beaurepaire? I think this may be the perfect opportunity for you to find out if the Angers circuit is being infiltrated and if so by whom. You'll be a hero Nigel!"

I could see by his expression that this was just what he feared. He's about to be drawn into a dangerous plan that could backfire terribly. And yet…

"How well do you know this pilot, Squadron Leader whatever?" I ask.

"Squadron Leader Cook. He's a good mate of mine. Another colonial like you, but despite that a decent fellow."

He's getting his sense of humour back. "D'you think he'd be willing to bend the rules a bit if we are likely to save agents' lives, including mine?"

"Maybe if…"

"Great, let's go see him. Can you arrange that?"

"No problem," says Miller, warming to the idea. After all he's got a vested interest. He doesn't want any more men being lost on his watch.

Three hours later we meet near RAF Tangmere at the Unicorn Pub in Chichester. Squadron Leader Cook, "Call me Cookie", turns out to be a 6'5" Canadian rugby player who joined the RAF as soon as the war started. Nigel Miller had met him on a training course and persuaded him, against the RAF top brass' wishes, to volunteer to fly SOE agents into enemy occupied territories once or twice a month.

I take to the man right away. A real trooper. This may be plain sailing.

We hatch a plan then and there.

9:00 p.m., Wednesday 9 February – RAF Tangmere

"Everything all set Cookie?" I ask as we walk from the SOE car to the hanger at RAF Tangmere.

"You bet Luc. Nigel's done his stuff."

"Great. Where's the bod?"

"Already on board. All wired up and ready to go."

"What time are we off?"

"9:30 Luc, half an hour to go."

"Let's get a beer."

9:00 p.m., Wednesday 9 February – Angers, France

Gilbert D'Ancourt lit a new Gitanes from the dregs of the old one and threw the fag end onto the cold, dry earth. He was unusually tense for what had become a common or garden experience for him; receiving an agent and delivering him into the hands of the Gestapo.

Another agent. Another $5,000.

Not today, he still had to kick himself. This time it was $50,000 dead or alive.

Luc was not just any ordinary novice agent but the man who had organized the largest, most secure and potentially devastating Resistance circuit in all of France.

He had over 10,000 men under his control, they say; from the Italian border to Toulouse, from the Mediterranean to Lyon. His men were devoted to him. Buckmaster, his boss, apparently says he is 'the best loved man in France'. The Maquis, so often an uncontrollable bunch of thugs, have apparently become a highly organized fighting force after joining the Rugby circuit.

No, D'Ancourt rubs his hands in expectation as much as warmth, this is no ordinary agent. The Germans, in particular Karl Metzger who promised him an extra $10,000, would pay dearly for Luc dead or alive. And if D'Ancourt had anything to do with it, it would be dead.

He doesn't want this guy around causing trouble. He wants his money. Easier to kill and collect.

At quarter past ten a car drives cautiously over the field, its milky headlights dance among the trees illuminating the ten armed Gestapo men hiding in the bushes. It draws up next to where D'Ancourt is standing, dims its lights, then turns them off.

Karl Metzger coming to watch the fun.

"Is all prepared Gilbert?"

"Yes, Sergeant. We've received the BBC message. They are due to leave as scheduled."

D'Ancourt enjoys calling him Sergeant. He knows it gets his goat.

But Metzger is in another place today. He smacks his lips, rubs his leather gloves together and adjusts his dark glasses. He feels as though he is preparing for his first date, or for giving a piano concert. All nervous expectation. This will be his crowning moment. Promotion at last, with a capital P! His fantasies increase. The Führer will personally pin the Iron Cross on Colonel Karl Metzger. Would Colonel be sufficient recognition? Perhaps not.

"Gilbert, nothing must go wrong with this. Is that clear? Are you certain

you have cleared everything with London?"

"Don't fret, Metzger. I got a message from London confirming the drop had been changed from Beaurepaire to Angers yesterday morning. Plus we got the BBC message. The weather's good. It's watertight. Unless the Luftwaffe chase him away of course."

"Don't underestimate Luc, Gilbert."

"Relax, Metzger. Everything is fine. They are due here any minute now. Have you got my money?"

"Be patient, my friend. You will get your reward in full."

9:00 p.m., Wednesday 9 February – Château de Julienne, Champs Martin, France

Jacques sits despondently talking to Claude and the Comtesse at the Château. They are concerned over the message that Xavier has sent confirming that Luc will not be arriving that night after all.

DUE TO CHANGE IN PLANS LUC UNAVOIDABLY DETAINED NO DROP 9TH AWAIT FURTHER INSTRUCTIONS STOP

The message was unsigned.

"Just doesn't sound right to me" says Jacques "I know Luc, I'm sure he would have sent us a message, coded, himself. This is not his style. Something is wrong."

"We can only wait and see" says the Comtesse.

Neither Claude nor Jacques respond.

"I think that he will contact us soon enough. Have faith young man" says the Comtesse. "Goodness, I'm beginning to sound like Father David. It must be time for bed."

She bids them goodnight.

"I guess there's nothing we can do Claude? Luc wanted you to become part of the reception committee. He hopes you will join us when he returns."

"If he returns."

"He will, Claude. He will."

But Jacques is not so convinced.

24

Cookie pulls back the Lancaster's throttle to just above stalling level as we approach the Angers dropping zone. The bomber hums along reassuringly.

"Is Joe all ready to go Luc?" he yells.

"Just adding the finishing touches."

I manoeuvre Joe, the life-size dummy dressed in my clothes that Nigel Miller has organized via Special Effects, into position over the hatch.

"Lights at one o'clock Boss" shouts the navigator, "I can see the torches clear as anything."

The Lancaster responds to the recognition light with that day's code and circles around once before coming in low for the drop.

The wireless operator and I open the hatch door and secure 'Joe' ready to 'jump'. I test the ripcord attached to Joe's parachute and to the hatch bar to make sure it's taut and will open automatically.

"Go!" cried the navigator.

I push 'Joe' through the hatch and moments later the rip cord yanks itself free from the hatch bar. The parachute opens allowing 'Joe' to glide gracefully through the hundred or so metres to the ground.

I join Cookie in the cockpit. Instead of flying off immediately, Cookie dips to the east and circles around once more over the dropping zone just in time to see repeated flashes of machine gun fire as poor 'Joe' is shot to smithereens.

"Case proven" yells Cookie, slapping me on the back.

"Looks that way" I say, my heart skipping a beat or two.

We plot our course south-east for Beaurepaire.

Metzger, a man demented, banged angrily on the feeble field telephone.

"Allo... Allo" he screamed. Was no one in this war fighting these fucking Bolsheviks but him! Where are all these morons?

Grenoble? Poitiers? Clermont-Ferrand... No, no Luftwaffe officer was available to speak to Sergeant Metzger.

Finally, through Abwehr contacts, he is able to rouse the local Luftwaffe Duty Officer in Lyon.

"Oberstleutnant Heine?"

"Yes?"

"Metzger here, Abwehr Headquarters, Paris."

"What can I do for you, Metzger?"

"An RAF Lancaster bomber is on its way to Beaurepaire. It is due to arrive shortly. I want it destroyed, Oberstleutnant. It is going to drop a very important British Agent HE MUST NOT BE ALLOWED TO ESCAPE, Oberstleutnant. I will personally see to it that you are recommended for the highest possible accolade if you achieve this."

"Most kind of you, Herr Metzger. I will alert the barracks at St Etienne, they will see to it I'm sure"

Oberstleutnant Heine cut Metzger off before he had to listen to any more.

Then he dialled the barracks in St Etienne.

"Shit.........Flak!" yells Cookie, quickly placing the Lancaster into evasive mode.

Not a total surprise. D'Ancourt was aware that the dropping zone had been switched from Beaurepaire to Angers. It didn't take a genius...

Moments later the Lancaster was hit. Then hit again. "We're on fire Cookie." The wireless operator could see the flames licking the fuselage.

"You jump Luc. With all this ammunition on board this baby will blow at any minute."

I have no choice. "OK Cookie" I hurriedly adjust the parachute "ready to go."

"Crew prepare to bale out!"

Moments later there is an almighty explosion as the night sky appears to catch on fire.

Oberstleutnant Heine picks up the phone and dials.

"Abwehr Headquarters, Paris" says an officious female voice.

"Heine here, Luftwaffe, Lyon. Put me through to Metzger will you?"

Metzger grabs the phone.

"Metzger here"

"Good evening Metzger. Oberstleutnant Heine here, Luftwaffe , Lyon. I thought you'd like to know that we have dealt with your little problem as requested."

"Wonderful, Oberstleutnant. Are you absolutely certain?"

"Yes, absolutely. The plane must have been loaded with bombs. My men in St Etienne say they have never seen such an explosion. There is no chance anyone could have survived. Absolutely none at all."

Metzger put down the phone a happy man. No one would even have to know about the embarrassing situation at Angers. All they needed to know was that Sergeant Karl Metzger had arranged the murder of Captain Joseph

Quantock or 'Luc' and, with his death, put an end to the most sophisticated Resistance circuit in France. That in turn would probably mean that any Allied invasion of southern France would be delayed for several months. It would also mean that forces of the Fatherland would be freed to go to the North where they would be needed in case of a British invasion across the Channel.

With his chest thus puffed out he pulled out a pad of paper and sat down to write the report to end all reports.

25

With the intense heat and ear–splitting noise from the exploding aircraft followed by the ice cold air at 7,000 metres and the thick low-lying cloud obscuring my view, it's several moments before I even start to make sense of what's happening.

The explosion shot me through the sky like a cannon ball. Cookie and his men never had a chance. They were still putting on their parachutes when I jumped.

All I know is that I am on my way down to God knows where. Searchlights are piercing the cloud, aimed at the disintegrating aircraft, not at me. I fight against the pressure to draw a deep breath. This fall seems endless. The clouds are falling faster than I am which makes me think I am going up. Perhaps I'm dead and floating to paradise? Unlikely!

Then, a break in the clouds, snow is falling, it feels even colder, a building is coming up at me through the snow. I feel a sharp jolt and a painful clutch at my groin. It takes me a moment to realize what's happened. The silk parachute has wound itself around the chimney of some building and left me dangling several metres above the ground, £20,000 worth of French francs and many forged documents in my pockets.

Hoping I'm not on top of Gestapo headquarters, I pull out my knife and slash at the parachute cords.

A young girl pushes open an upstairs window. She stares down at me. Then she squeals with joy "Papa, Papa, a man has come from the sky!"

A man runs out of the front door and stands dumbstruck at the sight of me dangling from his roof.

"British?" he asks.

"More or less" I mutter through my frozen lips.

"You must get inside quickly. The Boche are everywhere." He then reappears at his daughter's bedroom window.

I hand over my knife and he slashes at the remaining cords. I yank at the parachute to pull it off the roof.

"I have to bury this first" I say; but it's stuck.

"Un moment" says the farmer. Seconds later he returns with his school-age son and daughter.

"These two will help."

I pull at the parachute, attempting to get the twisted cords over the chimney pot to gather them together. In no time at all, the farmer's son scrambles up the roof and eases the parachute over the chimney.

"Voila," he says proudly, hurling the remains of the parachute to the ground.

I give him the thumbs up.

"Come inside" says the farmer "did you come from the plane that exploded?"

"Yup, I did."

"No other survivors?" asks the farmer, closing the door behind us.

"I think not, my friend. The plane exploded as soon as I jumped."

"Get the wine, make an omelette," the farmer commands

his frightened wife as he helps me into the house. Then to his daughter, "Louisa, get some blankets off of our bed and some dry clothes from my cupboard." My body is rigid with cold. My eyes are almost frozen shut. The farmer pulls up an armchair in front of the fire so I can thaw out before attempting to undress.

The boy is outside folding up the parachute ready to bury it.

"It looks like your children have been through this before?" I say, hearing my words a little more clearly.

"Yes, once. A British pilot was shot down and somehow ended up at our door. He was in very bad shape. We nursed him back to health. An American lady came and took him away, I think to Spain" he pauses "you'd better stay here for the night. Even before you were shot down the place was crawling with Nazis. I hate to think what it will be like now."

"It's a great risk you're taking."

"We know. Our family is very grateful for what you are doing."

"And the children?"

"The children won't say a word. Some in their school brag about hiding Resistance people in their home. My children know it isn't true. They would never breathe a word, don't worry."

This makes me feel very small. An honest, modest family, living off the land, all putting their lives at risk. It doesn't bear thinking about but it doesn't bear not thinking about either. Not if you are to keep an ounce of humanity during this nightmare.

"I will stay tonight but no longer. I will have to leave tomorrow, for all of our sakes."

I gratefully sip the glass of wine and munch on the omelette that the farmer's wife has provided.

"Well, we will have to find a very clever way for you to leave," says the farmer, "I think every house will be searched in the morning, if not tonight."

Warmed and fed I go upstairs with the farmer. A camp bed in the attic has already been prepared and fresh clothes are laid out. I thank the man, gradually pull my clothes off, dry myself and settle down for the night, marveling at the heroism of ordinary people.

I think of Cookie and the others, and fall asleep on the dampened pillow.

It's not until the following morning, sitting down to breakfast with the farmer's family, that I realize I don't even know where I am.

"By the way. Where exactly are we? Are we far from Beaurepaire"

"Very close. We're just outside the hamlet of Champs Martin."

"Good God, that's great." Good old Cookie, right on target.

The farmer's family stares at me.

"Not so great" says the farmer, "German patrols and dogs have searched every house in the village, even the château. We know they'll be here before too long."

Suddenly there is a loud bang on the door. We all look up. I grab my gun. Nobody moves. The door is thrown open.

An elderly lady, dressed in her nightgown, hobbles in with her stick.

"Grandma, you are supposed to stay in bed" the farmer's daughter rushes to turn her grandmother around.

"I heard a strange man in the house. Is he Boche?!"

"Mother, please go back to bed. He's not Boche, he's French" the farmer's wife says as she gently turns the old lady around and guides her back upstairs to bed.

Suddenly, I have a thought. I ask the farmer "Are you familiar with Father David at the Dominican monastery in Beaurepaire?"

"Only by reputation. He is the prior isn't he? Sometimes he comes into Champs Martin. I think he is a friend of the local comtesse. She is very famous around here. Her son, Claude, is a manager at the Beaurepaire hydroelectric station."

"What? He is? Claude?" I don't believe my ears.

"Yes, you know him? He is a very powerful man."

My mind is racing. Maybe we should forget the hydroelectric station at L'Argentiere and concentrate on Beaurepaire instead.

"Monsieur, back to Father David. I have an idea that might allow me to escape and leave you in peace."

"Tell me" says the farmer offering one of his rolled-up cigarettes.

"Would your mother-in-law be prepared to play along if we called the priest and said she was very ill and asked him to come and perform last rites?"

"What a good idea" replies the farmer a little too enthusiastically.

"If you could let her in on the plan and somehow get a message to Father David to come here with a young priest, that's very important, he must bring a tall, young priest, then I think we have a solution."

"I'm sure I can convince her she's dying, she's been telling us that for years. It's my interest in saving her soul which will arouse her suspicion." The farmer's wife shoots him an angry look.

I grin. "OK. This is what I propose. Can you contact Father David at the monastery. He is sure to be able to travel freely. Tell him that Ignatius, that's the name Father David and I agreed I would use if I needed to contact him in an emergency, has specifically requested that he come himself and bring along a young priest. Once they get here, Father David can perform extreme unction, if that's what it's called," the farmer nods "on your mother-in-law. The young priest and I can exchange clothing. Can he stay here for a day or two until the Germans lose interest?"

"Of course, but why?"

"Well I'll need to borrow his clothes so I can leave with Father David. Meanwhile the real priest will have to lie low."

"OK. I'll call the monastery."

At 1:00 we hear three no-nonsense raps at the front door. I hide in the attic where, pistol at the ready, I can hear every word even if I can't see what's going on. The farmer opens the front door to what sounds like two German officers.

"Herr Rey?"

"Monsieur Rey, oui."

I like this guy. He doesn't take any shit.

"We are here with two priests. I understand your mother is dying."

"Mother-in-law" corrects the farmer. Even under these trying circumstances he is loathe to have anyone think she might be a blood relative.

"We will have a look around. Who else lives here?"

"My wife and I, and our two children. They are at school."

"Where is the old lady?"

"In her bed, of course."

The farmer asks Father David and his fellow priest, respectfully waiting outside, to come in and take a seat at the kitchen table. He then leads the two officers upstairs to the old lady's bedroom.

The farmer's wife, with copious onion-aided tears trickling down her face, is kneeling by the bedside in the darkened room as the officers walk in. The farmer stays in the background. A faint trace of almonds scents the air. The frail old woman lies motionless in the bed, her hands wound around a wooden crucifix.

After a moment or two surveying the scene, the Germans open the curtains releasing a shaft of light onto the would-be death-bed.

The old lady sits bolt upright.

"Shut the fucking curtains you stupid bastards!"

It's hard to tell who is more startled. The German officers, genuine fear in their eyes, stop dead in their tracks. The farmer's wife, having never in her life heard her mother swear let alone use such awful words, stares open jawed. Luc, with his ear to the floor, tries hard to stifle his laughter. Only the farmer seems unsurprised.

The two officers quickly leave the bedroom, make a cursory search of the remaining rooms without searching the attic and go down to the kitchen.

"She's ready for you, Father, the sooner you dispatch her, the better" says the senior of the two officers as they walk out of the house.

I emerge from the attic to greet Father David and Brother François and to thank the farmer and his wife for their excellent work. As for the old lady, well it had worked out for the best in the end.

The priests go upstairs to the children's bedroom. Father David puts on his appropriate vestments as if actually performing extreme unction (an act which, if carried out, the old lady has made quite clear would be a step too far. And no one was in a mood to argue).

Brother François, remarkably similar to me in age and height, even skin complexion (Father David had clearly foreseen the plan) exchanges his priestly clothes for mine.

Half an hour later, two men in priestly garb emerge from the Reys' farmhouse and, under the semi-watchful eye of the two German officers waiting at the gate, get into the primitive cart and head down the road in the direction of the monastery – and the château.

"Father, it's good to see you" Claude says, opening the door "and... Good Heavens, Luc!.. But....we thought. God, Jacques won't believe it." He shakes hands with both of us. "We thought you might possibly have been involved in that plane crash last night even though we were told your plane had been diverted."

"Is Jacques here, in the house?"

"Yes, upstairs I suspect. We've been raided by the Gestapo twice in the past three days. He thought they were back again."

The Comtesse de Julienne is sitting next to a blazing log fire in the drawing room of the Château. She is all concentration, her eyeglasses balanced on the end of her nose, her legs comfortably almost horizontal on a footstool as she tugs at an unruly thread stuck in her embroidery hoop before plunging it back, killing a Boche with each stab of the needle.

Relinquishing her embroidery, the Comtesse greets us both while Claude goes upstairs to find Jacques. "Luc, this garb must mean you have finally seen the light? Father David's powers must be even greater than I suspected!"

I bend down to give her a kiss.

"No such luck, Comtesse. Merely a disguise. It's good to see you again."

"Likewise. Your friend has been very concerned about you. He thought you might have been in that plane last night."

"I was, I got out just in time, unlike my friends."

"I'm so sorry," said the Comtesse, "you'll have some lunch? I'm sure you must be hungry."

She goes out to the kitchen to alert Lucille to expect two more for lunch.

Jacques rushes in, grabs me and kisses me on both cheeks. "Luc, Thank God. I can't believe it" we hug.

"It's good to see you my friend. Been looking after things OK?"

"Sure, as best we could, Luc" he smiles "I can't believe it. But we need to talk."

"Sure Jacques. Let's have something to eat first, OK?"

"Of course."

We all four sit down in the living room. I am keen to find out what the story is with Claude and his new job.

"Claude, I hear you've become a successful capitalist?"

"Well, something like that. Not bad as a first job. I'm director in charge of operations, whatever that means, at the Beaurepaire Hydroelectric station."

"Sounds good to me."

"It's got potential," interrupts Jacques, "just think what damage he could do."

"How did this come about Claude?" I ask, delighted with this unexpected entrée into our new number one target for destruction.

"Mama of course. She put in a call to my uncle who runs the place and I was hired the following morning."

"Quite a powerful lady, your mother."

Over lunch we talk about the increasing German presence in the area. There is now a large garrison of Luftwaffe and Waffen S.S. at Grenoble. The quantity and quality of Resistance activities have attracted unwelcome Gestapo attention and an enlarging of the Gestapo's southern headquarters in Lyon.

Jacques recounts the Rugby circuit's accomplishments while I've been in London:

150 men recruited and armed at Valensole; six derailments in the Rhone valley between Marseilles and Nice; sabotaging of materials given to the Italians after the Armistice; destruction of the viaduct at Antheor; production cut at factories in St Auban resulting in only 30% productivity; sabotage of the railway bridge at Carnoules, petrol dumps sabotaged with water and abrasives; a German leave train destroyed near Montèlimar with 60 casualties; the tunnel at Manosque and targets at La Coucourde and Cagnes destroyed.

The Comtesse looks over her eyeglasses at me. "I'm afraid you and your people have developed quite a reputation young man. One might even say you are a celebrity in this region. In fact, from what Father David tells me, in the whole of southern France."

"That's not very good news," I reply, "I've tried to be as

anonymous as possible. It doesn't pay to be too well-known."

"Perhaps it is a mixed blessing," she responds, "the number of young men who have flocked to the Maquis or joined the Resistance because of your reputation has increased enormously, has it not Jacques?"

"Oui, that's right Luc. We estimate there are close to 5,000 men in the Rugby circuit area now, and hundreds, maybe thousands of others in the Vercors region. It is rumoured to be the largest Maquis base in France."

"Not much use without arms and ammunition" I add.

"Any news on that front?" asks Father David, "we keep hearing rumors that the Allies are about to invade. No one knows if it will be in the north or the south. Some say it will be next month, led by the British in the north. Others say it will be sooner, led by the Americans in the south."

"No, no news just yet. Everyone was very tight lipped in England. The general feeling is that it will be in the north. I don't think anything is imminent though. You can usually sense when something big is about to happen. I didn't see any signs."

After lunch, Jacques and I walk down to the summer house at the bottom of the garden. We extract a couple of chairs for the winter storage and sit down to talk.

"Have you heard any news from Montèlimar lately?" asks Jacques.

"No, nothing for several weeks. Why?"

"Bad news I'm afraid. Very bad."

"Tell me"

"After we got your message from London three weeks ago instructing us to blow up the goods train…."

"Wait a minute, I never sent you any message telling you to blow up a train."

Jacques is stunned. "What? Who did then? Xavier received a message signed by you, using your security codes."

I mentally sift through the possibilities. It doesn't take long to come up with the answer. I try to remain calm.

"What happened, Jacques?"

"We blew up the train, as ordered. Unfortunately young Marc was sick so Roger Bidou volunteered to help instead. After the explosion we dispersed, as before. Someone must have seen Roger Bidou and informed on him. The Gestapo came for him the next morning. He resisted and they blew his brains out, in front of Sylvie, on the front steps of his house."

"The bastards."

"They didn't give him a chance."

"I didn't mean the Gestapo bastards, I meant the British bastards."

"The British? I don't understand."

"It's clear to me now. The only people who have access to my security codes are the SOE top brass. It was a test, Jacques. A fucking test of my loyalty. To see if I was a double agent they decided to test out our organization by giving instructions out in my name. By pretending to be me. They must have known what happened to Roger Bidou while I was still in England but they didn't say a word to me. They'd have known I'd have hit the roof. The stupid bloody idiots. I'm pretty sure I know the guy responsible too. I have had my suspicions about him."

"What kind?"

"I think there's a double agent at SOE HQ in London who is in cahoots with this guy D'Ancourt in Angers. At least D'Ancourt's cover is blown now so it won't be long 'til they put two and two together. Poor Roger Bidou. I'll go and see Sylvie, is she still there?"

"Of course. She'll never move."

"I'm not surprised. Good for her."

I am sad and angry but we have to get a move on. I fill Jacques in on the events of the past 24 hours. He brings me up to date with the recruitment and training figures. The conversation turns to Claude.

"What has brought about this change in the poor little rich boy, Jacques? I thought he might stay tied to his mother's apron strings forever."

"Well you told his mother that we'd take him into the réseau, Luc, so that is what we did. He trained with our people for three weeks. He's a changed man. I have the feeling he's been looking for something to be committed to all his life. Now he's found it."

"That's encouraging. What exactly is he doing at the power station?"

"That's what we were discussing when you arrived unannounced this morning.

When Claude was in Montèlimar with us we told him that the power station at Beaurepaire was a target for the RAF bombers. He looked dismayed. Turns out that the guy in charge of the power station is his uncle. His mother's brother.

Anyhow, he agreed to do a deal. If we could persuade the RAF not to bomb the power station, he would volunteer to get a job there and personally place charges on the eight transformers to put them out of business. He figures it'll be at least six months before the station can become operational again, meanwhile it will require most of the spare transformer oil in France to fix things. What's more the lack of electricity supply could well hold up the electrically-powered German naval base in Marseilles and the surrounding factories for weeks. German attempts to use other power stations will result in their being overloaded and will cause fuses to blow all across the region."

"Brilliant, Jacques."

"Now all you have to do is to stop the RAF from bombing the power station in the meantime. And we may not have much time."

"I'll see to it. Can we get a message to London this evening?" I pause, "on second thoughts I'll go back to Montèlimar myself and give the message to Xavier. It'll give me a chance to see Sylvie Bidou and to catch up with the réseau."

"The bike's in the garage, here. I've been using it myself. Take it…"

"Excellent. I'll go right away. Tell the Comtesse thanks for lunch will you. I'll be back within a few days."

"Watch out for the Boche. Better change your clothes first, there aren't too many priests who travel around on motorcycles."

26

The Director's office on the fifth and top floor of the Beaurepaire Power Station was a conventional, sparsely furnished utilitarian room. It suited the Director, an oversized, middle-aged man in a grey suit with bad teeth and stains on his lapel.

It was ten o'clock on Tuesday morning. The Gestapo had already paid him a visit and he was in no mood for banter or tiresome interruptions. He suffered from dyspepsia which caused him intense stomach pains and necessitated catnaps at intervals throughout the working day.

He was not amused therefore when his layabout nephew, for whom he had only recently invented a job as Operations Director, insisted on seeing him.

"Claude I have work to do" he said walking up and down in front of his desk drinking a medicinal whisky and water out of a silver flask. "Why don't you go back to your office and ask your secretary to make you some coffee. That should be just about enough work for you for today, no?"

"Actually Uncle Thierry…"

"Monsieur le Director if you don't mind" he said, pausing momentarily, for added effect.

"D'accord, Monsieur le Director, I have a very important and urgent matter to discuss with you."

"I'll bet. The drinking water in the cafeteria not cold enough for the son of the Comtesse? Or perhaps the colour of carpet on his office floor is not to his liking?"

Claude showed no sign of reaction.

The Director slumped his oversized body down into his oversized desk chair and leaned forward condescendingly onto his desk.

"I'm all ears."

"I have an offer to make, Monsieur le Director. The Royal Air Force is planning to bomb the power station in the very near future. There will be much loss of life. The station will be destroyed, resulting in untold damage to the German war aims; confusion and mayhem throughout the south-east, devastation to our community and no doubt, should you survive, the loss of your job. My family and yours will be rendered homeless if not wiped out down to the last woman and child."

The Director could not believe his ears, or eyes. Had the little twerp lost his marbles completely? Doesn't he know he could be arrested and sent to work in a German labour camp for outbursts such as this? He dabbed the beads of sweat forming on his forehead with his handkerchief.

"Are you mad! How dare you come in here and say things like this! I've a good mind to call the guards and have you taken away for your own good."

Claude, unperturbed, continued.

"If you agree to do a deal with me then all of the above will still happen except for the devastation to our community. All lives will be spared and there will be no threat to you or your loved ones."

The Director picked up the phone to call the guards.

"I wouldn't do that if I were you, Uncle Thierry." The Director looked up and found himself staring into the barrel of a gun. He slowly put the telephone back on its cradle, and began to shake.

Claude continued, "My proposal is this. You provide me and a colleague of mine from the Resistance with a pass to come onto the site at night. I will place charges on each of the eight transmitters which we will then put out of action. As a result the power station will have to close down for several months at least and much of the industry in the south-east will cease to operate."

"Don't you think I know that, you idiot. The whole of Marseille would be plunged into darkness. The Germans would explode with fury! You cannot be serious. I suggest you stop playing these silly games, put away that toy pistol and go home to mummy."

"It is now twenty minutes past ten. I will wait for your answer until 11:30. I must warn you that if you do not agree I can assure you that the power station will be destroyed with much loss of life. Should anything happen to me, my friends in the Resistance have instructions to hunt you and, I regret to say, your family down and ... well I do not want to go into details but shall we say the ending would be prolonged and uncomfortable."

Claude replaced his gun, turned on his heels and left the room.

The dazed Director was now sweating profusely. Although his handkerchief was soaking wet he still dabbed at his throat, neck and forehead. He started to shake uncontrollably. His secretary, Mme. LeLonge, came in and, upon seeing the state of him, turned around and left.

Ten minutes later the Director, who never visited anyone else's office, walked down to Claude's office. A departure from character that did not escape the notice of Mme. LeLonge.

He opened the door, walked in, closed it carefully, strode up to Claude's desk and plonked down onto one of his two armchairs.

"Assuming for a moment that you are serious, what proof have I got that the RAF won't bomb us all anyway?"

"You can write out a message, just a phrase will do, and I will have it relayed back from London by the BBC tomorrow night. It will be confirmation that, if my sabotage is successful, they will not bomb."

"But this is blackmail!"

"Précisément"

At 7:25 the following evening, the Director of the Beaurepaire Power Station excused himself from the family dinner table, went down to the cellar and switched on his illegal radio set tuned in to the BBC.

He returned, ashen faced, ten minutes later. His message, Madame Souris a une Maison, still ringing in his ears.

It seemed he had underestimated his nephew.

The bitingly cold air aided concentration as Claude and Jacques gripped the perimeter fencing of the Beaurepaire Power Station with the flared-out jaws of their wire cutters at 9:00 on the night of the BBC broadcast. They removed just enough fencing for a man to crawl through. If this was to appear an outside job it would have to look convincing.

That done, they walked up to the main gate where the two German guards glanced at their passes.

"What brings you here so late in the day Herr Claude?"

"I've left my briefcase inside. I need to discuss the new requirements for additional generating capacity with my colleague here before your General Rumsteen comes on his inspection tour tomorrow." They let them inside.

Claude already knows the layout pretty well and Jacques had pored over the floor plans. They head to the north-eastern sector of the power station where the eight big transmitters are housed.

Apart from the two German guards on duty at the main entrance there is only a skeleton crew at night. Two Milice guards sit inside the massive control room, playing cards. An inspection was supposed to be made hourly but Claude knows that the guards rarely move from the control room, especially when it's this cold. They change over at 10:00 p.m. when the relief guards are due to take over.

Claude has bargained on the fact that they would remain in the control room tonight.

Of course he has an alibi of sorts for being there. He has a pass from the Director and after all, he is Director of Operations. But the fewer people that notice him the better.

Once they get to the room where the transmitters are housed, Jacques carefully opens the straps of his khaki knapsack and extracts eight SOE regulation delayed action fuses.

Each man takes four of these time pencils, inserts the detonator into the spring snout, squeezes the copper tube which crushes the ampoule containing the corrosive liquid and shakes it hard to make sure that the liquid is in contact with the steel wire that restrains the spring-loaded striker. When the corrosion is complete the striker will be released to fire a cap, thus igniting the detonator.

They then remove the safety strips; black for ten minutes delayed action; red for half an hour; white for two hours; green for five-and-a-half hours. They figure that three hours would be about right, that will mean the transmitters should blow around 12:30 a.m. At this cold temperature the ignition time may be delayed by up to an hour.

Then they remove the white safety strips on each pencil, check that they are all in place and leave the room without disturbing the guards.

"Jacques, wait here for me. I need to get the briefcase that I said I had forgotten."

"OK"

Claude walks up to the fifth floor, passes by the secretaries' office, and opens the door to his own office. His briefcase is lying on the floor. He picks it up and, walking by the secretaries' office without noticing Mme. LeLonge still at her desk, retraces his steps to the main staircase. He walks casually down the stairs to meet Jacques, waiting at the bottom.

It's ten minutes to 10:00 when they walk out of the front gate, thank the German guards and make their way, by a circuitous route, back to the château.

Back in the secretaries' office, Madame LeLonge is still at her desk waiting until 10:00 when her husband finishes his duty in the control room. Why, she asks herself, would the new Director of Operations be coming into the office at almost 10:00 at night to pick up a briefcase that she happens to know is empty?

Strange goings on. First the Director visits M. Claude's office, an event unparalleled in her fifteen years at the Beaurepaire Power Station. Then M. Claude arrives at night-time to pick up an empty briefcase.

She decides to mention this to her husband. After all he is a captain in the Milice. He should know about such things.

Father David and I are playing cards, trying to keep calm, when Claude and Jacques walk in the front door of the château at half past ten. Father David's plan is to whisk Jacques and me off to the monastery preparatory to smuggle us out of town tomorrow during the celebrations for the life of Blessed John of Fiesole, otherwise known as Fra Angelico. While this is not an obligatory feast day in the Dominican calendar, Father David explains, it's an optional one and Fra Angelico is a personal favourite of his, so in Beaurepaire it has become obligatory.

"Gentlemen, we'd best be on our way" says Father David, not wanting to stretch his curfew privileges too far.

"Be right with you, Father. Everything work out OK?" I ask Claude.

"So far so good Luc. All the charges have been laid. The German guards were relaxed. All is set for 12:30."

"Well done you two. Claude, you're going to need to get out of here as soon as possible. Can you join us in Digne? We're off there tomorrow."

"Yes, I've already talked to Jacques about it. I'll meet you at the monastery in the morning."

"I think you'd be safer coming tonight."

"I'll be OK. I have things to put in order here. Papers to burn and so on. I don't want the Gestapo to pin anything on Mother."

Reluctantly I agree.

"We'll wait up till the fireworks," Jacques yells as we hoist ourselves up into Father David's cart.

"Me too" says Claude as he waves us off.

At 12:20 a deafening explosion rocks the Beaurepaire power station, quickly followed by two more, then three more, then another two.

The night sky is unnaturally bright for the second time in as many weeks over Beaurepaire.

The monks, and non-monks, standing in the cloister of the Dominican abbey were lit up as if by a giant ethereal sunbeam.

The local Comtesse, her son and her maid, sitting out unusually late on their terrace, drank a toast to the brightened sky.

Two German guards deserted their posts rather than face the inevitable dispatch to the Russian front.

The pyjama-clad Director stared in horror out of his bedroom window and took a large un-medicinal gulp of whisky.

The Director's secretary, Madame LeLonge, cajoled her husband into getting up, getting dressed and, without delay, presenting himself in person at the house of Olivier le Duc, commander of the Beaurepaire Milice.

It was four o'clock in the morning by the time the Milice unceremoniously broke down the door of the Château de Julienne, ignored the insults of the rudely awakened Lucille and strode up the stairs in search of the Comtesse's son.

Half an hour later Claude sat, handcuffed to a chair, in front of Olivier le Duc's desk in a back room of the Beaurepaire jail. Having refused to answer any questions, he was informed that he would be taken the following morning to Gestapo headquarters in Grenoble where it was unlikely that his interrogators would be tolerant.

Claude's only request was that he be allowed to speak to a priest before being moved.

Le Duc, still clinging to his Catholic faith and vaguely intimidated by the thought that he had arrested the son of the Comtesse de Julienne, picked up the phone and made two calls.

Gestapo HQ in Grenoble would send one of their agents out first thing in the morning with a car.

The Dominican monastery, told simply that they had a nameless prisoner who had requested absolution, would send a Brother over at 6:00 a.m., immediately following the early-morning Liturgy of the Hours.

Brother Isidore, secretary to the prior, arrived promptly at 6:00 a.m. and was escorted into the cell where Claude, still handcuffed, lay on a bare mattress.

The consultation had lasted barely five minutes when Brother Isidore rapped on the door to signal to the guards that his visit was completed. Pulling up his hood for protection against the early-morning chill, he scurried purposefully through the town and up the hill to the monastery where he would report to Father David who, although he had his suspicions, was as yet unaware of the identity of the prisoner.

Gestapo Sergeant Frederick Mayer arrived at the Beaurepaire jail at 9:30 that same morning. He told his driver to wait out front in the car. Sergeant Mayer was of the opinion that the presence of a Gestapo vehicle in town had an agreeably intimidating effect on the local populace. He spent the next hour in conference with Olivier le Duc extracting every piece of relevant information he could obtain about the previous night's proceedings.

At 11:00 a.m. precisely, Gestapo Sergeant Mayer ordered Olivier le Duc to deposit his handcuffed prisoner in the back seat of the waiting Citroën preparatory to their leaving for Grenoble. With a stern warning to le Duc that he planned to return to question, among others, the Director of the Beaurepaire Power Station, Mayer himself got into the back seat next to Claude and instructed his driver to take the St Barthelemy road to Grenoble, due to the alternative route apparently being closed for roadworks.

At 11:00 a.m. precisely, Father David lifts his arms to quieten the Dominican monks assembled for their annual procession from Beaurepaire to the chapel of St Barthelemy in honour of Blessed John of Fiesole.

The local people have turned out in significant numbers to watch the procession, particularly well attended today. Normally only 40 or so monks turn out for the procession. Today it's 160. But if you count carefully, there are 162.

God of eternal beauty, in your providence you inspired Blessed Fra Angelico to reveal in images of earth the tranquil harmony of heaven. With the help of his prayers and by following his example may our lives reveal that same splendour to the hearts of all our brothers and sisters. We ask this through our Lord Jesus Christ, your Son, who lives and reigns with you and the Holy Spirit, one God, for ever and ever.

Father David finishes the short prayer and instructs the monks to start processing in the direction of St Barthelemy.

The virtuous assembly is barely four minutes into the procession before the monks perambulatory meditations are rudely interrupted by the claxon of a black Citroën.

Obediently the six-man-wide snake of monks parts to allow the Citroën, slowed now to a crawl, to proceed through the centre of the throng. They then close ranks behind the car. But as soon as the ranks close behind them, the ones in front divide so the Citroën's journey is slowed but not unduly impeded.

When the car penetrates through to the centre of the 162-man procession however, the ranks in front remain closed, thus enveloping the Citroën.

Obligingly, both the German sergeant and his driver roll down their windows to hurl orders and abuse at the monks. At that moment Jacques and I, one on either side of the automobile, slide short length, silent, single shot sleeve guns down our monastic sleeves and into our right hands. I press the muzzle against the sergeant's temple while at the same time pulling the trigger with my thumb. 'Brother' Jacques similarly dispatches the driver, pushes his body into the passenger seat and climbs behind the wheel. I clamber over the sergeant's body to undo Claude's handcuffs and Jacques applies gentle pressure to the accelerator. The procession of monks divides to allow the Citroën through.

Once out of sight of the procession the Citroën gathers speed.

"You OK Claude?" I ask.

"All the better for seeing you two. My God that was close," he rubs his freed wrists and relaxes for the first time that day.

"We're going to drive as far as Saint-Étienne and then dump the car," I explain, "we've got to make it look as though it's been ambushed out here to prevent any reprisals. This is near to a Luftwaffe base and it will be hard for them to pin the blame on anyone. Once we deal with the car, we'll make our way overland to Digne."

Twenty minutes later Jacques turns into a side road, stops the car and switches off the engine. The three of us jump out, reposition the driver's body behind the steering wheel and the sergeant's body in its appropriate place in the back seat.

I place three tyre bursters on a downward slope of the Grenoble road. Jacques and Claude manoeuvre the Citroën into position about ten metres up hill from the explosives. Turning on the engine he jumps quickly to safety as the car heads downhill and runs over the explosives. Only one of the charges works but that's enough to force the car off the road and into a ditch. The Germans' bodies slump over the far side of the car, facing the earth.

The three of us gather up any evidence left over from the bursters and take off across the fields in search of some sort of transport that will get us to Digne by nightfall.

27

Seyne-les-Alpes, an ancient market town, hugs the great Montagne de la Blanche, Louis XIV's great citadel, at 2,000 metres and provides impotent security for the town's fewer than one thousand inhabitants. The 13th-century church's mutilated sculptures speak of the region's troubled past. The spa town of Digne-les-Bains lies 30 km to the south. To the east is Barcelonnette and the Italian border. To the north-west, the Route Napoleon winds its way northwards through Gap and beyond, skirting the eastern edge of the ominous great plateau of Vercors. Romantics still hear the drum beats of the returning Emperor's gathering forces as he made his way north to his tumultuous welcome in Grenoble.

Under normal circumstances, Seyne-les-Alpes is a dozy town of blameless people, passed through, rather than visited, except by skiers practicing their manoeuvers on the slopes of Grand-Puy during the season.

But this is February, 1944 and circumstances are not normal. Although there are no German uniforms as such in Seyne, there is a garrison down the road in Digne and another in Barcelonnette now that the Italians have either been arrested or fled across the border. And of course there are Milice, ever vigilant in monitoring the behaviour of their fellow Frenchmen.

As the church bell, comfortingly familiar, strikes 6:00 p.m., Madame

Marie-George Turrel rests her bicycle against the shop window and fumbles in her pocket for the keys to lock the door of the tabac. It has been a hard day. The innkeeper's wife, Madame Dupard, in her usual obstreperous tone, lectured the tabac queue on the dangers that the Resistance, and in particular the Maquis, represent to law-abiding townfolk. Her words still ring in Madame Turrel's ears.

"The Germans are saving our country from being taken over by the Jews and the Bolsheviks. These so-called Resistance people and those draft-evading Maquis, with their Spanish masters, hiding up in the hills stealing and raping, they are putting all our lives at risk. The Germans will stop being benevolent masters if we don't turn these people over to them. You mark my words. They will come to our town, our homes, and pull our loved ones from their beds and shoot them unless we turn these gangsters over to them first. It is our duty."

As Madame Turrel cycles through the fading light towards her home in Selonnet, she thinks through the words of the innkeeper's wife. And the compliant responses of the townspeople in the queue, all except for old Monsieur le Môquet, the farmer whose son fled to the Vercors to avoid being sent to Germany with the STO. He was furious with Mme. Dupard.

"You do not deserve to call yourselves Frenchmen!" he harangued, "these young men are risking their lives for us, Madame Dupard. It is you, not they, who are collaborating with the enemy of France. Silence is the worst type of collaboration. That is the life of a whore not a hero…"

There was much nodding and tut-tutting. Even Madame Dupard, uncharacteristically silent, waited until M. Môquet left the shop before denouncing him as a man who had lost his senses since his son's treachery. "It's not surprising, is it dear, given the shame he has to deal with, now that his only son has let him down so?"

Twenty minutes later Madame Turrel, signaling to no one, makes a left turn off the Seyne-Gap road towards the hamlet of Selonnet where she has lived since marrying her husband, André, the mayor, twenty-two years ago.

For the last three years, André and Marie-George Turrel have provided food and lodging for the Maquis of the Vercors and a safe house for various Allied secret agents parachuted into the surrounding area. Their son, Pierrot, aged 16, has spent many a night meeting maquisards in the woods to hand over Marie-George's home-made provisions. He has been a proud member of the reception committee for nine of the eleven agents parachuted into the dropping zone so far.

Resistance is a family affair for the Turrels. Indeed it is a village affair. Such is the respect that the villagers of Selonnet feel for their mayor that not a single one of them would ever, or ever did, speak a word to the authorities about the goings-on in the Turrels' house. As far as the villagers of Selonnet are concerned, André Turrel is the true leader of the French Resistance. His friends are their friends. His values are their values regardless of what any Vichy marshal or foreign army may dictate.

Marie-George parks her bicycle in the garage of the old forge where they live. She notices that the lights in the little house across the street, usually just visible despite the blackout, have been extinguished. She wonders if the new arrivals have already departed. Two hunted Maquis leaders from Lyon had been staying in the Turrels' safe house across the street for a week while finalizing plans for their departure via the Spanish escape route.

André Turrel was sitting in the kitchen, smoking a cigarette, when Marie-George walked in. A freshly killed pigeon was lying on the table.

That evening the Turrel family ate well.

After dinner, André and young Pierrot put on their great coats against the strong north wind that so often brought a bitter cold to the Ubaye Valley at this time of year.

They fetched a sled from the garage, packed with food and clothing. It was a clear night. No one was about.

The two men made their way across the village square through to the track which would take them to the farmhouse almost a kilometre away. Unlike the Turrels' own house which was right in the heart of the village, *the farmhouse of Yves Lauchaire was isolated. Ideally situated for midnight visits from maquisards.*

The farmhouse was starkly silhouetted against the moonlit sky as André and Pierrot made their way slowly up the hill pulling their goods behind them. Tonight was a big night. Several members of the Vercors Maquis were to come down from the plateau to collect the Turrels' booty. They would bring news of developments up there.

There was a party spirit in the farmhouse as André and Pierrot walked in. There must have been fifteen maquisards there. Yves Lauchaire's wife and three daughters were handing out warm slippers and blankets. They had made shirts and socks out of rags and boots out of straw. Each man had a backpack of sorts, waiting to be filled.

André and Pierrot unpacked from the sled everything from chocolate to coffee, salted beef and cured ham to chickens and dried fruit, and of course, tobacco. The maquisards, impressively organized, gathered it all together, apportioned it out and packed it up for the long hike back. It would be daybreak before they were in safe country.

Once the maquisards had left, André and Pierrot bade goodbye to their friends and started back to Selonnet. This had been nothing unusual, a monthly occurrence, but a lifeline to the Vercors Maquis.

As the Turrels, père et fils, arrived back at the forge, Marie-George was just going up to bed.

"All well?" she enquired.

"Fine, as usual. The cigarettes were the stars of course" said André, "much more important than shoes and blankets."

Marie-George smiled while silently giving praise to her mother from whom she had inherited the tabac, thanks to the loi tabac which had granted widows of World War I officers the right to run tabacs throughout France.

"See you soon, love."

André and Pierrot had a quick restorative home-made liqueur before turning in. It was half past midnight.

"See you in the morning son. I'm just going outside for a pee."

"'night, Dad."

Pierrot went upstairs to the loft where he and his elder brother, long since departed to work with Henri Frenay's Lyon cell, shared a room.

As was his wont, André walked outside into the moonlit night for one last sight of the mountain, one last breath of mountain air and a final pee before going up to bed.

He finished peeing, pulled up his fly and turned to enter the house. But his way was barred by three armed men.

In an isolated field somewhere in northern France, a wireless operator finished receiving a message from Baker Street, carefully packed up his transmitting set, and hid it under the floor boards of an old shepherd's hut. By the light of a gas lamp he began to decode a message from the SOE HQ, just as he had done so often in the past three months:

ARNAUD AND MARINETTE ARRIVE DROPPING ZONE T85S TONIGHT

"Arnaud!" he said, in disbelief and out loud. He stopped decoding realizing the urgency of this information. The rest of the message would have to wait. It was already 5:00 p.m. and dark. He must return to Paris as quickly as possible and alert the others. It would take him at least an hour to organize the reception committee.

"Monsieur Turrel?" I ask, once the man has finished buttoning his flies. I have my pistol in my hand, just in case.

"Who are you?" He is annoyed; unsurprisingly.

"Friends of Carmen Dupré"

"Monsieur Luc?" he says, relaxing a little.

"Oui, bien sur" I say, replacing my pistol in its holster.

"We've been expecting you. But you've caught me a little unawares" he smiles, "come inside."

Jacques, Claude and I follow André Turrel into the darkened house.

For the past few months, Arnaud, much to his fury, had been ensconced in a training centre, supposedly to share his experiences and advice with new recruits. Instead, he had been so unruly, so unpredictable (obviously no one there knew him well) and rebellious that HQ decided they had no alternative but to send him back into the field.

Arnaud requested immediate transfer to Luc's Rugby circuit but he had one condition. Buckmaster was not minded to accede to agents' 'conditions' but felt he should hear Arnaud out.

Arnaud, perhaps for the first time ever, he certainly thought so, had fallen completely and totally in love with a young recruit named Marinette. His condition was that she act as his courier and be transferred to Luc's circuit with him.

For reasons best understood, perhaps only understood, by themselves, Buckmaster et al decided that this was a bad idea; that a Luc/Arnaud/Marinette triumvirate would be counterproductive. They insisted on their own condition; that Arnaud and Marinette could serve together but only if they started their own réseau. Arnaud reluctantly agreed.

Thus he and Marinette, the two star-crossed lovers, were assigned to resuscitate the Paris réseau and to be parachuted back into France (not to Angers) as soon as possible.

It was precisely ten o'clock as the Hudson responded to the day's agreed code flashed up from Arnaud's reception committee 1,000 metres below. Arnaud, and his courier/fiancée, Marinette, were thrilled at being able to return to France at last.

They positioned themselves above the hatch ready to jump on command.

The Hudson circled the site, dipped down a shade lower and the order was given to jump. Arnaud, clinging hard to his trusty wireless set, jumped first. Marinette was seconds behind.

The Hudson pilot glanced back and was gratified to see the two parachutes open as he headed for home.

In typical style, Arnaud boomed out a joyous welcome as he glided down. "Vive la France!" he and Marinette shouted to the people assembled below. Before their feet touched the ground they were both dead.

Metzger congratulated the team of Milice whose repeated, almost manic, machine gunfire had murdered the last remaining SOE agent from his list of four.

Chamberlain and Mathilde were in concentration camps in Germany; Luc was blown sky high above Beaurepaire and now Arnaud had been killed on the evening of his return to develop a new Resistance cell in the north of France.

"Mission accomplished my dear Heinz" he said, turning to the wireless operator who had faithfully decoded and responded to all the Baker Street messages for the past four months courtesy of the Gestapo's success in extracting both security codes from a tortured SOE agent.

"My pleasure, Sir."

"Now we must get back to Paris, Heinz. I have a report to write!"

The wireless operator shyly climbed into the back seat of the Citroën and sat next to Karl Metzger. The driver started the engine and they headed down to the Paris road.

After several minutes of superficial conversation, Wireless Operator Heinz mentioned that he had had a chance to decode the rest of the message on his way back from Paris to the dropping zone that evening.

"And what did it say?" asked Metzger, only half interested.

"Nothing too relevant now I don't think Sergeant. I'll read you the message in its entirety. He pulled a piece of paper out of his breast pocket and read it out loud as the car sped through the country lanes:

ARNAUD AND MARINETTE ARRIVE DROPPING ZONE T85S TONIGHT PLEASE ENSURE SAFE PASSAGE TO MEET LUC TOMORROW NIGHT SIGNED BUCKMASTER ENDS

Metzger felt his muscles contract and his nerves turn to liquid. He could hardly bring himself to gasp let alone speak. When he did speak, he screamed.

"You imbecile! You complete and utter fucking imbecile. Luc is still alive! And we have just shot dead the one man who could have led us to him. Out, Out, Out!"

Metzger kicked open the door of the moving car and pushed the hapless Heinz onto the road.

The driver screeched to a stop.

"Drive on, drive on," cried Metzger, deranged. The driver meekly obeyed.

A few minutes later Metzger thought better of his actions and ordered the driver to turn around and go back.

Heinz was stumbling along at the side of the road as he felt the oncoming Citroën's headlights pin him, immobile, against the forest.

The Citroën stopped.

Metzger opened the door.

A single shot rang forth.

Silence, but for a closing door.

The terrified driver turned the car around and sped back down the road towards Paris.

It's 2:00 a.m. in Selonnet by the time André Turrel, having fed and watered the three of us, takes us across the street to the small, two-storey guesthouse recently vacated by a couple of maquisards from Lyon.

We take over this innocuous-looking white-washed chalet on the edge of the nondescript village square as our temporary headquarters and home. Over the next three weeks the Turrel family caters for our every need. Not only do they provide food and lodging but introductions to influential maquisards and sedentaires, sympathetic gendarmerie and local functionaries. Forged documents are supplied virtually on demand. André Turrel seems to have the world at his disposal.

I send Jacques to Barcelonnette where there have been rumours that the local Maquis are getting so restless they are likely to do something silly that may put the whole area at risk. Claude, I send to the Vercors plateau, guided by young Pierrot Turrel, to make contact with André Turrel's friend the 'Patron', apparently the respected titular head of the Vercors Maquis.

And I spend several weeks in Digne, re-establishing contact with Marianne, the brave American vet, and with Theo Gautier, leader of the existing réseau. I persuade Gautier to incorporate his cells into the Rugby circuit and together we recruit more new members, a job that is becoming easier as news spreads of the explosion at Beaurepaire.

I encourage Alain, the wireless operator, to move up to Seyne to establish his base close to us. I also arrange for a new wireless transmitting set to be sent from England. It will be dedicated to communicating with the Free French in Algiers.

The night before Alain and I are to return to Seyne, we agree to eat supper in one of the restaurants in the old town of Digne, hugging the base of the prison now used as Gestapo headquarters.

Smoking a roll-up cigarette and reading the collaborationist press, I wait for Alain at a table outside. It's an unusually balmy April evening. I look up as Alain approaches and realize that something is horribly wrong. My first instinct is that he has been followed or compromised in some form and that he is trying to warn me. I feel for my gun. Alain approaches, pulls out a chair and sits down.

"Luc, I have some very sad news for you."

"Tell me"

"I just received a message from Buckmaster."

"Go on…"

"He says that Arnaud was killed by the Gestapo as he was parachuting down in Mayenne. They shot him before he even hit the ground."

I sit, stunned. Images of Arnaud flash through my mind. Arnaud at St Jorioz, sullen and resentful when first we met; Arnaud as laughing friend; Arnaud as noisy fornicator in Les Tissots; and Arnaud, crazy, mad, wonderful Arnaud, as Nazi foil and mischief maker organizing the Marsellaise and thus our escape from the streets of St Jorioz.

With moist eyes I look up at Alain. "I'm sorry Luc. I know he was important to you. He was on his way to see you, too."

"How do you know? Why?"

"Buckmaster says that they have discovered that the Mayenne réseau has been infiltrated by a double agent who, unbeknownst to Baker Street, has been sending them false information for at least three months and frequently shooting agents upon or soon after arrival."

"I'm not sure how 'unbeknownst' to Baker Street it really was, Alain. I'm not suggesting Buckmaster knew anything about it. But someone very close to him did. I'm sure of it. And he sent Arnaud to his death just like he tried with me. Mayenne is in the same circuit as Angers. The double agent is a guy called D'Ancourt. I've met him."

"Buckmaster says he is in cahoots with an Abwehr sergeant."

"Metzger?"

"Yes, Metzger. That was the name in the message. He says that he's on some sort of vendetta and you are the only one left."

"Thanks, Alain. Arnaud was a good friend; a one-in-a-million."

"His real name was Marc Weinberger apparently. For some reason Buckmaster includes that in his message. He thought you would want to know."

The following night was reunion time back at the Turrels in

Selonnet; Jacques, like me, devastated at the news of Arnaud's death, just back from Barcelonnette, Claude down from the mountaintop of Vercors, and Alain and I back from Digne.

Marie-George Turrel has found Alain a temporary home and perfect transmitting place with a friend who is the Guardienne of the Citadel of Louis XIV in Seyne.

The three Turrels, along with Claude, Jacques, Alain and myself gather around Marie-George's kitchen table.

I ask Claude to update the group on what's happening on the plateau of Vercors.

With the eagerness of the freshly converted, Claude explains the situation as he sees it. There are several thousand Maquis on the plateau, full of enthusiasm despite the privations of their living arrangements. All they lack is arms. The townships of the plateau all appear to be supportive of the Resistance. Such Milice as there are on the plateau come from the plains and return there as soon as their work is done. So far they have caused few problems. Only recently, though, a group of milicien arrived in the village of St. Martin-en-Vercors searching for M. Chavant, the 'Patron'. They didn't find him, but they said they'd be back and threatened reprisals should anyone be harbouring him.

The major problem in Claude's view is the lack of organization of some of the groups. Two if not three people are claiming leadership of the Maquis, thus the situation is very confused.

André Turrel supports Claude's analysis and warns of the danger of thousands of young men, possibly ill-disciplined and certainly poorly clothed, fed and armed, roaming the plateau without a clear plan and apparently without any real leader.

"My view, for what it's worth," says André Turrel, " is that the situation is dangerous bordering on critical. Unless these units can be brought under firm control and are properly provided for, the whole place will descend into anarchy. The 'Patron' is the natural choice for leader. I think you and he should get together as soon as possible, Luc."

Jacques then tells of a similar situation, albeit on a much smaller scale, in Barcelonnette. There are rumours that an Allied invasion is imminent. Loose talk on the streets and senselessly provocative and unproductive attacks on individual German officers have already resulted in serious reprisals.

Jacques says Barcelonnette is a time-bomb.

Having absorbed all they have said, I fill them in on the very positive situation in the Digne réseau, and we discuss the next course of action.

I will go to the Vercors. But first I need a courier, a female, to replace Monique. I ask Alain to send a message to Algiers with a formal request

Alain duly sends the message to Algiers. But as he finishes he receives another message:

REGRET INFORM YOU OF DEATH OF 700 HEROIC MAQUISARDS IN GLIÈRES AND MURDER OF TOM MOREL ENDS

Devastated by terrible news for the second time in a week, Jacques and I take time out. I try to comfort him, saying that to honour Morel's memory and that of Jacques' former colleagues gives yet more impetus to making our mission a success. But Tom Morel was, in many respects, Jacques' mentor and he is deeply affected by this new blow to our rapidly diminishing Maquis family.

A few days later the full picture emerges.

The British and Free French had been arming the Glières Maquis on a regular basis during the early part of the month of March. Aware of this, the Vichy had renewed their attempts to weed out and destroy Morel's 'army', to no avail. Eventually a sort of truce was agreed between them. But, ignoring this, the Milice took prisoners. This was too much for Tom Morel, man of principle. His men surrounded and captured a large group of Milice. Among them was their commandant, Gregoire Lefèvre.

Lefèvre, a fellow St Cyr graduate of Morel's, requested that, 'as an officer and a gentleman', Morel allow him to keep his gun.

Morel handed him the gun. Lefèvre put a bullet through Tom Morel's heart. The 'morality' of the Milice.

On 23 March, three battalions from the 157th Reserve Division of Wehrmacht and two German police battalions, consisting of more than four thousand men with heavy machine guns, 80-mm mortars, 75-mm mountain guns, 150-mm howitzers and armoured cars, arrived in Haute-Savoie. Captain Anjot, who had assumed command at Tom's death, prepared his men for the inevitable attack.

Three days later, after another air raid and shelling, the Germans took the offensive. There had been an unseasonal snowstorm the night before. Ski patrols dressed in white camouflage carried out the reconnaissance. One of the patrols with a Gebirgsjäger platoon made an attack on the main exit to the plateau and captured an advance post. Eighteen maquisards fought and resisted into the night, but were massively outnumbered and overwhelmed. At ten o'clock the following morning Captain Anjot ordered the Glières battalion to retreat.

In the days that followed, Captain Anjot and almost all his officers as well as the 150 remaining maquisards were systematically murdered.

28

Palazzo Rasini, Montigiano Alto, Italy, August, 1939

Gently decaying for over four hundred years, the once-grand Palazzo Rasini stands aloof on its own Tuscan hill looking out to the Ligurian Sea.

Forgetful of a world by whom they were forgotten, the inhabitants of the local commune spoke, until the turn of the 20th century, a dialect incomprehensible to strangers. They formed their own *isola linguistica* and isolated themselves in other ways too. Largely self-sustaining, their surrounding hills were rich in wildlife, their streams held plentiful supplies of trout, their olive harvest was rarely poor thanks to the area's unusually mild microclimate and their pigs were famed for providing the best prosciutto in northern Italy, enabling them to market their produce in the neighbouring hilltop village of Gombotelli. As a result, Gombotelli was soon recognized by cognoscenti as peerless among purveyors of premium prosciutto.

The Rasini family, whose position of wealth and influence had enabled them to travel and gain superior education, was unusual in having access to the wider world. Their fortune having come and gone through the wool trade, they had always maintained close and protective relations with the peasants who worked their lands. They were duly trusted and respected in return. It was, for all concerned, a pleasant, secure and bountiful life.

Count Giovanni Rasini, the current pater familias, was a widower. He was both bookish and blind which proved problematic. Luckily he had two sons and a daughter who took it in turns, when they were growing up, to read to him from his favourite philosophical tracts. He admired Marcus Aurelius and knew most of the Meditations by heart. He had a soft spot for the French philosophers.

In common with ancestors down the centuries, the present-day Rasinis attended the neighbouring universities of Pisa and Florence.

The eldest son, Massimo, at age 30 had gone on to study law in Bologna. A decision which, to his father's regret, had led him to practice law in Poland, where he now lived with his Polish wife.

Fabio, the middle child, on the other hand had pleased his father particularly by excelling in his studies of philosophy and had recently been awarded a scholarship to study in the United States. Propitiously, he had left for Harvard in July 1939.

The youngest was Giovanna; beautiful, outspoken, skilled and opinionated. At birth her father, being a Shakespearian scholar, had wanted to call her Caterina. Indeed the older she grew, the more she resembled Shakespeare's 'Kate' and the more the old man resented giving in to his late wife's insistence that she be named after her maternal grandmother, the late, sainted, Giovanna della Corte.

Nonetheless, Giovanna was the apple of her father's eye, or rather of his mind as he had never actually seen her, having been struck blind by some thus-far unidentified disease the year of her birth. Ironically, or perhaps predictably given her birthplace, Giovanna was a linguist. "A linguist from the place with no language" her university friends had teased her. In addition to her own language, she spoke Florentine Italian, French like a native, German, Spanish and English, the last in the perfect clipped accent of her professor, Rose Martin. The unloved wife of an aristocratic English art collector, Professor Martin lived with her notoriously selfish husband in one of the grand villas of Fiesole, overlooking Florence, and sought solace in the teaching of English.

Giovanna's mother died in childbirth, along with the baby, when Giovanna was just two years old. Thus Giovanna was brought up in a house of men. To avoid being taken advantage of in this vulnerable position, she learned to look after herself from a very early age. So successful was she that people used to mock that she had no need for a man because she could outperform them all. But in this, as in so many of people's assumptions about Giovanna, they were wrong.

The Rasinis were also widely known to be communists. Not hard-line Stalinist communists but soft, Italian communists living in the generally anarchical western Tuscany of the 1930s. Nobody much minded in the circles they travelled in.

But further afield there were rumblings. Mussolini's black-booted Fascists, the local branch of which was based some 25 km away in Livorno, had their eyes on Palazzo Rasini and its rich lands.

As time went by, and Mussolini the puppet master was yet to become the puppet, aggression became the norm for Italian Fascisti. Giovanna went to live and study in Paris for two years. But as the war clouds gathered over Europe, she returned home.

When she arrived she found that her family's house had been requisitioned by the Fascisti and her broken-hearted father exiled to the Mediterranean island of Lampedusa.

Assured by an elderly retainer that her father was alright, Giovanna made a quick decision. She would travel to Poland to join her brother Massimo who, through his wife's connections, had received a commission as a cavalry officer in the Polish Army based in Krakow. Despite the non-aggression pact signed with Germany in 1934, there were strong rumours that a German invasion of Poland was imminent. Incensed by this inhuman prospect, Giovanna wanted to fight to keep Poland free. She would persuade her brother to help make this possible.

But she was too late. By the time she got to the Polish border on 6 September, the German Army had taken Krakow. Her brother Massimo was dead.

As thousands of Poles poured over the border into Hungary, Giovanna went to Budapest to find work with exiles producing leaflets to encourage resistance. She also hatched a plan to smuggle escaping prisoners of war to safety.

Within three weeks of setting up shop with a group of refugees in Budapest, Giovanna met a well-connected Romanian writer named Gregor von Rizov. His mother was English and related to the British Ambassador.

Gregor, a larger-than-life man who warmed to Giovanna's feistiness and loved arguing against her strong opinions, quickly fell under her spell. The two became lovers. They worked together for the next six months printing leaflets, organizing an escape route for POWs and performing occasional sorties into Poland to rescue endangered individuals and spirit them out to England or to the United States.

At the beginning of 1941 they were married.

As Countess von Rizov, Giovanna approached the British Ambassador with a request for supporting, with funds and ammunition, her efforts in Poland. Impressed, the Ambassador put her in touch with a man on the embassy staff named Patrick Roper.

Roper was an Economic Attaché at the Embassy (i.e. Intelligence) with a particular brief to find and recruit people to foment resistance behind enemy lines.

He also became SOE's man in Hungary.

Roper was impressed with the young couple, convinced of their sincerity and appreciative of their plight. But there were more important demands on SOE's limited resources. Twice over the succeeding months he had to turn them down. Finally, despite his own best efforts, he was forced to tell them that regretfully there was no way SOE could help. Giovanna and Gregor rightly suspected it was due to their communist associations.

On 5 December Britain declared war on Hungary, the British Embassy was closed down and Roper left Budapest.

For almost two years Giovanna and Gregor continued their efforts. Funding came clandestinely from the US Government via an American contact in Budapest; from Polish expatriates and from Hungarians, always mindful of Poland's help to Hungary in the past. But operating clandestinely in the heart of an Axis partner, it became increasingly difficult for the two of them to survive. Personally, too, their relationship had gone through rocky patches. Although they had both had affairs, emotionally their relationship was still very strong. But times were difficult and they were frustrated at not being able to put their talents to better use.

Then, at the beginning of January, 1944, all that changed. A message delivered by an unknown hand was pushed through the letterbox of the apartment in Krisztinaváros, where Gregor and Giovanna were living. It came from SOE Headquarters in Baker Street.

IF POSSIBLE MAKE YOUR WAY TO CAIRO JOB OFFERS AWAIT YOU BOTH REGARDS ROPER ENDS

The couple left Hungary in a battered Opel and made their way through Romania and Bulgaria to Greece. There they paid a fisherman to let them stow away on his vessel during one of his regular trips across the Mediterranean.

They arrived in Cairo on 17 February, 1944.

Roper's informers hunted them down and at the end of the month Roper himself flew to Cairo to give them instructions. Gregor was to go to England for a period of intensive training at the SOE school at Arisaig.

Giovanna was to remain in Cairo for the time being and await further instructions.

Roper returned to London.

Cairo, April 26, 1944

The screen door banged shut behind the uniformed bar waiter as he descended the steps of Cairo's exclusive Gezira Club bearing a silver tray.

Built fifty years earlier, open only to British nationals or their select friends and home to the oldest 18-hole golf course in Egypt, the Gezira Club was carved out of the Khedivial Botanical Gardens and ideally situated on the island of Zamalek at the centre of Cairo.

A drop of sweat fell onto the tray from the waiter's forehead as he walked, in the stifling heat, towards a recumbent figure on a lounger. Crazy these foreigners the way they lay all day in the sun so they can look like beetroots in the evening, he thought to himself.

"Madame, your gin and tonic."

"Thank you Mahmood. Please just leave the tray on the ground."

Mahmood put the silver tray down next to the perfectly proportioned sunbather and made an admiring assessment of her body, strictly against staff regulations at the Gezira Club.

Yet who could blame him?

Countess Giovanna von Rizov was no ordinary sunbather. Her short dark hair framed a delicate yet strong face with piercing, almond-shaped eyes. Her beauty was already a subject of comment in Cairo, despite her having been in town for only a few months. It had to do with her bearing, her strength, a certain mystery that surrounded her. And a faint whiff of danger. No one was exactly sure where she came from. She had friends in high places, obviously. Otherwise what would an Italian/Romanian countess be doing at the Gezira Club, day after day, the gossipmongers asked themselves. And what about those rumours? They say she is insatiable in bed.

In conversation she gave little away. She disarmed men and women alike with her smile. She was fiercely intelligent, fighting fit and spoke five languages, fluently. She swam at least 7 km every day in the Gezira Club's pool.

She was opinionated, strong-willed, polite to servants, and no one knew where she lived.

The managers of the Gezira Club knew that she was there as a guest of the British Consul. The members were not privy to such information.

At precisely noon, the Countess gathered up her book and towel and walked into the clubhouse for a sandwich, and then a swim.

That evening, dressed in a man's shirt and tight-fitting slacks that emphasised her toned physique, she arrived as agreed at Shepheard's Hotel, a vast, old-fashioned rambling Colonial edifice with dark oriental halls and polished ebony ladies holding frosted lights beside marbled steps and endless corridors festooned with palms.

A piano was playing and Major Richard Dellafield of the SOE was leaning on the Long Bar, his customary Pink Gin in hand.

He stood up straight as he saw the Countess approach. Heads turned, male and female, as she passed through the bar on the way to the veranda and the seating area. Dellafield hurried over to introduce himself.

"Good evening, my dear. How good of you to come, and so punctually too. What's your tipple?"

"Just a soda water, Major, thank you."

"Fine, fine" he snapped his fingers to attract a waiter's attention.

"They are not dogs, Major" said Giovanna, settling into her chair.

Major Dellafield, his reddened cheeks turning redder, was not used to being spoken to like this. Especially by a woman. And a foreign woman at that.

"Of course. So sorry…" he mumbled as he manoeuvered his corpulent physique into the wicker chair. Too cocky by half, he decided.

Drinks were ordered followed by an uncomfortable silence, broken by Giovanna.

"How long have you been in Cairo, Major?"

"Two years. Too bloody long if you'll excuse my French. But there is light at the end of the tunnel. I am due to return to Blighty next month.

Unless the powers that be change their minds for the third time. What a business, eh…"

"Yes, what a business, as you say."

They sipped their drinks. Dellafield feeling more and more uncomfortable. Giovanna not taking her eyes off him. He shuffled nervously in his seat before speaking.

"Well I suppose you'll want to know why I arranged to meet you tonight?" he said with the self-satisfied air of a man in possession of confidential information.

"Naturally."

"I've had instructions from Algiers. You are to proceed there as soon as possible. Something about preparing you for a new mission."

At last. Two years of working as a courier in Poland and Hungary followed by three months 'in the cold'. "That's very good news Major. I do nothing here but read and keep fit."

That's not what I've heard, thought the Major. "Yes of course, dear. Quite understand. Would feel the same way myself."

"What is the next step, Major?"

"You'll find a ticket waiting for you with the concierge at the Continental Hotel, that's where you're staying isn't it?"

"Yes, this week I am."

"Very well. You're to report to Brooks Richards' HQ in Algiers tomorrow at 9:00 a.m. A room has been reserved for you at the Al-Jaza'ir under the name Christine Porter. That will be your nom de guerre from now on. You'll be given documents and further instructions by our contacts there. That all clear?"

"Perfectly clear, thank you Major"

" 'nuther drink?"

"No thank you Major. I think I'd better get back."

"Fine, fine. Think I'll stay and have the other half, ha ha. Nice meeting you." He waved her goodbye. His confidence slowly returned.

Algiers, 27 April, 1944

Algiers was buzzing with flies and rumours. Free French and British uniforms everywhere in evidence. Excitement in the air. Talk of an imminent invasion. Everyone could see that preparations for something major were well underway.

To confirm it all, de Gaulle was expected to move his headquarters to Algiers momentarily, a huge fillip for the Free French and a snub to Vichy remnants.

Christine (she had adapted to her new name enthusiastically) had taken a late-night walk in the immediate environs of the Hotel Al-Jaza'ir as soon as she arrived that night. Surrounded by palm trees and orange trees, the hotel was situated at the head of a grand boulevard with an impressive view of fine public buildings and a large square. All manner of people were out for evening promenades on the gas-lit streets. French and British soldiers and officers, Jews with dark-coloured turbans and sashes, Moors in embroidered jackets; bare-legged Arabs; Sudanese, Spaniards and Maltese.

The side streets were so narrow they were in permanent shade even at midday. The roads were so tortuous and the street names so confusing that Christine decided to stick to the boulevard.

At the apex of the triangular-shaped mass of Moorish houses was the Kasbah. The hotel porter had warned her it was unsafe to venture there without an armed guard. She was tempted to explore it anyway but it was dark and late and she needed to be up early.

The following morning, dressed in her new FANY uniform, Christine waited in the lobby of the Hotel Al-Jaza'ir.

At exactly 8:00 a.m. an eager young corporal arrived in a battered Jeep to pick her up.

She beckoned him over as he walked in the door.

"Good morning Corporal, have you come for me?"

"Christine Porter?" his eyes alight at the possibility.

"That's right."

"Yes, ma'am," he stressed with a Yankee inflection far removed from his native cockney.

"I'll collect your luggage."

"This is it," said Christine patting her knapsack.

"And I thought all women had masses of luggage!"

"Not this one," she said. They walked to the door.

"Hop in. We've got a 27-kilometre drive. Is this your first time in Algiers?" He held open the door of the camouflaged Jeep.

"It is."

"OK, I'll take you the scenic route."

They drove down to the bay where warships mingled with Arab dhows, past the grand 11th-century mosque in the Rue de la Marine and on to the outskirts of town to take the high road to the coast.

The corporal entertained Christine with stories of local colour.

"They still perform curious sacrificial rites on the seashore every Wednesday morning at sunrise. You should have a look sometime. It's gruesome!"

"What sort of rites?"

"Last time I went" said the corporal, warming ever more to his topic, "the Aissaoui, who are the fanatical religious followers of Sidi Mohammed bin Aisa, were beating their drums and tambours, then a young guy ran into the crowd yelling and screaming. He started to dance frantically.

Then the whole scene got much uglier when, obviously drugged out of their minds, a new batch of youths forced out their eyes with iron spikes, seared themselves with red hot irons, ate live scorpions and broken glass. They didn't seem to feel any kind of pain and all the while the crowd were cheering and drumming and egging them on."

By the time the Jeep reached the forest of Ain-Benan and turned down a rough road for the final nine kilometres, Christine felt quite ill. She also changed the subject.

"Corporal, tell me about Guyotville. Why are the SOE based out here?"

The Jeep swerved to the side of the road narrowly missing a laden cart.

"All I know is that when Algeria was secured by the Allies in November, 1942, the SOE decided to set up a mirror organization, code-namedd 'Massingham', here in Guyotville because of its easy access to Corsica, Sardinia, Sicily, Italy and the south of France. The place has been riddled with politics of course, like everywhere else; the Giraudists versus the Gaullists, everyone is confused. Some French Resistance people who were over here recently told me that there were masses of airplanes sitting here in the desert that could be used to drop supplies to them, but because no one agrees who's in charge, the planes just sit there. It's a mess. But, hey, what do I know. I'm a corporal."

As they rounded a sharp corner, the corporal nudged Christine "Right, this is it. Here's your beautiful view of the Mediterranean and over there is Massingham. Not bad, eh?"

The township of Guyotville lay stretched out before them, hugging the coast. A wire fence encased a large compound which seemed to include a hotel and several surrounding buildings right on the shore.

"Looks more like a country club than the SOE HQ" said Christine.

"Yeah, it is really. For part of the day. The rest of the time it's dead serious. Some of the 'visitors' have been here so long they have given up hoping for an assignment. If you're one of the lucky ones you'll be sent off to the Club des Pins… means you're mainstream if you're selected."

The corporal pulled the Jeep up to the gate and told Christine she'd have to get out here.

"Good luck old girl"

She responded with a rude sign.

The corporal, laughing, drove away.

Within three days Christine was posted to the Club des Pins and assigned to urgent parachute training and an emergency wireless operator's course.

When courses weren't operating, mornings were spent sunbathing and swimming and afternoons skiing in the Atlas mountains. It seemed like Saint Moritz in peace time.

But three weeks later, on 27 May, all that changed.

Christine reported to the office at 9:00 a.m. as usual but instead of being issued the day's training instructions she was called into Brooks Richards' office. Instead of Brooks Richards, a tall army colonel with a beak nose and insignificant chin was sitting behind the desk.

"How do you do Christine" he said, standing and shaking her hand, "do have a seat."

"Thank you, Colonel."

"Let me introduce myself. I am Colonel Maurice Buckmaster, head of 'F' Section, the French section of SOE. I'm based in London but I'm here for meetings with our Free French colleagues. It occurred to me it was an ideal opportunity to get to meet you."

"I'm flattered Colonel. I hope you have come with some good news."

"I have indeed. In fact I have a new and very interesting assignment for you. It's in France, down south. Our most successful circuit there, the Rugby circuit, was started up early last year by an American agent named Luc. He's assembled some enormously effective cells right across south-eastern France from Lyon to Montpellier and the coast, and all the way over to the Swiss and Italian borders. There are believed to be about 10,000 men, well they are mainly men, under his control. Both Maquis and Resistance fighters.

Sadly, Luc lost his courier several months ago and while he's managed without one for quite a while, the whole area is heating up given a likely Allied invasion in the near future. Long and the short of it is we would like you to be his new courier."

"When can I go?"

"Well not for a while I'm afraid. We need you here to help sort out the influx of Italian partisans. It shouldn't be too long though. A matter of a few weeks."

"The sooner the better as far as I'm concerned. Can you tell me where in the south of France I might be going, Sir?"

"The Vercors Plateau, near Grenoble. Not much happens there but it's important strategically nonetheless."

"Thank you."

"Well that's all. Good luck Christine and give my regards to Luc when you see him."

29

Seyne–les–Alpes, 26 April, 1944, 8:00 a.m.

Eugène Chavant, the civilian 'Patron' of the Vercors Plateau, a ruggedly square-faced, grey haired, moustachioed man in his mid-fifties, is crossing the village square. Dressed in his trademark short-sleeved jersey, baggy trousers and sturdy boots, he walks at a quicker pace than usual but still finds time to use his knobbly walking stick to displace stones that lie in his path. Drawing on his ever-present pipe, he heads towards the Turrels' house.

André Turrel sees him coming.

"Something's up, Luc. The Patron himself is on his way over." André opens the door.

"Eugène, come in. You look awful. What's wrong?"

The Patron acknowledges our presence without saying a word.

"Eugène, these are my friends, Luc and Jacques."

"Ah yes, you are here to help us they tell me?"

"We hope so."

"They will Eugène" says André "I'll make some more coffee but tell us your news."

We sit down at the kitchen table, the Patron at the head. He speaks quietly and methodically with the care of a school teacher. "Things have taken on a new dimension on the plateau my friends. How much do you know of the situation?" he stares intently at Jacques and me.

I respond. "Not enough. We know there are three or four thousand men up there mainly, people say, young men escaping the STO, a few former soldiers, some Spanish lumberjacks, in addition to local inhabitants of course."

"The 3,000 men constitute the major part of the Resistance at the moment but the number is gradually growing thanks to the army's realization, enfin, that the plateau is a natural fortress, virtually impenetrable given the right men and arms."

"How many trained soldiers do you have up there?"

"Probably a thousand but permit me to provide you with a little history."

The Patron is a man used to having his own way. André hands around fresh cups of coffee.

The Patron continues "Until December the plateau was under civilian control."

"That is to say under Eugène Chavant's control" interjects André with a wry smile.

"Just so" confirms the Patron, without smiling, "following the Italian armistice, the Germans, and the Gestapo in particular, took control of south-eastern France as you know. The civilians had controlled the entire plateau through a five-man 'military' committee of soldiers and civilians with myself as president. Colonel Descour, based in Grenoble, was in charge of the secret army covering our area. We got on well with his representative, Le Ray, who lived amongst us on the Vercors. He was not bad, for a military man. But he resigned…"

I get the picture. A strong-willed, wily, communist outlaw chief in gangster country coming up against the traditional, conservative military; not an easy alliance to imagine.

Chavant takes a sip of coffee, as if to lubricate the mouthing of the words he finds so distasteful "…and he was replaced by the appropriately named Captain Narcisse Geyer, a dangerous little man who parades around in full dress uniform, on a white horse displaying a great fondness for ceremony."

Avoiding the military/civilian conflict issue, I ask "How many men does Geyer have under his control? And what calibre of men?"

"Several hundred. Some of the cavalry from the 11th Cuirassiers whose barracks in Grenoble have been commandeered by the Wehrmacht; Russian deserters, a priest, some men from the alpine regiment. Some are good, some are not. They are hot-headed. Their antics put my people in danger. They take unnecessary risks. Overgrown schoolboys."

"Any trouble from the Germans yet?" asks Jacques.

"Almost immediately. At the end of January they attacked the village of Malleval in the north-west where a detachment of alpine troops were holed up. They killed thirty men and then set the village on fire, locking residents in their houses to burn alive. Last month the early warning system broke down and forty-five German trucks penetrated into the heart of the massif and blew up Colonel Descour's command post, shooting those who tried to escape. Their information was good. They knew precisely where to go…"

"Informed by the Milice?"

"… or collaborators, sadly even in the Vercors we have them."

"After Descour's HQ they went on to Narcisse Geyer's farmhouse and burned it and nine other farms in the area, as a warning. Then they left for the plain."

"And since then?"

"Since then we have had the Milice. Ten days ago a large force of Milice, accompanied by German troops, came up to the plateau and commandeered houses in Vassieux and La Chapelle. There they instituted, I can say, a reign of terror. The Chief of the Milice himself came, with his sadistic mistress, 'Colonel Maude'. They occupied the Hotel Bellier. They forced the owner of the Hotel, M. Bellier, to sit in a red-hot frying pan. But still he would divulge no information. They beat a farmer's wife who refused to say where the Maquis camps were and then dragged her along behind their car with her feet tied to the bumper. The night before last they rounded up three of our best men, took them to the hotel in Vassieux and, as usual, had them stripped naked. The perverted mistress always insists on this. She then acts as the judge and conducts a mock trial. In the past the priest or the doctor has been able to persuade her not to shoot the victims. But not yesterday. They took them into the street and shot them, one by one."

"I'm so sorry Eugène" says André "who were they?"

"Two men who had been with us from the start. Both friends. Sons of farmers on the plain near to St Martin d'Hères, the village where I was mayor. The third man had only been with us for a couple of months. His name was Claude. We didn't know a lot about him. He was from Beaurepaire."

Jacques shot a glance at me, then closed his eyes. I could feel the hairs rise up on the back of my neck.

"We know him, knew him," I say, "he organized the destruction of the power station at Beaurepaire. He was our friend. He joined the Maquis because of us."

"Eh!" says Chavant, opening his hands in supplication "c'est notre guerre."

"Oui, je sais, je sais" I agree, determined to avenge yet another friend's death. "So, M le Patron, where do we go from here? What do you want from us?"

"We cannot mount an effective resistance without arms and ammunition. The Americans and British dropped 7,000 tons of bombs over Germany in one night last month. Things seem to be moving fast towards an Allied invasion. De Gaulle is now firmly in charge. Giraud was demoted last week. General Koenig is now de Gaulle's Military Delegate and overall in charge of Descour and our region, or so I understand. That should make life easier. But our requests for arms and men are being systematically ignored."

"Has that got anything to do with your being a communist?" I ask "because we know de Gaulle's fear of the communists. Apparently he's given instructions that no arms are to be dropped where they could possibly fall into communist hands."

"Well he might as well stop supporting the Resistance altogether then as the majority, especially since Hitler invaded Russia, are communists. He can't do without us" replies the Patron curtly.

"How long do you think you can hold out with the men and materiel that you have at the moment?" I ask.

Jacques tosses me a cigarette and offers them around.

"For not very much longer. A question of weeks at the most" replies the Patron "I am to go to Algiers myself to put the case personally for support for our men before it is too late. Of course the Germans have the capacity, militarily, to wipe us out if they really want to. There are 40,000 of them in and around Grenoble. We have, at most, 3,000 poorly equipped and largely untrained youths; a few unreliable Sten guns, some World War I leftovers and a few impressive-sounding but ineffectual bombs. Fortunately General Pflaum, the Wehrmacht commander at the HQ in Grenoble, does not seem to be unduly preoccupied with the massif. At least not up until now. But all that could change."

Silence in the Turrel kitchen.

"It sounds to me as though, potentially, given the men who are living in the plains and waiting for your summons to join them, you may have enough manpower" I say.

"Potentially", the Patron agrees.

"But what you need is arms, supplies and training."

"Precisely."

"Well that's why we are here, to provide training and materiel so that everyone's prepared when the invasion comes. If we can't get that for you then what purpose are we serving?"

"That's correct. But our requests for arms go unanswered from Algiers. No arms or supplies have arrived. Just empty promises. They have no idea what our men are going through or what dangers they face. That's why I plan to go there myself; to force them to do something."

"Meanwhile, we've got to do our damnedest to get things moving, huh Jacques?"

Jacques, wide-eyed, nodding, always the optimist is raring to go.

"I think the best plan is for us to come up to the plateau as soon as possible" I suggest, "Once there, we can assess the situation then I'll be responsible for getting supplies."

"Very good" replies the Patron. He's a man of few words and distrusts most people, but he's clearly decided to give us the benefit of the doubt.

"Jacques will have to go to Beaurepaire first" I explain, "he needs to see Claude's mother; tell her what happened. Then he can go on to Montèlimar to check up on the cells there. The Gestapo have targeted much of the Resistance in the south over the past few months. So far Rugby, our circuit, is secure but it could be blown any minute. Especially with Metzger so involved."

"Metzger?" enquires André Turrel.

"He's the Abwehr sergeant who arrested the two SOE agents in St Jorioz. He's been pursuing the wireless operator Arnaud and me ever since. They got Arnaud recently, shot him as his parachute opened on his return to France. He'd been shopped by a collaborator. I think Metzger has lost the scent now" I say, not really believing it but not wanting to divert attention from the Vercors.

I turn to the Patron. "We'll be there in a few days, M. Chavant. I need to spend a little time with my people in Digne and when Jacques gets back from Montélimar we'll be up. Shall we say on Monday 8 May?"

"I should still be there. Come to St Martin en Vercors and go to the Hotel Breyton; ask for Mme. Breyton. I will alert her to expect you."

With that the Patron stands up – as do we all, instinctively.

"André, my old friend. We will be in touch. Thank you once again for your help. Messieurs Luc and Jacques, we will meet again, on the plateau." He walks to the door, turns, waves his hand behind him as he does so and makes his way back across the village square.

"Quite some man" says Jacques.

"The best" replies André.

Jacques leaves for Beaurepaire. I depart the following morning for Digne. Marie-George Turrel continues her days behind the counter at the tabac; André looks after the town and organizes supplies of food and drink for the Maquis. Young Pierrot attends school and helps his father at weekends.

By the time Jacques and I return a week later, life has returned almost to normal. Or what passes for normal these days. No German uniform has yet been spotted in the village of Seyne-les-Alpes. But André warns his people not to be complacent. Milice are usually visible; but collaborators don't wear uniforms.

Just after dawn on Monday 8 May, Jacques and I, packed like donkeys for our trip up to the plateau, take leave of the Turrels. Jacques still has his cousin's motorcycle. André has somehow procured another, on loan, for me. The silence of the early morning is shattered as we cross the town square and join the main road to Gap.

Shortly after Gap, we get our first view of the plateau.

It's a crisp and clear morning. We stop at the side of the road, light a cigarette and sit there, legs astride, just staring. Like a limestone death ship floating on a sea of granite, the 900-metre high Vercors plateau juts abruptly out of the soil of La France Profonde, dwarfing all around.

"Christ, what a spooky place" Jacques says, enunciating both of our thoughts.

"You're talking about our new home, buddy! But you're right. No wonder the Germans don't like going up there."

At Die, we cross the River Drome and take the winding path towards the Col de Rousset. Jacques says he's grateful we're together. The high cliffs bear down on us as we ride ever higher.

"Talk about remote," I yell to him "this is surreal!"

Jacques nods. "Oui, can we leave now please?" he shouts back.

We laugh and ride on.

Some twenty minutes later we think we've made the plateau. We take a corner expecting to find a wide sweep of farmland but instead find a narrow, deep-sided gorge and twenty men, some armed, blocking our path.

We bring the two motorcycles to a stop. The men look quizzical rather than fierce. I assume they are the Patron's men.

"Welcome, Messieurs Luc and Jacques?"

We nod.

"We have been watching your every move. Very impressive

riding" says a young man of perhaps nineteen who carries a Sten gun which, although it turns out to be unloaded, sets him apart, establishes his credentials with the others.

Half an hour later, we pull into the main square, the only square, in St Martin and park our bikes next to the imposing Hotel Breyton, a white stucco building opposite the church. A sign says that the 300-year-old lime tree in front of the hotel was planted on the instructions of the Duc de Sully, the man who put Henry of Navarre on the throne of France.

Although basking in the name of hotel, the Breyton turns out to have only three bedrooms. Nevertheless, it is the most famous building in the area. Managed by Mme Breyton, its café-bar is, we are told, the informal, and only, headquarters of the civilian government, and therefore the only one recognized by the majority of the inhabitants of the Vercors plateau.

Jacques and I find the Patron, Eugène Chavant, seated at a table next to the bar, affording him a clear view of the door while allowing him to be well-positioned for a quick departure out the back if necessary, I assume.

He welcomes us "Bienvenu, mes amis, to the St Martin Elysee," and introduces us to Mme. Breyton, who is asked to bring coffee.

There are three tables of men sitting in the room, all staring at us. We smile, somewhat awkwardly, and sit.

"So, we meet again. I have some news" says the Patron, wasting no time. "The government in exile in Algiers, de Gaulle's people, have agreed that I should come. Officially I am a courier charged with taking a secret plan on behalf of the American O.S.S. but I plan to use the occasion to get a firm commitment of support from de Gaulle, and a promise of arms. Without that I will refuse to return."

Mme. Breyton brings our coffees.

"Are you sure they want you to return; maybe they think life will be easier for the military if you stay in Algiers?"

Chavant snorts, "They need me here alright. You will see evidence of that as you go around the massif over the next few days. I want you to meet everyone, even Geyer. Especially Geyer. So you will see what we are up against."

Just then a military man walks in. He isn't wearing a uniform but is nevertheless easily identifiable as a military man.

The Patron looks up. "Ah, now here is the acceptable face of the military. Gentlemen, meet Captain Costa de Beauregard, military commander of the Vercors, northern sector… we confine Geyer to the south" he adds as an aside.

"Patron" says the soldier taking a chair from a nearby table and joining us "I hear you are off to see our Masters? Give them hell from me will you."

"Certainment, mon ami." Chavant explains to us "The captain has shared my frustration over the lack of arms," he turns to de Beauregard, "by the way mon Capitaine, this is M. Luc and M. Jacques. They are, how shall we say, independent agents with good contacts in London and Algiers. They have come to solve all our problems…"

I am getting the measure of Chavant; a charming rogue who nevertheless, and despite all his apparent egocentricity, holds the people of the Vercors close to his heart. It becomes clear that Roland Costa de Beauregard, a bright young captain from an intellectual family, respects Chavant for his socialist principles. A fact which Chavant recognizes and appreciates. But de Beauregard is also a former instructor at the military academy of St Cyr and an aristocrat. There must be times when the two men are at loggerheads.

"We will do our best to help" I say, "by the way Captain, could we come and spend a few days with you and your men to get a better idea of requirements?"

"Bien sur, why not? Come tomorrow. The Patron will arrange it I'm sure and will give you the grand tour."

Chavant nods.

"Great, that's settled." We finish our coffees and as we make to leave the café-bar, I turn to Chavant "By the way, Patron, will you do me one favour when you are in Algiers."

He raises his eyebrows, cocks his ear.

"Find out what the hell has happened to the replacement courier I was promised."

"Of course, my friend."

The following morning Jacques and I take off, with a couple of the Patron's men, towards St Nizier on the north-east slope of the massif. As we approach de Beauregard's roadside villa HQ we get a perfect bird's eye view of Grenoble. I borrow a pair of binoculars. It's like looking down on a three-dimensional map, so clearly visible are the city, its streets, vehicles and even its people. Especially visible is a black swastika flying on the mast above the barracks that serve as the headquarters of General Karl Pflaum and the 157th Wehrmacht's Reserve Division.

A few days later, a battered Renault draws up in front of the Hotel Breyton and Chavant and a comrade climb in. The townspeople turn out to wave them off, such is the portent of this trip with its high expectations for salvation in the shape of men and arms. The old car drives past the burned-out village of Les Barraques and down the steep winding road to the plain.

Five days later, at 2:00 a.m., the Patron of Vercors is standing on a deserted beach at Cap Camarat, near St Tropez. He can just make out the signal from the intermittently flashing light of a torch. He responds with the pre-agreed code and shortly thereafter a rubber boat pulls up on shore, manned by a US naval lieutenant. Chavant is whisked to a waiting motor-launch bound for Corsica where he will board a plane for Algiers.

Algiers, 22 May, 1944

Over the past few weeks, Algiers had become enormously important. De Gaulle, having outmaneuvered Giraud, was now the undisputed leader of the Free French. He was based here, on French colonial soil. No longer could he be slighted by Churchill or ignored by Roosevelt. In recognition of his new stature, all Resistance departments: the British SOE, the American OSS and the French BCRA were being merged into a single unit called SPOC (Special Projects Operations Centre) under three SPOC colonels, one American, one British and one French. All parties were to act in unison to prepare France for Operation Anvil, the Allied invasion of the south.

Within hours of his arrival in Algiers, Chavant found himself waiting outside the office of the French SPOC colonel, Jean Constans, who was to be responsible for providing arms and supplies to the Maquis in south-eastern France. At last Chavant felt that he was getting to the heart of the operation.

Colonel Constans, a balding 40-year-old professional soldier, listened attentively as the civilian Patron of the Vercors explained the significance of the plateau and described its potential as an impenetrable natural fortress from which the Maquis, and army, could mount withering attacks on the Germans. Chavant explained the objective of Operation Montagnards, the plan hatched by the Patron and his friends three years earlier to turn the plateau of the Vercors into a Free French fortress in the heart of hostile territory.

The proposal was very simple. On the day of the Allied invasion in the south, planned, according to all informed military intelligence, to occur simultaneously with the invasion of the north, the three thousand maquisards in the Vercors camps would be joined by several thousand more Resistance members from the plains.

All the plateau's passes would be closed so that parachutists could safely be dropped onto the airfield presently being constructed on the massif at Vassieux. They would be in a perfect position to mount attacks on the Germans who would by then be occupied with fighting the invading armies south of the plateau. The Vercors' location near to the Route Napoleon and road, rail and air services made it an ideal position from which to operate.

Constans was impressed. He pulled out a large-scale map of the Vercors and for the next hour or so he and Chavant huddled over the map while the Patron explained how the Vercors would benefit the Allied cause if they had the necessary men and arms.

Constans communicated his enthusiasm to his British and American counterparts and invited Chavant back to give his colleagues a similar briefing the following day. Indeed throughout the rest of the week, Chavant went from meeting to meeting with the top military brass spreading his message, repeating his plea for arms and men and his insistence that Operation Montagnards be given the go-ahead from the very highest authority. The only man in a position to give the go-ahead was General Charles de Gaulle.

On 3 June, Jacques Soustelle, the well-known archaeologist-turned-minister in de Gaulle's cabinet, handed Chavant a letter signed under de Gaulle's name, authorising Operation Montagnards to proceed.

His mission achieved, Chavant departed by Lysander on 4 June and headed for a remote field in the Ain Department outside Lyon. In his pocket he had the signed order approving Operations Montagnards which he would hand over to Colonel Descour as soon as possible. He also has 2,500,000 francs and a new set of signal codes.

In addition he had a promise, from Constans, that Luc's new courier, an Italian girl with the nom de guerre of Christine Porter, would be sent to the Vercors within 24 hours.

One of Luc's Rugby circuit cell leaders in Ain conveyed the news to Descour that Chavant had returned and wanted an urgent meeting.

Descour agreed to meet with Chavant the following day, 5 June, at the crossroads in the Lyon suburb of Villeurbanne.

30

Monday 5 June, 1944

The turning point for the Vercors and for each and every person whose life is bound up with the plateau.

The critical events take place in four different locations…

Café Noir, Villeurbanne, a suburb of Lyon, 10:00 a.m.

Colonel Marcel Descour, commander of Region 1 of the twenty districts into which France's Secret Army is now divided, is dressed in a felt hat and an unironed, grey suit. His Chief of Staff, a Benedictine monk named Dom Guétet, is similarly attired, as are most businessmen in this unprepossessing suburb of Lyon.

The two men, sitting in the nondescript café, listen with increasing excitement to Eugène Chavant as he relates the story of his trip to Algiers.

Descour found it difficult to contain himself as Chavant recounted his discussions with the top brass and the positive, nay enthusiastic, reactions of everyone involved. Descour knew that the Patron was not given to hyperbole which made his news all the more impressive. After all the doubts and prevarication, the 'grand plan' was to proceed at last. Descour's men, who had managed to maintain their morale despite being poorly sheltered, fed and clothed and lacking arms, ammunition and training, were at last to be given the chance they had yearned for; to restore France's glory and to play a significant role in removing the German Army from French soil.

Descour read and reread de Gaulle's Order. "Well my friend, at last the day we have been waiting for has come. You'd better return to your plateau and prepare!"

Even the normally taciturn Chavant managed a grin.

"Oh, by the way Patron, I think you'll be pleased to hear that I have appointed a new Military Commander of the Vercors. His name is Major François Huet. Costa de Beauregard will continue to look after the northern sector and Geyer the south, but Huet will be your main contact and in overall control."

Chavant was not pleased to hear that yet another military man would be vying for control of the plateau but at least it would help to keep Narcisse Geyer in his place.

Chavant thanked Descour, said his goodbyes and headed off to catch the bus back to Ain to prepare for his return to the Vercors the following day.

Hotel Breyton, St. Martin en Vercors, 11:00 a.m

Major François Huet, the new Military Commander of the Vercors, was no stranger to the massif. In the summers of his youth he and his family used to travel up there for picnics and games. In the winters they would take annual ski trips to the Vercors.

But now he looked at everything with a very different eye. Which is why his face probably showed his concern when, after climbing off the bus from Grenoble, he was greeted by a motley group of de Beauregard's under-clothed and under-fed troops with barely a weapon between them with which to offer a salute to their new commander.

Huet, a former training officer at the elite military academy of Saint Cyr, tried to hide his shock. After a formal inspection of the 'troops' he was taken by de Beauregard to have lunch at the Hotel Breyton.

They sat down at the table next to the bar.

"No, not there. That is reserved for the Patron" boomed the voice of Mme. Breyton.

Even though they both knew that Chavant was out of town, de Beauregard and Huet moved to another table without complaint.

The picture was gradually becoming clearer to Huet. Over lunch de Beauregard was able to bring him up to date with developments. He explained the tension between Chavant and the military, especially Geyer, which tallied pretty much with what Descour had warned would be the case. He also filled him in on the arrival of Luc; the man, it was now well known, who represented the SOE in this area and was responsible for cells of 10,000 able-bodied men in south-eastern France, and of his deputy Jacques Villaz, formerly of the Glières Maquis.

Huet had known the Glières Maquis commander Tom Morel and had met Jacques in early 1943.

At 1:30 a white steed pulled up in front of the hotel. Sitting atop it was the diminutive figure of Capitaine Narcisse Geyer who couldn't have contrasted more starkly with his four-man mounted escort of six-foot-tall cavalry officers. All five men were in full uniform, with highly polished boots. One carried the standard of the 11th Cuirassiers even though their Grenoble barracks were now commandeered as the HQ of General Pflaum and his 157th Reserve Division Wehrmacht.

On seeing this dramatic display, Huet began to understand Chavant's antipathy toward Geyer, and indeed the military in general. Nevertheless, Geyer was a war hero who demanded, and was granted, great loyalty from his men. He had already proven himself to be a canny commander in the southern region of the Vercors. Geyer joined his new commander and Captain de Beauregard for coffee. Unlike the other two, Geyer was not a St Cyr graduate, which foretold friction between them. But all were

BING TAYLOR

professional military men. Huet outlined the chain of command and insisted that Chavant and the civil department be on equal footing with the two regional commanders. All of them, Chavant, Luc and Jacques included, would in future report to Huet.

"Bonne chance" said Geyer as he stood up to leave. He clearly felt as much antipathy towards Chavant as did the Patron towards the 'Poseur'.

Huet ordered two more coffees and quizzed de Beauregard as to where he could find himself a suitable headquarters.

General Pierre Koenig's HQ, Duke Street, London, 2:00 p.m.

General Colin Gubbins, head of the SOE, and Colonel David Bruce, head of the London branch of the American OSS, were walking the short distance from Grosvenor Square to the Duke Street HQ of General Pierre Koenig. General Koenig had taken up his new position as Commander-in-Chief of the Forces Françaises de l'Intérieur (FFI) four days earlier. Thus he was now in charge of all Resistance forces in France.

Koenig welcomed the two Secret Service heads into his office and offered them cigarettes and seats. "I'm sorry we had to arrive at such short notice" said Gubbins "but Colonel Bruce and I have a message of the utmost secrecy and importance to deliver in person."

First, they told Koenig that the Allied invasion of Europe would be launched in a few hours' time. As previously agreed the Resistance should be mobilized to coincide with this.

Koenig was thrilled.

Second, they informed him that the invasion of the south, originally intended to happen simultaneously, would have to be delayed.

Koenig was concerned.

But it was the third, and final, message that caused the French general the greatest consternation.

"General Eisenhower" Gubbins continued, "wants the Resistance in *the south mobilized as well. It is essential that the Germans are not given advance warning of the likely point of attack, or indeed that we will only be attacking in the north."*

General Koenig, like de Gaulle, had become a symbol of victory for France. The hero of Bir-Hakeim, he had held off two divisions of Rommel's Afrika Corps for three weeks of day and night attack and then broken through German lines to join up with the British Army. As a military man, he could perfectly well understand the need to deceive the enemy. But he was being called on to deceive his own men as well; a deception that could cause the sacrifice of many hundreds, even thousands, of lives.

Koenig was horrified. He sat there, ashen-faced, as the enormity of what he was being asked to do sank in.

"I hope" Koenig told the visitors "that I will be able to issue an order for the Maquis in the southern sector to withdraw from combat at the very earliest opportunity?"

"We only need a couple of days" replied Gubbins.

A field near Vassieux, Vercors 02.30 a.m.

Jacques and Alain, the 'pianist' from Digne, are waiting with me at Dropping Zone B, some three kilometres outside Vassieux, one of the major towns of the Vercors.

Surrounded by flat land ideal for dropping arms and people, it's here that the airfield, at present little more than a landing strip, is being constructed in the anticipation of the arrival of supplies.

Late last night, Alain arrived at the Turrels' house in Seyne-les-Alpes with a message he had just received from Algiers:

NEW COURIER CHRISTINE PORTER ARRIVES DROPPING ZONE B 03:00 HRS 5 JUNE REGARDS CONSTANS ENDS

Being in desperate need of a reliable female courier, I am delighted. The three of us waste no time in returning to the plateau. We head straight for Vassieux and Dropping Zone B.

Shortly after 03:00 the roar of a Hudson echoes across the valley. A single pass, a sharp turn and a lower pass this time. Christine jumps free and in no time at all the Hudson is heading back towards Africa.

The silken chute opens beautifully but a gust of wind catches the parachute and drags Christine off in the direction of the forested hills to the west of Vassieux.

"God, I hope she doesn't land in those woods" Jacques says "they are treacherous." The three of us jump onto our motorcycles, Alain riding pillion on Jacques', and head for the forest.

It's almost 10:00 a.m. before we find her. She has been suspended from a tree for seven hours, her parachute cords are tangled in the branches, and she's dangling five metres above the ground, semi-conscious.

I throw off my knapsack, remove my jacket and climb up an adjacent tree from which I figure I'll be able to untie the cords. Jacques and Alain remove their jackets, tie them together with mine and wait for her to fall. Three minutes later she does.

By the time I rejoin the others Christine is already recovering her wits. Swearing like a trooper, she stands up, refuses any help and sweeps back her hair. All three of us gaze, motionless, speechless, transfixed by this dark Latin beauty with her high cheekbones and deep brown almond-shaped eyes. Even after seven hours of semi-conscious suspension from a tree, the effect is startling.

Christine, preoccupied with gathering together her scattered belongings, is unaware of the effect she's having on her 'saviours'.

"Welcome to the Vercors, Christine. I'm Luc. This is my deputy Jacques and our wireless operator Alain."

"What took you so long? I could have died up there…" she says angrily, still brushing bits of the forest off of her.

"We had to decide whether or not you were worth saving."

"Ha, ha" she says, giving an involuntary smile. "OK, thank you."

"Shall we head off? Are you up to riding pillion on my motorcycle?" I ask.

"I'd rather you rode pillion" she replies, still smarting from the indignity of her landing.

"Well too bad. Not today." Not your run-of-the-mill courier, this one.

Jacques and Alain jump on the Peugeot 25 and head south, down the valley towards the road to Digne. They are going to spend a few days at Seyne-les-Alpes organizing the last of the pre-invasion sabotage plans.

Christine and I head up the valley to St Martin. I have arranged with Mme. Breyton for us to stay at the hotel for a couple of nights to give Christine a chance to meet the main players before moving down to Seyne-les-Alpes to coincide with the anticipated invasion.

We arrive at the Hotel Breyton after lunchtime.

Costa de Beauregard and a tiny military man are huddled over their coffees when we walk in.

"Ah Luc, welcome" says de Beauregard "we weren't expecting you for another couple of days. Come meet Major Huet, our new Military Commander."

"Good to meet you Sir," I say "let me introduce you to Christine Porter, my new courier, just fallen out of the sky."

Christine takes off the unbecoming hat she's been wearing for the bicycle ride and shakes hands with the two military men whose reactions are predictable.

"We're delighted to have you with us" says de Beauregard

kissing her hand "you provide a welcome relief from having to look at the likes of Luc all day. Have you any good news from Algiers, Christine? The invasion perhaps?"

Huet orders cognacs all round.

"The best news for us Italians is that the Americans reached Rome yesterday" she lowers her voice as Mme. Breyton brings the tray of drinks and some bread and cheese, "but as for the invasion, there were lots of rumours that it was going to be at the start of this week; then the weather put paid to that."

"So, it looks as though we'll have to wait a while longer."

"Who can tell?" replies Christine, consuming her meagre meal with relish "there are so many rumours and counter-rumours. We thought it looked as though there would be a simultaneous invasion attacking Calais and Marseilles on 5 June. Perhaps it really is just better weather they are waiting for."

Christine finishes her cognac and excuses herself. "I think I will go and get some sleep gentlemen. I am a little tired. "

"OK" I say "we'll meet here in the café at 6:00 p.m., OK?"

"OK." She walks over to Mme. Breyton to collect her room key.

"Congratulations M. Luc. She is a real beauty" says de Beauregard.

"That she certainly is" I reply "let's hope she's also good at her job." But somehow I feel there is no cause for concern. She may be beautiful but she's also intelligent and has more than an air of confidence about her. "She certainly knows her mind."

They all laugh. "M. Luc, please stay a while" says Major Huet "It will give us a chance to get to know one another."

"Of course, as long as I can have some coffee."

Mme. Breyton brings over two more coffees and two more cognacs.

The two of us talk for the next hour or so until de Beauregard comes to collect Huet to take him up into the hills above St Martin to inspect a possible headquarters. Suddenly overcome with tiredness, intensified by the cognac, I say I'm going to have a nap.

"I'll see you down here before the radio broadcast Luc, d'accord?" says Huet. I go up to my room, collapse on the bed and immediately fall asleep.

At 6:30 I wake up, have a quick shower and go downstairs. No sign of Christine, but Huet and de Beauregard are standing at the bar and chatting. I join them.

"The radio is on in the back room. The BBC broadcast is in ten minutes." Mme. Breyton announces.

We adjourn to the private dining room.

The news of the Americans' triumphant occupation of Rome, the first Axis capital to fall into Allied hands, is followed by an unusually large number of messages personnels even by the standard of the last few weeks which has already seen a significant increase.

Immediately I realize what's up. The 'personal messages' of the last few weeks have been dummies, to fool the Germans, but now the invasion is ON. Any shred of doubt was dispelled when I hear my own coded message ordering the Rugby circuit and all Resistance movements throughout France to mobilize and to immediately cut all railway lines, telephone lines, destroy high tension pylons and mount guerilla attacks on all sufficiently small German convoys.

Huet, de Beauregard and I stare numbly at each other for an instant and then break out into broad grins. "At last" says Huet "at last our moment has arrived!"

"We have no time to lose" I say "I must get off the plateau immediately and ensure that all the Rugby circuit cells will have heard the broadcast."

"Fine" says Huet. "We will coordinate activity here. My orders are to mobilize the Maquis on the plain and to bring them up here. It will be a massive undertaking. Our numbers will increase from 400 trained soldiers to possibly 4,000 within the next few days," he turns to de Beauregard "Captain, send a messenger to Geyer and ask him to come here as quickly as possible." De Beauregard leaves us. " Luc, we will see you back here in a few days?"

"Sure, I'll be back as soon as I can." I go upstairs to awaken Christine. She's about to get a baptism of fire.

31

At 11:55 on the evening of 5 June, 860 km to the north of the Vercors, six gliders containing British infantrymen from the 6th Airborne Division, land on a field outside the village of Bénouville, near Caen.

The Allied invasion of Europe has begun.

By dawn, 18,000 British and American parachutists were on the ground in Normandy securing essential roads and bridges and disrupting German lines of communication.

In Paris the previous evening the head of SD wireless security received fifteen messages telling him that D-Day was to be that night. He went to see Field Marshal von Runstedt who said "Look out of the window, you fool." It was raining hard.

Field Marshal Rommel's headquarters had also intercepted a message indicating that an invasion was imminent but it was not considered sufficiently credible to be passed on to the Field Marshal who had flown back to Germany to celebrate his wife's birthday.

At 6:30 a.m. American troops came ashore at 'Utah' beach in amphibious tanks. An hour later British troops landed at 'Sword' and 'Gold' beaches followed by Canadians at 'Juno' beach. It wasn't until 10:15 a.m. that Rommel was finally given the news. He flew back to France immediately, charged by Hitler with driving the invaders back into the sea by midnight.

It is 11:55 on the evening of 5 June. With Christine holding tightly onto me I manoeuvre the Peugeot 25 off the massif and pull the sturdy motorcycle onto the silent, moonlit road to Digne.

Carrying fresh papers identifying me as a French civil engineer responsible for roadworks and thus free to travel at night (in an emergency), I've given Christine instructions to say that she is my wife if we're stopped. She reluctantly agrees. As I drive the bike at full throttle along the deserted road, determined to make Seyne-les-Alpes before dawn, I go through the orders in my head. As soon as D-Day is launched, with its planned, massive and simultaneous invasion of both the north and south, we are to disrupt German lines of communication; breach the critical railway lines from the south coast, the majority of which are in my territory, and unleash massed sabotage designed to prevent the Germans from reaching the invading troops in the north and, especially in our case, the south, while keeping essential routes open for the invading Allied forces.

Once that's achieved I'll return to the 'fortress' Vercors from where, in conjunction with Huet's forces (which by that time will have increased tenfold), we should be in a position to attack the Germans from behind.

My priority is to ensure that the 10,000 men and women under my control are mobilized without delay. I'll get Jacques to leave immediately for Montèlimar to organize the western side of the Rugby circuit; Christine will go to Barcelonnette and the Italian border to ensure that access roads from German-occupied north-western Italy are made impassable, and I'll go to Digne to mobilise resistance along the coast.

My one major preoccupation and concern is my fear that the

maquisards, after years of frustration and increasing feelings of impotence, will take foolish chances in their euphoria. There's a real danger that, despite all their efforts, the invasion will proceed less quickly than we hope. Should that be the case the Germans, assisted by the increasingly desperate Milice, will exact a terrible revenge. It doesn't bear thinking about. Once again I will insist that my people obey the cardinal rule of the Resistance:

NEVER, NEVER TRY TO HOLD A POSITION. DO AS MUCH DAMAGE AS POSSIBLE, THEN DISAPPEAR

By the time Christine and I pull up to the Turrels' house in Seyne-les-Alpes my plan of action is clear.

A beaming André Turrel opens the door. Inside Alain and Jacques are glued to the radio. Alain alerted Jacques immediately upon hearing the coded message on the BBC. Jacques got word to the cell leaders in the eastern section to ensure that they were fully mobilized and is preparing to leave for Montèlimar in anticipation of my instructions.

I introduce Christine to the others and then send her off to bed. She's had hardly any sleep in the last thirty-six hours and she needs to be wide awake in a few hours' time.

I tell the others of my concern about premature celebration and insist that the message is passed on to each and every one under Rugby circuit control. André Turrel agrees to contact all cells north of Seyne-les-Alpes and south of the Vercors. Christine will depart in three hours' time for Barcelonnette and the Italian border. Alain and I will return to Digne and organize the southern cells. There's no time to lose. Though there's been no confirmation as yet, it's entirely possible that the Allies may already have landed on the south coast.

By midday Jacques is already in Montèlimar. I am meeting the heads of the southern cells in a pre-arranged safe house south of Digne reiterating the plans already put in place from D-Day to D-Day-plus-5 and emphasizing the need for continued discipline lest over-enthusiastic cell members take the law into their own hands. Alain has collected two additional wireless sets and is cycling back the 21 km to Seyne-les-Alpes. Christine, armed with her new Red Cross identity card (by fortunate coincidence she is a fully-qualified nurse), is with one of the Barcelonnette cell members in his Renault 'ambulance' on her way to the Italian border.

All cells within the Rugby circuit are in full mobilization mode by the end of the day. Mountaineers have already engineered an 'avalanche' to descend on a detachment of German troops heading from Grenoble south on the Route Napoleon; Alpine Maquis, among whom are former ski instructors, once again disrupt the Rhone valley links in line with my instructions to destroy all links with Italy. Railway workers, always among the most vigilant and creative of resisters, organize mass derailment of troop trains.

By midday in St Martin en Vercors, every man woman and child able to move was in the town square. Captain Narcisse Geyer, with his mounted guard, was resplendent in full uniform astride his white horse. Major Huet, along with Colonel Descour, newly arrived from the plain to take up his position at his temporary headquarters in a forest seven km south of St Martin, were mobbed by tricolor-waving citizens.

Huet did his best to respond positively to the assembly yet, cautious by nature, he was concerned at the lack of news of the southern invasion. Even though Colonel Descour had emphatically reinforced the order that the Vercors was to be mobilized, Huet felt uneasy that he had had no direct order from General Koenig in London. Descour reassured him by showing him the de Gaulle letter from Algiers. He was certain, too, that once Chavant returned the following day, Huet would be completely satisfied. But for the moment the military commander of the Vercors remained concerned.

Huet established his HQ at the Hotel Breyton, reassuring Mme. Breyton that he would find a suitable place, perhaps the local school, for the Patron when he returned. Geyer, with his love of regimental tradition combined with his unparalleled understanding of guerilla tactics and desire to distance himself from his more traditional commander, established his own HQ in a remote farmhouse at La Rivière, several kilometres south-east of St Martin.

By nightfall on 6 June, 155,000 Allied troops had landed in the north. Hitler, in common with the French Resistance, expected a simultaneous invasion in the south and perhaps in Belgium and even Norway, and therefore hesitated to commit more troops to the north of France. Nevertheless, the British and American casualties amounted to over 10,000 men that day.

But throughout France, wherever possible, people had been sitting by their radio sets: Luc in Digne, Alain and the Turrels in Seyne-les-Alpes; Jacques in Montélimar and Father David at the Comtesse de Julienne's château; and Christine, with ten escaped Italian prisoners of war whom she had convinced to come over the border to join the Resistance, in a mountain lodge retreat near Barcelonnette. That afternoon General Charles de Gaulle broadcast to the nation.

The supreme battle is joined!
After so much struggle, so much rage and pain, now at last comes the decisive blow, the blow we have so long hoped for. Of course, it is the battle of France and it is France's battle ! Massive attacking forces, for us the forces of rescue, have begun to pour from the shores of old England. Here, at this last bastion of Western Europe, the tide of German oppression was once halted. Today it is the base from which is launched an offensive for liberty. France, overrun

for the last four years but never reduced or vanquished, is standing up to play her part.

For the sons of France, wherever they may be, their simple, sacred duty is to fight with all the means at their disposal. Our task is to destroy the enemy, the enemy that crushes and defiles our native soil, a detested and dishonoured enemy.

That enemy will do his utmost to escape his fate. He will ravage our native land as long as he possibly can. Yet for some time now he has been little more than a wild beast being driven back from his prey. From Stalingrad to Tarnopol, from the banks of the Nile to Bizerte from Tunis to Rome, he is now becoming used to defeat.

France will fight this battle with fury. She will fight with discipline. Just as each and every one of our victories has been won for fifteen hundred years, so will this victory be won.

With discipline! For our army, navy and air force, there is no problem. Never have they been in better spirit, better prepared, better disciplined. Already Africa, Italy, the seas and the skies have witnessed the rebirth of their strength and glory. Soon it will be the turn of their native soil.

For our nation which struggles, bound hand and foot, against an aggressor armed to the teeth, good order in the battle requires that certain conditions be met.

The first is that the instructions given by the French Government and by the French leaders whom it has designated for the task must be followed exactly.

The second is that our action in the enemy's rear should be combined as closely as possible with the frontal action of the Allied and French armies. Everyone must expect the task of those armies to be both hard and long. This means, therefore, that the action of the Resistance forces must be continued and intensified right up to the moment when the Germans are routed.

The third condition is that all those who are capable of action, whether by force of arms, by means of destruction, or of intelligence, or of refusal to carry out work useful to the enemy, should not let themselves be taken prisoner. Let all such individuals avoid imprisonment or deportation. Whatever the difficulties, anything is better than to be put out of action without having had a chance to fight.

The battle of France has begun. Throughout the nation, the Empire and the armed forces there is now only one determination, only one hope shared by all. Behind the cloud, so heavy with our blood and tears, behold! – the sun of our greatness is shining forth once again!

Any lingering doubts as to whether or not we should mobilize are finally dispelled by General Charles de Gaulle's stirring call to action. In Digne, I crack open a bottle of cognac and offer it to the assembled cell leaders.

32

By the following morning, 7 June, it became even clearer that the tide of the war was turning. Thanks to the breaking of the Enigma code used by the Germans for sending secret messages, the Allies learned that the Germans were running critically short of fuel. Hitler still believed, and would do for at least another week, that the Allies' main thrust would be south of Boulogne and that there would be a simultaneous invasion in the south, so German troops remained close at hand, hundreds of kilometres away from the action. This included General Pflaum, at Grenoble, who remained in his quarters, ready to move south at a moment's notice.

Shortly after 10:00 a.m. the ageing, battered bus carrying Eugène Chavant started its ascent onto the massif at St Nizier. The Patron could barely control his excitement. The spectacular invasion in Normandy had been just the fillip that his men needed and now he would at last be able to tell them that the arms and support they so desperately required were on their way. And not only that but he had it on reliable information that de Gaulle himself was considering making the Vercors his headquarters. It was full speed ahead for Operation Montagnards.

Nevertheless he was alarmed to see the tricolor flying from the top of Le Moucherotte, the three fingered granite rock shooting heavenwards above the pass of St Nizier. And in plain sight of General Pflaum's headquarters in Grenoble. Chavant felt it was needlessly provocative and would have it taken down.

As the bus arrived in the square at St Martin en Vercors it was mobbed. Seemingly every man woman and child in the area had turned out to meet their Patron. Chavant, visibly moved as he climbed down from the bus, was smothered in kisses and hugs as he made his way to the Hotel Breyton.

Planes flew overhead dropping posters. The joyous people clamoured for the bright yellow pieces of paper. It was a message from General Eisenhower praising the Resistance for their valour and sacrifice and asking for their continued help in the struggle ahead.

Having fought his way through the crowds, Chavant made it into the hotel where he greeted Mme. Breyton and his friends. He asked where Luc was and was told he had gone to Digne and wouldn't be back for a few days. He wasted no time in telling the assembled throng of his success in Algiers; of the 4,000 paratroopers who would be arriving shortly once the landing strip being built at Vassieux was complete. Arms would be arriving in substantial numbers very soon and, he told them, de Gaulle himself may well move his headquarters to the Vercors, so impressed was he with the plateau's impregnability.

That evening, as arranged by Colonel Descour, Chavant was introduced, by the local priest who had been specifically selected for the purpose given the delicacy of the situation, to Major Huet, the new military commander of the Vercors.

Despite the fact that Chavant was a life-long socialist with a disdain for church and army and Huet was a professional soldier, graduate of the elite St Cyr military academy and practising Catholic, they were bound by a mutual cause. Besides, Chavant had the great news of his success in Algiers. To the people's delight, Huet openly expressed his admiration for Chavant. The two men quickly agreed a 'modus operandi'. Chavant, realizing that the military phase of the operation was about to begin in earnest, willingly accepted that he, along with everyone else in the Resistance, would come under the command of Major Huet. In recognition of Chavant's importance to the success of his mission, Huet asked him to serve on the military council governing the plateau. Henceforth all their energies would be devoted to the successful mobilization of the Vercors and to the defeat of the German invaders.

Throughout the day, new recruits arrived in droves from the villages on the plain.

Busloads of sedentaires left their jobs and families, boyfriends and girlfriends and took to the massif. In the town of Romans, a large percentage of the male population suddenly downed tools and travelled through town, on bicycles, horse and cart, in gazogènes with their wood-burning washboilers bolted onto the trunks, in commandeered buses and on foot, waving the tricolor and shouting insults at the assembled Milice, as they headed for the Vercors.

The Milice meanwhile casually pulled out their notebooks and noted down names.

Elsewhere, the Germans were exacting terrible and easy revenge for the insult of the Normandy invasion. On Crete they took 400 Greeks, 300 Italian POWs and 260 Jews 100 km out to sea and then scuttled the boat.

Closer to home, in the prison at Lyon, the Gestapo decided, on the spur of the moment, to shoot all 300 suspected Resistance members rather than waste rations and paperwork by keeping them in jail or sending them to Germany.

But German brutality and nervousness was countered by French exhilaration and joie de vivre.

The following morning, 8 June, Colonel Descour, satisfied that the mobilization was working well, sent a radio message to Algiers:

REMIND YOU URGENCY TO PARACHUTE MEN AND ARMS REGION VERCORS STOP COULD RECEIVE AT LEAST ONE REGIMENT OF PARATROOPS STOP MOBILIZATION CARRIED OUT AT VERCORS BUT

ARMAMENT AT PRESENT INSUFFICIENT STOP
CANNOT RESIST IF ATTACKED STOP LACK LIGHT AND
HEAVY ARMAMENT FOR 2000 AT VERCORS STOP IT
IS URGENT TO ARM AND EQUIP THEM STOP THREE
MAIN DROPPING ZONES READY TO RECEIVE DAY AND
NIGHT ENDS

*At noon, Eugène Chavant and Major Huet met at Descour's farmhouse
headquarters south of St Martin en Vercors, in anticipation of the response
from Algiers.*

No response was forthcoming.

*Chavant's old suspicion of the military was beginning to resurface. The
prospect was of thousands of unarmed men, unable now to return to the
plains for fear of arrest and worse, who would be sitting ducks in the event
of a major German onslaught.*

Descour sent a second message:

TWO THOUSAND VOLUNTEERS TO BE ARMED AT
VERCORS STOP INITIAL ENTHUSIASM FADING OWING
TO LACK OF ARMS STOP DISPATCH OF MEN ARMS FUEL
TOBACCO EXTREMELY URGENT STOP HEAVY ATTACK
POSSIBLE STOP IMPOSSIBLE TO RESIST EFFECTIVELY
UNDER PRESENT CONDITIONS STOP DEFEAT WILL
ENTAIL MERCILESS RETALIATION STOP WOULD BE
DISASTROUS FOR RESISTANCE IN THIS REGION ENDS

*Chavant's thoughts turned to Luc. Surely with his contacts in London,
Luc would have a good chance of getting some response.*

*He spoke of this to Huet. "I think Luc may be our best chance of getting
some joy out of these bastards. I am happy to go to Seyne-les-Alpes and find
him, or at least get word to him. With his contacts in London, and Algiers,*

I think he could get some response. What do you think? It's worth a try, n'est ce pas?"

"Anything is worth trying if it gets some action. Patron, I think we may need you to be here, however. Could you not send someone else to Seynes-les-Alpes. Or could we not send a radio message?"

"I believe Luc said he was moving his wireless operator to Seyne, let's try" said Huet.

So a third message went out that day, this time to Luc, in Chavant's name.

Luc meanwhile had just received a message from Christine, delivered by courier:

Luc, we have a problem here in Barcelonnette. The Maquis have taken control of the town in the name of the Free French declaring a Republic of Ubaye. Tricolors flying from town hall. Situation perilous given proximity of German troops and presence of Milice. Colonel Zeller in charge. Will he listen to you? Please come.

This was just what Luc feared. He decided to leave immediately for Barcelonnette. He left Alain in Seynes-les-Alpes and borrowed the neighbour's black Citroën gasogène.

As I drive the lumbering vehicle towards Barcelonnette a terrible thought is gnawing away at me and, try as I will, I cannot dismiss it. I feel the empty pit in my stomach as it re-emerges.

We are being set up and it's going to result in disaster, torture and death for many of us. We're going to be sitting ducks for the Boche. And there's nothing we can do about it but play along.

I have become increasingly convinced over the past 48 hours that the mobilization of the south is a ruse to trick the Germans. And I figure the Germans will be coming to the same conclusion themselves.

I know there is probably no alternative. I may well have taken the same decision had I been in their shoes. But I have a terrible sense of foreboding. All we can do is to minimise the inevitable damage. It may be too late to prevent a bloodbath in Barcelonnette.

It wasn't until midnight that night that Alain decoded the Patron's message to Luc from the Vercors:

NEED YOUR HELP URGENTLY TO REQUEST ARMS FUEL MEN TOBACCO FROM LONDON ALGIERS STOP 2000 UNARMED MEN HERE RAPIDLY LOSING FAITH AND VULNERABLE TO MASSIVE ATTACK STOP SITUATION DESPERATE REGARDS PATRON ENDS

Luc had already left. Alain had instructions to stay by his wireless set. It was André Turrel who offered to go to Barcelonnette to deliver the Patron's message to Luc.

He was too well-known in the area to travel by breaking curfew. Instead he left in a terrible rainstorm at dawn.

As I approach the little 13th-century town in the Ubaye valley, surrounded by mountain walls, maquisards with Sten guns and tricolor arm bands stop me at a checkpoint.

"What the hell is going on here?" I yell to the men.

"The Liberation of France is going on" one of them replies, accompanied by the others all with grinning faces, "and this is where it begins, in the Republic of Ubaye" he adds proudly.

"Who's in charge?"

"Colonel Henri Zeller. His HQ is in the town hall."

I drive as fast as possible to the town square. After being stopped by two more barricades I pull up in front of the town hall. A large tricolor with the Cross of Lorraine hangs over the entrance, guarded by armed men.

"Where is Colonel Zeller?" I ask a guard as I run up the town hall steps.

"First room on the right."

Barely able to contain my rage, I open the door without knocking and find a group of men gathered around Colonel Zeller, Free French commander of the whole of south-eastern France and thus Colonel Descour's superior officer. There appears to be a heated discussion with someone seated at the table. Now I see that it's Christine.

"Luc, thank God you're here" she says "they won't listen to me. Please tell them how mad this all is."

"They'll find out soon enough."

"Welcome Luc" Colonel Zeller shakes my hand "your reputation precedes you. I am delighted you have come to share in our joy. Sadly your colleague here does not share our enthusiasm."

"Colonel, unless I am missing something, she is right. Just what do you base your enthusiasm on?"

Zeller sits down, somewhat disconcerted, and offers me a seat next to Christine.

"Well, if I may say so, I believe you are missing something Monsieur Luc. You may not have heard the news. The Allies are going to invade the south within the week."

"And who told you this?"

Zeller turns to one of the young men standing around the table. "Allow me to introduce you to Captain Edgar, recently arrived from Algiers. The Captain will explain."

"How do you do, Sir" says Captain Edgar, a young British staff officer.

"Well, Captain, I'm all ears."

"I have been seconded to Colonel Zeller's command in readiness for the Allied invasion of the south, Sir."

"When did you arrive?"

"Three days ago, Sir"

"How did you come?"

"I was dropped by parachute."

"I know of no landings from Algiers within the last three days."

"I was dropped to a Gaullist réseau, which is perhaps why you didn't know about it?"

Colonel Zeller interrupts the interrogation. "Surely this is proof enough of the Allied plans? They drop one of their own officers here specifically to alert us!"

"Colonel, I have had no indication from London or Algiers that an Allied invasion of the south is imminent, or even planned for the near future. I am certain I would have detected signals had that been the case. In fact I suspect the invasion may not be for weeks."

Captain Edgar pales visibly.

I continue "I suggest Colonel that you recall your men and get them to a place of safety as soon as possible. The Germans will not wait long when provoked. And you are certainly provoking them."

Now Zeller too is getting nervous. And not before time.

"If you are right, Luc, we have been badly misled. 600 men are at risk of losing their lives. I suggest you get hold of London or Algiers as soon as you can and get us out of this mess."

"What arms do you have, Colonel?"

"250 men have arms, the rest have nothing"

Suddenly a loud explosion rings out from up the valley.

"It looks like we may be too late, Colonel. I suggest that those men who do have weapons should try and fight their way out of town. The rest should take to the hills and do their best to escape.

We can always regroup on the Vercors."

"You mean we should retreat? Abandon the town?"

"I mean exactly that. You have no choice it seems to me." I turn to Christine who has been silently observing the situation.

"Christine, I want you to take your Italians and any other Resistance members and make your way back to Seyne. Can you do that?"

"Of course."

Suddenly André Turrel bursts into the room accompanied by an irate soldier who tries to prevent him entering.

"Luc" André Turrel shouts "a column of German tanks is on its way to Barcelonnette. They will be about 10 km away by now. I passed them an hour ago."

I'm impressed to see that Zeller moves into action instantly. He assembles the maquisards with weapons of some sort and instructs them to fight their way out of town. He doesn't tell them that they've been misled. That there is to be no imminent invasion. That they are bound to die.

I quickly read the Patron's message given to me by André Turrel. The two of us walk outside.

"Thanks André. You must get out of here as quickly as possible. Christine and her Italians need to go back to Seyne too. If you go with them I'm sure they'll be faster, and safer."

"Of course, Luc. But what about you?"

"From this message it looks as though I need to go to the Vercors. I'll probably take Zeller with me as he's supposedly the man in overall charge."

By 6:00 p.m. the firing has died down. There's no sign of a German attack. Zeller and I discuss the situation. We decide that most of the unarmed Maquis and André, Christine and her Italians should have been able to get out of town unscathed.

Captain Edgar has volunteered to lead a group of twenty men to try and stall the Germans as they approach the main road on the outskirts of the town.

Shortly after dawn the following morning, 10 June, Zeller and I and three maquisards escape in the Citroën. We strike out for the Vercors.

Captain Edgar was among the first to die as he attempted to prevent a German advance patrol getting through the barricades. By noon, 150 men have been killed or captured and German tanks are occupying the town square. The Tricolor has been replaced by the Swastika and jackbooted Wehrmacht soldiers stand where maquisards stood 24 hours before.

33

On the Vercors plateau itself there is widespread elation.

At last Descour has had a response to his increasingly desperate pleas for arms and men. It comes from his old military academy friend Colonel Jean Constans in Algiers who's now in charge of communication with the Resistance for General de Gaulle's office:

ONLY OBSTACLES AT PRESENT ARE ATMOSPHERIC CONDITIONS STOP WILL DO OUR BEST TAKING INTO ACCOUNT LIMITED AIR TRANSPORT FACILITIES

Not quite the immediate, action-filled response he would have liked, but a positive reaction nonetheless.

All across the plateau, in all the Maquis camps and among the villages and farms, the news of Chavant's promise of arms and men had spread like wildfire. Coupled with the increasingly optimistic news from the Normandy front and the stirring words of de Gaulle and others, this had the effect of motivating the people as never before. Spirits were raised, hearts were light, the end was in sight. For the Maquis it was validation for their years of fighting and suffering; even the 'attentistes' ventured out with light in their eyes, as if recovering from their self-inflicted comas.

Colonel Descour held a breakfast meeting in his farmhouse headquarters at Rang-des-Pourrets. The Patron, Huet, Geyer and Costa de Beauregard were all in attendance. The atmosphere was unusually convivial. For once, the anticipation of action, not to say victory, concentrated everyone's attention on a shared objective.

Huet reported that the Vercors was now fully mobilized with all passes guarded. There were now more than 2,000 new recruits on the plateau. While a lot of these men, and a handful of women, were sleeping rough (and it had been particularly trying due to the constant rainfall over the past few days) they were at least being fed. The villagers were being very supportive of the Maquis. Even those who may have had reservations in the past were providing food wherever possible.

Geyer was having difficulty restraining his men from executing raids on the plains. They had already commandeered two petrol tanks and kidnapped a number of German soldiers whom they had set to work building shelters. At Chavant's insistence they had reluctantly removed the Tricolor from the top of Le Moucherotte. But so far Geyer had been able to persuade his men to hold back from performing serious unauthorised attacks.

Costa de Beauregard painted a similar picture. The Milice had not been seen on the plateau for almost a week now. Some of his men had taken the law into their own hands and had shot two collaborators in Méaudre. Otherwise all seemed under control. The dropping zones were under observation day and night in expectation of the promised arms. Geyer confirmed that work on the landing strip at Vassieux was proceeding apace.

Only the Patron seemed preoccupied and lacked the enthusiasm of the others. Partly this was his nature but partly it was a growing suspicion that he may have been misled in Algiers. His mind kept on replaying that frightening scenario of thousands of unarmed men stuck on the plateau, easy targets for the German Army should they decide to attack in force. It concerned him too that General Pflaum was still entrenched in Grenoble *when by rights he should have moved to the south coast by now to ward off the expected invasion.*

After Huet, Geyer and Costa de Beauregard had left to return to their own HQs, Chavant communicated his concern to Descour. The two men decided to send another message to Constans in Algiers:

TWO THOUSAND ADDITIONAL VOLUNTEERS NEED TO BE ARMED AT VERCORS STOP DO NOT UNDERSTAND YOUR LACK OF SUPPORT STOP DISPATCH OF MEN ARMS FUEL TOBACCO EXTREMELY URGENT STOP HEAVY ATTACK MORE LIKELY BY THE DAY STOP IMPOSSIBLE TO RESIST STOP DEFEAT WILL ENTAIL MERCILESS RETALIATION STOP INSIST YOU HELP END

It's almost 2:30 that same afternoon by the time we turn off the road to Gap and start to ascend the pass to the Vercors plateau. I've warmed to Zeller now that I've had a chance to get to know him better but I find it hard to forgive him for his naiveté in permitting the carnage to happen in Barcelonnette.

"What an eerie place" says Zeller upon seeing the Vercors for the first time, "it looks like it has landed from another world."

"That's what we thought the first time we saw it. And it only gets worse."

I edge the Citroën around a tight curve in the road and 20 metres later we are confronted by a very professional-looking barrier. No unarmed teenagers this time but 20 armed men.

"Oh God" I say to Zeller "You know what this means. The Vercors too is declaring its 'Independence'."

"Christ" responds Zeller "with 2,000 men here this could make Barcellonette look like child's play."

"More like five thousand" I say as the leader of the barricaders approaches the car.

Zeller turns white.

Recognizing me, the maquisard says "Welcome, Monsieur Luc, to the Free French Republic of the Vercors, Sir."

"Thank you" I say, resigning myself to the inevitable "any action yet?"

"Not yet, but we are all prepared."

"I hope so" I say. But I doubt it

The Maquis leader signals to the others to lift the barrier and let the car pass.

Long before we encounter the next manned barricades my mind starts racing ahead thinking of the likely consequences from this devastating turn of events.

"I'm afraid we've been used as pawns" I finally say to Zeller as we make it up to the plateau and head towards Vassieux.

"It looks that way to me too" he says. And this from the Commander of the French Forces of the Interior for the whole of south-eastern France. Shit.

Descour was still talking to Chavant and waiting for an answer to his latest message to Algiers when he heard the old Citroën pull up to his farmhouse at 4:30.

"Mon Dieu" he muttered to Chavant as he looked out of the window. "It's our friend Luc accompanied by my boss, Colonel Zeller. They do not look very happy with life." He involuntarily patted down the hair on his head before opening the front door.

"Welcome. This is a surprise. I hope everything's OK?" Descour says quizzically as Colonel Zeller and I approach the house.

"First of all a cup of tea my friend" says Zeller "and then tell us what the situation is here. After that we will go over our news."

I greet Chavant with a warm hug. "How are you Patron?"

"That depends" replies Chavant.

"On what?" I ask, retying my shoelace.

"On what you have to say, I suspect. And what your friends in Algiers and London have to say."

"I thought they were your friends now?"

"For a moment I thought so too" says Chavant "but they do not act the way friends do here in France!"

"Welcome to the world of international politics" I say "I suspect Colonel Zeller here will be able to shed some light on the situation, from first-hand experience."

"Humpf" replies Chavant quietly "he's one of them. Don't expect much from him."

Descour's aide brings in tea for everyone and the five of us sit down to talk.

Descour starts. "Ever since the invasion the Germans have been very quiet. No patrols up here. Not even any Milice visitations. They are still at their HQ in Grenoble. We had expected them to move south by now."

"And what about mobilization? Judging from what we have seen on the way up here the Vercors is fully mobilized?" says Zeller.

"Yes it is. Our instructions were explicit and Major Huet has done a very effective job. He has also had to deal with hundreds of new recruits who have been arriving daily from the plain."

"How many men are up here now?"

"Over 4,000." Descour replies.

Zeller looks anxiously at me. Chavant, wily as ever, doesn't miss the significance.

"Colonel Descour" the Patron interrupts "I believe our friends have some bad news for us. Let them talk."

"Well, you're right" I say "there is no sign of an Allied invasion of the south. And there may not be for a week or more in my view."

Descour looks horrified. "But we can only hold out for a few days at the most. What if the Germans attack? We have no arms. We are expecting a large consignment of arms and ammunition and of course the 4,000 paratroopers that the Patron was promised in Algiers. So far the buggers haven't even answered our messages."

"We have just come from Barcellonette" I reply, "where the Maquis proclaimed a Free French Republic. I hear there's nothing left of it now. Most of them are dead. The rest have taken to the hills. We only just managed to escape ourselves."

"The bastards" mutters Chavant. "They lied to us. The bastards"

Descour's aide knocks on the door.

"Oui?"

"Major Huet is here, Sir."

"Send him in" Huet joins the group. Descour starts to bring him up to date when in come Geyer and Costa de Beauregard as well.

"I see the Vercors telegraph system is working well" says Descour, telling the new arrivals to find seats. Descour describes the situation thus far and relates his concerns about holding out if the invasion, as I suggest, might not happen for several days or maybe even weeks.

Huet and the others are aghast. All three of them had the same fears. Their units had increased in size enormously since the call for mobilization. But the new recruits are largely untrained and almost wholly unarmed. It is all they can do to provide them with the bare minimum of food and shelter, and often not even that. And now there is the danger of being attacked by a vastly superior, professional, fully armed, well-fed German Army.

The euphoria of the morning has been replaced by deep apprehension.

The gloom is broken by the arrival of Descour's aide once again.

"Alain has a radio message for you Colonel. Can he bring it in? It's urgent."

"At last" says Descour "This may be the good news we've been waiting for.

Of course. Send him in."

But the news could not be worse.

The radio message was not from Constans in Algiers promising men and ammunition.

It was from General Koenig in London. Descour read it aloud to the assembly:

CURB TO THE MAXIMUM ALL GUERILLA ACTIVITY STOP IMPOSSIBLE AT PRESENT SUPPLY YOU WITH ARMS AND AMMUNITION IN SUFFICIENT QUANTITIES STOP BREAK OFF CONTACT WITH THE ENEMY AS MUCH AS POSSIBLE TO PERMIT REORGANIZATION PHASE STOP AVOID LARGE CONCENTRATIONS STOP REFORM IN SMALL ISOLATED GROUPS ENDS

There's a moment or two of total silence as the full impact of Koenig's words sink in.

As the senior man present, Koenig's deputy in effect, Colonel Zeller breaks the silence.

"Gentlemen, we appear to have a crisis on our hands. A crisis brought about knowingly by our own leaders. A crisis that has used us as pawns to be sacrificed, if necessary, for the greater good.

It is clear to me now that General Koenig would have had no choice but to order the mobilization of the whole of France. Anything else would have alerted the Germans to the area of the invasion. This would have resulted in the German Army committing many more troops to the north and could well have lost us the war. Instead, the decision has meant that the bulk of Germany's forces have been kept away from the landing zones and that the Allies have made significant progress in their quest to restore the independence of France.

The problem we now have to confront is how best to limit the damage that has been done and inevitably will be done to our cause here in the south, and specifically here on the Vercors.

Colonel Descour, you are the commander of the French Forces of the Interior with responsibility for this area. I have complete faith in you, and in your subordinates here. I leave it to you to decide how best to handle the situation. I will support you in whatever decision you make."

Although intellectually each man present can appreciate what Colonel Zeller is saying, their specific responsibility is not the north of France and the invasion of Normandy. It is here on the Vercors. And their own general and supreme commander has put each and every one at risk of losing his life. We need to decide what action to take without delay.

"It seems to me" says Descour "that to obey General Koenig's order to disband and regroup in small isolated units would be impossible. We have thousands of men protecting all the passes in the Vercors. Similarly, how could we not engage with the enemy if they attacked, which they are now certain to do?"

Chavant, barely able to control his rage at having his beloved Vercors put in such danger by the politicians and the military, interrupts.

"To disband would be to send thousands of young men to their deaths. They would be tortured and killed as soon as they left the massif. As it is, the Milice will have had many of their names and could well be taking revenge on their families as we speak."

No one says a word. We all know he's right.

"What about explosives? Could we blow up the passes as Luc's men have done before?"

"We have no dynamite, only plastic" says Huet "and engaging the enemy with the few meagre weapons we have would be tantamount to sending our men to be slaughtered."

"Whatever happens we need more weapons, that is clear" responds Descour. "I suggest, no matter what, that Colonel Zeller, Luc and I try everything within our means to obtain men and ammunition."

"Of course, right away. I need to get back to my HQ at Seyne as fast as I can in any event to make certain that everyone in my circuit is aware of the new situation. I should be able to send messages to both London and Algiers tonight."

"Good" says Descour "that is a priority for sure. When will you be back?"

"Hard to say. I have a lot of ground to cover. A few days. Maybe a week. But I'll get word to you as soon as I hear anything."

"OK. And we will see to it that you are informed about our decisions here. Au revoir."

I leave Descour's headquarters, get back into the ageing but reliable Citroën and start back down the road to the Col de Rousset.

Descour continues his discussions with the others.

"The Germans don't appear to have sufficient soldiers to mount a major attack on the Vercors at present, but of course they could always get reinforcements."

"They can't be sure how many men we have up here. Or how much armour for that matter" says Huet.

"I think the Milice would be able to give them some sort of idea, don't

you?" says Chavant, packing his pipe with tobacco to calm his fury.

"I haven't seen any Milice since the invasion" interjects Costa de Beauregard "all they know is that thousands more men have come up here in the last few days."

It's Geyer who brings everyone's attention back to Koenig's order.

"Gentlemen. We have to decide first and foremost how to respond to General Koenig's order. It seems to me we have only two choices. Number One, we disperse and send all the newcomers, all two-and-a-half thousand of them, back to the plain where of course they will be subjected to torture and death. Number Two, we stay put and rely on Algiers, the British and the Americans to give us the necessary support."

"Number Two would mean disobeying the order" points out Costa de Beauregard.

"It would" replies Geyer "but I suspect not one of us would vote for Number One."

And of course none of them would.

"It seems we have no choice but to disobey the order of General Koenig" says Colonel Descour.

"Bravo c'est le grand boum!" says Geyer enthusiastically "Il va y avoir du sport!"

I pull the Citroën off the road just south of Vassieux and head up a mountain track to the storehouse where the Maquis' supply of fuel is kept. As I pull into the farmyard I notice another person getting fuel for his motorcycle. Even in the early darkness I recognize Jacques. He waves.

"Just getting back from Montèlimar?" I ask.

"Luc, thank God. I was just on my way to St Martin to find you."

"What's up?" I say, detecting the nervousness in his voice.

"The Germans are massing for an attack on the Vercors. Two

Panzer divisions and S.S. units are on their way to join Pflaum in Grenoble. They have Tiger tanks. Our people in the Drôme also report unusual activity in the airfield at Chabeuil which would be a logical base from which to launch an air attack on the plateau."

"Just as we expected I'm afraid. General Koenig has sent a message ordering us to demobilize throughout the south. You need to get to Colonel Descour's headquarters as fast as you can. They are even now deciding what action to take in light of Koenig's order. This may help sway them, although I suspect their minds are made up to ignore it."

"Mon Dieu, what chaos" replies Jacques. He immediately gets back on his motorcycle. I finish filling the car with fuel.

"Goodbye my friend" I say "and good luck. I'll see you in a few days. I'm leaving for Seyne but will return here with Christine once everything is sorted out. I'll get word to Montèlimar and make sure they know the latest."

"OK, and ask them to monitor the airport at Chabeuil too." We hug.

"Luc, just a minute, I want to give you something" Jacques walks back to his bike, fumbles in his knapsack and pulls out an envelope. "This is a letter addressed to you but you must promise only to open it if I'm dead. OK?"

This is getting a bit maudlin, I hope it's not an omen, but I agree. He hands me the envelope which I put into my own knapsack. By the time I turn around he has disappeared down the Vassieux road.

34

Jacques weaved his motorcycle through the town of La Chapelle en Vercors past a straggling group of fifty or so young men just up from the plains in answer to Eisenhower and de Gaulle's call for mobilization.

He responded animatedly to their calls of "Vive la France!" and heard, for the first time, "Vive la Republique du Vercors." His heart was heavy and he had visions of these young men just marching to their deaths.

As he arrived at Descour's HQ he noticed it was protected by a similar group of earnest young recruits. He brushed them aside authoritatively and hurried into the house.

The grand men of the Vercors were all still there. The Patron in his short-sleeved sweater and plus-fours; Geyer in the dress uniform of the 11th Cuirassiers and Costa de Beauregard in army fatigues. Huet, upright as usual, in a clean but ordinary-looking uniform, sat at the side of Descour's desk holding a cigarette between his right thumb and forefinger, as if he were aiming a dart. Descour, looking preoccupied, was huddled in a corner with Colonel Zeller.

A strange tableau that etched itself into his mind's eye.

The stillness, however, was due to be shattered with Jacques' news of the German attroupement on the plain.

For a moment or two, following the announcement, the room remained dead silent.

Then Zeller spoke. "At least that reinforces the decision we have just made. There can be no question of us demobilizing now. We might as well just offer up every man, woman and child as sacrificial lambs. No, on the contrary, we must muster all the men and arms we can and defend the plateau."

Descour and Huet nodded their agreement. Chavant, still furious, insisted that an urgent message be telegraphed to Algiers.

Chavant and Descour quickly concoct yet another message which they hand to Descour's wireless operator for immediate transmission:

FOR VERCORS REPEAT URGENT DEMAND FOR LIGHT ARMAMENT FOR 18 COMPANIES AND HEAVY ARMAMENT FOR 6 COMPANIES STOP MOBILIZATION WAS ORDERED FOLLOWING FORMAL ASSURANCE OF ARMS DELIVERY STOP IF PROMISE NOT FULFILLED IMMEDIATELY SITUATION VERCORS WILL BECOME DRAMATIC ENDS

Only Narcisse Geyer seemed to relish the news positively. He wanted to get back to his men as quickly as possible to prepare them for what he was certain would be an imminent German attack.

"Want to come with us?" Geyer said to Jacques as he buckled up his jacket, ready to leave.

"Why not?" said Jacques "Luc will not be back for a few days."

And with that they were off. Jacques left his motorcycle at Descour's HQ at the express request of Huet who, as Military Commander of the Vercors, might well need a faster way of getting around over the next few days than the gazogène Citroën he had been allocated.

Geyer and Jacques made their way to Geyer's HQ at La Rivière, a hamlet a few kilometres up in the mountains. They arrived at the camp around midnight. Jacques couldn't believe the sight; several hundred men queuing up at a makeshift kitchen where a young maquisard named Joseph La Picarella had spent all day making more than 400 pancakes.

"Picarella's pancakes have a mythical quality" explained Geyer "they give people courage."

"I think he'd better keep on cooking" replied Jacques.

The weather was wet and miserable. Many of the men were sleeping rough with only a motley collection of rags and blankets to provide some warmth at night. Food supplies were barely sufficient to keep body and soul together.

Jacques thought it made the conditions of the Glières Maquis look positively luxurious in comparison.

And yet morale seemed very high; and even higher the following morning when Narcisse Geyer told the men that, finally, the chance to exact revenge on the Germans was at hand.

Resplendent as usual in his sparkling uniform, Geyer stood on a soapbox and spoke to an assembly of 400 men representing the 1500 under his command.

"Mes amis, all eyes of France are on you, the courageous men of the Vercors Maquis and the 11th Cuirassiers. Within days, perhaps hours, we will meet the enemy and the hour of France's return to glory will be upon us. Our part is clear. We will show them that Frenchmen do not lie down and let the venemous Boche walk all over us. We defend our country to the last drop of blood. Let there be no misunderstanding. We will triumph. Each and every one of us will fight to the death for our mother country.

Remember the proud motto of the 11th Cuirassiers 'Toujours au chemin de l'honneur' Vive la France! Vive de Gaulle!"

"Vive la France. Vive le général de Gaulle. Vive le capitaine!" the crowd shouted back.

Stirring stuff, thought Jacques, if it works. It was very different from the traditional, restrained control of Huet and Descour but Jacques thought it was wrong of the others to mock Geyer. He clearly had the devotion of his men and was undoubtedly brave, if impulsive.

An example of which Jacques was to experience the following day.

Monday 12 June, 1944

Sleeping on a camp bed in the corner of Geyer's office, Jacques was shaken awake by the captain himself at 6:00 a.m.

"Mon ami Jacques, are you open to some sport today?"

Jacques cleared his eyes, shook his head and pulled himself up onto his elbows. "What have you in mind mon capitaine?"

"Have you heard of Chambaran?"

"Yes, of course. The German prison camp about sixty kilometres away. Why? Are we going to liberate it?"

"I am reliably informed there are three 25mm anti-tank guns in a garage on the outskirts of the camp. Plus Brens and enough ammunition to have ourselves a pretty spectacular time. What do you say we go and relieve the Germans of those guns?"

"I guess we may well need them" replied Jacques, jumping out of bed "and as we don't have any ourselves it makes perfect sense to me."

"D'accord. On y va" replied Geyer "get yourself a wash and one of Picarella's pancakes and join the rest of us in the yard."

Half an hour later the group of fifteen Maquis and two soldiers descended the plateau in two clapped-out trucks loaned to them by the Huiller Brothers, owners of the only trucking company on the Vercors.

Sticking to the back roads, which the Germans were increasingly loath to use thanks to Luc's successful sabotage campaign, they made their way through German-occupied territory to Chambaran. They didn't arrive until dusk.

A local maquisard met them on the outskirts of the area where the camp was situated and jumped into the truck to act as their guide.

Five minutes later he told Geyer's driver to turn off on to a dirt track.

Geyer, Jacques and two other maquisards were led across a field towards a large wooden garage just inside the perimeter of the camp. The local maquisard and his friends had already cut the barbed wire surrounding the camp in preparation for their visit.

The five men then climbed through the wire and ran to the side of the garage, out of range of the camp searchlight. The lock to the garage door had been picked an hour previously. The door gave, revealing, as promised, three 25mm anti-tank guns; a stack of Brens and several hundred rounds of ammunition and dynamite. Geyer went to the window of the garage and, using a small hand torch, signalled to the other men waiting in the brush across the road.

Within quarter of an hour all the guns and ammunition had been liberated from the now-empty and relocked garage and placed on the trucks.

In the early hours of the following morning the group reached the Vercors with their booty.

Now all they needed was a chance to use it.

It came soon enough.

Tuesday 13 June, 1944

By the break of dawn on 13 June, the weather had cleared markedly. Costa de Beauregard stood on the balcony of his farmhouse base looking through a pair of binoculars trained, alternately, on General Pflaum's Grenoble HQ with its Nazi eagle and black, white and red swastika flag clearly visible, and then on to the road from Grenoble to St Nizier. He had been informed that Pflaum had issued a curfew the previous day: no gatherings of more than three people anywhere, cafés and public places to close, everyone to stay inside from 8:00 p.m. until 6:00 a.m.

De Beauregard knew that this could only mean one thing. Pflaum intended to attack.

Huet too had heard the news and was on his way, on Jacques' borrowed motorcycle, to de Beauregard's HQ. The people of Saint-Martin, seeing Huet driving so quickly through town (Huet never rushed) also knew that something big must be brewing.

Back at his headquarters, Descour mulled over another non-reply from Constans. The same excuses about the weather but at least there was the promise of a few arms to be dropped as soon as possible, 'Wait for the BBC message', perhaps the following morning.

"And perhaps that will be too late" remarked Chavant who stopped in for an ersatz coffee and to check if there had been a response.

"No news on the invasion I don't suppose?"

"Rien" said Descour.

"When is Luc back?"

"Not for maybe a week" replied Descour. He understood the older man's worry, they all shared the same concern, but he knew that the Patron felt it more acutely. Chavant made his indignation clear. He had been promised 4,000 paratroopers and sufficient ammunition. Where were they now that they were so desperately needed?

But this particular morning Chavant was too preoccupied to complain. He too had been told about the curfew. And about the massing of reinforcements.

Just then Geyer arrived in a state of agitation. He had seen the early-morning issue of Le Petit Dauphinois, the German-controlled local newspaper. It announced that the tramway service on the St Nizier line was suspended until further notice.

"This means, I am certain, that the Germans will attack today via St Nizier!"

"Oui, bien sur" said Descour "and St Nizier is in the northern sector under the control of Captain Costa de Beauregard. You, Capitaine Geyer, are in charge of the southern zone. And you will have time enough to be involved when the attack moves to the south."

Chavant, who had never hidden his disdain for Geyer, nevertheless felt uneasy at not having him involved. In a combat situation Geyer's behaviour was, by all accounts, exemplary.

"Capitaine" he said "given the number of reinforcements that General Pflaum now has at his disposal I shouldn't think it will be long before they invade the south."

Geyer was hardly mollified. "What reinforcements does he have? Do we know, exactly?"

Descour replied that Jacques had already told them of a number of reinforcements.

"And today there are more" interrupted Chavant, "my people tell me that the bulk of the reinforcements are made up of S.S. together with the Wehrmacht's 157th Reserve Division, the butchers who massacred 700 Maquis on the Glières plateau."

"All the more reason why my trained men should be involved from the start, mon Colonel" said Geyer, directed to Descour.

"Your time will come Capitaine Geyer."

Geyer stormed out of Descour's office, mounted his horse and took to the hills.

It was around 8:30 that same morning that farmers working in the fields alongside the road to Vercors caught sight of the column of soldiers, four of five hundred of them, marching up from Grenoble towards St Nizier.

Some of the farmers wondered how to get word to the Maquis, but there was no need.

De Beauregard's men were placed all along the pass and had seen them too.

And so too, by 9:00, had Costa de Beauregard and Huet from their vantage point on the massif.

De Beauregard's Maquis had been given orders not to open fire until the enemy was close. Most of the men had Sten guns which were only accurate at very short range.

De Beauregard and Huet watched as the heavily-armed German

column, dressed in ominous grey, started up the pass. Shortly thereafter they heard the first staccato sounds of the Sten guns followed by the louder, deeper sound of the German 6.3s.

The German advance was rapid. Within an hour, two Wehrmacht soldiers had placed a machine gun at a strategic vantage point above the train track, protected by sandbags. De Beauregard ordered his men to try to take it out. It soon became apparent that the gun, its heavy 13.7mm bullets finding their mark all too frequently, was cover for a further group of soldiers planning their advance under its protection.

Thereafter a battle raged for three hours before Huet decided to send a messenger for reinforcements. "We need Geyer's crack commando team. Get Sergeant Chabal and his commando unit."

Geyer was fuming back at his headquarters at La Rivière following his contretemps with Descour.

He and Jacques were talking inside while Geyer's men tried to assemble the three stolen guns. It turned out that significant parts were missing rendering two of the guns inoperative. The third, however, could be made to work by cannibalising the other two. They were working on this when the messenger arrived by car at La Rivière.

"Capitaine Geyer, we are under attack" shouted the distraught messenger "hundreds of German troops are advancing up the pass towards St Nizier. They are already surrounding Charvet Hill. Major Huet has asked for your help. He needs Sergeant Chabal and his commando unit."

"Well, well" said Geyer "Captain de Beauregard has found the Wermacht 157th too much for him has he?"

Jacques, who had jumped up to start packing his few belongings when he heard the news of the attack, dropped everything.

"The Wehrmacht 157th. They're the bastards who massacred Tom Morel and the Glières Maquis."

"Yes" said Geyer "the Patron told me that this morning, I meant to tell you."

"There is no question then" replied Jacques "I am going with Sergeant

Chabal and his commandos."

"This isn't kid's stuff, mon ami."

"Get lost, Captain Sir" said Jacques much to the amusement of Geyer and horror of the messenger.

Geyer became serious. "Very well, tell Major Huet that Sergeant Chabal is on his way with twenty crack commandos and one green maquisard!"

Jacques smiled "Not so green."

"Do you have transport, Sir?" enquired the messenger.

"Certainly, the best, we have a bus. We shall transport our men by bus. It will show solidarity with the people."

Within twenty minutes a bus carrying Sergeant Chabal, 20 commandos and Jacques, drove through St Martin. Everyone on the bus was singing the Marseillaise. The townspeople waved them through, some with pride, some with hope, all with fear.

De Beauregard's men couldn't believe their ears when they heard the Marseillaise booming loudly from the bus as it wound its way down the mountain pass towards Charvet's Hill where they were still under fierce fire from the Germans.

De Beauregard halted the bus and gave Chabal his orders. "Seize the machine gun and instil fear into the enemy. Make them feel we are much stronger than we are."

"That we will do. Look at this" he uncovered the anti-tank gun. De Beauregard stared in disbelief.

"Stolen" said Chabal, grinning "by Jacques here and Captain Geyer from the German camp in Chamberan!"

"Bravo, Sergeant. Now let's get on with this battle."

Chabal and half of his commandos were going to take out the machine gun by utilising the cover of the forest and attacking from behind. Jacques and three others would try to secure the railway embankment which was giving the Germans an unwelcome vantage point. The remaining men would fire the anti-tank gun wherever it would do most damage as a show of strength.

The Maquis were clearly outnumbered two to one but de Beauregard was determined to tie up as many German troops as possible. After all, that was part of the master plan of Operation Montagnards, indeed of the whole Resistance. De Beauregard suspected that the real purpose of the German attack was to get a fix on the likely strength of their opponents. He was confident that Chabal, particularly with the aid of his anti-tank gun, would help to give the impression of strength.

Within half an hour, Chabal and his commandos had achieved their objective. Approaching from the rear they attacked the German gun post with their machine guns. The Germans quickly withdrew. Chabal and his men made their way back to try and join up with Jacques' group and secure the railway embankment where German troops were still in control. As they crossed the fields below the embankment they were fired upon by snipers from within the farm. Two of Chabal's men were wounded. One was killed.

Meanwhile Jacques and his three companions, having killed two Germans protecting the embankment on their way, emerged from the woods above the embankment. Two of the men, crawling along the open ground, attempted to take out two Germans manning a machine gun outpost on the northern side of the embankment. Jacques and the third man kept to the edge of the woods as they headed towards the southern outpost.

Suddenly there was a rat-tat-tat of machine gun fire in their direction. Jacques felt a searing pain in his leg. The force of the bullets knocked him back a couple of metres. His companion was killed.

Jacques crawled back into the woods as best he could, covering his path by brushing back the undergrowth with his hands as he edged backwards.

Moments later he heard a shrill, aborted scream from the northern section of the embankment. He knew what was happening without looking. The Germans were cutting a wounded man's throat.

He lay quite still. The adrenalin pumping through his body helped to numb the pain in his leg. Two or three minutes passed. Still no sign of German soldiers coming for him.

Gradually he hauled himself up on his elbows and looked around. Nothing; the Germans had retreated. Gradually even the sporadic firing ceased. Then he passed out.

It was several hours before he finally came to. Disorientated and losing blood he tore a piece of shirting off and bound his wound with it. He then started limping away from the scene of battle and found himself getting deeper and deeper into the forest.

He spent two days stumbling through the forest trying to find the Goule Noir. He knew if he could follow the gorge it would eventually lead him to civilization.

The pain of his leg wound, now infected he felt certain, coupled with intense hunger, caused him to hallucinate. He had moments where he thought he would faint and just willed himself forward. He knew there were likely to be Boche in this area although he had seen no sign of human life for two days, just the bleak, forbidding Vercors, its high rock outcrops pressing down on him like the closing lid of a coffin.

His mind kept wandering. He tried to bring it back by playing memory games with himself but it was becoming increasingly difficult. He fleetingly recalled childhood memories only to find them eluding his grasp once he tried to recapture them. He forced himself to recount conversations with his mother; pieced together the last moments he had seen her and attempted to resurrect them. He thought of his young nieces and felt guilty that they would not have him to provide for them. He played with puzzles in his head until that too started to drive him crazy.

All the while he fought to stay upright. His leg was dragging, slowing him down even more and making him unsteady. Every two or three minutes he would pause, straining to hear any unusual sounds, human sounds above the din of the water rushing down the gorge several hundred metres below. Nothing. It was hard to imagine there could be anyone within many kilometres of this god-forsaken spot. Still Luc's words intruded on his thoughts: 'Never let your guard slip. It is when you feel most secure that you are most at risk'.

Jacques continued like this for another hour. Dusk was descending on the gorge. He would have to find a cave in which to shelter for the night. He gave himself half an hour to find one. Still hugging the side of the escarpment he was surprised to see how close to the gorge he suddenly was. He must have been going downhill gradually without being aware of it. He stopped to survey the scene; a clear drop of 30 metres to the river below; no sign of any let-up in the sheer rock face; not even any flat land. He turned to make his way into the woods but as he did so he lost his step.

As Jacques fell, desperately clinging to the rock face, he knew this was the end. A strange calm and numbness overcame him.

But it was not the end.

He lay, trying to come to his senses, for some thirty seconds before he was able to pull himself halfway up.

A voice rang out like a shot from the woods above.

"Halt!"

Soaking wet, dead tired, famished and having just narrowly survived what he was convinced was his fall to certain death, Jacques slowly turned and stared lazily up at the woods as if to say "What now?" A torch beam almost blinded him but not enough to stop him seeing the barrel of a sub-machine gun.

Aiming it at Jacques' heart was a single camouflaged German soldier.

"Stand up and throw your weapon in the water!" the German said in perfect, controlled French.

"I am wounded and I don't have a weapon" said Jacques as he cautiously stood up. He was shivering helplessly, his soaking shirt and trousers clinging to his body.

The German didn't let his torch beam move from Jacques' face.

"Move down the bank four metres and climb onto the fallen tree" said the German.

"I cannot see where I am going with that thing in my face" said Jacques.

The German lowered the torch beam so Jacques could pick his way clearly to the tree. He was half tempted to risk plunging into the gorge below but knew he would have no chance of surviving even if he were able to get to the edge before the German shot him. He could feel the sub-machine gun trained on him. The torch beam showed no sign of wavering. This man was not frightened.

A large tree trunk lay horizontally and somewhat precariously on the bank, sticking out above the escarpment. Jacques hauled himself up onto the trunk with the last ounce of effort he had in him.

He slowly stood up.

The last thing he was aware of was swaying and slowly collapsing onto the bank, glancing at the end of the sub-machine gun barrel as he landed in slow motion at the feet of the camouflaged soldier.

As he came to, he felt as though he was being shaken like a salt cellar. His mind gradually cleared and as he regained the power to focus he realised he was being hauled up a steep bank hung over a man's shoulder. And then it came back to him; the German. He was being taken back to the Nazi camp. What could he do? He could hardly move let alone make a run for it. The German was clearly fit and strong.

He decided he best be quiet. At least he was compos mentos.

He made no noise. His head was turned away from the German but he could see nothing except for passing rock and trees, like everywhere else along the gorge.

He felt they were on flat land. The German quickened his pace. They reached a hut. Door opened. Light. Warmth. Silence.

Jacques was flung down onto something softish. A couch? A bed? He kept his eyes closed for the time being, deeming it safer. There were noises of cups and dishes of some sort. Cupboard doors opening and shutting. But no other voices. Were they alone? One on one, even in his current state, would give him a fighting chance. He had expected at least three or four. Strange.

"You! Stand up!" the German prodded with a stick? a gun? "I know you're awake. I am a doctor. I felt your limbs contract as soon as you came to while we were coming up the hill. You cannot fool me. Stand up!"

Jacques slowly stood up. His wet clothes clung so tightly to his body that he clearly carried no weapon.

He moved his head in an uncontrolled manner both to try to convince the German that he was not really alright and to take in the scene about him. Two beds, table, chair, fire… signs that there must be at least one other German.

"Who are you?" the German demanded "French? Spanish? Maquis? What are you doing here? Don't you know the war is over for your lot. You are finished. The Fatherland has triumphed!"

"Fuck the Fatherland!" said Jacques, fully expecting to be beaten, or worse. But there was no immediate response. Just silence.

After a minute or so the German, still with his sub-machine gun trained on Jacques said "What are you fighting for? Don't you know it is hopeless? Why carry on?"

"You have invaded my country, you and your Fascist friends. You have killed my mother and father and most of my friends. I will fight you with every last fibre of my being." He spat out the words and then spat on the floor.

The German made no reaction.

"Take off your shirt" said the German.

"Why?"

"You are wet and cold, take off your shirt!" He nudged him with the sub-machine gun.

Slowly Jacques unbuttoned his soaking wet shirt and took it off, holding it by his side.

"Give it to me" said the German.

Jacques duly handed him the shirt. The German took it and hung it on a chair in front of an ancient, small, gas-operated fire all the while keeping his gun pointed at Jacques.

Jacques stood stock still in nothing but his trousers. His body was still wet, his heart was still racing.

"Now give me your trousers" the German motioned with his gun.

Slowly, Jacques removed his trousers and handed them to the German.

Given this inexplicable situation, Jacques retreated somewhat from the fear that had gripped him until now. In his almost naked state he watched the German carefully hang his sodden trousers over the back of the chair in front of the fire.

"And now the rest" he commanded, gun still at the ready.

Jacques didn't move. He had little enough dignity remaining and what he had he wanted to keep.

"Now!" the German said pulling himself up to his fullest Nazi height.

Reluctantly, Jacques pulled down his wet underpants and let them lie where they landed.

"Move!"

Jacques took a step back and the German picked up the underwear, all the while retaining eye contact.

The German took the underwear and hung it over the fire screen. He then put down his gun for the first time, picked up a towel and a blanket from the bed and gave them to Jacques.

Cautiously Jacques dried off and then wrapped the blanket around himself. He stayed where he was.

"You'd better sit down on the bed," said the German "let me look at the wound."

Jacques, perplexed at this unexpected turn of events, sat down and pulled his leg free from the blanket. The wound was still covered in the primitive bandage that he had put on days earlier. It was now caked red despite being soaking wet.

"My name is Hans" said the German as he bent down to undo the bandage "I am Austrian, not German. I was a doctor in civilian life."

He cut off the bandage to reveal a dangerously infected wound on Jacques' fibula.

"I need to redress this. Don't move. I will get some disinfectant and clean bandages."

Even now, wearing nothing but a blanket, Jacques' mind was rapidly thinking of ways to escape; but something kept him where he was. Perhaps it was the unexpected. This German, or Austrian, guy was different. He seemed seriously concerned. And where were his comrades? There were knives and forks and mugs lying around; clearly there were others somewhere, but where?

Five minutes passed. Hans, unarmed and in shirt sleeves, returned with a bowl of boiling water and fresh bandages. He also had two ham rolls and a cup of coffee which he offered to Jacques, who cautiously took them.

Silently and professionally, Hans bathed the wound and redressed it.

Jacques, now somewhat sustained, warmer and reassured that his wound had been carefully bandaged, sensed from Hans' benign treatment, that he was in no immediate danger. An unlikely calm enveloped his body. How strange, he thought, that for the first time in ages he felt warm, fed, comfortable and secure – and he was a prisoner of the Gestapo.

"I think you should try to sleep" said Hans.

Taking this incongruous situation to its limit, Jacques felt his body almost involuntarily go limp as he collapsed into a lying position and almost instantly fell fast asleep.

A deep sleep gradually gave way to bouts of intense dreams. At first they were carefree dreams of summers fly-fishing with his father, of schoolboy pranks and family suppers.

Then they changed direction.

Great waves of sensual warmth emanating from below enveloped Jacques' upper body. The overpowering flush of sexuality rendered his upper limbs limp. He felt the blood rushing downwards from his head and arms. It felt as though his groin was on fire. Fully aroused, he felt a moist warm organ surround his own drawing it into its depths and then releasing it, repeating the action in pleasurably similar yet varied ways, caressing every nerve ending, stimulating every blood vessel he had.

With mounting anticipation he waited to see what part of his body would surrender next to this sensual invasion.

Each time Jacques thought it was over and started to relax back into dreamless sleep the sensation would grip him again. Now a gentle and loving caress, lulling him into a floating limbo. He felt himself gently writhing in tune to the limbs that were enveloping him. Just as he would get used to the rhythm, it would stop. A period of quiet relaxation followed and then another, different, series of sensations would take over.

And then the time for gentleness was over. Jacques felt his organ being sucked away from his body and momentarily suspended in moist mid-air. Arms grasped his body and turned him over. Fingers and then a tongue followed his spine down to the base and beyond. He was turned back over again. The organ that had gently played with his own before now took him all inside so that Jacques felt he might disappear altogether. It pulled him in. Released him. Pulled him in. Released him and then wouldn't let go at all. It clung tightly around him. Faster and faster it moved up and down never releasing its grip. Jacques had lost all control of his body. He felt nothing but total surrender as his body tensed; his muscles tightened, his torso lifted upwards, outwards and offered itself into the abyss that encircled him.

Within moments the arousal was too strong to contain. At the point of climax Jacques became fully awake and aware of everything around him. All his sensations were on red alert.

Hans did not lessen his grip until he too was spent.

Jacques watched as Hans climbed out of bed and walked across the room, the light from the fire highlighting the Austrian's muscular body as he made his way to the sink.

Hans returned with a warm, wet cloth and wiped Jacques' body clean. He turned off the fire, climbed back into the bed and kissed him.

"I don't want tonight ever to end" said Hans. Jacques smiled and put his arm around him, pulling him down so Hans could lay on his chest.

Then, his naked limbs intertwined with those of his enemy, Jacques fell into a deep sleep.

Seven hours later, Jacques awoke to the smell of freshly brewed coffee. He was surprised to see that Hans was already up and dressed.

"I hope you slept well" said Hans "you'd better get up now. You must be out of here by 08:00. My replacement is due here at 10:00."

Jacques got out of bed. Even after the night's exertions his newly bandaged wound seemed a lot less painful. He pulled on someone's dry clothes, his own were torn and still damp, and washed his face in the basin next to the fire.

"Why are you here all alone?" asked Jacques. "I thought you Gestapo men always travelled in pairs?"

"My partner was shot by the Maquis two days ago. They took his body away" said Hans pouring out two cups of black coffee. "I managed to escape. He was the wireless operator. I don't know how to use the wireless so I couldn't call for help. I decided to stay here until today when our replacements are due to arrive."

They sat down together at the table where Hans had already put out bread rolls and cheese.

Jacques decided to probe a little further. "Why did you join the Gestapo?" he enquired, sipping his coffee.

"They advertised for people who could speak French. The pay was better and I had the chance to come back to France where I spent my summers as a child."

"You make it sound as though you are a tourist! In fact you have come back to kill us."

"I have killed no one. And I don't intend to. I volunteered to be a lookout. I never really expected to see anyone in this inhospitable place. It was an easy option.

I am just really doing my duty like everyone else, French, British, American, we are all doing our duty. If you had been born in Austria instead of in France you would be where I am now, doing your duty too."

"So you are just going to let me go? Aren't you breaking some Nazi rule? What if they find out? What if I tell them? What if I come back here and kill you?"

"I'll take my chances" said Hans. They both knew that he would be safe.

"Well, you know I am very grateful" said Jacques "but I pray I do not see you again. I think the war is almost over, don't you?"

"Since June I have thought it would be over but still it goes on. I think people underestimate Hitler's determination. Powerful men do not see straight any more. They are blinded by their own ambition and a misplaced confidence in themselves. They are convinced they are right despite all the evidence to the contrary."

"What will you do when it's all over?" asked Jacques.

"I will return to Bad Godesberg and resume my life as a doctor. And you?"

"I will return to Annecy and study to be an architect" said Jacques.

"Funny" said Hans "here we are, an architect and a doctor stuck in the middle of the forest, in the middle of a war that neither of us wants, preferring to make love when our masters want us to kill each other. Funny"

"Yes, funny" said Jacques.

"Will you come find me after the war?" asked Hans.

"How could I not?"

It was eight o'clock. Armed with provisions, an illegal map, wearing dry clothes from Hans' dead partner and carrying a German revolver, Jacques made his way back down to the gorge.

35

As soon as Jacques and I part, after filling up our respective transports at the Maquis' fuel depot, I head for the Turrels' house in Seyne–les–Alpes, arriving shortly after midnight.

Christine is still asleep in the little 'mother-in-law' house across from the Turrels' that has been allocated to us as our safe house. As I quietly open the front door I call out to Christine, anticipating that she may well be crouching behind the bedroom door, pistol at the ready.

I'm right. Naturally cautious, she emerges, armed and wearing nothing but a man's open necked white shirt (one of my shirts I notice) her dark locks accentuating those devastating almond eyes. To my surprise and delight she flings her arms around me.

"It's good to see you, Luc."

"Can't think why" I say, throwing down my knapsack and taking off my jacket "I'm hot, sweaty, tired and very bad company."

Christine lights a candle and turns on the stove "I'll make some coffee while you clean yourself up. Then you must tell me everything."

"I'll have a quick wash but I have to be in Digne before daybreak."

After I freshen up and change into some clean clothes, Christine sits down with me on the primitive bench that serves as our couch and we sip coffee as I bring her up to date on the latest developments on the Vercors.

We spend a half hour or so going over plans for the next few days before it's time for me to go. Christine is going to leave in the morning, taking the Italians with her, to join Jacques in St Martin. The Italians can be assigned to one of the Maquis groups. Christine and Jacques can then report to Colonel Descour or to Major Huet. I will concentrate on ensuring that all cells know to revert to sabotage and disruption. I am certain, though, that the mobilization order will have meant that many of our people will already have exposed themselves irretrievably to the Milice or the Germans. They will find it impossible to return safely and will have to take to the Vercors. Many will have been killed of course.

As soon as I get to Digne I head for the American vet's house and her spare bed. Six hours later I meet the 'pianist' Alain in a café and hand him the following message for transmission:

SUPREME HEADQUARTERS HAS LED ALL OF US INTO THINKING THAT THE LANDING IN THE SOUTH WOULD FOLLOW WITHIN TWO WEEKS OF D-DAY AT MOST STOP WE HAVE BEEN FORCED INTO PREMATURE ACTION STOP DELIVERANCE ONLY POSSIBLE IF LARGE SUPPLIES OF MATERIEL ARRIVE IMMEDIATELY FAILING WHICH ENTIRE RESISTANCE ORGANIZATION IN SOUTH-EAST WILL COLLAPSE STOP NEED HEAVY AND LIGHT MACHINE GUNS RIFLES GAMMON GRENADES NOT STEN GUNS STOP TWENTY PER CENT OF AMMUNITION SUPPLIES DESTROYED STOP NEED TEN MILLION ROUNDS AMMUNITION MINIMUM AND COMPANY OF PARATROOPS ENDS

I then spend the next week criss-crossing the Basses Alpes and the Isère as far as Lyon meeting all the cell leaders I can. Despite the feeling of anger that they had all been let down and the nervousness concerning the non-invasion in the south, morale is remarkably high, mainly because the news from Normandy is getting better.

But it's almost the end of June and no sign of an imminent invasion here in the south. Rumours abound but I think an invasion is highly unlikely while Allied forces still encounter significant resistance in the north. This, coupled with the lack of response from Algiers to our pleas for help, make me increasingly apprehensive.

Back in Saint-Martin en Vercors, Dr Fernand Ganimède, a 70-year-old physician, is taking delivery of a truckload of medical supplies and equipment seized at gunpoint from a hospital in Grenoble by the Groupe Vallier, one of the daring but virtually uncontrollable 'terror groups' also based on the plateau. Doctor Ganimède has set up a makeshift hospital in a house in Saint-Martin which is already full with the wounded and dying. He needs additional space but for the time being he is coping, just about. He is being helped by his wife and by their young son Jean along with two nurses and a trainee doctor. He desperately needs more help. The Groupe Vallier has provided sufficient supplies for the time being but he needs nurses and doctors, not just supplies.

Christine heard from Colonel Descour about Dr Ganimède's plight. As luck would have it, two of the Italians she has brought back to the Vercors are trained doctors, and she herself is a trained nurse. The three of them present themselves at Dr Ganimède's hospital in Saint-Martin the morning after their arrival.

Dr Ganimède is delighted at this virtual doubling of his staff and puts them all to work immediately.

At around 2:00 that afternoon Christine administers a sedative to a young man who has had his appendix removed. She glances over at the dozing patient in the next bed and is sure she recognizes him. "Jacques, is that you?"

Jacques quickly comes to his senses. "Christine! Thank God. What are you doing here?"

"Just helping out but what are you doing here, more to the point?"

"It's a long story, Christine, but …"

"OK, tell me later. I've got work to do now. You look OK to me. It's a bullet wound isn't it?"

"Yes, Dr Ganimède removed it yesterday. I feel a lot better today. He says I must stay until tomorrow unless they need the bed."

"He must be getting soft. I'm going back to Seyne tomorrow" she said quietly to Jacques "to meet up with Luc. Let's meet tonight at the Hotel Breyton. I'll tell Dr Ganimède that you are needed."

"Fine by me."

Dr and Mme. Ganimède thank Christine profusely for her help and for providing the two Italian doctors who have been assimilated quickly into the team. Christine says she will be back whenever time permits, maybe even with some more Italian doctors, and leaves to meet Jacques at the Hotel Breyton.

Stalwart Mme. Breyton provides them with a meal on the house and pastis for two. Jacques fills Christine in on the details, all those that he figures she needs to know, about his escape following the German attack, and his meeting with, and nursing by, Hans.

"And the bullet wound?" asks Christine, impatiently.

"After leaving Hans, I made my way back in the direction of Saint-Martin. Not too far from the outskirts I was accosted by one of the Groupe Valliers; they're a bunch of hired assassins who…"

"I know who they are. They supplied the hospital with medical equipment and supplies."

"Well, they're still a bunch of terrorists. True terrorists. Anyhow one of them jumped me and pinned me to a tree and held a gun to my head. He thought I was from the Milice. I was wearing a German Army shirt and trousers given to me by Hans which didn't help of course. In any event he refused to believe me. I had no choice but to kick him in the balls. As he grimaced in pain he pulled the trigger. The bullet went clear through my shoulder."

"And then?"

"Then I killed him."

"I see, best not to broadcast that. What did you do with the body?"

"Buried it."

"Good. Anyhow, enough of that Jacques, I'm off to Seyne in the morning, just for a few days I think. Meanwhile there is something you could do if you wouldn't mind?"

Christine was so skilled, so talented and so willing to get involved in the most dirty and dangerous business herself, a sort of female version of Luc, that Jacques was happy to do anything she asked.

"Tell me" he replies.

"There is a desperate need for vehicles. The Huilliers' trucks were almost completely destroyed by God knows who last week. Milice probably. We need replacement trucks and cars and motorcycles. Is there any way you could take a few men and get some for us?"

"Of course I will" said Jacques.

"Va bene, you're a good man Jacques. I'll see you in a few days."

"Va bene? You're spending too much time with those Italians."

Christine smiles, says "Bonne nuit" and goes upstairs for a proper night's sleep. She has to leave for Seyne at dawn.

Jacques goes in search of four or five men to accompany him on his mission to steal vehicles.

I get back to Seyne from Digne at 11:00 p.m. the following evening. I spot a light coming from underneath the door in the Turrels' house so I go in for a late-night brandy.

André is talking with his son, Pierrot, in the kitchen. Pierrot has been monitoring the transmitter sets. No news from Algiers. Nothing from London.

"It's looking pretty grim isn't it Luc" says André,

"It is."

"Well morale is still high nonetheless. So you must keep yours up Luc. Speaking of which there's a young lady over in your house whom you'll probably be pleased to see," André grins.

My feelings for Christine must be a tad more transparent then I thought.

"All is not lost then" I say, thereby admitting defeat. I polish off my brandy and head for the door, "Bonne nuit, mes amis"

"Bonne nuit."

Ten minutes later

I have never been submissive in bed. Nervous sometimes. Unsure now and then. But submissive never. Until now. Naked, I lie on my back staring, dumbstruck at the sheer beauty of her.

Christine removes her shirt, my shirt, in which she now sleeps, revealing, in tantalizing slow motion, her naked body. It's unnerving having your every fantasy revealed as fact. God she's gorgeous.

My eyes trace the perfect line from her eyes to her mouth as it makes its sensual way downwards following the chin and under her neck and then descends briefly only to be thrust outwards and upwards by her gently undulating breasts.

The tension in my limbs becomes unbearable. She is completely naked. Her breasts now firmer. Her hair shimmering in the candlelight. And those eyes, always those eyes. Her rapid heartbeat sends tremors throughout her body that whet my appetite even more.

Christine's aura of unconquerability, her self-assuredness in her womanhood and her physical courage make these minutes of seduction so sublime that I feel swept away. Oddly, as this most elemental of moments draws closer, I lose all sense of worldliness. I have been taken to another sphere altogether. I am hers completely. She can do whatever she wants with me. I am helpless under her spell. I am floating, orgasmically, in space.

Complicit in my anxiety, Christine straddles my body. Total control. She gently kisses my eyelids. She brushes past my expectant mouth on her way down my body, stopping at the navel. She returns to my face and rapidly changes gear. We kiss, tenderly at first and then with increasing power as our tongues entwine and fight for domination, depth, intensity. I bury my face between her breasts and begin to kiss and caress them. She pulls away, sits upright, and moves her hand determinedly down to my groin and seizes me. Moving her straddling body lower down my legs she wraps her mouth around my cock.

I fight back the desire to come, but then she looks up at me, those almond eyes penetrating my soul while her mouth is engorged with my cock. And I almost lose it.

She releases me just in time, takes hold of me and gradually guides me inside her. She is worryingly professional. Her vaginal muscles tense on demand and understand implicitly just when to relax.

She lowers herself down now, all the way. I reach a point inside her that unleashes a flood of pleasure that renders her too, momentarily, helpless. She stares down at my body, traces her finger under my left nipple and follows a line up under my armpit, down my chest, across my stomach, circling my navel to the point where our bodies are molded into one. Then she lowers her face and kisses me, this time more gently. While we kiss lovingly above, our bodies below are demanding animal satisfaction. We release our lips.

I cup her breasts in my hands gently caressing them with my

tongue. She lifts her head and moans. She contracts her vagina and writhes her body to our ever increasing mutual stimulation.

I feel her succumbing to my power now and move her beneath me. Putting my arms under her thighs I penetrate even deeper. She moans and moves her head to and fro as if inebriated.

I move slowly upwards and we kiss, deeply and lovingly as if uniting our mutual desires. Our bodies now move in concert as if orchestrated by some all-knowing choreographer. Our eyes lock in dual acknowledgement of mutual submission.

I pull out and kiss her. She grabs my cock and guides it back in. Fast and furious now our basic instincts take over and we gratefully submit. Like the two animals we are, we thrust and moan, stare and sweat, gasp and, finally, come.

The calm after the storm. Silence. We speak only with our eyes.

Ten minutes later, relishing those most beautiful of all post-coital cigarettes, we lie together damp and hot, exhausted and thoroughly happy.

I have never felt more at one with myself, with the world, with human nature, with a woman than I do now, with Christine.

A feeling of ethereal lightness pervades our bodies, lingers there, immobile, until we both fall asleep.

At 5:00 a.m. there is a loud rapping at the door, to the tune of Beethoven's 5th. Although I recognize the signal, I get the rapper to identify himself before opening the door.

"I am Jean-Marie from Xavier, M. Luc. I have an urgent message." I remember that the 'pianist' in Montèlimar occasionally enlists the support of his neighbours' son, Jean-Marie.

Wearing only the shirt that Christine usually wears to bed, I open the door to see a boy barely 13 years old standing before me. "Come in" I pull him inside while shaking his hand, "want a drink, something to eat?"

"No Sir, thank you I must get back."

"OK, what does Xavier have to say Jean-Marie?"

The boy is out of breath and speaks rapidly. "He asks that you meet him as soon as possible in Chabeuil. There is a great assembly of planes and trucks there. He says they are destined for an attack on the Vercors."

Christine, wearing my motorcycle jacket, materializes from behind the door. The boy politely averts his eyes.

"It's OK, she doesn't bite; not you anyway."

He steals another glance.

"Tell Xavier I will meet him at Café Carrefour by the crossroads into Chabeuil centre off the ring road at 3:00 this afternoon will you."

"Yes Sir, I will do."

How did this kid make it here I wonder? He's anxious to leave. "Hey, Jean-Marie. How did you get here from Montèlimar?"

"My uncle trades rabbit skins in this area. He brought me here. I must meet him at the road into Seyne in ten minutes. We must make it back before it is too light. Au revoir Sir, Mademoiselle."

Chabeuil airport lies near the southwestern section of the ring road that encircles the Vercors massif, barely 5 km from the plateau. Only moments away by air. Any build-up of aircraft is very ominous.

At three o'clock that afternoon I drive my Highway Department Citroën into the parking lot of the Café Carrefour, a natural stopping off place for traveling businessmen and regional employees. Its owner, Henri, is an experienced Resistance man.

Xavier is already there, pointedly reading a newspaper from the collaborationist press.

I nod hello to Henri and drop my satchel on the chair next to Xavier before greeting the 'pianist' with four kisses, the norm in this part of France.

"Coffee Xavier?"

"Please." I go to the bar, exchange a few words with Henri, and collect our two coffees.

Xavier, clearly perturbed, explains that the small and usually quiet airport where normally three or four planes are parked near the runway, is now rumoured to be bulging with more than 60 aircraft. In addition Rugby circuit members have reported that several convoys of trucks have been spotted heading in the direction of Chabeuil. Perhaps they are just heading for the south coast and the anticipated invasion but it is suspicious that they have taken a route that brings them directly by Chabeuil instead of the more direct route south.

I decide to go and have a look for myself. Just to double-check before raising the alarm back at the Vercors, and hopefully getting those buggers in Algiers to respond.

"How easy is it to get close to the airport?" I ask Xavier.

"At the moment it's still pretty easy, but the Boche are gradually sealing off the surrounding roads. If we try tonight we should be OK."

"Good, we'll go and have a look tonight then. I'll get the name of the contact with a house near the airport and we can meet there and then go on by foot after dark. OK by you?"

"D'accord."

"Wait here"

"OK" Xavier picks up his paper. I walk over to the bar and have a quiet word with Henri. A minute later I return to Xavier.

"OK Xavier. There is no need for you to hang around. Henri says that a young couple that I know live close to the airport. They both work with us. I am sure that Guy, the husband, will come with me. Best that just two of us go I think. You head on back to Montélimar. And thanks for getting in touch. If it's true, it's critical news."

We say goodbye and Xavier leaves. I finish my coffee, wave thanks to Henri and leave the café.

With my mind preoccupied with the problem of the airport I realize I have forgotten my satchel. I return to the café. Henri is on the phone. He looks up at me. I motion towards my satchel, grab it and wave goodbye.

As I drive towards the airport something gnaws at me. Something I can't put my finger on. It's not just the situation at Chabeuil. In the end I dismiss it as a sudden case of nerves.

Guy and Gine Beluze are a young couple in their early twenties. Their house backs onto the perimeter road of Chabeuil airport. They live in uncomfortable anticipation of the Luftwaffe ordering them to evacuate the house but so far they've been allowed to remain.

As I drive by their house, Guy is in his driveway working on a small gazogène van. He looks up and seems to recognize the Highway Department Citroën coming down the road in the early evening.

I drive on by and park the car a mile or so down the road, in a garage forecourt, disused as almost all of them are these days. I then return to Guy's house on foot.

Guy is still working on his car when I stroll up the road.

"I thought it was you, Luc" said the beaming Guy, "but I couldn't understand why you drove right past."

"Natural caution, Guy. Just in case anyone recognizes my car I don't want to implicate you."

Guy, an enthiusiastic little man whose visible belly is testimony to his love of life and of his wife's cooking, is already an experienced engineer working in the Highway Department. His wife Gine is heavily pregnant and looks after the house and their small vegetable garden. Outwardly it appears as though the war has had but little effect on their way of life. But inwardly Guy is in turmoil about the Occupation and the implications for his unborn child. It was the expectation of fatherhood that above all persuaded him to work with the Resistance. To make the world, his world anyway, a safer place for his wife and child was his motivation. The same is true for people like Guy all over France.

"Gine is just making some soup for supper. Will you join us?"

"Wonderful, it's been a while since I had a good home-cooked soup."

Gine looks radiant in her expectant motherhood. Rosy cheeked, with a seductive smile. The three of us enjoy our soup as I outline my hastily prepared plan. Guy says that he has noticed a bit more noise than usual and that there are certainly a few more planes parked along the runway but nothing like the 60 or so that I fear.

"Is there some way that we can get close to the runway without being seen?"

Guy thinks for a moment.

"We could go through the forest. I haven't been there for ten years or so but when I was a kid we used to spend time in there. As I recall it backs right up to the eastern rim of the airport. It's quite thick forest. I can't see why any Germans would be in there and it should give us plenty of shelter."

"Sounds ideal" I check my watch. It's 8:45. " Can we go? We should be ok. It's a clear night and looks like there'll be a bright moon if we need it."

We finish supper. Gine says she'll clear up so Guy and I leave for the forest, on foot.

After half an hour's walk we head into the forest taking a rarely-used path that quickly becomes almost impassable. Guy figures we'll need to walk for a good mile or so before we are even close to the perimeter of the airport.

We're only about a quarter of a mile into the woods when we come across a sign HALT above the outline of a soldier and a dog.

"Let's hope not," says Guy. There's no sign of a fence of any sort and we keep on walking, though more slowly and cautiously than before. The undergrowth looks like it hasn't been disturbed for some time. A steady breeze blows in the night air. We continue on for another 300 metres or so when I put my hand on Guy's shoulder to stop him.

"Look" I lower my voice "over to your right, beyond those oak trees. Notice anything peculiar?"

Guy stares in the direction I am pointing. "Yes, I do."

There is a large, dark mass of something that doesn't look natural. More like a large smooth rock and yet it's gently flapping in the wind.

"I think our friends may be trying to hide something from us. Let's go take a look."

As we move towards the unnatural mass I think there is no need for us both to risk our lives, just in case whatever it is is booby-trapped. I tell Guy to stay where he is and that if I get into trouble he should get the hell out of there as fast as he can. Sensibly he agrees.

I stealthily approach. Whatever it is, it's a good size and covered in a tarpaulin of some sort. I creep right up to it and move around until I find an opening. I pull back the tarpaulin to reveal the fuselage of a Fokker Wulf FW 190, one of Germany's newest and most deadly fighter planes.

I replace the tarpaulin and creep back to Guy and relay to him what I've seen.

"I think we'd better have a look and see how many more they have hidden here, Guy. You go clockwise as far as you can and I'll go anti-clockwise. We'll meet back here at exactly 11:00. If you haven't finished by then come back anyway. All we need is an estimate of the total number. I'm sure what they have done is hidden the bulk of them in these woods which is why Allied reconnaissance wouldn't have seen anything unusual."

Sure enough, when the two of us meet just before 11:00 we figure that there must be at least 150 planes hidden in the forest. Time to get back and spread the alarm.

We make it back to Guy's home shortly after midnight. As we are saying goodbye at the entrance to his front garden I notice that the door to the house is open.

"Does Gine always leave the door open for you, Guy?"

Guy swings round and runs into the house. I follow him. Guy opens the door into the front room and then we both hear moaning coming from upstairs.

"Oh God no, it's Gine. Maybe she's having the baby!"

Something tells me not.

We race up the stairs and into the bedroom.

Gine is lying, naked, bruised and bleeding on the floor. It is immediately obvious that she has been beaten and raped, repeatedly. Probably by the Gestapo or Milice.

Probably as the result of my presence in Chabeuil.

"Guy, we've got to get her to the hospital in Valence as soon as possible. I'll drive."

Guy, intermittently sobbing and fuming, and working as fast as he can to comfort and clean up his wife, says "No Luc. They'll be expecting you to do just that. I'll take her myself. You get out of here. Use the back door."

I know he's right.

"At least let me help you get her dressed, then I'll go."

It takes us twenty minutes to get Gine into a fit state to get her down to the car. I leave them at the door.

"I'm so sorry Guy. I hope to heaven she's alright. I'll check back with you somehow tomorrow."

"Au revoir Luc. Take care."

And now, unfortunately too late, I realize why something was gnawing at me as I drove into Chabeuil.

I go back to the empty garage forecourt where I find my Citroën. After a quick check to see that it hasn't been tampered with, I drive for a few kilometres and then pull the car off the road into a field where I will sleep until 6:00, the time when the Café Carrefour opens for the day.

It's the beginning of July and the sun will rise early. I sleep fitfully stretched out on a blanket beside my car.

At a few minutes past 6:00 a.m. I throw my blanket into the back of the car, get in and start the motor. Ten minutes later I pull into the lay-by across the road from the Café Carrefour and wait. Two old-timers go in for their morning brandy. No sign of any other cars. I get out, walk across the street and climb the steps to the café. I pull out the gun from my shoulder holster and throw open the door.

Henri looks up from the bar and stares as though he has seen a ghost. My revolver is aimed at his head.

"Get outside" I motion to the two old men. They jump up from their seats. "And don't come back." They flee.

Henri is shaking like a leaf. He hadn't expected to see me ever again. Not after his phone call to the Milice. He had rather expected a fat reward.

"Collaborators are one thing" I say, still pointing my revolver at the whimpering man "but comrades from the Resistance who turn in one of their own are the lowest of the low."

Henri looks up at me, pleading with watery eyes.

The bullet that kills him embeds itself in the mahogany cabinet behind him, a permanent reminder.

As I head back to the Vercors I feel a finger prodding my soul. But I know I've done the right thing. I had no choice.

But what about justice? What about a fair trial? An unwelcome voice inserts itself.

Did I kill this man out of anger? Out of fear, even? If I had let him live what would have been the consequences? A repeat performance I reassure myself. I have to, if I am to live with myself.

By the time I get to Vercors I am convinced that I had no choice. But I also know this act will haunt me for the rest of my life.

The situation on the Vercors plateau, when I get back that morning of 10 July, is a heady mixture of elation and panic.

Elation at the arrival, by parachute, of two American commando units, each with fifteen officers and men and thirteen containers of rifles and ammunition. Not quite the 4,000 parachutists promised to the Patron but enough to significantly raise the spirits of the citizens of Vassieux and La Chapelle as the Yanks pass through those towns on their way to Saint-Martin.

Panic at the increasingly apparent signs that the Germans are planning a major offensive. Aerial reconnaissance flights are becoming more and more frequent; curfews and suspension of road, rail and tram services in and around Grenoble are now everyday affairs and my men are sending in reports of significant troop movements. Away from the south coast. Towards the Vercors.

The sense of panic is not abated by the news from Chabeuil. Huet ages ten years as he absorbs the information with horror, and helplessness.

"Luc, we have to do something, and fast. Many of our men are now armed, although a good many still have no idea how to use their weapons properly. But we have only Sten guns. We need field guns, mortars, machine guns."

"And we need someone to bomb Chabeuil" I add." I'm going to send a message to Algiers demanding they bomb the airport. Plus, as we have had no help at all from Algiers and very little from London, I'm going to send a message to the Americans direct and get them to supply weapons. I'll need to use Descour's wireless operator, OK?"

"Sure" says the despondent Huet "Bon courage."

"By the way" I add " I've sent Christine to Barcelonnette on a mission to the Italian border. Have you seen Jacques?"

"Ask Geyer, he doesn't tell me what he's up to but he and Jacques were talking about some way of getting more vehicles."

I leave Huet to his worries and go to find Bob, Descour's 'pianist'. We send the following message:

YOU MUST BOMB IMMEDIATELY AERODROME CHABEUIL STOP IT IS CERTAIN THERE ARE MORE THAN 150 AIRCRAFT THERE FROM SALON AND AVIGNON WITH MUCH MATERIEL STOP VERCORS IS MENACED FROM THERE STOP THIS IS ABSOLUTELY ESSENTIAL STOP VERY LARGE QUANTITY OF BOMBS HAS NOT YET BEEN PLACED IN HOLDS STOP HAVE COPIED THIS TO LONDON ENDS

Guy knew the plan was to bomb Chabeuil so he will have remained with his wife in Valence. I ask Bob to send another message to the USAF commander for the Mediterranean region requesting the immediate supply of heavy weapons, machinery and ammunition.

Half an hour later I am on my way over to Geyer's HQ to look for Jacques when a convoy of trucks, cars (including a police car), motorcycles and assorted small vans comes towards me from the direction of St Nizier. A Cross of Lorraine flag, fluttering on a makeshift pole, is stuck in the side window of the lead car.

Driving it is Jacques.

It transpires that Jacques and twenty of Geyer's men had set up a road block on the main route from Grenoble, on the east of the massif. They hijacked almost every vehicle that came by, including that of the Chief of Police of Romans, for under an hour and forced all the occupants to walk. They then drove the vehicles back up onto the massif just as German troops were heading out of their garrison at Grenoble in response to an alarm.

Things are looking up. The ranks of the Maquis have now swollen to 5,000 men most of whom have some sort of weapon, no matter how primitive. There is now plenty of transport and enough petrol, thanks to a daring raid by the Groupe Valliers earlier in the week. A skeleton crew of Americans has arrived indicating at least that the outside world is aware of our plight. I realize of course that this is a double-edged sword. The Vercors has already become something of a legend in France, particularly since the public declaration of the Free French Republic of the Vercors several weeks ago. But the more the outside world talks of the Vercors Resistance, the more attention the Germans are likely to devote to the problem. The more likely they are to mount a major offensive.

For the moment though, things are looking good.

A message from Alain in Digne confirms the sabotage operations that Rugby circuit men, particularly in the Isère region, have carried out. All have achieved their objectives.

I cable Algiers with the news as follows:

DEPARTEMENT ISÈRE REPORTS COMPLETE INTERRUPTION RAILWAY TRAFFIC GRENOBLE-CHAMBERY GRENOBLE-VALENCE GRENOBLE-VEYNES GRENOBLE-LYON STOP ALL TELEPHONE AND TELEGRAPH COMMUNICATIONS CUT STOP

Unlike all the previous messages, this elicited an immediate response from Algiers:

BRAVO FOR SPLENDID RESULTS ANNOUNCED IN YOUR SIGNAL WE ARE PROUD OF YOU STOP ONCE AGAIN MY LONGSTANDING FRIENDSHIP AND MY CONFIDENCE STOP

For fuck's sake. I show the response to Zeller and Huet.

"Look at this crap. What sanctimonious nonsense. They are perfectly capable of rapid response when they don't actually have to get off their asses and do anything."

"It's their asses they are trying to protect" remarks Zeller. He, better than anyone, understands the political in-fighting whirling around de Gaulle wherever he goes. And nowhere more so than in his new headquarters of Algiers.

At dusk, a squadron of Focke Wulf FW 190s from Chabeuil fly low over the trees of the Forêt de Lente and swoop on Vassieux. They kill fifteen people, destroy shops and, partially, the church. They then fly on to La Chapelle and strafe the streets of that town too.

The following day, 14 July, the people of the Vercors awake early to celebrate Bastille Day. Despite the menacing presence of the Germans on either side of the massif, the villages and towns across the plateau have turned out en masse. For the first time since 1940 it really looks as though victory is within our grasp.

At Saint-Martin, by 7:30 in the morning, Narcisse Geyer, predictably resplendent, has already assembled his cavalry for a formal celebration in the square opposite the Hotel Breyton. Also present are General Zeller, Major Huet, Captain Costa de Beauregard, Jacques, Christine, having just returned from Barcelonnette, and me. A contingent of 50 men representing the 5,000 now based on the plateau, are also crowded into the little square. Saint-Martin, indeed the whole Vercors, has seen nothing like it before.

In Vassieux and La Chapelle, despite the tragedies of last night, spirits are not dampened. The old, the young, all marching and singing together with the Maquis, with whom relations have not always been that close. Certainly a good number of villagers feel that the Maquis presence on the plateau has put them all at risk. And there are many farmers who have lost livestock and valuable produce to marauding maquisards from time to time. Still the fraternal feeling is to the fore on this Bastille Day.

And then a miraculous thing occurs. Here in Saint-Martin and, I suspect, all across the plateau, in the towns, villages and hamlets and in the isolated dwellings high up in the forests, the people stand still and silently listen. It's as if the earth has begun to shake. Doors and windows rattle, china plates fall off their stands, dogs bark and coffees spill.

The inhabitants cover their ears at the deafening sound and, as one, turn their heads to stare at the sky expecting God knows what. I grab Christine's hand and squeeze it. Only I know what is happening. For these are American Flying Fortresses. And this is in response to my message.

No fewer than seventy-two of these monsters, the biggest bombers in the US Air Force, come roaring over the peaks of the massif. They are flying in tight formation of groups of twelve escorted by fighter planes. They fly the length of the plateau in what seems, and probably is, a matter of seconds. They then turn more slowly and fly back. As they approach the as-yet-unfinished runway at Vassieux they drop more than 800 containers of arms and equipment. All supported by parachutes in red, white or blue. The brilliantly clear sky acts as a theatrical backcloth to this magical, colourful display.

The celebrations at Saint-Martin continue. Major Huet, stickler for military precision in all he does, is determined that nothing should interrupt the order of the day. He also realizes that there are more than sufficient numbers of people in Vassieux to collect and distribute the arms and equipment.

And, just as he expected, as soon as the last American plane disappears over the peaks of the Vercors, men, women and children, especially children, rush, elated, from every direction on to the dropping zone to recover the containers with their red, white and blue parachutes now lying limply on the ground.

Within minutes the Germans attack.

Flying low over the dropping zone they machine gun as many people as possible and destroy as many containers as they can. The scene of people desperately trying to pull the heavy containers into safety whilst being hammered from the air by the planes from Chabeuil is devastating and tragic.

And the attack doesn't let up once the dropping zone has been destroyed. In the Hotel Bellier at La Chapelle, where a celebratory lunch is just getting underway, there is an enormous explosion. The assembled people all stand and sing the Marsellaise. And still the bombing continues. The Groupe Vallier, in their house on the outskirts of the town, fire their three Thompsons from their garden at every passing plane until both they and their house are utterly destroyed.

In Vassieux, in Saint-Martin and in virtually every village and hamlet in the Vercors the story is the same. And when people try to flee by car, cart or foot they are machine-gunned from the air.

It was rumored in the streets of Grenoble that the Germans were planning on giving the upstart Free French Republic of the Vercors a Bastille Day they would never forget.

And they never will. Those that survive.

36

The rollercoaster of emotions resulting from the dramatic events of the day are having a strange effect on the group of men sitting around the table in Colonel Descour's headquarters this evening. Some are more edgy than usual; all have reverted to type.

Huet, cool, traditional and collected, sits solemnly and upright at the head of the table, chain smoking. Despite the recently promoted General Zeller's presence, Huet is chairing the meeting in Colonel Descour's absence. Geyer, defensive, fidgety and frustrated at any indication of inaction is sitting next to him. Opposite Geyer is Costa de Beauregard. Normally calm and alert, tonight he is up and down like a yo-yo. I, pensive and preoccupied, sit between Geyer and Eugène Chavant, now formally President of the Free French Republic of the Vercors. The Patron feels the death of every one of 'his' people personally and today has been one of the worst days of his life, so far. General Zeller, focused and listening intently, sits at the other end of the table, opposite Huet.

Taking control of the proceedings, Huet recounts the day's events, and counts the cost in human lives at over one hundred. We all know this is an underestimate.

Then Huet turns to Costa de Beauregard, knowing that his HQ high above St Nizier gives him a vantage point from which he has a perfect view of General Pflaum's HQ.

"Captain, what is your analysis of the German presence around the massif?"

"Clearly" says de Beauregard, jumping up from his seat and pointing to the map stuck on the wall, "Pflaum's reinforcements have arrived, from Strasbourg and elsewhere, and they are based inside the German compound. There are so many of them that they have had to erect a tent city in the compound in order to house them all."

"Do you have any precise estimate as to their strength?"

"Our informants estimate there are around 6,000 in Grenoble alone."

"But still there is only one way up here" Geyer interrupts "for any sizeable force requiring transport."

"Yes," responds de Beauregard "and we have shown that we can make life pretty difficult for them if they try to use the pass up through here" he says, thumping the map at St Nizier.

"And what about German forces elsewhere on the plain?" asks Huet.

It's my turn. "My people say there are signs of more troops coming down from the north to join the German garrisons at Valence and Romans. They estimate perhaps an additional 1500 men and we know that Chabeuil is already reinforced. Not to mention the planes and heavy ammunition reported there."

At the mention of Chabeuil, the Patron, still smarting from the knowledge that the promised arrival of his paratroopers is now looking less likely than ever, turns to General Zeller, "Mon general, what do your people in Algiers say now about bombing Chabeuil airport?"

"I am as frustrated as you are, Patron. I am going to Algiers as soon as possible to try to sort this out. I am sure that political infighting is responsible for the inaction and I cannot deal with that from here. General Cochet is very aware of our plight. But unfortunately, although he has been given responsibility in Algiers for the southern sector, he has not been given responsibility for the Vercors."

"And who has?" asks the Patron.

"General Koenig, in London."

"Oh Mon Dieu" are the only words the despairing Patron can muster.

A moment's silence ensues. The Patron's disenchantment has this effect on people.

"Luc, as far as harassing the enemy on the plain and keeping them occupied there, how do we stand?" asks Huet eventually.

"As you know, all major rail and telephone links are being targeted daily. Most have been destroyed. But the Germans, using forced French and Italian labour, are repairing and rebuilding at quite a pace. We are ahead of them however and within, I would say, three weeks we should have disrupted every significant road, rail and telephonic communication facility. The Germans only stick to the main roads now, using women and children as human shields more and more. Certainly no German vehicle travelling alone ever reaches its destination."

"Well at least that sounds encouraging" says Huet.

"For the greater good of the Allies it is, but I don't think it's necessarily going to be of great benefit to the Vercors" I say.

"And Captain Geyer, in preparation for the eventual arrival of the paratroopers and supplies from Algiers, how is the building of the landing strip proceeding?"

"Almost finished. Corporal Tourara and his team have been working day and night to get it completed."

Huet's deputy interrupts the meeting to announce that a

messenger has arrived at the villa wanting to see Luc urgently.

"Where is he from?" I ask.

"He says he's from Montèlimar and has a message from Jacques. He is clean. We have his gun." I excuse myself from the meeting and go out to meet the messenger.

Moments later I return.

"Gentlemen, I am not quite certain what this means yet, but I do have a strong suspicion. Jacques has been watching the airfield near Montèlimar. He says German gliders are making practice descents. What particularly alarms Jacques is that instead of circling in the usual manner they are practicing with parachutes attached to check their speed. This can be for various reasons, I know. But it could also enable them to land in a restricted place."

"Such as the Vercors plateau" says Huet, nodding.

"As you know Montèlimar is only 100 km from here" I emphasize.

"That possibility makes it all the more vital that we secure the landing strip. It may well be our only hope" adds Huet.

No one wants to contemplate the possibility of a major German-landing from the air. The consequence, as Huet has hinted, is obvious. Massacre.

"On the basis of our discussions gentlemen," resumes Huet "I suggest that we pursue the following course of action…

1. Captain de Beauregard, please ensure that you have men day and night guarding the pass to St Nizier and monitoring the activity of the Boche. It is clear that following the day's activities the Germans may already be in control of St Nizier. We need to check that they get no further.

2. Captain Geyer, you will do the same for the southern sector as there is still a possibility that the garrison at Digne will be reinforced significantly and they may try to attack from the south via the Col de Rousset, the only other feasible way onto the massif

for heavy transport.

3. Patron, apart from trying to maintain morale amongst the civilians I think it would be wise, just in case of a major attack, to move Dr Ganimède's hospital with the wounded, both French and prisoners, down to a hospital on the plain, perhaps at Die?

4. Luc, I think that you would be most valuable to us by ensuring that the enemy is continually harassed here in the south-east and by providing regular and up-to-date intelligence, particularly by monitoring the activities at the Montèlimar and Chabeuil airfields. You might also reinvigorate your attempts to get more men and ammunition. This time hopefully they will drop it at night.

General Zeller, I think you have the picture clearly of the dramatic and potentially disastrous situation we're now in on the Vercors? We are up here, maybe 5,000 of us, as a result of Generals Eisenhower and de Gaulle's mobilization order. Once that was rescinded it was impossible for us to demobilize. To send people back down to the plains would have been tantamount to sending them to their deaths. We've been resisting the enemy in every way possible, harassing and destroying their men and supplies wherever we can, but we need the reinforcements and supplies that the Patron was promised when he went to Algiers. You must get de Gaulle to help us. He is obliged to. Unless of course he wants the deaths of 5,000 Free French martyrs on his conscience."

Five minutes later Colonel Huet sends yet another message to Colonel Constans in Algiers:

RECEIVED DAYTIME PARACHUTE DROP JULY 14 ABOUT 72 PLANES VERY SUCCESSFUL STOP HAVE BEEN MACHINE GUNNED ON THE GROUND EVER SINCE DEPARTURE OF ALLIED AIRCRAFT THANKS ENDS

As Huet's uncharacteristically sarcastic telegram was making its way across the Mediterranean, General Pflaum, Commandant of the 157th Wehrmacht Reserve Division and Colonel Schwab, his anti-terrorist expert, gathered together their senior officers for a final briefing at the HQ in Grenoble.

In the hall that served as a meeting room sat General Pflaum, tall and elegant with those Teutonic good looks that so often serve as a prerequisite to promotion in the Third Reich and Colonel Schwab, short, bald and with the unprepossessing appearance that guarantees he will not be promoted in line with his abilities or certainly his ambitions. Behind them was a large map of the Vercors massif pinned to the wall. Their senior officers were seated in serried rows in front of them.

General Pflaum opened the proceedings:

"Gentlemen, I want to congratulate you on the day's achievements. We have inflicted major casualties on the terrorists of the Vercors plateau and we have taken control of St Nizier thus enabling the next phase of our attack of the plateau to be put into effect immediately."

The assembled officers stole each other excited glances. At last they were to get rid of this 'Free French Republic' that was such an insult to their honour and which, with its waving Tricolor flags from Le Moucherotte, had made them the laughing stock of Grenoble.

Pflaum, satisfied with this reaction, continued:

"Over the next three or four days, troops of the Third Reich will take up their positions all around the plateau penetrating inland wherever there is little or no resistance and protecting all access routes as the first phase of our assault.

The attack will start at 0600 hours tomorrow morning and will commence from four directions. In the north, from St Nizier, troops will proceed to take all towns in the northern sector and, once that has been accomplished, move on to the southern sector.

In the south an armoured division will move from Valence along the

Drôme River to Die from where they will advance up to the plateau via the Col de Rousset.

From the east, Gebirgsjägers will break through the walls of the massif using the mule tracks.

From the west we will attack from Pont-en-Royan under cover of artillery."

The atmosphere in the room was tense with concentration and emotion. Regardless of the increasingly worrying news from Normandy there was now a feeling of real confidence that a major victory was within their grasp. For Pflaum, the Vercors' importance was not just strategic but its conquest would also be an important propaganda victory as the defence of the plateau by the Resistance had by now achieved mythical status throughout France.

"Our reconnaissance planes indicate that the landing strip being constructed by the terrorists at Vassieux is nearing completion. In our view it is already capable of handling large enemy planes. It is vital that we secure this as a major priority and retain it for our own use. Therefore, four hours after the commencement of the ground attack, airborne troops will be dropped in the area of Vassieux and will seize the landing strip. Once the landing strip is secure our troops will head both north and south to attack the terrorists from the rear. I will now hand over to Oberst Schwab who will conduct you through phase two of the operation."

Schwab, a man with considerable experience in dealing with (and extracting information from) terrorists, pulled himself up to his full 1.5 metres. He surveyed the room relishing his ability to demand the total attention and, he hoped, awe of the cream of the Wehrmacht, those self-satisfied officers who had so often mocked him in the past. Well, no more. Now it's Schwab's turn to show them what he's really made of.

"Gentlemen" he started, (how he wished he could do something about his squeaky little voice, but he couldn't) "I will now conduct you through phase two of our plan of attack. Once the plateau is secured all exits will be blocked. Anyone attempting to escape will be shot. Every house is to be searched. Any house which has harboured terrorists or provided food or storage or comfort in any way, or that you suspect may have or may intend to, you will destroy. All cattle will be removed for transport to the plain leaving only the bare minimum to sustain civilian life."

As he said those words he was aware that it showed a sign of weakness but Pflaum had insisted that he keep them in.

"All men between the ages of 17 and 30 will be arrested," that's better, he was getting back into his stride now "unless of course they are terrorists or you think they may have been or may intend to be, in which case they will be shot. If they are likely to have information of use to the Reich then they will be interrogated by a unit under my control." A universal look of impatience and disdain spread across the faces of the assembled officers.

"Once the villages are secure" continued Schwab "you will search the massif from the highest mountains to the deepest forests." He then pinned a new map of the Vercors on to the wall behind him.

"Men can live for many days without food. But not without water. This map identifies where every river, stream and waterfall on the Vercors is situated. The terrorists are most likely to attempt to locate these at night. Therefore we are providing teams with flares that will illuminate the area for several hundred metres. Anyone found trying to steal water will be shot on sight.

Are there any questions?"

There were none. At least not for Schwab.

Pflaum was aware of the effect that Schwab had on his officers and found it tactically very efficient. He also knew when they had had enough.

"Thank you Oberst Schwab. You may sit down now." Pflaum pulled Schwab's map off the board and dropped it on the floor to reveal his own map. "Just to emphasize Gentlemen" he said pointing at Vassieux, "this landing strip must be secured at all costs and kept secure. As long as it remains unprotected it is the only place the enemy can land their planes."

Everyone knew, of course, that it was also the only place the Germans could land their planes.

Pflaum returned to his office to put a call in to the Luftwaffe Commandant at Chabeuil Airport. As he approached his office door his trusted personal secretary stopped him.

"You have a visitor, Herr General, he is waiting in your office."

"Who is he?" said Pflaum, irritated. He didn't like people assuming he would see them without an appointment.

"His name is Metzger, Sir. Sergeant Karl Metzger. He is from the Abwehr."

Pflaum particularly didn't like people from the Abwehr assuming he would see them.

General Gabriel Cochet, Commander-in-Chief of the French forces within the southern sector of France, looked out of his fourth-floor office window onto the bustling street traders in Algiers' famous Kasbah. He was holding the latest message from Major Huet in his hand, at least he assumed it was the latest. Messages from the Vercors were taking anything up to three days to reach the right person in the political and bureaucratic nightmare that was the seat of the provisional French government in Algiers.

He blamed the Gaullists, even though he had been one himself. Their vision was to land triumphantly back on French soil in the Massif Central when the time was right, and that ought to be very soon now. They were so obsessed with their 'grand projet' that they weren't interested in anything that stood in their way. Otherwise why were there perfectly serviceable planes, planes that could be used to bomb Chabeuil, sitting in the desert? And why were there hundreds of parachutistes who could have been dropped in Vassieux, sitting impotently in Trapani?

Those parachutistes who were so incensed at their inaction that they had christened themselves 'the paratouristes'.

The answers to these questions, from Colonel Constans and Jacques Soustelle, directeur général des Services d'action en France and de Gaulle's right-hand-man, were the same old negative prevarications… 'Our reconnaissance planes show only 29 planes at Chabeuil, not 100'; 'The landing strip at Vassieux is not yet capable of taking Allied planes'; 'Planes and parachutists will be dispatched as soon as weather permits'. Well the weather has permitted German planes to bomb Vassieux, La Chapelle and virtually every other town and hamlet on the Vercors, but it is not good enough for Allied planes? And today the weather was crystal clear all over the south of France.

Cochet himself had been reduced, like his colleagues, to sending platitudinous messages to the Vercors Maquis. But what made him especially angry this Sunday morning was that he had just been informed that the message in his hand should never have come to him in the first place as General Koenig wanted responsibility for the Vercors to be taken by the northern sector, even though it was clearly in the south.

Cochet had a better understanding than most people of the needs and the potential of the Resistance. When he was based in Clemont-Ferrand in the unoccupied sector during 1941 he had arranged anti-Pétain leaflets to be distributed throughout the region. He knew how they operated, how they thought, what they were up against.

Was he, he wondered, the only person in Algiers who cared about the precarious situation of the Resistance in the Vercors? Intelligence had confirmed that troops were encircling the massif in very significant numbers. Far outnumbering in men and weapons the 5,000 men on the plateau. And this on the day that German resistance to the Allied invasion of Normandy had clearly crumbled!

Just then his assistant came in with a message from Colonel Caffey:

COCHET LAST NIGHT 74 ALLIED PLANES BOMBED CHABEUIL AIRPORT HURRAH CAFFEY END

'Enfin' said a relieved and elated Cochet. He quickly sent a message off to General Zeller on the Vercors, confirming the good news.

By midday on 18 July it was increasingly clear to Huet, as he looked out over St Nizier from Costa de Beauregard's vantage point, exactly what the Germans had in mind. Over the past few days, General Pflaum's men had blown tunnels and bridges, mined other approaches, thrown barriers across all access roads, set up machine gun positions along the ring road and established troop encampments in the hills. They were clearly here until their business was finished.

Huet returned to his HQ determined to call up every able-bodied man in the region, including the remaining sedentaires who were working on the farms, and prepare them to defend the citadel. General Zeller had given him the good news about the bombing of Chabeuil earlier that morning. This, of course, meant that at least 100 enemy planes and their cargo of bombs had finally been put out of commission. But Huet knew that the Vercors was still very vulnerable. The sheer number of German soldiers amassed around the massif was testament to that.

Geyer in the south and Costa de Beauregard in the north were already preparing for attack. Luc had left the plateau via mule tracks in the south early that morning to meet with his cell leaders. They were to report all German troop movements and to hamper them wherever possible. Soon Jacques would return from Montélimar bringing with him the latest information on the gliders. Luc had not yet heard the news about the bombing of Chabeuil airport.

Huet had asked Christine to visit the hospital run by nuns in Die to see if they could handle Dr Ganimède's wounded. They would not be safe in Saint-Martin. The Gestapo would have a heyday with them.

As dawn broke over the cliffs of the Vercors on 20 July, Christine and two maquisards made their way up via the mule paths from the road to Die. All other access routes up to the plateau had been barricaded by the Germans.

Her news was not good. The nuns told her that the last doctor had left that morning because a German attack was expected imminently. There was no possibility of their being able to handle Dr Ganimède's thirty-eight wounded men (including four Wehrmacht prisoners) and women.

"There is another possibility" Huet said to Christine on being told of the news, "we have been scouring the area for places to hide the wounded.

Two days ago, near Rousset, we discovered a vast network of caves, seven metres high in some places and about 400 metres deep. It's known as the Grotte de la Luire. It's just possible that we could move everyone there. We'd have to do it at night because the Germans would notice the increased traffic. The last 600 metres would have to be by foot."

That evening, as Huet was conducting a final tour of the plateau's defences before the expected attack, Christine and Dr Ganimède's team of three doctors, six nurses and a Jesuit priest, carried the wounded out on stretchers and loaded them into Huillier buses that had been stripped of their seats.

The convoy headed out of Saint-Martin towards the Forêt du Vercors. It was a still, moonless night. Rain was expected. The buses passed though the shattered towns of the Vercors and, just before ten o'clock, they arrived at a lane at the foot of a steep mountain path that would have to be covered by foot. Those that could walk did so. The others were carried on stretchers by the nurses, the Italian doctors, the Huillier brothers and by Dr Ganimède's young son Jean.

As Dr Ganimède surveyed his makeshift hospital, lit by candlelight, he reflected on their chances of survival. Very slim, he thought, very slim indeed. But he felt reassured by the presence of Father Yves, the Jesuit priest who had come down from Paris to offer his services. The following morning he would hold a Mass in the cave.

Christine returned to Saint-Martin in a bus driven by 16-year-old Daniel Huillier. It was almost midnight as she walked through the door of the Hotel Breyton. Huet was sitting at a table smoking and drinking a cup of coffee with Jacques who had just arrived back from Montèlimar.

"Ah Christine, come join us," said Huet. Christine thanked him, gave Jacques a peck on the cheek, pulled up a chair and sat down. "And how did the hospital move go?"

"Fine – all arrived safe and sound."

"Jacques here has just returned from Montèlimar. I wanted to hear what he had to say before going back to the house and going to bed" said Huet.

Mme. Breyton brought over cups of coffee for both Jacques and Christine, said goodnight and went to bed.

Huet discussed with them the likelihood of an attack within the next thirty-six hours and went over the plan as agreed at the meeting with General Zeller five days earlier.

He was worried, of course, but felt that they were as prepared as they could be under the circumstances.

"And what news from Montèlimar, Jacques?" asked Christine.

"More gliders. Around thirty of forty airmen, it was difficult to tell exactly. But most worrying of all, Gestapo. Lots of them."

"What's that all about?" asked Huet.

"Well it looks to me as though the Germans are planning on landing their gliders on the plateau with a cargo of Gestapo inside. I can't think why else they would be there."

Huet had thought the same but hoped there might be some other explanation.

"Speaking of planes, how is the landing slip going?" asked Jacques.

"Well I received another fatuous message from Algiers this morning saying they had surveyed the landing slip and it was too short and too thin for their planes to land there."

"Mon Dieu," said Jacques "I hope the Germans will decide the same thing, but I doubt it."

"Oh, you haven't heard" said Huet "the Chabeuil airport has finally been bombed. Everything destroyed!"

"Really? Fantastic" replied Jacques "When?"

"Three days ago. I received a message confirming it from General Cochet in Algiers."

Jacques glanced first at Christine, then at Huet. "I came through Chabeuil this afternoon on my way up here. The airport is fully operational and loaded with planes."

The blood drained out of Huet's face.

Algiers had bombed the wrong airport

37

After sleeping fitfully, Major François Huet got up from his makeshift bed at 5:00 a.m. on the morning of 21 July. He had spent much of the restless night going over and over the plans, attempting to find the flaws; anything left unaccounted for given his miserable resources. He had all but given up hope of getting any help from Algiers or London. Was he doing the right thing? Or was he laying his men open to massacre and the village and townspeople of the Vercors open to the inevitable reprisals?

Quite possibly, yes, he thought.

But that was destructive thinking. All he could really hope for was for this seemingly interminable wait for the attack to end.

The dawn sky was overcast. Rain was on the way. Yet another advantage for the well-clothed, fed, armed and protected Germans.

Huet made himself a cup of coffee, lit a cigarette and waited.

In their rooms at the Hotel Breyton, neither Jacques nor Christine had slept well.

Jacques was worried to the point of despair about their total inability to defend themselves in the event of an air attack which, having seen the activity at both Montèlimar and Chabeuil, he thought was inevitable. Ironically, he thought, the new landing strip at Vassieux had made them more vulnerable, not less. He looked at his watch. 5:30 a.m. He decided he'd go and see Huet to get his permission to mine the airfield.

Christine's concern over the security of Dr Ganimède's 'hospital' vied in her mind with something new and unexpected… she couldn't stop thinking about Luc. God knows she had had many men in her life, but never one quite like this. All the others had wanted to own her, to subjugate her to their will. But Luc was not like that. He was independent, strong-willed, sometimes infuriatingly so, but he never tried to control her. On the contrary, he seemed to encourage her free-spiritedness.

She punched the pillow and turned over to try to get some sleep. Then she felt herself worrying that maybe he didn't want her enough. Maybe he didn't need her?

Alain, the 'pianist' from Digne, and I drive silently along the La Chapelle road in the direction of Saint-Martin. Alarmed by the news, corroborated by every cell leader in the vicinity of the Vercors, that the German build-up is much larger than originally anticipated.

I have plans to be with Christine once more before the attack. I'm constantly distracted by thoughts of her intruding on my supposedly military mindset. I give myself a mental slap on the face.

My information indicates that the German forces lined up in preparation for an attack on the Vercors consist of (at least): four battalions of Reserve Gebirgsjägers, the feared Alpinistes; two companies of parachutists; 11,000 Wehrmacht soldiers; 4,000 S.S. troops; and the 45 or so gliders at Montèlimar, each capable of carrying at least ten men.

Yesterday I spoke to Guy Beluze. His wife lost their baby, but she would live. Guy also confirmed that Chabeuil was fully operational. No one had bombed it. That means that over 100 bomb-carrying aircraft are also at the enemy's disposal.

To top it off our contacts in the Haute-Savoie confirm that two Panzer divisions are due to arrive any day now from Strasbourg. The odds are so insurmountable that it doesn't even warrant thinking about. I just want my people to survive.

"Remember" I told them earlier today "that you have succeeded brilliantly in diverting troops and attention away from the Normandy invaders. That, as far as the outside world is concerned, is our primary objective. For the next few days your own safety is paramount. We need you all to survive and be healthy; please make certain that we'll all meet again as soon as the expected German attack is over. Of course if you can do more damage to the German cause in the meantime, so much the better. But you'll be able to do most good by surviving."

It is almost 6:00 a.m. as Alain and I arrive at the Hotel Breyton.

Madame Breyton is busy putting the clean red and white oilcloth tablecloths onto the café tables as we walk in. I give her a kiss on the cheek.

"Room 16" she says, ignoring the kiss.

"Merci Madame, please give my friend here a coffee."

"We will join you shortly" I say to Alain as I bound up the stairs to Christine's room.

When Jacques walked into Major Huet's office at 6:00 a.m. he found him sitting in front of the large map of the Vercors that he had stuck onto his wall, marked with both German and Resistance troop positions. He was wearing his beret tilted to one side in a characteristic manner and smoking his third cigarette of the morning.

"Bonjour Jacques, join me for a cup of coffee. It may be our last for a while."

But a phone call interrupted his mission to boil the water.

Jacques walked over and looked out of the window. It was starting to rain. He listened to Huet's conversation

"Oui" "Oui" "Combien?" "COMBIEN??" "Mon Dieu" "Deux colonnes?" "de Saint Nizier?" "a?" "D'accord" "Merci, merci"

Jacques, fearing the worst, waited for Huet to speak.

"A force of two thousand men is advancing from St Nizier along the road to Lans. I expect they will split at Lans. Half will go on towards Villard and the other half towards the Gorges de la Bourne from where they will try to storm the southern sector."

"What shall we do?" asked Jacques.

"At the moment, nothing. All the defence positions are manned. They have been every night for a week now. We can only wait."

They both stood, looking out of the window. Jacques took the opportunity to tell Huet of his concerns about the vulnerability of the landing strip, particularly in view of the news about Chabeuil that they had discussed the previous evening.

Huet agreed with Jacques that the landing strip should be mined.

Another call came through. As Huet had foreseen, the enemy column was splitting.

Gradually the office filled up with Huet's staff. News was spreading fast.

"Take my motorcycle" said Huet, forgetting that he had borrowed it from Jacques in the first place "I cannot move from here as I will lose touch with the others. There are no reports so far of other enemy troop movements but I must wait and see."

Jacques looked at his watch. It was 8:30 a.m. If he drove fast he could be in Vassieux by 9:15.

Christine and I are just out of bed when I see Jacques speed by the window on a motorcycle. I wonder what he's up to.

Despite my exhaustion from climbing all night, I managed to muster up the strength to fulfil my, and Christine's, objective.

Bleary-eyed, we descend the stairs and take our seats at the table Mme. Breyton has laid for us, in anticipation.

"Bonjour my lazy lovers" is her greeting "you had better have a good meal, it may be your last."

"That's cheery Mme. Breyton," I say.

"Well, two thousand German soldiers are on their way from St Nizier. It won't be long until they are here."

I glance at Christine.

"No other sign of attack? Nowhere else on the massif?"

"Apparently not" answers Mme. Breyton giving us bread, confiture and black coffee, "which is some good news at least" she mutters as she waddles off to her kitchen.

"I'm not so sure that's good news" I say to Christine "it could mean they are waiting for an air attack to pave the way. We may as well eat this as it's here. We don't know when our next meal will be, she's right."

"Now who's being cheery?"

Moments later the phone rings. It's 9:30 a.m. and Mme. Breyton takes the call. It's Huet, for me.

"Hullo?"

"Luc?"

"Yes"

"Huet here" he sounds excited, "we've just received a call from Bob Bennes from his transmitting hut near the Rousset. He says there are planes approaching from the south."

"They can't be from Algiers. We'd have been warned" I say.

"Well they might be from England. We weren't warned on Bastille Day were we?"

"But if they were from England they'd be coming from the north." I sit down to finish my coffee as the Patron walks in to join us.

Bob Bennes, Descour's radio operator, tapped out a signal to Algiers in his radio hut near the Col de Rousset:

WE ARE UNDER ATTACK BY PARATROOPERS. WE ARE DEFENDING OURSELVES STOP BOB ADIEU END

The normally serene Bob Bennes had used the word 'Adieu' instead of his usual 'au revoir.' The significance would not be lost on Algiers.

Jacques sped into Vassieux just as the first planes cleared the southern horizon.

"Planes, planes" yelled the excited townspeople "the Yanks are here! Come see, come see."

Jacques pulled his motorcycle off the road as the planes flew overhead, the black crosses painted on their wings visible for all to see.

"It's the Boche!" he yelled; others yelled, the people scattered from the streets. Wave after wave of aircraft flew overhead. Focke-Wulfs and Dorniers screeched over the town and the surrounding open country, dropping bombs and machine-gunning whoever and whatever they saw moving. Four hundred people – Maquis, civilian volunteers, women and children – were working desperately to get the landing strip ready for the arrival of the Allies. Over 100 of them were killed as they ran hither and thither trying to avoid the machine-gunning.

It took less than three minutes to level the four hamlets on the outskirts of Vassieux.

Jacques watched helplessly as the planes circled the town again and again coming in low each time to bomb and shoot. Bodies littered the main street and the fields between the town and the landing strip. He took shelter amongst the ruins of the bombed out Nouvel Hotel, protecting his motorcycle which would, he hoped, be his ticket to freedom.

And then he saw what he had feared most. Enormous transport planes towing gliders, some forty of them. Gradually the gliders were released, some at the airstrip; the others at the access roads. Jacques knew what those gliders contained. It was time to leave.

Jumping onto the Peugeot 75, he headed as fast as he could back down the road towards Saint-Martin. He passed by the first glider just as it landed. Its cargo of S.S. killers jumped out before the glider had come to a standstill. Bullets whistled by his head as Jacques disappeared down the road.

Christine and I are discussing the best way of handling the advancing Boche with Chavant when the telephone rings again. This time it's from Jacques who has stopped off at Descour's HQ, which General Zeller is using as his command post.

I take the call and listen. Christine is watching as I feel my face turn white. But not a muscle moves or even twitches.

The café falls silent. All eyes are on me as I hang up the phone.

I address the room but look at Chavant as I speak, knowing that what I have to say will be devastating for him.

The planes have finally landed. They are not the planes that the Patron has been promised. "German fighter planes from Chabeuil have bombed Vassieux killing hundreds. Around 40 gliders, carrying S.S. troops, have landed around Vassieux and three-engined transport planes have landed on the airstrip."

Chavant, a man who rarely raises his voice, lets out a roar of pain that is so loud and terrible it sounds as though it comes from deep below the surface of the earth.

We all stand, silent, stunned.

The Patron has finally accepted that he has been betrayed and that all he has striven for is lost.

Huet had seen the planes as they came over the horizon. He quickly realized they were not from Algiers or England.

Reports arrived of S.S. troops throwing hand grenades out of gliders as they came in to land and then jumping out with their machine guns blazing, shooting at everything that moved, and people that didn't. News of other attacks began to flow in.

In the east, enemy troops were progressing rapidly up the mule passes, protected by the heavy machine guns and mortars of the Gebirgsjägers.

In the south, the 9th Panzer tank division was advancing towards Die.

In the north, both German columns were now attacking the maquisards. The northern column had already reached the approach to the Gorges de la Bourne that separated the northern from the southern sectors of the Vercors.

The S.S. troops at Vassieux were the biggest threat, however, and newly promoted Colonel Huet got on the phone to Geyer.

"Captain, the enemy have landed at Vassieux"

Geyer restrained himself.

"I am aware of that Maj… uh Colonel. We are closer to Vassieux than you are."

"You must surround the enemy and attack" said Huet, somewhat irked.

"I have already issued that instruction Colonel, but it is proving impossible. The enemy is protected by constant bombardment from the sky. I have told my men to wait until nightfall."

"Very well" said Huet, biting his tongue but forcing himself to add encouragingly "I have faith in you."

Then came news from the west. The Germans had already attacked the villages nestled at the foot of the massif and some two thousand alpine troops had been seen proceeding along the ring road, presumably heading for the mule passes on the western side of the massif.

Huet's staff plotted the German advances on the big map in his office. With the exception of a few bright spots (the Maquis were holding the enemy at the Gorges de la Bourne) the news got steadily worse as the day progressed.

Huet called another Conseil de Guerre for nine o'clock that evening. Geyer sent in his apologies. He had planned his attack on Vassieux for nine o'clock.

Apologies accepted.

Christine and young Daniel Huilier had kept their promise to Dr Ganimède and transported the remaining equipment from the hospital in

Saint-Martin to the Grotte de la Luire. To do so they had to take the road via St Agnan, bypassing Vassieux and hoping they wouldn't attract the attention of either the planes conducting the onslaught on Vassieux or advancing German troops coming up via the Col de Rousset. Luckily they were able to do both. They returned to Saint-Martin by 8:30 that evening.

As we walk up the hill in Saint-Martin on our way to Huet's 'Conseil de Guerre' the Patron and I are discussing what each of us could contribute now that the die has been so firmly cast. We have spent all day criss-crossing the Vercors, boosting morale and redistributing arms.

The Patron explains that his role as President of the Vercors means that he has no choice but to stay with his people. He would in any case. "But, you and Christine should get back to the plain as fast as possible, Luc. You have done all you can here, mon ami. There is no point in your remaining to be killed when you could be down there where you are needed, organizing more cells, more sabotage, preparing the way for the Allies. That way you could really help to speed up the end of the war."

Then he stopped, put his hand on my shoulder and looked deep into my eyes as he spoke.

"By staying here you will only be in the way. Go." This is not a suggestion but an order.

"I guess you're right. I don't think there is anything more we can do up here except to make the situation worse."

Chavant nods and together we walk into Huet's office.

Gathered at the Conseil de Guerre are Jacques and General Zeller; Chavant, Christine and myself; our 'pianist' Alain, Costa de Beauregard; representatives from Geyer and Dr Ganimède, and Huet's senior staff.

Given that we are assembled in the centre of a plateau that is being attacked from every conceivable angle by an enemy that is superior in every respect, except perhaps willpower, we are surprisingly calm.

Huet, ever the professional soldier, formally opens the proceedings by reading out the apologies. Hard to believe, but true. Descour is still down in Grenoble; Geyer is preparing to attack Vassieux. He then welcomes us one by one. I see the Patron raise an eyebrow (Chavant-speak for 'For Christ's sake get on with it').

"Gentlemen, and Christine, as you are all I am sure aware, the Vercors is now virtually surrounded by German forces." He goes on to recount the situation in each part of the massif, although it's unlikely at this stage that there is anyone present who is unaware of even the smallest detail.

Nevertheless Huet continues, "Even as we speak, our comrade Captain Geyer is leading a counter-attack on the German force occupying Vassieux. The spirit of the Montagnards is still very much alive but we are forced now to confront the likely outcome and to decide what our next move should be. In my view we have the following alternatives:

First, we can take the view that we have done all we can. Defeat is inevitable. We disperse as quickly as possible.

Second, we stay and fight for as long as we can hold out and then we disperse.

Third, we fight to the last man.

Gentlemen, and Madame, your views please!"

A hush falls over the room. Then the Patron stands up and, somewhat to people's surprise, says "I favour your first option." Quick glances back and forth, everyone gauging the general reaction.

"I say this for the following reasons. One, without the promised help from our so-called government in Algiers we are so outnumbered that it makes victory inconceivable. Two, we have done all we can to achieve the overall mission which is to pin the German Army down in significant numbers in order to stop them reinforcing troops in the north or helping to counter the Allied invasion, when and if it comes, in the south. Three, one way in which we are superior to the enemy is in our knowledge of the Vercors. Before the enemy penetrates any further we have the opportunity to escape via tracks unknown to the Germans. Luc has men who are protecting an escape route across the Drôme river at the Pont-de-Quart, east of Die. Four, and my final point, is that the sooner the Maquis leave the plateau, now that their work is done, the more likely it is that the Germans will temper their treatment of the civilian population. The longer we stay and fight, the more fierce will be the German reprisals."

With that the Patron sits down, lights his pipe, and waits.

Huet, not wanting to reveal his own feelings until everyone has had their say, thanks the Patron, formally, and asks for more responses.

Geyer's representative, a young cavalry officer, volunteers that it was inconceivable that members of the 11th Cuirassiers would retreat while there was still any chance of engaging the enemy.

General Zeller, reluctant as ever to interfere in what he considers Huet's territory, expresses his view that strategically the Vercors Maquis have achieved their objective and have nothing more to gain by continuing the fight.

"And what about you Luc?"

"I agree with the Patron and General Zeller. We have achieved all we can. We have pinned down a very considerable enemy force. It has enabled us to make headway in paving the way for a rapid Allied advance once the invasion of the south takes place. I think our continued presence here is counter-productive. I can see nothing but bad coming from it. I am in favour of dispersal."

The rest of the assembly divides roughly into two camps; one camp wanting to stay and fight, the other in favour of immediate dispersal.

Huet is clearly tempted by the idea of staying and fighting to the bitter end. He would go out in a blaze of glory. A martyr for La France! But he realizes the futility of the situation.

In the event, a compromise is agreed. We would stay and fight until it is clear that we will be overpowered. Then we will disperse. Huet's staff are tasked with allocating a list of dispersal routes for each area within the next few hours.

Huet tells me confidentially that he has picked the fall of Valchevrière as the trigger for issuing any dispersal order. Valchevrière is positioned high above the Gorges de la Bourne in dense forest. It has a viewing terrace built to provide a spectacular 'belvedere' for tourists but also, crucially, it dominates the lane up through the forest from Villard which gives access to the southern sector. If Valchevrière were to fall then all would be lost.

As the others are leaving, Eugène Chavant hands me a crumpled piece of paper.

"Luc, would you be good enough to ask your man Alain to send this message to Algiers for me? I don't want it to go through ordinary channels."

"Of course, Patron, of course."

Christine and I watch as Chavant walks slowly down the hill to Saint-Martin. We both wonder if his disillusionment has finally broken his will. Then we read his message:

LA CHAPELLE VASSIEUX SAINT-MARTIN BOMBED BY GERMAN AIR FORCE STOP ENEMY TROOPS PARACHUTED AT VASSIEUX STOP WE PROMISED TO HOLD OUT FOR THREE WEEKS STOP TIME PASSED SINCE TAKING UP ACTION STATIONS SIX WEEKS STOP MORALE OF OUR PEOPLE EXCELLENT BUT THEY WILL TURN AGAINST YOU IF YOU DO NOT TAKE ACTION IMMEDIATELY STOP THOSE IN LONDON AND ALGIERS UNDERSTAND NOTHING

ABOUT THE SITUATION IN WHICH WE FIND OURSELVES
AND ARE CONSIDERED AS CRIMINALS AND COWARDS
STOP YES REPEAT CRIMINALS AND COWARDS

*Even before Narcisse Geyer received the telephone call from Huet
ordering him to attack Vassieux his men had been pouring in from what
remained of the surrounding hamlets to take up their positions on the hills
around the town. Men from the renegade Maquis, from camps deep within
the Forêt de Lente and answerable to no one, also responded to Geyer's call.*

*By 9:00 p.m. that night, as Huet had been calling his Conseil de
Guerre to order, Geyer had 400 men in position. He figured this number
would equalize, or possibly outnumber, the German force in Vassieux.*

*As dusk turned to darkness Geyer gave the order to attack. His men had
the town completely encircled and slowly, stealthily, they made their way down
from the hills. From north, south, east and west they moved towards Vassieux.*

*No sooner had the first patrol, from the north, entered the town than
they were spotted by a German sentry.*

*"Halt" yelled a solitary German. They shot him dead. No further obstacle,
they proceeded cautiously along the side streets towards the centre of the town.
Within five minutes some forty men were 100 metres inside the town when
suddenly a flare was sent up behind them illuminating them just as clearly as
it illuminated the forty Waffen S.S. troops at their rear. They had little time to
take in the scene for within seconds the Germans started shooting, supported
by a machine gun placed in the steeple of the ruined church which gave a 360
degree coverage of the approaches to the town. Every last maquisard was killed.*

*The Germans, now on full alert, dispatched men armed with machine
guns to every house around the perimeter of the town. Geyer realized that
the situation was hopeless and, wanting to preserve what was left of his
dwindling force, ordered a retreat.*

*The following morning, 22 July, the Germans were still fully in control
of Vassieux.*

38

It started, that fateful Saturday 22 July, with the inevitable reprisals. By 6:00 a.m. the Gestapo had rounded up twenty young men in La Chapelle, all pulled from their beds.

They took them to one of the few intact public buildings, the elementary school. The boys, ranging in age from 13 to 22, were held there throughout the morning.

Their parents, friends and lovers could hear the screams as they were tortured.

At noon they were taken out into the public square and forced to stand with their hands in a Nazi salute. If they refused, as several did, they were bludgeoned with rifle butts until, inevitably, they obeyed.

At 1:00 p.m. the Gestapo shot dead the first boy in the line. Then they killed one boy a minute until, nineteen minutes later, they all lay dead.

Later that afternoon they arrested the baker's son, 16-year-old Pierre. They suspected him of carrying messages for the Maquis. They had no proof but he would serve as an example. He was tied upside down to the rear bumper of a Gestapo Citroën, his face on the ground.

By the time they had dragged him through the town for twenty minutes he had no face left.

In Vassieux, if anything, things were worse. Men, women and children were picked at random from their houses and rounded up in the town square where they were systematically mown down. Only one 12-year-old girl, Lisette, survived. She lay under her parents' bodies for two hours before being discovered by her grandmother who had come to search for her after the Germans had left.

The village priest, who had devoted much of his time to ministering to the wounded and dying at Dr Ganimède's 'hospital', was arrested and taken to the Gestapo headquarters, located in the mayor's house. After he refused to answer their questions, the Gestapo dug his eyes out and then took the time to fill the empty cavities with insects before arranging for them to be sewn closed.

The Gestapo were still not satiated. They tied the Red Cross driver and his 18-year-old son to a rope that they had slung over a branch of the lime tree in the town square. The two men were tied in such a way that if one person's feet were on the ground, the other was suspended, the rope slowly strangling him. The father and son took turns to rest. Eventually they ran out of strength and hanged each other. The Boche cut off their genitals and shoved them into their mouths. They were left on public display, the people being forbidden to touch them.

Huet and I listen with horror as Lisette, the sole survivor of the morning's slaughter in the Vassieux town square, and her grandmother, recount these tales of German reprisals.

At 8:15 that morning news came in that the Germans had smashed the defences in two of the south-western passes, giving them access to Le Grand Veymont, Vercors' highest peak. Gebirgsjägers had ascended the mountain. They now had a perfect position from which to fire on the defenders of the passes below.

In the south, the Germans had progressed well through the

night so that Panzer forces were barely 7 km from Die. Unless the Resistance blows up the tunnel at the Col de Rousset pass, German tanks will climb up to the plateau within a matter of hours.

In the east, close to where my men were protecting the crucial bridge at Quart, we got reports that another Panzer division was making quick headway despite constantly being impeded by Maquis. If the bridge falls, we know there will be no escape route except through the mule passes. Certainly there will be no hope of removing Dr Ganimède's wounded from their cave in the Grotte de la Luire.

And at Valchevrière, where, almost single-handedly, Chabal had repulsed a German attack the previous evening, they were once again under attack. But Huet has lost communication both with Chabal and with Costa de Beauregard. He has to get a messenger to them fast to see if they needed, or could spare, any men.

"I feel as though I am playing chess, Luc, constantly moving men around the board, constantly under threat, with fewer and fewer squares in which to take refuge."

"It seems to me, Colonel, that the time for dispersal is drawing very near."

Huet shrugs his shoulders.

"But if you are determined to remain fighting then I think that the best way my people and I can help is for Christine to go to Dr Ganimède's hospital. She will see if there is any way that they, at least, can be removed to the plain as long as we still have control of the bridge at Quart.

Jacques, I'm sure, will be happy to go to Valchevrière. He knows the Gorges pretty well after having been stranded there. He can locate Chabal and report back.

For my part, I would suggest that I go to the Col de Rousset and organize for the tunnel to be blown. What do you say?"

Huet is reluctant for the tunnel to be blown as it's the only way out by road to the south. But he agrees it would have to be, if the tanks were to be prevented from coming through.

He approves my plan. He escorts me to the door of his office where we confront a breathless messenger. "Mon Colonel, Junker Ju 52s have landed at Vassieux airstrip. They are off-loading supplies and taking away the German wounded."

Huet turns to me with a look of total incomprehension and says "How ironic, the runway is too small for the Allied transport planes but quite sufficient for the Germans' much larger ones! Mon Dieu these guys in Algiers have a lot to answer for."

Some guys in Algiers felt the same way. Chavant's telegram had hit Soustelle's headquarters in the old Arab palace below the Kasbah like a bomb. As was its intention.

Once again General Cochet was left out of the loop. He knew it wasn't his responsibility but he still felt he should do everything he could to help. He was getting nowhere with all the red tape in Algiers. As soon as he found out about Chavant's telegram he cabled his superior officer, General Koenig, in London:

VERCORS YOUR ZONE I CAN DO NOTHING MORE

Within half an hour Jacques Soustelle called General Cochet and asked him to organize a commando team to be sent immediately to the plateau. Although relieved at last to be involved in matters relating to the Vercors, Cochet pointed out that a commando team, while no doubt helpful, would not be sufficient to repel an invasion of 11,000 German troops. He wanted more. He wanted the planes sitting in the desert to be immediately mobilized and ordered to bomb Chabeuil.

"*But these are being held in reserve for Force C and the landing on the*

Massif Central" came the reply.

Cochet wanted to send in the French paratroopers stationed near Algiers.

But De Gaulle's unfathomable hierarchy made quick, or even slow, decision-making a laborious and lengthy process. This, combined with politics and rivalry and a tendency towards political opportunism, resulted in no clear decision being made by the end of the evening on 22 July.

Meanwhile, back in the Vercors massif... intrepid, resourceful Christine was terrified of only one thing in life: riding a bicycle.

When Luc came to her and asked her to go to Dr Ganimède's hospital in the Grotte de la Luire to see if they could remove any of the wounded and dying down to the plain that night before the tunnel at the Col de Rousset was blown, she instantly agreed.

"I'm afraid it's too dangerous for the Huillier bus to take you, you'll have to go alone. I've organized for a bicycle to be dropped by in a few minutes' time," he told her casually.

"Oh, uh, fine" replied Christine. "OK, you go now. I'll report back later."

As Luc left her waiting for the delivery of the bicycle in front of the Hotel Breyton he was disturbed by the quick dismissal.

Although Christine quickly mastered the technique she didn't get over the fear, nor would she.

The Germans still had not broken out of Vassieux but planes were criss-crossing the skies and frequently swooped low above her. They left her alone, a lone girl on a bicycle not being a high priority at the moment.

It took her an hour to make it along the St Agnan road and down to the lane leading to the Grotte de la Luire. On approaching, she heard gun shots. She backtracked, dumped the bicycle and climbed above the cave so as to get a view of the entrance.

As she climbed she heard another shot. Convinced that something was very wrong she lay down and pulled herself to the edge of the cliff overhanging the cave. Her worst fears were confirmed. A truck was parked on the lane just where the steep climb up to the cave's entrance began. Outside the entrance itself were four bodies. Two of them she recognized as two of the French male nurses. She could only just make out that the third body was a woman, probably another of the nurses. Then she watched in horror as two Gestapo pushed her friend Franco, the Italian doctor she had brought to Saint-Martin to join Dr Ganimède, prodding him with their rifles and stood him up against a tree. He yelled something inaudible before being silenced permanently.

Christine felt helpless. Her mind was racing, trying to think of something she could do. Then she saw the wounded being brought out on their stretchers by the less seriously wounded. They walked, limped, fell down the steep incline as they made their way to the waiting truck. It was clear what fate lay in store for them.

Finally Dr Ganimède and his wife and their son Jean were taken out of the cave, marched down the ridge and shoved into the back of the waiting Gestapo Citroën.

Five or six Gestapo then did a final search of the cavern. They missed one young medic who had hidden deep inside the cave. When the Gestapo emerged they brought with them a neatly dressed lady. They talked with her for a few minutes and then put something into her hand, it looked like a wad of money to Christine, before saluting to her and leaving.

Once the truck and car were out of sight, the well-dressed lady turned and started down a path beside the cave.

Christine had taken that same path when she and Daniel Huillier came the previous time. She knew that it went to a lane about a hundred metres below the cave. Wasting no time Christine made her way around the cave so that she would end up on the same lane; before the elegant lady who was clearly not dressed for the occasion.

And so it transpired.

As Christine approached the lane she found a Renault parked to one side sheltered under a tree. No one inside. Keeping to the protection of the scrub she made her way up the lane, past the Renault, and got to *the entrance of the path just as the elegant lady was coming down. She recognized her immediately. It was 'Colonel Maude' the sadistic mistress of the Chief of Milice in Die.*

"Going for a stroll, Madame?" said Christine emerging from the shade of the trees.

"Oh my goodness. You startled me."

"Did I? So sorry."

'Colonel Maude' gradually regained her composure. "Yes, I'm a botanist, I often come up here, it has such a variety of wild flowers." As she talked she fumbled in her pocket.

"No note book? No magnifying glass? No nothing; except I believe you have a good amount of cash in your pocket, no?"

The lady lost her composure and started to shake. "Why, why… how did you know… a friend owed me some… how did you know?"

"I saw you being paid off by the Boche. How much did they pay you for turning over your countrymen to their deaths?"

"Please, please I can explain… here take the money."

"Save your breath. You only have a few left" said Christine as she pulled out her pistol "you are lucky, your death will be short and sharp, unlike those you betrayed."

'Colonel Maude' gave an unladylike scowl and said "They were scum, they were nothing, they were…" The bullet quickly put an end to her jabbering.

Christine had run out of patience. She removed the car keys from the wretched woman's pocket, climbed into Colonel Maude's Renault and drove back to Saint-Martin in style, the symbol on the roof of the car protecting her from attack by German planes.

I make my way through the Forêt de Lente, accompanied by one of Chavant's most trusted men as my guide. Our progress is slow for we are constantly on the alert. There are rumours that

Gebirgsjägers have already penetrated deep into the forest. Huet has sent a message for Pierre Reynaud, the cell leader in command of the bridge at Quart, to meet me at the Col de Rousset as long as there are enough men left to protect the vital bridge. He has alerted cells in Die and Chabeuil to bring explosives up to the Col de Rousset.

It takes us seven hours to reach the bridge. Geyer's men have the pass pretty well defended and as yet there has been no sign of Germans attempting to come up the pass.

Pierre and the men from Chabeuil are already here, waiting. Three men from Die join us. They quickly fill me in on the situation in each of their areas. The Germans have occupied Die, the hospital has been evacuated, most of the doctors have long since fled. There is clearly no point in taking Dr Ganimède's wounded down there.

I feel a pang of guilt at having sent Christine on a pointless expedition.

The men say that Chabeuil airport is as busy as a Paris airport. Planes are leaving around the clock for sorties to the Vercors and returning to refuel, offload wounded, pick up provisions and depart. A Panzer division left Chabeuil early this morning and would be approaching the massif any time now.

Pierre Reynaud reports that the bridge at Quart was secure, for the time being. But he warns that the Panzer division coming from the south-east is due within the next 12 hours. He doubts his men can hold out against such a force. They would be outnumbered by ten to one. Pretty average odds for the Vercors Maquis.

"Just remember, Pierre, we are a guerrilla force. I need you to live another day. If it becomes clear that your position is hopeless then for heaven's sake withdraw and disappear. We have too much important work still to do to risk losing you now. Leave the battles for the armies."

Pierre looks at me and smiles. He will do exactly what he wants. I shake my head knowingly. His men are well trained. I can only hope for the best. "Meanwhile, let's get this tunnel wired. What explosives do you have?"

"Chargeurs de F.M." say the men from Chabeuil. The men from Die have grenades.

"OK. There are empty boxes of tuna and paté left over from the Bastille Day party in the tunnel. Let's fill them. We'll blow the tunnel as soon as the first tanks make it into the entrance."

Within half an hour the preparation is accomplished. We leave the boxes inconspicuously where they were found. I give Geyer's men guarding the tunnel instructions to blow it when the time comes. I make arrangements with the men to visit them within the week and leave with Chavant's guide for the walk back through the forest. We should be in Saint-Martin shortly after midnight.

As soon as Luc had left his office for the Col de Rousset, Colonel Huet called Jacques with the request that he go to join Chabal and his men at Valchevrière.

"Communications have been lost both with Chabal and with Costa de Beauregard" Huet explained "We have no way of knowing if they are still alive, if they need men and weapons or if they have any to spare. Luc has agreed that I could ask if you would make your way to Valchevrière and then report back."

"Of course, Colonel. Do you want me to go right away?"

"Please, Jacques. If you leave now you could be back by, say, noon tomorrow."

"OK, Colonel. I'm on my way."

Jacques left Saint-Martin by bicycle half an hour after the departure of Christine and Luc.

He arrived at the outskirts of the Gorges three hours later, hid his bicycle and started the long climb towards Valchevrière on foot. As he made his way along the Gorges he suddenly realized why it all seemed so familiar. Two minutes later he passed the hut where he had spent the night with Hans. He knew that the Germans had left the area once Chabal's men had taken up their positions but he decided to look inside out of curiosity.

A few sticks of furniture remained, nothing more. Most things had been burned or vandalized. On the wall was written Hans Müller, 43 Eleanorstrasse, Bad Godesburg, Germany. And then several words were just discernible... j'espere .... rendezvous ...

A bientot... Jacques paused for a second or two and then closed the door.

It was nightfall by the time he got to Chabal's post on the belvedere.

Colonel Huet and three of his night staff sat drinking coffee and staring at the map on the wall of his office as midnight approached. It was clear from the pins on the map that his whole line of defence was crumbling fast.

Only one pass remained open, the Pas de l'Aiguille in the south. Otherwise the entire massif was encircled. The enemy were making substantial inroads on every front. Huet had ordered a second attack on Vassieux earlier in the evening but that, too, had failed. His men were becoming disheartened. To many of his staff the situation appeared completely hopeless. But Huet decided to soldier on. There would be no dispersal yet.

At dawn on Sunday 23 July a squad of Gebirgsjägers climbed to the ridge above the cave where the maquisards were positioned to guard the Pas de l'Aiguille. They lowered down a box of explosives into the cave, detonated it and killed every man inside. The last pass off the Vercors was now closed. The only way out were the mule passes and many of those were now occupied by Germans.

Also at dawn, the Germans attacked Valchevrière under cover of a barrage of mortars. They launched assault after assault at Chabal's men. Jacques delayed his return to Huet to help repel the German attacks. Chabal, dragging on his pipe, fired his bazooka as the Germans approached the belvedere. He killed twenty-seven men before being shot in the head. Moments earlier he had taken a list of men under his command from his pocket, crumpled it up and hurled it into the Gorges below.

Jacques picked up the bazooka and continued to fire, withdrawing into the forest behind to join the remnants of Chabal's men as he went. As he retreated into the woods he heard a voice behind him scream "Run, Jacques, run!" He swivelled around, crouched down and found himself facing a Wehrmacht unit that had already arrested Chabal's twelve remaining men.

A single shot rang out from the woods and the German officer who had yelled for Jacques to run, fell to the ground, dead.

Jacques bit his tongue, dropped the bazooka and put his hands up. He was marched over to join Chabal's men. The deafening sound that had surrounded the belvedere since dawn was gone. The prisoners were all made to lie spread-eagled on the open ground below the belvedere. They were kept there for two hours; presumably awaiting a decision as to their fate.

German soldiers gradually appeared from everywhere. They sat on the belvedere eating their bread and cheese and drinking coffee. Every now and then someone would make a remark and they would laugh and jeer at the prisoners.

It was late morning before the prisoners were allowed to move. Six or seven Wehrmacht soldiers forced them on to their feet and marched them to the edge of the Gorges. They were made to kneel, facing the Gorges. Jacques was at the far right end of the line. A thousand images flashing through his head, from his early childhood to the death of his mother; the smiling faces of his sisters the last time he saw them in Annecy; warm baguettes; Luc's friendship and finally the brave but senseless attempt of Hans to save his life a few hours earlier.

As the first shot was fired, and the first of Chabal's men fell headlong into the Gorges below, a strange calm came over Jacques. This was not how he expected the end to be. If anything he thought he would go out in a blaze of fire, not kneeling beside his comrades and being picked off one by one to give the German soldiers some final amusement and target practice to while away their time before receiving their next orders.

As the shots got closer, and the man next but one fell into the ravine, Jacques' mind closed down into what he imagined was a kind of Buddhist dharma, somewhat akin to ecstasy.

Another shot rang out, and then another.

News of the fall of Valchevrière reached Huet as he was discussing his options with Chavant, General Zeller, Luc and Christine in Saint-Martin at 3:00 that afternoon. He had feared the worst when Jacques failed to return that morning, as promised.

The maquisards who brought the message had, along with two others, escaped from the escarpment opposite the belvedere just before the final onslaught. They had seen Chabal killed and knew that Jacques and twelve others had been arrested. They reported the lull in the shooting, then confirmed that the men had all been executed.

Christine grabs my hand and squeezes it tight. I feel the tears well up in my eyes. She tightens her grip. Chavant too grips my arm. "I understand Luc, I understand" and he does, for all his gruff exterior. Once again I have lost my best friend...

General Zeller breaks the mood. "Colonel, I think the time has come, n'est ce pas?"

Even Huet knows now, with the fall of Valchevrière, that it's hopeless to continue. Only sheer dumb pride would keep him from issuing the dispersal order now. And General Zeller had as good as given the order himself.

"Oui, mon General... oui."

Huet calls his team together and instructs them to issue the "Dispersez et nomadisez" order that he's been keeping in his top drawer. Each group of Maquis knows what part of the plateau, or indeed the plains below, they should make for. Huet had, of course, forbidden them to return home. He knows that a few foolhardy ones will, only to be tortured or shot.

As previously agreed, General Zeller confirms to Huet that he, Christine, Alain, the 'pianist' and I will depart directly for the Col de Rousset and then leave the plateau and head back to Seyne-les-Alpes. Colonel Descour, still unaware of the death of his young son at the airstrip in Vassieux, is due to return to the plateau this afternoon. There is no longer any need for Zeller's presence on the Vercors and my team have many pressing demands elsewhere.

Zeller tells Huet to outline his plan.

"D'accord, mon General. Each man has a specific position to go to once the dispersal order has been received. You do not need the detail but rest assured they are all accounted for. Once we have re-established contact with Costa de Beauregard, he and his men will head for the heights of Plenouze in the far north of the massif.

Captain Geyer will leave his headquarters at La Rivière and fall back into the Forêt de Lente. From there he can resume the guerrilla tactics that he loves so well."

Even now the regular soldiers' distaste for the flamboyant, unconventional Geyer shows no sign of abating.

"I will take my men to Forêt de la Sapine in the far west. Smaller groups will be situated in inaccessible places across the plateau. We can only hope that the Allied invasion will take place imminently."

"And you, Patron? What will you do?" I ask Chavant.

"I will not go far from Saint-Martin. They will not find me. You will see" he has the suggestion of a smile as he draws on his pipe.

Before we all leave, Huet asks if Alain could send one final message on his behalf to London:

WE HAVE HELD ON AGAINST THREE GERMAN DIVISIONS FOR FIFTY-SIX HOURS STOP UNTIL NOW WE HAVE LOST ONLY A TINY PIECE OF TERRITORY STOP THE TROOPS HAVE FOUGHT COURAGEOUSLY BUT DESPERATELY FOR THEY ARE NOW PHYSICALLY EXHAUSTED AND ALMOST OUT OF AMMUNITION STOP DESPITE REPEATED REQUESTS WE ARE STILL FIGHTING ALONE AND HAVE RECEIVED NEITHER SUPPORT NOR AID FROM THE START OF THE BATTLE STOP IT WAS OBVIOUS THAT SOONER OR LATER THE SITUATION WOULD BECOME DESPERATE AND DETERIORATE INTO TERRIBLE MISFORTUNE ON THE VERCORS PLATEAU STOP WE HAVE DONE ALL THAT COULD BE EXPECTED OF US BUT ARE FILLED WITH SADNESS FOR THE ENORMOUS RESPONSIBILITY OF THOSE WHO FROM FAR AWAY DELIBERATELY ENGAGED US IN SUCH A VENTURE ENDS

I leave the others inside to finish their preparations for the journey, collect my knapsack from the hook by the front door and walk down the road a bit to sit on the wall. It's time to fulfil my promise to Jacques. I reach into the pocket of the knapsack and pull out the envelope he gave me those few short weeks ago.

My dear friend,

As I know you are true to your word, by the time you read this I will be dead. Surprisingly, for someone who once had ambitions to be a playwright, I am finding this the hardest letter I have ever had to write. But I have to write it.

Luc, my friendship with you was the most important relationship of my short life. You were my guide, my protector, my mentor, sometimes my chastiser, my foil, and always my friend. I felt closer to you than to anyone living. Whenever I thought of your smile, your laughter, your warmth, my heart, now stilled, beat faster. I loved you Luc; I could never have told you so, and that's my failing, for you would not have minded. But I truly loved you Luc. Like many others, I would have followed you anywhere. I trusted you implicitly. Before you read the rest of this letter (which you must promise to burn as soon as you have read it) I want you to know that.

It would be easier if I just left it at that and then you could forget about me and get on with your life, for I know you will survive, I promise you that. But I need you to know the real me before you forget me. I need to close the circle with a clear conscience.

I don't want to attach a label to myself because whatever I may be I do know who I am and part of who I am, or who I was, is a man who loves men. I love women too, of course, but not in the way I love men. It is something I have tried to overcome, and then when that was impossible, to hide ever since I first discovered the attraction when some friends and I were playing football at the school playground. I was seven years old. I suddenly was overcome with an overwhelming desire to kiss my friend Michel when we found ourselves alone in the playground after the game. All I knew is that some powerful urge had overtaken me. From then on, until I met you, I felt like I had been cut adrift from the world. I spent the rest of my life trying to prove myself. Since meeting you I have felt more at one with myself than at any other time in my life. It would take a brighter man than me to explain why. All I know is that this is the truth and that is miracle enough for me.

So this is not only a confessional note but a thank you note, my dear Luc, for the companionship, joy and love (may I call it that?) that you gave to a young Frenchman you once knew called Jacques Villaz.

Numbed, I sat motionless on the wall for what seemed an eternity but must have been a minute. The tears that had welled up inside burst forth. Strangely the emotion I felt most along with the loss was anger. Anger at having this beautiful friendship stolen from me; it was like losing François all over again but even stronger. I didn't give a fuck about his loving men. Anger too at a world that would force such a good, brave man to feel guilt and surely loneliness all his life. And anger at Jacques for not having told me before, seeing as it had obviously been eating away at him. And anger at war, stupid, fucking, senseless war…

"Luc" Christine, suddenly beside me, startled me "darling, we've got to go." She bent down, wiped the tears off my cheek, and kissed me.

It's three o'clock. I take the wheel of General Zeller's car and with heavy hearts we drive away from Saint-Martin. We take the road to Saint Ange which is still held open by the Maquis. We half expect the German garrison at Vassieux to have made a breakout attempt by now, but I am assuming they are waiting for the heavy armour to arrive via the Col de Rousset.

As we pass groups of Maquis heading for the hills on our approach to the Col de Rousset, Geyer's men warn us that German tanks have been spotted ascending the pass. We will have to ditch the car and walk.

As we drive around the last sharp bend towards the Col de Rousset we see the tunnel explode. The blast knocks the car off the road. Zeller and I yank open the back door and pull Christine and Alain out. I then douse the car with petrol and set fire to it.

We emerge back onto the road to see delighted Maquis punching the air as they make for the hills. Bits of tunnel, tank and body parts are all around us.

We start down the steep slope and see the Panzer division in deep disarray. At least two of their tanks have been destroyed and a couple more put out of action. They will have to find an alternative way of getting their hardware onto the plateau.

Stopping frequently to take cover (an enemy plane is searching above) we gradually descend the plateau. By nightfall we should make it to the ring road. If we manage to get across without being seen by German patrols we should be able to wade across the Drôme and reach Seyne-les-Alpes by the first light of dawn.

Not long after General Zeller's car pulled away from Huet's headquarters that afternoon, the first German troops appeared on the heights above Saint-Martin.

Chavant had seen to it that the town was alerted immediately Valchevrière had fallen. Most of the buildings were empty. Fearing the worst, he had taken the precaution of dispatching Mme. Breyton to his sister's house in Grenoble the previous evening.

The Patron himself, with a heavy heart and eternal bitterness at his betrayal by Algiers, was one of the last to leave the town. As he made his way off into the forest to resume his life as a fox, the first shells landed on Saint-Martin.

39

By the first week in August the mood in the HQ of the Wehrmacht's 157th Reserve Division was decidedly positive, not to say celebratory. General Karl Pflaum had telephoned Field Marshal von Runstedt the previous week to inform him that the backbone of the Vercors Resistance had been broken, that the camps and villages previously harbouring terrorists had been evacuated and burned and that the enemy was now split up into small groups, desperately trying to escape through the encircling lines of the Wehrmacht.

Soon the news was even better; so much so that Pflaum decided it was an appropriate occasion for a little well-deserved gloating for the 157th, a necessary fillip since the news from the north was getting steadily worse.

As Pflaum, in great good humour now, was on his way to address the assembly of officers, he saw the Abwehr sergeant, whom he had been studiously avoiding for the past few weeks, talking to his secretary.

"Sergeant" he barked at Metzger "we have some entertainment laid on this morning. Come and join us."

Metzger, unable to believe his luck, followed General Pflaum into the crowded auditorium. Directed to a chair in the front row, he gazed contentedly around the room and took his seat with the others.

"Gentlemen", the general began "today I bring you the personal congratulations of Field Marshal von Runstedt, Commander-in-Chief of German Forces in the West. He wants me to assure you that the Führer himself has heard of your success in routing the enemy and destroying the enemy's will by exposing the mockery of the Free French Republic of Vercors."

General laughter ensued.

"The so-called Vercors Resistance has been a symbol for terrorists across the country. Now it is no more. You, the combat troops of the 157th Reserve Division, supported by our colleagues in the Luftwaffe, have put paid to that. The Führer is proud of you. The Fatherland is proud of you."

Satisfied noises all around.

"However, our brothers in the north have not had the same success. The news from Normandy is not good. The Americans are within 80 km of Paris. 35,000 of our comrades have been taken prisoner. The massed troops of the German Army are looking to us to prevent the enemy from attacking from the south. There are rumours that an invasion is imminent. We have been called upon to repel it."

The mood in the room was getting more sombre now. It was unusual for a German general to give out bad news. But Pflaum wanted to put the fear of God into his troops while maintaining their morale. He let what he'd said sink in. Now it was time for specifics. Pflaum turned to the large map behind him. Colonel Schwab, fresh from his successes in the Vercors, took up the pointer as Pflaum resumed speaking.

"The enemy is likely to land here in Provence," Schwab indicated the coastline from Marseilles to Cannes, "our navy base in Marseilles will no doubt be a primary target. We assume the navy itself will be repelling any attempts to land by sea, probably from Italy, here, or from the north coast of Africa" Schwab pinpointed Algiers. "Their destination will be Grenoble. Our Intelligence is that the enemy is likely to plan on reaching Grenoble in 90 days. We will of course prevent this and push them back into the sea."

Concentration was intense now. Pflaum could sense the communal flow of adrenalin.

"In order for the enemy to progress inland they need to have access to these major roads" Schwab indicated the Route Nationale 85 from Nice to Digne, the Route Nationale 7 from Marseilles to Lyon and the Route Napoleon. "Not only is the Route Napoleon the major link between Grenoble and the sea but it is the road that Napoleon took when returning from Elba and as such it would have special significance for an invading French army."

Pflaum took a long sip of water, then resumed.

"As you know, the British air force bombed Chabeuil this week, two weeks after our victory in Vercors. So much for their timing! But the remaining airports are intact and must remain so. It is our responsibility to safeguard all airports for the Luftwaffe.

The Port of Marseilles will be protected by the 146th Reserve Division. However the 157th may well be called in if reinforcements are needed."

Pflaum then ordered Schwab to turn the map around so it was facing the wall. On the reverse side was an enlarged image of Luc. The same one that had appeared on the station platform at Albertville. The assembly all looked puzzled.

All, that is, except Metzger who stared, aghast, at the image and then at Pflaum. Was Pflaum going to announce that he had captured Luc? Was his prize about to be taken from him just as he sensed he was closing in for the kill?

Silence. Then Pflaum resumed.

"However, the news I have for you gentlemen today is that the enemy has already landed. This is the face of the enemy. This man, known to the approximately 10,000 French so-called Resistance under his command as Luc, is an American terrorist; real name Joseph Quantock."

Metzger gulped. So Luc hasn't been caught. Is this general now going to spill the whole can of beans? Will he now have to compete with the entire

157th Wehrmacht Reserve Division to capture Luc?

"This Luc is the brains behind the destruction of factories, power stations, armaments trains and the train links from the entire south-eastern section of France and the border; the man who has made it impossible for our soldiers to use any of the smaller roads leading from the sea to Grenoble; the man behind the destruction of the hydroelectric station at Beaurepaire; the man who has overseen the murder of several hundred of your friends and colleagues; the man who aims to capture and kill you. He must be captured at all costs."

Every man in the room sat there and scrutinized the drawing of Luc in front of them.

"There will be a reward of one million Reichsmarks for his capture, preferably alive."

A communal intake of breath. Beads of sweat appeared on Metzger's forehead.

"This reward is offered exclusively to people in this room. Including our friend the sergeant from the Abwehr. If you need to pay others to aid you then you will have to use your own funds.

Oberst Schwab will now continue the briefing and will introduce you to the Abwehr sergeant who will be able to give you a detailed breakdown about this man Luc."

Metzger glared in fury at Pflaum. The general allowed the trace of a smile to steal across his lips.

Schwab cut short his planned lengthy recounting of 'his' successes on the Vercors; villages razed to the ground, livestock removed, young girls raped, young men rounded up and killed. He decided to leave out the torture accounts, although privately he had found them particularly exhilarating. Schwab was aware of the hatred for him, and for his tactics, in the room.

But the main reason for cutting short his presentation was that he, like Karl Metzger, had been temporarily non-plussed by the General's reward offer for the capture of Luc. It hadn't taken long for Schwab to realize that he was in a better position than anyone, except perhaps for Metzger, to track down this man Luc and claim the one million Reichsmarks.

Nevertheless his general had told him to brief the officers on Luc and he would do that, although he would be careful to withold a few significant pieces of information.

"We now turn our attention to the terrorist Luc." It was a much cherished sensation of Schwab to engage such rapt attention from the officers of the 157th Wehrmacht Reserve Division. "Our information is inevitably somewhat sketchy but I will ask Sergeant Metzger of the Abwehr to come up and join me here. Sergeant Metzger has made something of a hobby out of tracking down this man Luc so he will no doubt want to share his information with you. Sergeant?"

Metzger rose reluctantly from his seat, feigning a smile, and joined Schwab on the platform.

Pflaum, sitting in the shadows behind the two men, privately thought woe betide the Reich if it is to be controlled by such despicable specimens as these two.

Schwab continued "Luc is over two metres tall, strong and, as you can see, good-looking in an American sort of way. He works for British Intelligence and does not wear a uniform. He is therefore a terrorist and would normally be shot on sight. But he is not to be shot. He must be captured alive if at all possible. He is the only person who knows all the cell leaders of the so-called Resistance organizations throughout south-eastern France. He is the only person who is aware of the invasion plans and when and where it will take place. He is the only person who knows what acts of terrorism and sabotage are planned in order to pave the way for an enemy invasion. We must capture him and interrogate him thoroughly before killing him." Schwab paused. "Any questions so far?"

An officer in the second row put up his hand.

"Ja, Oberleutnant?"

"What information do you have on his whereabouts?"

"If we knew where he was we would not be here, Oberleutnant."

Silence. Another miscalculation on Schwab's part. How to rescue the situation?

"I will call on Sergeant Metzger of the Abwehr to bring you up to date on Luc's 'whereabouts' as Metzger will know that better than anyone."

Metzger, loath to provide information even to his hand-picked assistant, was now called upon to reveal his secrets to the entire German Army. But he knew his Machiavelli. Subterfuge was called for. In particular he would have to outwit Schwab whom he deduced quite quickly would be after Pflaum's booty and would no doubt prove to be his greatest rival.

Metzger spoke in staccato. "Luc is a terrorist working for the British Special Operations Executive, a group of spies sent in to organize French resistance. He speaks excellent French. He was almost arrested in Annecy when two major ringleaders of the Resistance cells were arrested by my men." Pause for effect.

"Since then he has moved down to the south where he has been organizing groups of deserters, communists, homosexuals, Jews and Spaniards into terrorist cells. He has been responsible for the murder of many good people who have been working with us for the good of the Fatherland. He has a female assistant named Christine who is Italian. And beautiful. They are reputed to be lovers. He was on the Vercors but regrettably was allowed to escape." Pause for a sip of water and a sideways glance at Schwab.

"He has been sighted in Marseille and Montélimar and various points in between over the past month. He has a second in command called Jacques Villaz, a Frenchman who is a so-called Maquis formerly with the Glières Maquis before they were destroyed. We know no more than that."

Schwab, resuming, said "We thank the sergeant for his contribution. It is a little out of date in some respects; the Jacques you speak of was actually shot by one of our firing squads last week."

"What a pity" retorted Metzger as he sat down "that you didn't think of capturing him alive as that would have led us to Luc."

There were noises of agreement in the auditorium. Even Pflaum found himself thinking 'Advantage Metzger'.

"That will be all Gentlemen" said Schwab, too disconcerted to ask for questions.

Pflaum announced that Schwab would arrange for images of Luc to be distributed to everyone at the door, reaffirmed the one million Reichsmark reward for his capture alive and called the meeting to an end.

Metzger, feeling he had nothing to gain and everything to lose by sticking around with the Wehrmacht, took advantage of a car provided by the local Abwehr office and ordered the driver to take him to Montèlimar. A local agent had sent him a message the previous evening confirming the rumour that Luc was expected in Montèlimar within 36 hours to hold a meeting with the heads of the various cells.

The local agent in question was actually working for the Resistance. Luc, defying his own rule about assembling all the cell heads together under one roof, had indeed called for just such a meeting to be held but not at Montèlimar. Instead it was at a farmhouse near the village of Champourçin, not far from Digne and 200 kilometres from Montèlimar.

40

8:00 p.m., 3 August, 1944

News is coming in from the coast that American bombers are scorching and softening up potential landing areas suggesting that the long-anticipated invasion is not far off.

General Zeller, Christine and I are sitting, with the ten cell heads, in the living room of a house owned by Aristide, code name of the local farmer, head of the Champourçin cell.

Also here are Marc, from the Bidous' farm in Montèlimar; a pharmacist from Oppede in the Vaucluse; a teacher from Le Pouget, west of Montpellier; a bar manager from Albertville in the Haute-Savoie; a tabac owner from Valence; a garagiste from Apt; a gendarme from Lyon, a hotel manager whose hotel had become the headquarters of the Milice in Grenoble; and a restaurateur from Aix en Provence.

The farmer's mother and wife hover at the kitchen door. Every now and then they interject comments, always taken very seriously, and make certain we all have enough to eat and drink.

The smoke-filled room echoes with the sound of laughter,

arguing, drinking; sometimes all three at once. An outsider could easily mistake this scene for a birthday party. But it is the preamble to possibly the most momentous meeting of all the participants' lives.

At 9:00 p.m. I call the meeting to order.

"Mes amis, we are facing what will possibly, no, probably, be the most decisive week of the war." The faces around the room, some comic, some prematurely gnarled, others scarred, one burned, gradually settle into their individual versions of composure.

"Xavier from Oppede tells us that American bombers are already softening up the coast line in anticipation of a landing. The Germans in Marseille and Grenoble are fully mobilized and dangerously jittery according to Etienne who has just come down from Grenoble." What I don't mention is that Etienne has also brought a copy of the picture of me that is being handed out to people on the street with an offer of a reward. It is even more substantial than before.

"I have had no direct orders to confirm that the invasion will take place this week but the signs are increasingly strong that it will. Which places an enormous responsibility on us. One which we have already proven we can meet. General Zeller here is leaving for Algiers in the morning to meet with General de Gaulle and others. It is vital that the Allies get to Grenoble as quickly as possible. I have told him that, given the talent, resolution and resources at our disposal we should cause enough disruption to the German forces that we can clear the way to Grenoble to allow them to take the city within ten days. Maybe even fewer. A delay would be disastrous for us. It would allow the Germans time to mount similar attacks to the massacre at Vercors. As you know, no solitary German vehicle ever reaches its destination. Small units no longer leave the security of the Wehrmacht compound. Even large convoys are very vulnerable thanks to your efforts. The Germans may have superior arms to us but they are confined to where they can operate on a very large scale, as in Vercors. This means they do not control vast parts of the country. That is our strength."

I address Zeller directly.

"General, the message you must take to de Gaulle is that every day the Allies spend getting to Grenoble will cost French lives, maybe many French lives. The German garrison towns, Digne, Sisteron and Gap, are surrounded by mountains. Our men control virtually the whole of the French Alps. The Germans will not be able to mount a challenge against the combined forces of an advancing army and the Maquis."

From what he has seen and heard over the past week, I know that Zeller is already convinced that I am right, although even he thinks ten days is a little optimistic.

"Luc, I am convinced. And I am certain that de Gaulle would not disagree with a plan that would shorten the war by almost three months and save hundreds, maybe thousands, of French lives. I leave at dawn tomorrow morning. I will persuade him."

Determination has returned to the assembled faces. Time for me to outline the plans.

1. Raymonde from Grenoble and our host Aristide will be responsible for ensuring that the Route Napoléon is kept open and free of Germans for the Allied advance.

2. François from Le Pouget and Xavier's cells from the Vaucluse will take responsibility for the roads between Marseille and Toulon and for the continued disruption of the rail lines.

3. Aristide's cells between Digne and Nice will take charge of the coast from Toulon to the Italian border.

4. Max from Valence will be in charge of the Route Nationale from Marseille to Lyon which is the most likely route for significant German troop movements.

5. We need to ensure the routes from St Tropez and Toulon to Draguignan are protected. That will be up to Michel from Aix.

6. Christine will cross the Italian border and find reinforcements there from both Italian partisans and Polish POWs so they can hold the border from Ventimiglia to Barcelonnette and deny all road and rail access to the Germans.

7. The Haute-Savoie mountaineers under Georges in Albertville will protect the borders north of here to prevent German reinforcements getting through and others retreating across the border.

8. Jean-Louis from Apt will continue to act as liaison with the Maquis from the Vercors and ensure that they are reassigned to active cells as quickly as possible.

9. Marc from Montèlimar will protect the roads and airstrips around Montèlimar which is likely to be a flashpoint for German forces given its strategic location on the main route north.

10. And I will visit you all during the next ten days. Are there any questions?"

A few need additional weapons. Others, materiel. I promise them as soon as possible.

"The light is at the end of the tunnel mes amis. I know that you all know what you have to do. In most cases you are already doing it. But bon courage. We will meet again soon and celebrate properly."

Xavier proposes a toast. Aristide and his wife offer their house as the party venue once the war is won. We mingle for half an hour then each man goes his separate way.

I am returning to Seyne, hoping Christine will come too before leaving for Barclonnette. But no, she says she wants to leave right away for the border.

I watch her go. Her small, deceptively fragile figure making its way down the path to the road. I have never come across a girl like her before. She too is a loner. Apparently needing no one. A female version of myself. And I don't like it one bit.

The following day General Zeller flew, via Corsica, to Algiers. As soon as his plane landed at the Aeroport de Maison-Blanche he made his way to de Gaulle's headquarters. De Gaulle agreed to see him that evening at 6:00.

Zeller checked in to his hotel in the Kasbah, had a wash, a shave and a change of clothes before returning to de Gaulle's HQ.

"I can give you fifteen minutes General" said de Gaulle as he sat down at his imposing desk in the Palais de Justice. Zeller, sitting opposite him, quickly outlined the situation in south-east France. It became clear to him that the Vercors was a sensitive subject and best avoided. But de Gaulle was keen to hear about the state of preparedness in the south-east. After five minutes de Gaulle handed Zeller a large, blue file "This is the Operational Plan. Sit down at that table there and study it. I'd like to know your view."

Zeller read through the introduction, an outline of Operation Dragoon, the planned assault by American, Australian and Free French Forces on the beaches of the Cote d'Azur. From just west of Cannes landings would take place all along the coast to St Raphael, St Tropez and driving on to capture Toulon and Marseille before heading north up the Rhone valley.

Good, thought Zeller, just as Luc had guessed. Then, to his amazement, he saw that the plan called for the Allies to take 90 days to reach Grenoble.

"General," said Zeller placing the bulky file on the table, "this is far too cautious. If the Allies advance north through the mountains, in particular by the Route Napoleon, they will be virtually unchallenged. They'll be in Grenoble in days, not months."

De Gaulle looked astonished. Acutely aware of the Vercors tragedy, and no doubt feeling somewhat responsible for letting it happen, he was determined not to have another debacle on his hands, particularly at this crucial juncture in the war. He grilled Zeller for details. The fifteen-minute interview lasted two hours as de Gaulle and Zeller pored over maps of south-eastern France. Zeller identified the areas controlled by Luc's Maquis, including the French Alps and pointed out the vulnerability of the German garrison towns. He explained how, by advancing up the Route Napoleon, the Allies could reach Grenoble in a matter of perhaps ten days. They could then strike west across the Rhone valley and cut off the enemy's retreat.

De Gaulle's incredulity changed to conviction. "This is extremely important" he said, pulling himself up to his full two metres "you must leave for Naples immediately and explain what you have told me to General Patch."

By ten o'clock the following morning Zeller was in the office of the American General Patch, the Corps Commander, in Naples standing before an enormous wall map and explaining to Patch and his senior staff exactly what he had said to de Gaulle. He was bombarded with questions about the location and size of the German forces, about the numbers and effectiveness of the Maquis, about the ability of the Resistance and Zeller's capacity to control them.

"I'll give them their orders by radio and direct them to execute the operations you want" Zeller assured Patch.

Zeller left for Algiers shortly after the meeting. That evening Patch sent a signal to de Gaulle saying that he would follow Zeller's advice.

Zeller sent a coded message of confirmation to Luc.

41

Colonel Schwab, Butcher of Vercors, in the company of his two most trusted assistants, studied the somewhat hysterical report received from the hotelier in the small Basses Alpes village of Seyne-les-Alpes.

The hotelier, threatened with deportation by the Germans for black-market activity, had agreed to pass on information of interest to the local Gestapo in order to save his neck. Not much was reckoned to happen in Seyne-les-Alpes but nonetheless Colonel Gerster, the Gestapo chief in Digne renowned for his cunning and thoroughness, had thought it prudent to have at least one frightened pair of eyes there. Just in case.

So Gerster had added the hotelier's name to the list of people to be supplied with a drawing of Luc. Anything to increase his chances of getting what he understood to be a fairly substantial reward for Luc's capture.

When the hotelier's report came in, maintaining that not only had he seen Luc but had done so on many occasions over the past eighteen months, Gerster thought it worthwhile to pass on the report to Colonel Schwab at Gestapo HQ in Grenoble. Privately though he was highly sceptical. Many such reports had come across his desk in the week since the drawings of Luc had been sent out.

Schwab, however, was less sceptical. It made a lot of sense to him that

Luc would be in the Digne area. And he was damned if that guttersnipe Metzger was going to lay his hands on Luc first. He knew Metzger had been dispatched to Montèlimar but he also knew it wouldn't be long before he'd return. And he'd probably return to Grenoble and go running to General Pflaum. Schwab hoped Pflaum would give him short shrift.

Meanwhile, decided Schwab, it was time to get on more intimate terms with Colonel Gerster. He picked up the phone and dialled Gestapo HQ in Digne.

After an infuriating delay he was finally put through to Gerster.

The act of controlling his anger had produced the unfortunate side effect in Schwab's already embarassingly squeaky voice of making him sound uncomfortably sweet. Gerster could hardly believe this was the famous Butcher of Vercors on the line. He instructed Schwab to hold the line for a minute and ordered his telephonist to double-check that the call was indeed from Gestapo HQ in Grenoble.

By the time he got back to Schwab the Colonel's fury had erased all traces of sweetness.

"Gerster what in God's name are you up to? I'll have your balls fried for supper if you try anything like that on me again!"

Ah, thought Gerster, that's better. That's the man we know and love.

"I'm sorry Herr Oberst, I apologize. It was unavoidable. The line is very problematic. It is fixed now Herr Oberst."

"Very well. Now I want you to listen and listen carefully."

"Of course, Herr Oberst."

"This report you have sent to me from the hotelier in Seyne-les-Alpes may or may not be reliable. But it is very plausible. Our information is that this Luc person is likely to be in the Digne area. He may well have some sort of safe house in this village of Seyne. I want you to go up there and assess the situation yourself. Talk to the hotelier. Talk to the people in the town, the gendarmes, the tabac owner, the butcher and so on. Let me know what you find. By tomorrow night. Is that clear?"

"Very clear Herr Oberst."

"And Gerster?"

"Yes, Herr Oberst."

"There is a very good reward for you if you capture this Luc alive. He must be alive."

"Substantial, Oberst?"

"Yes, Gerster. 100,000 Reichsmarks."

Schwab heard an intake of breath through the phone. Good, he thought, he's impressed.

But Gerster's mind was running along different lines.

42

On 10 August the remaining German troops started their withdrawal from the Vercors. The manhunts, murders, destruction of hamlets and farms, stealing of livestock and harassing of villagers of the past two weeks gradually petered out.

Eugène Chavant, Patron of the Vercors, had made his way to the small house that Costa de Beauregard and his men were using as a refuge in the remote hamlet of Barraque-les-Feneys. A bitter but unbroken man, he had spent the previous three weeks living in the woods, off the land, moving cautiously and slyly, mainly at night. His anger at the 'treason' of Algiers had merely stoked the fires within.

As he sat there alone that evening, staring out at the peace and quiet that lay so unnaturally on the land, he thought of the hundreds of brave men, women, and children who had died because the plan of the Montagnards, his own plan, had gone so terribly wrong. It should not have. If only Algiers had delivered on their promises... if only they had bombed the airport at Chabeuil on time... if only... but it was pointless to pursue such thoughts. He knew that. But in the loneliness of the night he allowed himself this lapse. An escaping tear of unredeemable guilt trickled down his craggy face.

The Patron was lost in thought when a quiet but firm knock at the door startled him. He turned and faced the door as it opened.

Standing before him was the emaciated figure of a young man. Dressed in shabby, ill-fitting clothes with a wispy, straggly beard and shoulder-length hair it was hard to distinguish what type of man this was.

But then the man smiled. And immediately the Patron knew him.

"Mon Dieu, Mon Dieu" cried the Patron, temporarily taken aback at the sight of this resurrected figure, "c'est pas possible!"

"Oui, c'est moi". An infectious smile radiated out from the sunken visage that was his face. "C'est moi." The Patron grasped him with both arms and hugged him tightly.

"Careful" said Jacques "you'll break a bone."

"Sit down, sit down" said the Patron as he pulled a chair over and gently lowered the weakened man into the seat "let me get you something. Water? Bread? Wine? I don't know what there is here but I'll find something. Mon Dieu Jacques, it is good to see you" the Patron said as he sourced some wine and bread from Costa de Beauregard's cupboard "but you have a lot of explaining to do. Otherwise my years as an atheist are over."

Jacques, who had lived off the land for three weeks, rather less successfully than the Patron, nibbled at the bread and sipped the watered-down wine as he recounted his harrowing story to the Patron. "It was Sunday 23 July" he began "the day that Valchevrière fell."

The Patron nodded.

"I was on my way back to Huet's HQ when Chabal's men came under fire. I made my way back to the belvedere and found Chabal standing there smoking a pipe and firing his bazooka. He must have killed more than twenty Germans before he was finally shot. He died instantly. I picked up his bazooka and started firing," Jacques's voice started to falter, "there were only 12 or 13 of us and we were eventually forced back into the woods. The Boche were in front of us and behind. They cornered us all and took us prisoners."

"Rest, Jacques, don't overdo it" said the Patron feeding him some more bread and water.

"No, I'm OK, I'm feeling better already." The Patron settled back and lit his pipe while Jacques resumed.

"We were made to lie down for several hours while the Germans, more and more of them, hung around and smoked and drank and poked fun at us. We thought they might actually let us go, they seemed to be so relaxed. Then a senior officer came over and everything went quiet. Next thing we knew we were forced at gunpoint to go over to the side of the gorge and kneel down. Then they started to shoot. Very slowly, one by one, they shot each man and his body fell over into the gorge. They were very brave. Hardly a whimper. Just a few prayers. I was at the far end; the last to be shot. I don't know what came over me but as soon as the guy next to me was shot I just tumbled over, head first, into the gorge hoping that I would hit something soft and out of view of the Germans. And I did."

The Patron shook his head and smiled "Incroyable… Incroyable."

"The Germans, and their dogs, spent several hours looking for me but my fall had been broken 100 metres above the gorge. I didn't move until that night and even then I moved very slowly. By the morning I had made it down to the gorge."

"You must know that gorge pretty well by now!" said the Patron having heard an account of Jacques' previous experience in the Gorges de la Bourne.

"Yes, and it helped because it wasn't far from where I was last time. I made my way along the river and found a deserted hut which had been used by the Germans at one point but hadn't been lived in for many weeks. I risked staying there for three nights, leaving it at dawn each day when I went foraging for food and only returning late at night." Pausing for a sip of the watery wine, he asked the Patron for a cigarette, his first in three weeks. He took a deep drag and coughed so hard that he had to stop talking for several minutes while he regained his composure.

"I saw no one for two weeks. I left the hut after three days when I felt well enough to walk. I had hurt my back and hip pretty badly with the fall but it felt OK by then. So I started walking. It was eerily quiet. I sensed that something had gone terribly wrong long before I came upon the hamlet of Escoulin en Vercors. It had been burned to the ground. It was like a horror film;

dead, dismembered bodies lying in the streets, hanging on the trees. The houses all gutted. The stench of burning flesh was still everywhere. I walked through the village, or what had been the village, and followed the road towards Saint-Martin. On the outskirts of the village I stopped and looked behind me. I just caught a glimpse of someone, someone small, a child, as he ran behind a wall. I walked back and, I'm not sure why, started singing the Marseillaise. A boy, aged about eight, came out from behind the wall and walked tentatively towards me.

It turned out he was the only survivor. He had been off hunting with an uncle when the Germans came. The uncle ran towards his burning house when he saw what was happening. The boy stayed in the woods, terrified, but he survived. His uncle did not."

The Patron had heard that Escoulin had been destroyed, like so many others. His own uncle and aunt had once lived there. They had died just before the war, mercifully.

Jacques resumed. "The boy, Pasqual, has another uncle who lives here in Les Barraques. He knew the way very well so we decided to come here. It took us several days. We saw troops of Germans in the distance moving down towards St Nizier so we got the impression that they were in retreat. Since then we have learned that they were just going home after finishing their job."

The Patron nodded. "Along the way we met several maquisards and some of de Beauregard's men. Just outside Barraques I met de Beauregard. His men had told him they had found me. He was very surprised to see me. He told me where you were so I took Pasqual to his uncle's and came here. Fin!"

"Marveilleux," said the Patron "I'm glad at last that something good has happened. You must rest up Jacques. There is a bunk in the room by the kitchen. Once you are recovered we will go together to see Luc. I have to make contact with him anyway. We think the Allies are about to land on the coast. Two months too late but welcome nevertheless. We need to coordinate our plans. I think the Vercors' contribution to this war is not over yet."

"It is good to see you Patron" said Jacques "I have faced certain death twice now. I don't want to have to do it again."

43

On the same day that Jacques was walking through the burned-out village of Escoulin en Vercors, Christine was crossing the snow-covered Alps into northern Italy, still occupied by German troops. She had left Luc the previous evening. Her heart had beckoned her to stay but her mind told her that she had a job to do and to clutter things up with emotional attachments at this stage in the war she knew would be a mistake. She walked away from him, determined not even to turn around. But she knew herself well enough to know that this was a ploy; and knew he did too.

By nightfall on the second night she had got as far as the upper reaches of the Alps, close to the Italian border. She had been climbing all day. Although she found plenty of fresh water to drink she felt tired and hungry. She decided to go on until she had crossed the border and then find refuge somewhere, she hoped.

It was nearly 10:00 p.m. when she arrived at the pass from Col de Larche, which she knew as Maddalena, into Italy. It was a cold night. Visibility was almost zero. Having seen or heard no one all day, she stuck to the mountain pass, for it would have been all too easy to get lost elsewhere. Half a mile or so before she reached the border she heard voices, German voices. Three or four men talking animatedly coming towards her. She dived behind a snow bank and waited. The Germans passed close by and a minute later an Alsatian dog pounced on her. She calmly put her arm around his neck. He sniffed at her, licked her hand and lay down beside her. His handler whistled for twenty minutes or so; the dog didn't move. Finally the handler gave up. She named the dog Taboo. He stayed close to her all night.

By mid-afternoon the following day she had made it to Argentera. There she met with the 25-year-old head of the Italian partisans, Angelo Galimberti, a veteran of the Spanish Civil War who had returned to Italy, with his Spanish bride, to organize the Italian resistance to Mussolini. Angelo and Christine, and Taboo, met in a safe house just out of town and hatched a deal. He and his group of 100-strong partisans would join her for a month if she, in turn, would provide them with weapons and ammunition sufficient to return and rid Italy of the remaining Germans (and Italian Fascists).

"Done" she said. Within 24 hours the Italians were all safely over the pass and into France where they would position themselves at strategic points along the border. Their acts of sabotage and harassment of German troops over the next few weeks could well prove decisive. Her mission having been achieved, Christine and Taboo started down the road back to Barcelonnette.

When she arrived at the safe house, she received the news that she feared most of all.

44

The hamlet of Le Selonnet, on the outskirts of Seyne-les-Alpes, had been restless ever since Mme. Turrel's questioning by the Gestapo. It was the first time that a German uniform had been seen in Seyne-les-Alpes. Everyone was unnerved.

The black Citroën, belonging to Colonel Gerster, the Gestapo Chief from Digne, had been parked across the street from the Turrels' tabac that day. Two sinister-looking men in black uniforms sat in the car or leaned against it, smoking and waiting for their boss who had been inside the hotel since shortly after breakfast time.

No one wanted to come near the shop. Especially when they saw Gerster go in and not come out for twenty-five minutes. It had a devastating effect on the morning's takings. Not that they were ever very much, but something at least.

By the time the tabac opened up again at 4:00 that afternoon the Citroën had long gone and the shop immediately started to fill up. They were only there to gossip. Mme. Turrel closed the shop early and headed home.

André and I are in the kitchen when Mme. Turrel returns and tells us of the Gestapo encounter.

"So, the result of the Gestapo visit to Seyne is that your picture is now everywhere in the town."

"Then I must get out and not return" I say immediately "I've already put your family at risk more than enough. We most certainly have overstayed our welcome."

"Don't worry about us. The whole village knows you are staying here and no one has squeaked" André Turrel lights his pipe "if they had we would not be sitting here now. But equally nor would they. The townspeople would see to that."

And I believe him. No one in Seyne would dare risk incurring the wrath of André Turrel, the Mayor-cum-Father Confessor of Le Selonnet, Seyne and beyond. But even so I need to find alternative lodging as soon as I can.

"In any event" I say, pulling a piece of paper from my pocket, "according to my interpretation of a message received this morning from General Zeller, the Allies should be landing any day now."

I read the message to the Turrels:

DE GAULLE AND AMERICANS CONVINCED OUR PLAN STOP RAPID MOVE NORTH GUARANTEED STOP CONFIRM DATE AS DISCUSSED STOP YOU TO BLOCK ENEMY MOVEMENTS SOUTH OF LYON AND HARASS ALL ROUTES STOP MAJOR AIR SUPPORT FORTHCOMING BONNE CHANCE MON AMI ENDS

Because Zeller is aware of the invasion plan he is now considered a security risk and will not be allowed to return to France until after the invasion. This is common practice. I've also received another message from Algiers, this time from de Gaulle's office, informing me that Colonel Constans had been appointed de Gaulle's Commissioner for the area and would be arriving by plane shortly. I am ordered to meet with Constans at a safe house south of Digne in two days' time. I don't relish the prospect. Constans is the man who ignored all our pleadings for support for the Vercors maquisards. I wonder how the Patron would react if he knew I was meeting him.

As I explain to André Turrel that I'll gather up my things and head down south to check on preparations before meeting Constans on 12 August, Mme. Turrel, looking as though she's seen a ghost, puts her head around the door and announces that the Patron is here.

Neither the Turrels nor I have seen Eugène Chavant since the dispersal order and I'm elated at the prospect of seeing him, but disturbed that something awful has happened to him by the look on Mme. Turrel's face. Moments later a healthy, smiling Patron walks into the room.

"Patron" yells André Turrel and hugs his old friend.

"Luc" says the Patron "how good to see you."

As I embrace the Patron I look over his shoulder and, seeing another person, gasp.

"What the Fuck!"

"Typically warm American welcome" says Jacques, tears streaming down his face.

I grab him and shake him just to make sure he is real. "Jesus H Christ, I don't believe it. You're dead! What the fuck happened!"

Losing all my composure, crying like a baby and laughing at the same time, I stare at Mme. Turrel who is now beaming as if to ensure that we all see this apparition. "But you were shot. Dead. Killed. We have witnesses. We've been mourning you for Christ's sake!"

"Well" responded Jacques, looking none the worse for his day long walk from the Vercors, "it's what comes of being a good Catholic."

"Cut the crap!"

The Patron intervenes. "OK mes enfants. I suggest the two of you go into the kitchen and do your catching up. André and I have business to discuss."

Jacques and I walk into the kitchen. Before we even sit down he says to me "Did you read the letter?"

"No" I lied "I never really believed you were dead" I lied, again. He looked relieved, which made me sad.

Half an hour later we returned to the living room to join the others.

"Satisfied?" asks the Patron.

"Well, it's a good yarn but I'm still suspicious he's a double agent."

I get a strong kick on my rear end.

Mme. Turrel supplies us all with a magnificent spread of meats and vegetables the like of which the Patron says he has not seen since before the war. During the meal we discuss, ever more enthusiastically, the imminent invasion. I tell them all I know. "The likelihood is that the Allies will land this week. Zeller has persuaded them to drive up the Route Napoleon in order to get to Grenoble in the shortest time possible to minimize the losses on our side. They will also take Toulon and Marseille and then drive up the Route Nationale to Lyon. The plan, at least as far as we have suggested it and the indications are that it has been agreed, is then for the Americans to move off west of Grenoble towards Montèlimar and cut off the enemy's retreat."

The Patron interrupts "We still have around 1,000 men hiding out in the forests of the Vercors. Geyer and his men are mounting daily raids on the plains. We are perfectly able to continue that, on both sides of the massif, but as always we need more weapons."

"Good, that's what we thought. We have enough men covering the eastern side of the Route Napoleon but not the west. I will get Raymonde, our cell leader in Grenoble, to liaise with you. And

Jacques can tell you where there might still be a cache of weapons on the Vercors."

We all spend the night at the Turrels'. In the morning, after a breakfast of rolls and homemade apricot jam, the Patron starts on his way back to the Vercors. Jacques and I say our goodbyes to the Turrels, promising to return after the liberation, and head off towards Digne in the Red Cross car that Claude Renoir, the artist's son, has procured for us.

45

An agitated Sergeant Metzger sat outside General Pflaum's office at the Wehrmacht HQ in Grenoble. Convinced that he'd been hoodwinked on the orders of Colonel Schwab, he was determined to register a strong complaint.

General Pflaum, increasingly concerned about the direction the war was taking, had far more important things on his mind than the amour-propre of an irritating sergeant in the Abwehr. The Abwehr no longer existed officially, its director, Admiral Canaris, having been imprisoned for anti-Hitler leanings and the organization incorporated into Reichssicherheitshauptamt under Heinrich Himmler. But Pflaum liked to retain its usage, finding it pleasingly denigrating. He directed his secretary to send Metzger away. Permanently.

Infuriated, Metzger decided to take matters into his own hands, yet again. He went to the Reich Security main office in Grenoble and placed a call to Colonel Gerster, Gestapo chief in Digne. He would make him a proposal.

Colonel Gerster walked over to the window of the fortified prison in Digne which served as his HQ. It was a beautiful summer's day. A light breeze fluttered the makeshift dresses of the school girls as they marched in a snake along the canal. A couple of boats headed for the ports in the south. A bevy of old ladies sat on the wall outside the cathedral, gossiping.

But Colonel Gerster was not thinking about these sights. He was *mulling over the conversation he'd just had with the Abwehr sergeant. He was also considering the phone call from Schwab; and the testimony of the frightened hotelier in Seyne who still maintained that he had seen Luc in Seyne, regularly. He had even thought he might be living there. But the woman in the tabac, a simple French peasant, not the lying type, was adamant that she had never seen anyone looking like Luc in Seyne.*

Still, Gerster's hunch was that the hotelier could well be right. Perhaps he should pay another visit to Seyne-les-Alpes? Apply a little pressure? But he thought it unlikely that Luc would still be there now that his picture had been distributed far and wide. Surely the whole town couldn't be covering up for him? Someone would let him know.

The meeting between Jacques and me and Colonel Constans, de Gaulle's representative and the scourge of the Vercors Maquis, plus his entourage of three, is strained. Constans wants reassurance from the horse's mouth that Zeller's information is correct. I reassure him, in so far as I can, with the proviso that there should be no more meetings, such as this one, which would take me away from my job at this critical time.

At a small supper our group is joined by an SOE man, David Fellows, a veteran of the Greek campaign. Apparently Buckmaster thought Fellows might be useful to us as he speaks perfect French, albeit with a heavy accent, and had asked Constans to give him a ride. I need this like a hole in the head but it's a fait accompli so we have no choice but to take Fellows on board.

At dawn the following morning, 13 August, the four of us — Jacques, David Fellows, the driver Claude Renoir, and I — set off on the road to Digne.

Ten kilometres before Digne, Fellows suddenly says "I say Luc, what is the likelihood of our being stopped and searched?"

"Possible, but unlikely. Why?"

"Well, I've just realized that I have several hundred thousand francs in my pocket. It might look a bit suspicious don't you think?"

"I certainly do" I say "you'd better divide it between us three. Leave Claude out. It would look a bit odd for the driver to have so much money."

"A bit odd for us too" says Jacques.

"Well, we don't have much choice. It would look even worse if we hid it in the car, although they might just think we were black-marketeers. Divide it into three, David."

Fellows does so. As we approach Digne an Allied air raid begins. Suddenly German soldiers (or rather soldiers in German uniforms for these men were Tartar, Georgian and Armenian members of the Wehrmacht's 'Oriental Legion against Communism') appear, shouting and threatening.

I have learned that it is wise to avoid these characters as they can't speak German or French and thus get easily frustrated and resort to indiscriminate violence. I decide that it's best if we split up rather than risk being questioned by the 'Mongols'.

"Claude, take the car and meet us on the other side of town, where the road divides to Seyne."

We watch as Claude leaves and takes a side road around Digne. He is much less likely to be stopped travelling by himself in his own car, not that the 'Mongols' will be able to read his papers; but the Gestapo will.

"David, you had better stick with Jacques as you don't know the area. I'll go on alone and we should all meet up at the car in half an hour or so. OK?"

"OK, see you there."

I watch as the two of them make their way through the town, side stepping the 'Mongols'. I take a different route, through the upper part of the town passing just below the Castle and Gestapo

HQ. I stop off at the house used by Alain, the 'pianist', when he's in Digne. The sight of my own face on posters outside the Gestapo offices persuaded me of the necessity to wear some type of disguise. Alain's emergency supplies include regulation SOE disguise materials: false moustaches, wigs, make-up. The door is open. The room has been ransacked. There hadn't been much there in the first place but what there was is now strewn over the floor. Nothing particularly incriminating, however, I do find the 'make-up' box.

Five minutes later I emerge from Alain's former flat wearing a peasant's jacket, carrying a small suitcase of assorted dirty clothing and sporting a Hitlerian moustache, unlike the elegant version on the 'Wanted' poster.

Twenty minutes later all three of us reconvene at Claude's waiting car. Breathing a sigh of relief, we all set off on the road to Seyne. As we take the first bend of the road we run into a road block, manned by yet more 'Mongols'.

"Damn, best let Jacques and me do the talking David."

The 'Mongols' start gesticulating, pointing to our pockets.

Jacques, Fellows and I, looking self-important and suitably put out by the intrusion, all grudgingly produce our papers. The 'Mongols' glance at them and wave us through.

As we get back into the car, Jacques looks into the rear-view mirror and mutters "Uh, oh."

A Gestapo car, its horn blaring, pulls up behind us.

"Merde."

"Maybe they've just come to dismantle the roadblock after the air raid?" says Jacques.

Three officers get out, wave the 'Mongols' aside and the senior officer, speaking fluent French, asks to see all four of our papers.

The Gestapo chief looks at the papers. Claude Renoir's genuine Red Cross papers are in order. Jacques' and my papers also pass scrutiny. The questions seem routine. Fellows' papers are the last.

"What is your name?"

"The same as on the identity paper" replies Fellows.

The Gestapo chief snarls. "And what is that?"

"Jean-Jacques de Courville".

"Where are you from?"

"Montpellier"

"Why don't you have a southern accent?"

"I lived for many years in Brittany when I was a boy and it has stayed with me".

"Your job?"

"I work for the Electricity Board."

"Now?"

"Yes, now" Fellows is getting irritated, clearly.

"Then why are your papers out of date? And why do they not have a stamp?"

Fellows shrugs, "I must have forgotten to renew them."

The Gestapo chief isn't having this.

"Get out of the car, all of you."

The Gestapo men level their machine guns. I realize it's hopeless to make a run for it. In any case we may still get away with it. All four of us get out, still affecting the appearance of important people who are being unnecessarily inconvenienced.

"What are you doing here?" The Gestapo chief holds on to Fellows' papers as he continues questioning him.

"Going to visit my sister in Barcelonnette."

"All four of you are going to visit your sister?"

"Listen Corporal, or whatever you are, this is all getting rather tiresome."

"Shut up and answer the questions."

"No, I don't know these gentlemen. They were just kind enough to offer me a ride."

"Hmm…"

"Empty your pockets, all of you."

The Gestapo chief motions to his subordinates to take our belongings and show them to him.

"You say you've never met these men before?"

"Never seen them before, no"

"Then why do three of you have several hundred thousand French Francs, all numbered consecutively?"

Fellows, at a loss for words, starts to splutter.

"Enough lies. All three of you are under arrest. The driver can go. But don't let me catch you back here again or you too will be arrested."

Jacques, Fellows and I are then bundled into the Gestapo car and driven back into Digne, not to the prison but to the Gestapo HQ in the Villa Marie Louise, an imposing, heavily guarded villa set back from the main road and surrounded by wooded parkland.

Once there, we are ordered out of the car and, escorted by the three Gestapo officers, taken into the villa, marched past a door with Oberst Gerster written on it and taken to a desk manned by two Gestapo officials who immediately jump to attention on seeing us approach.

"These are three enemy agents. Take their papers and their belongings and put them into holding cell Q. I will deal with them later."

The formalities, such as they were, being over, the three of us are escorted to an assembly line of concrete cells that have been constructed in an obscure corner of the park.

Holding cell Q is a dark, windowless room, stifling in the midday heat of a Provençal August and stinking of the excrement of the twenty or so other occupants. Fellows, his arrogance undiminished by his predicament, yells abuse at the parting Gestapo.

I turn to Jacques. "Fuck" I say, in English, the first English word I have used in months. After all the emphasis I've put on security, discipline and caution in training Maquis throughout the southeast of France I've gone and committed an unpardonable sin of carelessness myself. I don't blame Fellows. A new boy, arrogant, silly behaviour with the Gestapo. I am furious at the SOE in Algiers for providing Fellows with out-of-date papers. But I blame myself. How could I have been so careless as not to have noticed that the money was consecutively numbered; and how stupid of the SOE to have given them to him in the first place.

Still, here we are. The Allies will land in a day or two and could well be in Digne a couple of days later. Far from relieving our situation I realized that this will make us even more vulnerable. The Germans are already very twitchy. I noticed packing cases in the hall of the villa. There are also signs of a recent bonfire near our cells in the park. They are clearly preparing to pull out, there is little doubt about that. And judging by past experience I know that instead of taking the trouble to process prisoners and send them to concentration camps they are much more likely to summarily execute them.

And they haven't even discovered our identity yet. Once they do, it will narrow the odds against our survival significantly.

Fellows spends his time squatting on the floor eyeing the other prisoners with disdain. Jacques starts to say something to me and I interrupt him. "They've made a terrible mistake my brother, soon we will be released when they realize we are Milicien."

Momentarily taken aback Jacques realizes what I am saying. The Germans are more than likely to have planted a stool-pigeon amongst us. Someone who would be given preferential treatment, or maybe even freed, in exchange for information. We must speak in code, if at all, from now on.

Just before two o'clock in the afternoon, four hours since our arrest, two Gestapo men open the door to our stinking cell and yell out "Jean-Jacques de Courville."

"Oui, c'est moi" replies Fellows.

"Viens ici."

Fellows goes to the door, casts a backward glance at our darkened room, and is taken away by the guards.

The screams persist for forty minutes.

"God knows what they are doing to him" I mutter to Jacques "poor Fellows."

Jacques nods silently, busily contemplating his own fate no doubt. We are both wondering if we'll have the strength to survive such torture or if we'll blurt out what they want to know.

This is the closest I've come yet to contemplating my own death; death by torture. I know I owe it to my dead companions, let alone the living ones, to remain silent. But as Fellows' screams became ever more blood curdling I face the fact that maybe I won't have the strength of character to withstand the torture.

All suddenly goes quiet. The panic in the room, though visibility is all but zero, is palpable. The communal breathing is rapid, sharp, tremulous. Five minutes later the door is thrown open, casting a shaft of light on our stinking group. We are huddled together despite being covered with shit. Then Fellows' horribly mutilated and unrecognizable body is pushed into the room.

Jacques covers his mouth to stop himself throwing up. I put my arm on his shoulder. "I think we've just seen an example of an indignant Gestapo officer getting his revenge."

An hour later the Gestapo guards return to take Jacques and me away.

46

Claude Renoir is still unable to control his shaking by the time he arrives at the Turrels' house in Seyne-les-Alpes.

"What is it Claude? What's happened? Come in…" implores André Turrel. "It's Luc and Jacques" Claude blurts out "we were stopped by the Gestapo as we drove out of Digne and they were both arrested along with another guy. They let me go."

André Turrel closes his eyes and takes a deep breath, partly to retain self-control and partly in response to the inevitable. Luc had been miraculously fortunate thus far. Even André himself was beginning to believe in his invulnerability. He pours two glasses of whisky and hands one to Claude.

"Drink this, my friend. And then we'll decide what to do. In any event we must let Christine know as soon as we can. Do you have any idea where she is?"

"Yes, I know where she is, I think. Luc said that she is due back tomorrow. She's in Barcelonnette."

"Then we must go and collect her right away. She will know what to do, whom to contact and so on. By tomorrow it may be too late."

André Turrel knows, too, that the Boche will very likely execute Luc and Jacques rather than wait around for the Allies to land.

Wasting no time, André and Claude take off for Barcelonnette, arriving *there by three o'clock. Christine is out but due back at the safe house any moment now according to the owner.*

Twenty minutes later André Turrel watches as Christine, accompanied by a dog, walks casually up to the house. André gears himself up to break the news.

Christine takes it surprisingly calmly. She's had so much bad news, seen so much horror over the past few years, that she knows the only way to deal with this kind of news is to remain coldly logical and calculating. She turns to André.

"Luc is the most important agent in France. The information he has, if he succumbs to Gestapo torture, would put everyone's lives at risk and even jeopardize the invasion. We have to get him out."

André, not normally a man to shirk an opportunity, no matter how impossible it may appear, is incredulous. Before he has time to show it, Christine turns to Claude.

"Claude, how quickly can you get me to Digne?"

"I don't dare Christine. The Gestapo said that if they find me, or my car, in Digne again they will arrest me."

"Well, can you take me close? Then I'll try to hitch a ride."

André Turrel, beguiled as are all men by Christine, smiles encouragingly at Claude Renoir.

"Yes, I can take you close. I can drop you at Le Brusquet. It's about ten km away."

"Fine, that will do."

"Are you sure about this Christine?" asks André "wouldn't it be better for a man to do it?"

Christine's withering look needed no vocal support.

The three of them start down the primitive, winding road from Barcelonnette to Digne.

"How are you going to get back from Digne, Christine?" queries André as they sit in the back of the Citroën, their minds racing backwards and forwards over past and possible future events.

"Bicycle!" she says "do you know anyone in Digne who has a bicycle

they could loan me?"

"Of course. My brother-in-law. He lives on the hill, near the cathedral."

"And near the Gestapo barracks," points out Christine "actually that will probably be convenient."

"OK. He lives at 26 rue de l'Eglise. His name is Christian Du Fleur. If he is not there his wife will be. Just say you are my friend and that you want to go bird watching in Seyne. They will understand. They are used to helping us out."

"Thank you," says Christine who is busy writing something in a notepad. Claude stops the car on the outskirts of Digne.

"I must leave you here Christine. I'm sorry I can't take you further."

"Don't worry, Claude. I may need you again before this is all over. Where can I contact you?"

"At my house" interjects André "we'll none of us rest until this is over." Claude agrees.

"Good, I'll contact you there. One more thing, André. Your son knows the code for sending messages to Algiers doesn't he? Can you make sure he sends this message to Brooks-Richards," she hands André a carefully written note, "it tells him to listen in every half hour and to be prepared to send a lot of money, tonight. If my plan works we'll need it."

"Of course, Christine. Good Luck!"

She smiles and gives him a peck on the cheek. "Look after Taboo for me."

The dog seems to understand, and happily stays with André Turrel as Christine leaves.

Forty minutes later, walking nonchalantly into Digne, she looks like any young lover on the way to meet her beau. Passing by a patrol of German wolf-whistlers, she responds with a coy smile and climbs up the steep hill to 26 rue de l'Eglise. Christian Du Fleur is at home. He lends her his bicycle. Then she heads for the prison.

There is a feeling of something about to happen in the air. The previous day, US planes had attempted to knock out the bridge across the Drôme near Crest. They had missed the bridge and destroyed much of the town of Crest, killing 36 people in the process. This had caused resentment, but elation too at the nearness of the invasion.

Among those getting nervous about likely developments over the next few days and weeks are the gendarmes in Digne. Aware that Digne is near the likely landing areas, and on a likely route north for any invading army, they have given much thought lately to their personal safety, and to that of their families. While all around them signs of a strong German presence are still very much in evidence, there is nevertheless a feeling that they have to be cautious, have to make some overtures to the 'other side' as a sort of insurance policy. Christine hopes to capitalize on this. But at first her plans are thwarted.

She walks around the castle searching for gendarmes. She accosts several and explains that her husband is being held inside and that she is desperate to get some food to him, is there any way they can help? It's more than their life is worth they explain. Of course they would if they could but they hope she understands. She does. They are scared. Finally she comes across an elderly gendarme sitting on the wall, smoking.

"Monsieur, I am desperate to see my husband. He has been arrested by the Gestapo. I want to see him and to give him some food. Please will you help me?"

"Madame, the Germans do not allow visitors into the prison. So many people have been arrested lately that it is full." Her helplessness, and beauty, touched the old man's heart.

"You could try and ask Willem Schenck, the liaison officer. He is on good terms with the Germans. He might be able to help you, but it would cost you money!"

"Where can I find him?"

"His house is that building across the street. Number 10, rue Grenette. But don't tell him I sent you!"

"Thank you" said Christine. She walked to the building across the street. It was 4pm on Monday 14 August.

47

Jacques and I have been waiting outside Gerster's office for twenty minutes.

An hour ago we were brought by car to this prison where Colonel Gerster of the Gestapo keeps an office. He likes to be near to the business, we were told.

They washed us down for the occasion, "Oberst Gerster doesn't like excremental smells in his office." We were given clean prison uniforms, and handcuffed.

A pudgy Frenchman in a Milice uniform emerges from the office "The Commandant will see you now."

Jacques and I are pushed into the room and made to stand in front of the Commandant. The two guards who have been with us the whole time take up positions on either side of the door.

Colonel Gerster sits behind his oversized desk. A cigarette holder bearing, I notice, the finest Albraine cigarette, is poised in his right hand. Gerster is apparently a man who likes the finer things in life. Slowly he stands up and walks around in front of his desk.

Jacques and I stare straight ahead, avoiding eye contact with the man. Gerster finds this irritating.

"I suggest you cooperate with me gentlemen, unless you want to suffer the same fate as your Mr. Fellows. I gather he paid rather a high price for his insolence?"

Gerster, his back to us, and staring out of the window, continues talking. His French is depressingly fluent.

"A most interesting situation this is. I didn't catch your names, at least the names that you are using, so I'll call you, let us say, Luc and Jacques." He swivelled round in time to catch both of us staring at him. "Ah, eye contact. Yes I thought that might cause a soupçon of interest."

He's clearly done his homewrok. I'm certain that the Gestapo officer arresting us wasn't aware of our identity. Our identity cards had false names. Then I remembered, Fellows. Of course. Fellows probably told all he knew under torture. And what did he know? Not a lot. Just names, and my SOE connection. At least Jacques may be safe.

"You seem to have caused rather a lot of trouble between you. You were almost picked up in Annecy, I believe that is where you met, n'est ce pas?"

I realize he knows a lot more than Fellows could have told him.

"No need to answer. I am certain of the details. There was that little matter of arming a large band of terrorists in the Glières. Naturally they were wiped out but it was annoying for us and a number of good German soldiers gave up their lives. That alone is enough for me to have you shot but we want to have a little fun with you first.

And there was to be more wasn't there? German agents disappearing in Montélimar, in the Vercors, Chabeuil. Trains being derailed all over the place. Hydroelectric plants blown sky high. Ammunition stolen. Not to mention hundreds of acts of sabotage up and down the country. Need I go on?

I thought the idea of putting itching powder in the underwear of German brothel visitors quite ingenious I may say. Congratulations.

You've left a trail of destruction behind you and no doubt you have more planned for the arrival of your invaders. Did you know that your American friends bombed Crest yesterday? They killed most of the population but missed the bridge over the Drôme that was their mission. I don't think we will have much of a problem repelling such incompetents, do you?"

I'm taken aback by the depth of Gerster's knowledge. Who, other than myself, is aware of all this? I wonder why, if Gerster had all this information on us, we hadn't immediately been taken to a high-security prison in Grenoble or Lyon. Digne is just a small provincial prison by comparison.

"Anyway gentlemen, as you probably know there is quite a price on your head. At least on yours Luc, or should I call you Joseph Quantock? No, let's stick to 'Luc' for the time being. As I was saying, there is quite a price on your head and it is my duty to ensure that you are, against my better judgment, kept alive until I have what I want from you."

He pauses, puts on his glasses and, looking down at some paperwork, says "Jacques Villaz will be shot."

Jacques glances at me with his eyebrows raised as if to say 'not again'.

"Tomorrow morning at 5:00 a.m. The locals have come to expect it. They find the sound of a firing squad reassuring first thing in the morning. Luc will be transferred, also tomorrow morning but only after he has had the privilege, rarely accorded, of seeing his friend shot."

Gerster removes his glasses and leans back in his chair.

"Do you have anything to say gentlemen?"

I decide to see if he's bluffing. "You're very well informed

Colonel. I am indeed who you say I am. But this man here is not the Jacques you are talking about. He was killed by your soldiers at Valchevrière on the Vercors. I am sure you can easily verify that."

"I don't think that will be productive, Herr Luc. You see we have already verified that he is indeed the Jacques that we think he is."

"And how do you think you have verified it?"

Gerster picks up the phone. "Bring Brandt in please."

Jacques and I keep staring ahead as the door behind us opens. Reflected in the window we can see it is a burly officer in the uniform of an S.S. Hauptsturmführer.

"Ah Brandt, come here. I want to introduce you to two friends of mine. But then, of course, you've already met!"

The officer walks to Gerster's desk and turns around to face us.

It's David Fellows.

48

Christine knocks on the door of Number 10 rue Grenette. Presently a heavy set lady answers the door. "Ja, what you want?" she asks in a thick German accent.

"Frau Schenck?"

"Ja"

"May I please speak with Captain Schenck? I am a British agent."

A shocked Frau Schenck says nervously "Wait here" and disappears upstairs. A minute or so later wide-eyed Willem Schenck himself appears at the door, holding a pistol.

"Who are you? What do you want?"

"Captain Schenck," responds Christine calmly, "as I have told your wife I am a British agent. I am a niece of Field-Marshal Montgomery. The Gestapo are holding three important British agents. One of them is my husband. I want your help in getting them all released."

"Are you mad?"

"Captain, the Allies will be landing any moment now. It will be a matter of days at the most before they get to Digne. If my husband and his friends are killed and if the American soldiers don't shoot you, then you can be certain that the local Maquis, who are watching us at this moment, will

see to it that you and your wife are shot."

Realizing he was standing at the front door, with a gun and talking to an enemy agent in full view of the Gestapo, as well as, apparently, the Maquis, he nervously motions Christine into the front hall and hurriedly closes the door.

"Listen, it's more than my life is worth even if I could help you. But I can't. I am just a liaison man."

"Then you must be liaising with someone? Tell me who? Maybe he can help?" Christine is conscious of creaking floorboards above. Schenck, aware that his wife is probably listening, takes Christine into a small ante-room and shuts the door.

"The only person I know who might be able to help is a Belgian called Max Waem. He is 'officially' an interpreter for the Gestapo, but I think his role is a bit more shady than that."

"He sounds a likely person."

"He would want a lot of money" says Schenck "but I suppose if you are as well connected as you say that will not be a problem?"

"Just arrange for me to meet this Waem, Captain, then we can discuss the money."

Schenck, perspiration rolling down both cheeks, agrees. They both get up and walk to the front door. Schenck opens it and cautiously looks up and down the street. "If you come back at 5:00 p.m. I will make sure that Waem is here."

By 5:00 p.m. Christine is sitting in the front room of the Schencks' flat, talking to Frau Schenck. Ten minutes later Captain Schenck, accompanied by a small, mean-looking man in a Gestapo uniform, carrying a pistol, enters the room.

Frau Schenck pours coffee and leaves the three of them to talk.

For two hours Christine talks, persuasively, flirtatiously, threateningly, to Waem. There is no point in appealing to higher ideals with men like Waem, she decides. Only self-interest will really make an impression. As her patience, and the time, is running out she delivers her ultimatum:

"Monsieur Waem, I am informed that by this time tomorrow the Allies will be in Provence. Both you and Captain Schenck are well-known to the local Maquis, who despise you. If you do not help me I can guarantee that you and your families will all suffer a terrible end. I suggest you consider your situation very carefully."

Schenck and Waem leave the room to discuss their response. When they come back, Waem starts talking.

"If I do get your men out, what will you do to help me?"

"If my husband and his friends are released, alive and well, then I will guarantee that both of you and your families will be spared. I will make certain that the Allies know what you have done for their cause. They will not hurt you, or imprison you."

"I will need two million francs and safe passage out of the country" replies Waem.

"I will see to it" says Christine without blinking. "How soon can you get them out?"

"They are being held across the street. They were brought over this afternoon. Something unusual is going on because normally prisoners as important as this are transferred immediately to Lyon. I know they plan to shoot one of them at 5:00 a.m. because it is my job to take prisoners to the firing range when they are sentenced to be shot. The other one will be taken away, probably to Lyon, tomorrow morning."

"And the third?"

"There is no third. Only two."

Christine is worried. Maybe Luc has already been shot, or taken away. Claude Renoir had confirmed that there was another man taken with Luc and Jacques. Where is he?

"Do you know the names of the two men?"

"Yes, of course. They are well known. The commandant is expecting a large reward I think. The English one, your husband I suppose, is Luc.

The other one is French, Jacques. He is the one to be shot."

"So we must move quickly. Before 5:00 a.m."

"But I will do nothing without the money and the guarantee."

"If you want to live, you will. I will return here with the money by 4:00 a.m. at the latest. We can meet here can't we Captain Schenck?"

"Yes, yes" Captain Schenck is now so worried and confused and frightened that he will agree to anything. Especially as he has already agreed with Waem that they will split the money. He's just preoccupied as to how he will get out of Digne in one piece, and with the money.

Christine, a lightweight scarf tied around her neck, closes the Schencks' door and mounts her bicycle. She has no idea if she can get the money in time but she'll give it a damned good try.

49

Colonel Schwab, in his office at the HQ of the Wehrmacht's 157th Reserve Division in Grenoble, ponders the situation. He had sent one of his best men, Hauptsturmführer Brandt, a fluent English speaker, to Algiers to infiltrate the Free French HQ. He knew that with the disarray, political rivalry and general chaos amongst the opposing French factions in Algiers, a well-spoken SOE agent asking for a lift on the next available flight to France would have at least an even chance of getting it, especially with the faked letter from Maurice Buckmaster.

When Brandt had sent him a message saying that he was hitching a plane ride with de Gaulle's personal emissary, he couldn't believe his luck. But where is Brandt now? Schwab hadn't heard a word since his arrival. Perhaps the French got wise to him? Perhaps he had been killed? Not for the first time that day Schwab put through a call to Gestapo offices in Montélimar, Gap, Crest and Digne and asked for an update on the Luc affair.

No one reported any sighting. Montélimar confirmed they had rounded up several maquisards who had reported seeing him locally but they could find no sign themselves. Gap, likewise. Crest, nothing. In Digne that conniving Gerster had tried to get a bigger share of the reward 'in the event he found Luc'. But Schwab would have none of it. 100,000 Reichsmarks was quite enough for the Commandant of a small Gestapo bureau like Digne. He had told Gerster so. And he had added a codicil suggesting that he try and live at a standard becoming a commandant of a small Gestapo bureau and not like the Czar of Russia.

In Digne, Colonel Gerster was pursuing a high-risk strategy, and he knew it. He had tried to get General Pflaum's man Schwab to increase the reward money 'in the event that he found Luc'. This was even more important now that he had offered part of it to Brandt on condition that he kept his mouth shut until Luc had been handed over. Of course Brandt could always be put out of the picture.

It was almost midnight when Gerster decided to call the Abwehr Sergeant Metzger.

"Metzger, hello. Oberst Gerster here."

"Yes Oberst. What news?"

"Nothing as yet, Metzger, but I think we are close to arresting your friend."

"You are? Is he in Digne? My people here say he is in Montèlimar!"

"We are 90% certain he is here in Digne. We arrested Jacques, his number two."

"You have? I thought he was dead. I want to interrogate him!"

"Too late, he's been shot" Gerster lied. He didn't want Metzger coming down prematurely. Only after they agreed a deal.

"Damn" cried Metzger.

"Metzger, this mission has become a little more dangerous for my men. It may be a little more costly than I thought."

There was quiet at the other end of the line.

"Besides, Oberst Schwab is determined to beat you to the finishing post so to speak and has increased his share to me."

"How much?" asked Metzger.

"200,000 Reichsmarks" Gerster lied.

Silence. Then Metzger spoke.

"Alright Gerster. 250,000 and that is final."

"Alright Metzger. I go with you then, once I find him."

"How soon do you think?" Metzger had seen the reports of an expected invasion within the next 36 hours. He was determined to get to Luc before it was too late.

"Possibly tomorrow. Why don't you come down around 2:00 p.m.?"

"Very well. I'll be there."

"Good" said Gerster, and rung off.

Metzger had no intention of waiting until tomorrow. Gerster was playing Metzger off against Schwab.

Gerster already had Luc. Metzger was certain of it. He would order a car to take him to Digne. Now.

50

Christine cycled the 20 kilometres to Seyne, uphill for much of the way, arriving in darkness. Her preoccupation with getting Luc and Jacques out of prison had finally overpowered her fear of cycling.

By the time she arrived at the sombre Turrel household it was already 9:00 p.m.

Fortunately the Turrel's son, Pierrot, was at home. He confirmed that he had sent the message and that Brooks-Richards was standing by, awaiting her instructions.

"OK" said Christine "We have to move very quickly. I think there is a chance we can get them both out but we need to get two million francs to Digne by 2:00 a.m. at the latest. What is the dropping zone closest to Seyne?"

"Le Grange's fields, 2 km west of here. I've got the map reference here."

"You're certain it's safe? At least it's a clear night, thank God."

"As safe as any other" replied André Turrel.

"Where is Claude Renoir?"

"In the house across the street, sleeping."

"Does he still have the car?"

"Sure."

"OK, we can let him sleep for a while longer but he's going to have to drive me back to Digne. We'll need the car to get the men out of there. Pierrot can you send this message right away?"

LUC DUE TO BE SHOT AT 5AM STOP TWO MILLION FRANCS IS PRICE OF LUC'S LIFE ESSENTIAL YOU DROP MAP REFERENCE GN20S NO LATER THAN MIDNIGHT STOP CHRISTINE ENDS

Pierrot Turrel took the message and cycled the 2 kilometres to the safe house where he kept the Algiers transmitter. He sent the message and waited for a reply. It was a quarter to ten.

Christine took the opportunity to wash and change her clothes and then ate a small supper in the Turrels' kitchen.

At half past ten she heard Pierrot's bicycle on the path outside. The youth burst into the room with a message from Brooks-Richards:

DOUBLE ANTICIPATED AMOUNT BUT ON ITS WAY STOP PLANE LEFT 10:00 FINGERS CROSSED STOP B-R ENDS

"Wonderful, well done. Don't think Algiers have ever acted so quickly. About time too" said Christine as she tied the laces on her shoes. "Time to wake up Claude"

"I'll get him" said André as he went out the door.

Ten minutes later Claude, Christine, Pierrot and André, armed with flares and torches, were in the car heading for Le Grange's field. By 11:00 they were in position, watching the night sky.

51

Before retiring for the night, Colonel Schwab, at the subdued Wehrmacht headquarters in Grenoble, decided to put in one final call. The disappearance or at least non-communication of his man Brandt was disturbing him.

"Gestapo HQ, Digne" confirmed the voice on the other end.

"Schwab here. Put me through to Captain Reitsch."

The night operator located the extension for the deputy commander of the Digne Gestapo.

"Captain Reitsch I have Oberst Schwab for you."

Reitsch had been hand-picked by Schwab for the role. The natural successor to Gerster. He looked at his watch. Almost midnight.

"Good evening Oberst. What can I do for you?"

"Reitsch, are you alone?"

"Yes Oberst."

"Reitsch, I have lost trace of an important officer, Hauptsturmführer Brandt. He flew over from Algiers recently in the company of a French colonel. He hasn't been heard from since he landed. I want him found."

"Yes Oberst. I will make enquiries. I've only just returned from Stuttgart this evening."

"You are to call me as soon as you know anything, understand?"

"Yes Oberst."

Schwab rang off. Reitsch scribbled down a reminder to talk to Gerster in the morning.

Meanwhile, two floors beneath Reitsch's office, in a three-man cell with a bunk bed and a single mattress on the floor, Luc and Jacques lay awake. Sleep was out of the question. When they spoke they spoke in murmurs, careful not to let the third man hear what they were saying.

My mind is racing; desperately trying to come up with solutions.

"I'm pretty sure some sort of bartering is going on" I whisper to Jacques. I can think of no other reason why we haven't been immediately transferred to Lyon or Grenoble "and I think Fellows or Brandt or whatever he's called is involved."

"He certainly made a quick recovery from being beaten senseless and left for dead" says Jacques.

"Maybe he too is a good Catholic?"

"Fuck you."

"OK, darling, but be gentle."

Jacques shoots me a glance and sees my barely suppressed smile.

"Bastard, so you did read the letter?"

"Of course I did." We both burst out laughing. He flings his arms around me.

Another milestone reached in his life. At least with me he has no more secrets and he knows I love him for who he is. Better still I can kid him about it.

"The Boche probably threw any old body into the cell." I say.

"Yeah." Jacques is subdued again, convinced that finally his end is just hours away.

I want to reassure him. "We'll come up with something before 5:00 a.m." I say, only half believing it myself. A couple of possibilities occur to me; we're both big men, perhaps we can overpower the guards who come to collect us? Maybe we can also try and do a deal with Gerster? With the Allied invasion imminent he doesn't have much of a future here. I'm certain Claude Renoir will have gotten news to the others by now. Perhaps the Maquis will even spring us?

The Germans took my watch but I guess it must be almost two o'clock.

"Luc, I want to ask you a favour? If you make it, will you see to it that my nieces in Annecy are looked after? Just ask the postmistress in Annecy how you can find the nieces of Jacques Villaz. She will take you there."

"Of course Jacques, but don't think like that. We're both going to get out of here. One way or another we'll get out of here."

We have to think that.

But I can see Jacques feels the situation is hopeless. Especially for him.

52

The plane from Algiers flew over the Le Grange field at 11:45. André and Pierrot held flares while Christine signalled the code. The pilot circled back over, slowed for a moment or two, and then flew away leaving one small parachute sinking rapidly towards the earth. The rubber pouch landed metres from Christine. She quickly checked inside. Two million francs.

"We're in business" she beamed at the others "let's go." They dropped André and Pierrot Turrel off in Seyne and then sped down the road to Digne. Claude knew that this was highly dangerous for him but he was willing to risk it. Christine's powers of persuasion were already legendary.

Barely 100 km north of them, Sergeant Karl Metzger's Citroën was also heading for Digne. The Maquis had taken control of the main roads and Metzger's driver was forced to use slower, side roads. That, coupled with the damage done by the Allies' recent bombing waves, was slowing his progress considerably.

Impatiently, Metzger looked at his watch. Just past midnight. With any luck they should be in Digne by 3:00 a.m., certainly by 4:00 a.m. He would demand that Luc be handed over to him. He had a formal letter from S.S. Colonel Ritter in Paris authorizing Luc to be given into his custody. He clapped his hands at the prospect, startling his driver.

As Christine approached the outskirts of Digne, Claude Renoir slowed the Citroën down so it was barely creeping along the darkened road. Christine reached into the rubber pouch, removed one million francs, and handed it to Claude.

"Keep this very safe Claude. If all goes well we will collect it when next I see you."

Claude dropped Christine at the unguarded crossroads. He then drove into the woods where the Gestapo executed their prisoners, parked the car and waited.

Avoiding the main streets, Christine weaved her way across town, up the hill by the cathedral and onto the rue Grenette. Quietly she knocked three times, the agreed signal, at Number 10. Instantly the door was opened, not, as she had expected, by Schenck, but by Waem himself.

"Good evening Fraulein. You have the money?"

"I have half of it Herr Waem. The other half is in the hands of the Maquis and will be handed over when you hand over Luc and Jacques."

Waem's left eye twitched.

"Very well" he replied "plans have changed somewhat. We need to move quickly."

"All the better" replied Christine.

"Where is your car?"

"In the woods as we agreed. By the firing squad wall."

"And what provisions have you made for me?" Waem wanted final reassurance before committing himself.

"You have nothing to fear as long as the men are safe and in good health."

"Well I cannot guarantee their health, they have been in the care of the Gestapo after all, but I will get them to you."

"If you don't Herr Waem, I have issued instructions for your immediate execution."

"I thank you for your confidence Fraulein. And if I do?"

"Then you and your family…"

"I have no family."

"Then you will be given safe passage to southern Italy under protection of the Allied forces. From there you can go wherever you want. The same goes for the Schencks."

"The Schencks have already departed. They made alternative arrangements."

"I see."

Christine handed Waem one half of the agreed two million francs and confirmed their meeting place. She then left and made her way back through the sleeping town to the woods of St Lazaire.

Five minutes later Max Waem, the one million francs placed in a money belt around his waist, replaced his cap with the skull and crossbones insignia of the S.S., checked his appearance in the mirror and walked out into the street, quietly closing the door on the Schencks' house and their strangled bodies.

The town was eerily quiet thought Waem as he made his way to Gestapo HQ that Tuesday morning on 15 August. He vaguely wondered who might be on the night shift. Not that it really mattered. He routinely went down to the cells in the early hours to question prisoners one last time before escorting them to the firing squad. You never know. Fear does funny things to people. Some of them blurt out everything they know. Waem guessed it was their last vain attempt for a reprieve. Of course it never worked.

At first his visits were a weekly routine. Lately it had become an almost daily event. He supposed the high command were panicking now that the Allies were so close. In fact he thought as he looked into the south, the lights on the horizon were unusually bright tonight. Perhaps today was D-Day for the south. If so the timing couldn't be better. He could take his money and run. Maybe he wouldn't even be missed in the ensuing mayhem.

He checked in at the desk, writing his name in the log that the keen new corporal insisted on keeping, and then walked to the main office to see who was on night shift. Usually it was some middle-ranking officer but tonight it was different. Captain Reitsch, the deputy Commandant, was on duty. On account of the importance of the prisoners, Waem assumed.

"Good evening Captain" Waem saluted, half-heartedly.

"Hello Max." Waem looked through his in tray. Nothing interesting.

"No news tonight Captain?"

"No good news Waem. The Americans might be causing a bit of trouble down south by the looks of it."

"Yes, looks like it" replied Waem, "Brandt said that an invasion was imminent. And he should know."

Reitsch sat up straight. "Brandt, Waem? Is Brandt here?"

"Yes, he's been here for a few days now. Well I saw him yesterday anyway. That's when he told me about the invasion."

"Do you know where he is?"

"No, but Oberst Gerster will know. They are practically inseparable."

Waem finished sifting through his papers and went downstairs to the cells.

Reitsch picked up the phone to call Gerster then hesitated before putting it down again. He thought for a few moments and then dialled Grenoble instead. It was 2:00 a.m.

The night duty officer answered "Wehrmacht, Grenoble."

"Captain Reitsch here, Gestapo Digne. I need to talk to Oberst Schwab urgently."

"The Oberst doesn't hang around the office at 2:00 a.m. Captain."

"I know that you fool. This is urgent. Put me through to Schwab."

"I'll locate him and call you back."

"But…" the phone had gone dead.

An avalanche of rocks had blocked the road to Digne from Sisteron. Metzger's driver was forced to take a detour to les Mees, adding 45 minutes to their trip. It was 2:00 and they were still at least 45 minutes from Digne.

The more Metzger thought about the likely scenarios the more he was convinced that Gerster was still playing him off against Schwab. But if he got there first and claimed the prize it didn't really matter. Gerster had screwed more money out of him but it wasn't the money that mattered to Metzger. It wasn't even the promotion any more. It was his pride. He had been pursuing

Luc for 18 months now. He had invested time and energy and he was damned if he was going to be foiled by some trumped-up Gestapo chief.

"Can't you go any faster!" he yelled demonically at the driver.

"Do you want to drive?" the man replied.

"What!" was all Metzger could muster, taken by surprise .

"Then shut up."

The blood vessel in Metzger's forehead throbbed as he fought to regain control. He would have the man disciplined once he got to Digne, he decided. That would teach him.

Wearing his Wehrmacht tunic against the cool of the night, Waem ordered the guard to open the Number One holding cell.

It's the middle of the night but Jacques and I are both wide awake. Someone is opening our cell door.

"Out, you two. Now." A small man in an S.S. uniform yells at us.

I slowly raise myself from the bottom bunk. Jacques is already standing. He seems confused that both of us are being taken out. Obviously wondering why we are both going to be shot. Then he remembers, I am being forced to watch.

I follow Jacques out of the door. Considering the S.S. man's stature, or lack thereof, I consider the possibility of overpowering him then and there but think better of it upon seeing two armed guards standing at the entrance to the cell block.

"I have a gun gentlemen. I suggest you do exactly as you are told" says the S.S. man, unnecessarily loudly.

He holds the outside door open and orders us to walk through into the cool night air.

As I pass him he says to me quietly "You have a very resourceful wife."

Wife? What's he talking about?

Jacques mutters to me "Shall we take him?"

I indicate the two guards standing at the compound entrance. Then I whisper to Jacques "It may not be necessary. Wait and see."

The S.S. man gives a Heil Hitler-style salute to the two guards at the gate.

"Bit early aren't you tonight Max?" says one of them.

"Need to get my beauty sleep" replies the S.S. man.

"It will take more than sleep, Max" they laugh as they let the three of us through.

Reitsch's phone rings. It's Wehrmacht HQ in Grenoble returning his call. Colonel Schwab is on the line.

"Reitsch. What is it?"

"Oberst, I thought you might like to know that your missing agent Brandt is here in Digne. Apparently he has been staying with Oberst Gerster for a few days."

Schwab was silent for a moment or two then he spoke.

"Reitsch, listen to me very carefully. I am appointing you Commandant of the Gestapo HQ in Digne with immediate effect. You are to place Oberst Gerster and Hauptsturmführer Brandt under arrest, you understand."

"Of course, yes Oberst, but on what charge?"

"Disobeying orders; undermining a senior officer, anything. Just do it."

"Yes, Sir"

"But before you do that, do you have prisoners in the holding cell at Digne?"

"Yes, Sir, two"

"Who are they" asked Schwab, furious that he had not suspected this before.

"One British agent and one maquisard, due to be shot."

"Reitsch. You are to go downstairs yourself, now, personally, and ensure that both men are there. Double the guard with people you trust. Under no circumstance must any harm come to these men or heads will roll, especially yours. That clear?"

"Quite clear, Sir."

"Then go, now. I will stay on the line."

Reitsch, adrenalin rushing, ran downstairs to the holding cell.

"Oh my God! Oh my God! NO".

He walked slowly upstairs, sat down at his desk and, without speaking a word, gently replaced the phone on its cradle.

The S.S. man, Jacques and I walk a couple of hundred metres into the woods and out of sight of the guards. There in front of us is the firing squad wall.

Standing next to it, radiant in the moonlight, is Christine.

I think that I've never seen a sight of such beauty. Jacques gapes open-mouthed in disbelief.

Christine smiles. "It worked" she says, kissing us both "quickly, into the car. We need to get out of here."

The S.S. man removes his uniform, which he's worn over civilian clothes, throws it into the woods and climbs into the car between Jacques and Christine. I sit in front next to Claude.

"Head for the coast, Claude" says Christine. Then she turns to Jacques and me. "The Resistance in Marseille have confirmed the invasion has begun. Six battleships and 21 cruisers began barraging during the night. Five thousand tons of bombs fell on coastal gun emplacements. They think the Allies will have taken Marseille and Toulon by nightfall."

Claude Renoir manoeuvres the Citroën onto the road to Mezel in the direction of the coast.

Just where the road branches right to Oraison we see another car coming towards us.

As it passes I pick out the profile of a maniacal little man sitting in the back seat wearing a beret and dark glasses, exhorting his driver to go faster.

EPILOGUE

After carefully refilling my glass, then his, with his favorite Burgundy, Joseph Quantock sunk back into the wingback chair and slowly marshaled his thoughts. He was quite infirm now and in considerable pain. It was several minutes before he started to speak.

"The story I told to you long ago in Africa was my story, a deeply personal story I've told to no one. I was not a hero and don't want you to portray me as such. A team has no single hero. It's like a game of football. No one plays alone. In my little corner of the war I believe every Maquis was a brave person who contributed to our success, whether recognized or not. No one ever betrayed me though some withstood inconceivable torture by those attempting to persuade them to do so. I was never tested myself. Who can tell how I would have fared?

Arnaud, Jacques and Christine were only the most obvious heroes in my story. There were thousands of unsung heroes, thousands."

"We know of the fate that befell Arnaud, but what about Christine and Jacques?' I ask.

"Jacques still lives in St Jorioz. His nieces look after him. We meet twice a year. Once in St Jorioz and once in Le Pouget. We spend the time laughing, in tears sometimes or in silence. Just remembering. My daughter cooks us a meal when he's here, and we eat well and drink too much good wine. We are still the best of friends.

Christine came to London after the war. After a lot of inexcusable dithering she was finally awarded the George Medal (only men could be given the George Cross at that time) for her immense contribution to the war effort. She got a job working in several hotels as a chambermaid."

"Couldn't you have helped her get a better job?"

"You have to understand something about Christine. She was a very determined woman as I'm sure, by now, you know. She wouldn't accept help from anyone. She wanted to do everything for herself. She was happy to do something seemingly secure and mundane. While she was working at the hotel an Irish kitchen steward fell in love with her and proposed marriage. She turned him down and, rather than stay there, she got a job on a cruise liner. While she was on leave she stayed in a seedy hotel off the Cromwell Road. One time when she was back from a cruise the kitchen steward arrived at the hotel and begged her to marry him. She said she wouldn't. He pulled out a knife and killed her. She was forty-three years old".

The old man stared into the distance. His eyes glazed over. He was silent. I left him alone.

I went back to Le Pouget two weeks later. The wingback chair was empty.

Bing Taylor
Rome
August, 2014

ACKNOWLEDGEMENTS

I would like to thank Adam and Nellie Munthe, Rod Bailey, Mary Magill, Tanis Taylor, Patsy Taylor, Marco Calvani, Francesca de Sapio, Chloe Waters, Joanie Taylor, Sam Beazley, Dom Agius, Pam Rose, Clemence Watt, Jasper and Daisy Gibson, Chuck Berry, Killian Strong, Alessandro Spina and Ilaria del Seppia, Zachary and Masa Taylor, David Hills, Slav Todorov, Jay Cammaerts, Gary Pulsifer and Wole Wey for their friendship, comments, advice and, in many cases, hospitality too.

Les Tilleuils Hotel, St Jorioz; Hotel Bellier, La Chapelle en Vercors; Hotel le Relais de la Forge and the Turrel family in Selonnet for their hospitality and for their generous sharing of photographs and memories.

Special thanks to that brave publishing venture Middle Farm Press, especially Kate Taylor and Sam Gray, for their support and encouragement, and patience.

CAST OF CHARACTERS

GROOMBRIDGE, KENT, UK

Joseph Quantock, 'Luc' American SOE agent
Lord Horley, minister in Churchill's government

BURGUNDY, FRANCE

Uncle Sam, Joseph Quantock's uncle
Mme. Joupin, the housekeeper
François, her son
Philippe Morseau, the school bully

SOE HQ LONDON

Maurice Buckmaster, Head of F Section, SOE
Vera Atkins, his Intelligence Officer
Selwyn Jepson, novelist and recruiting officer
Nigel Miller, in charge of Agent Coordination
Martin Bettinson, number two to Buckmaster
Major-General Colin Gubbins, Head of SOE, 1943-1946

SOE ARISAIG

Willy Ferguson, silent killing instructor, Arisaig; formerly, Shanghai police
Macpherson, small arms instructor, Arisaig; formerly, Shanghai police

SOE PILOTS

Hugh Verity, Lysander pilot ferrying agents into France
Squadron Leader Cook, Canadian Lancaster pilot

FRENCH RESISTANCE
Lyon
Charles Decosse, leader of Lyon circuit
Henri Frenay, Resistance leader, publisher of Combat!

Compiègne
Jean Besson, wireless operator
Mme. Sainte-Beauve, owner of hop farm used as dropping ground

Paris
Gilles Marchais, Resistance leader in southern France
Suzanne, his secretary
Alice, secret 'double' agent

St Jorioz
Mme. Marchais, wife of Gilles
Robert Bardot, Marchais' number two
Louis 'le Belge', colleague of Bardot
Jean Cottet, proprietor of Hotel de la Poste
Simone Cottet, his wife

Annecy
Tom Morel, former St Cyr graduate, leader of Glières Maquis
Jacques Villaz, Quantock's number two
Capitaine Anjot, leader of Glières Maquis after Tom Morel
Thierry de Rôme, ambulance driver

Montelimar
Roger Bidou, farmer
Sylvie Bidou, his wife
Alain Bidou, their son

Benoit, a cousin, farm worker
Laurent, a cousin, farm worker
Marc, farm worker
Raymond Daujat, corn merchant; 'post box'
Father Thibault, local priest
Anne-Marie, telephonist

Digne
Marianne, American vet; 'post box'
Theo Gautier, leader local Maquis

Seyne-les-Alpes
André Turrel, Mayor of Selonnet
Marie-Georges Turrel, his wife; Tabac owner
Pierre Turrel, their son
Claude Renoir, friend of Turrels'; son of the artist

Chabeuil
Henri, café proprietor
Guy Beluze, Highway Department engineer
Gine Beluze, his wife

Toulouse
Jean-Paul Cassis, factory worker making aircraft parts for Luftwaffe

Montrouge, Paris
Carmen Dupré, friend of Selwyn Jepson; safe House

Rugby circuit cell leaders
Pierre Reynaud, Quart
Aristide, Champourçin

Xavier, Oppede
Etienne, Grenoble
Raymonde, his number two
François, Le Pouget
Max, Valence
Michel, Aix
Georges, Abbeville
Jean-Louis, Apt

NATIONAL LEADERS
Winston Churchill, Prime Minister, Great Britain
Franklin D. Roosevelt, President, USA
Adolf Hitler, German Chancellor and Head of State
Maréchal Philippe Pétain, Chief of State of Vichy France 1940-1944
General Charles de Gaulle, Leader, Free French Army and French
Government in Exile

COMMAND AND CONTROL, LONDON
General Dwight D. Eisenhower, Supreme Commander Allied Forces,
Europe
Colonel David Bruce, Head of London branch of US Intelligence Agency, OSS
General Marie-Pierre Koenig, Chief of the Forces Françaises de l'Intérieur, FFI
High Dalton, UK Minister of Economic Warfare 1940-1942; minister in
charge of SOE
Lord Selborne, Minister of Economic Warfare 1942-1945; minister in
charge of SOE

SOE IN FIELD
Joseph Quantock, 'Luc'; American, leader of Rugby circuit
Giovanna Rasini, 'Christine'; Italian, his courier
Gregor von Rigor, her husband

Roger Chamberlain, 'Paul' former organizer of Cannes Resistance circuit
Mathilde Chambrun 'Claudine' his number two
Marc Weinberger, 'Arnaud' their wireless operator, St Jorioz
'Alain', wireless operator, Digne
'Monique', courier Montelimar
Gilbert D'Ancourt, organizer Angers circuit,

VERCORS RESISTANCE

Eugène Chavant, 'Patron'
Capitaine Narcisse Geyer, Commander, southern sector, Vercors plateau
Capitaine Costa de Beauregard, Commander, northern sector, Vercors plateau
Major Huet, Military Commander, Vercors
Colonel Marcel Descours, Commander, Region One, French Secret Army
Colonel (later General) Henri Zeller, his boss; Free French Commander
S.E. France
Joseph La Picarella, maquisard; pancake maker
Huiller Brothers, truckers, Vercors plateau
Sergeant Chabal, Commando leader
Groupe Vallier, uncontrollable but patriotic "terrorists"
Dr Ganimède, doctor
Father Yves, Jesuit priest from Paris
Bob Bennes, Descour's wireless operator
Corporal Tourara, in charge of Vassieux airport construction

CIVILIANS, FRANCE
Beaurepaire

Father David, Prior, Dominican Monastery
Comtesse de Julienne, Champs Martin, near Beaurepaire
Claude, her son
Lucille, their ageing retainer
Guillamme, cousin of Jacques, les Varilles, outside Champs Martin

M. Rey, farmer harbouring Maquis outside Champs Martin
Brother François, Dominican monk
Thierry Claude, Director, Beaurepaire Power Station
Mme. Lelonge, his secretary

Vercors
M.Bellier, hotel owner, La Chapelle en Vercors
Mme. Breyton, hotel owner, Saint Martin
Lisette, 12 year old girl, Vassieux
Pasqual, boy courier

ABWEHR HEADQUARTERS, PARIS
Colonel Hans Froehling, Head of Abwehr, German Military Intelligence, Paris
Karl Metzger, sergeant; linguist, musician; counter-espionage agent
Heinz, wireless operator

GERMAN ARMED FORCES
Paris
Field Marshal von Runstedt, Commander in Chief German Forces West, Paris
Field Marshal Rommel, Commander of German Army Group B, Paris

Grenoble
General Karl Pflaum, Commander 157th Wehrmacht's Reserve Division
Colonel Schwab, anti-terrorist expert

Digne
Colonel Gerster, Gestapo Chief, Digne
Brandt, S.S. Hauptsturmführer
Willem Schenck, Gestapo liaison officer
Max Waem, Belgian interpreter, Gestapo

Lyon
Oberstleutnant Heine, Luftwaffe Duty Officer

Algiers / Naples
General Henri Giraud, Commander-in Chief, Free French Forces, demoted by de Gaulle
Colonel Jean Constans, the French SPOC Colonel
Jacques Soustelle, archaeologist and head of Special Services Bureau
General Gabriel Cochet, Commander-in-Chief, French forces Southern Sector
Colonel Eugene Caffey, US Commander 20th Engineer Regiment
General Alexander Patch, US Corps Commander, Naples

FRENCH MILICE
Gregoire Lefèvre, Commandant Glières Milice
'Colonel' Maude, wife of leader of Vercors Milice
Philippe, school teacher turned milicien
M. LeLonge, milicien, husband of secretary at Beaurepaire Power Station
Olivier le Duc, Commander Milice, Beaurepaire

ITALIANS
Giovanna Rasini 'Christine'
Giovanni Rasini, her father
Massimo Rasini, her brother
Fabio Rasini, her brother
Angelo Galimberti, partisan leader

BRITISH ARMY
Major Richard Dellafield, SOE Cairo
Commander Francis Brooks Richards, Head of F Section, SOE, Algiers
Captain Edgar, British Army captain dispatched to Barcelonnette